THE WOMAN SHE WAS

The Woman She Was

ROSA JORDAN

BRINDLE
& GLASS

Brindle & Glass Publishing Ltd.
www.brindleandglass.com

LIBRARY AND ARCHIVES CANADA CATALOGUING IN PUBLICATION
Jordan, Rosa
The woman she was / Rosa Jordan.

Issued also in electronic formats.
ISBN 978-1-926972-46-6

I. Title.

PS8619.O74W66 2012   C813'.6   C2011-907167-3

Editor: Kathy Page
Copy Editor/proofreader: Heather Sangster, Strong Finish
Design: Pete Kohut
Front cover photo: Celia Sánchez (detail) courtesy of Wisconsin Historical Society Image ID 85353
was taken by Dickey Chapelle, who spent time in the mountains with the Cuban
rebels before going on to Vietnam, where she was killed.
Photo on page ii: Memorial of Celia Sánchez, taken by Rosa Jordan
Author photo taken by Derek Choukalos

BRITISH COLUMBIA ARTS COUNCIL   Canada Council for the Arts   Conseil des Arts du Canada   Canadian Heritage   Patrimoine canadien

Brindle & Glass is pleased to acknowledge the financial support for its publishing
program from the Government of Canada through the Canada Book Fund, Canada
Council for the Arts, and the Province of British Columbia through the British
Columbia Arts Council and the Book Publishing Tax Credit.

FSC
www.fsc.org

MIX
Paper from
responsible sources
FSC® C103214

This book was produced using FSC®-certified, acid-free paper, processed
chlorine free and printed with vegetable-based inks.

1 2 3 4 5 16 15 14 13 12

Dedicated to the memory of Celia Sánchez
and those Cubans still working to realize
her humanitarian vision of their homeland.

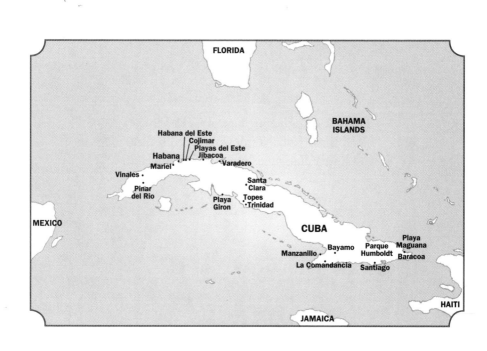

FLORIDA

BAHAMA
ISLANDS

Habana del Este
Cojimar
Playas del Este
Jibacoa
Habana
Mariel
Varadero
Vinales
Santa
Clara
Pinar
del Rio
Topes
Playa
Trinidad
Giron

MEXICO

CUBA

Playa
Maguana
Parque
Bayamo
Humboldt
Manzanillo
Baracoa
La Comandancia
Santiago

HAITI

JAMAICA

ONE

CELIA was sure that she had not fainted, hallucinated, nor suffered an altered state. She had simply—what? Carefully, as if reviewing a patient's case history, she tried to reconstruct what had happened.

As on previous visits, she had first examined the small museum's paltry exhibits: a few articles of clothing, a worn leather purse, the dented aluminium canteen that Sánchez was said to have carried during her years as a rebel leader. Then she had turned her attention to the portraits. Although done by different artists, each had rendered the face with a flatness that stripped the subject of personality. Celia guessed that this was because the paintings were copied from photographs, Sánchez having never posed for a portrait. Still, what was the matter with those men? Couldn't they see who she *was*? Celia turned away from each painting with the feeling one gets upon discovering that essential parts of an important book have been blacked out.

The museum contained not a page of Sánchez's writings, no description of her role in bringing Cuba from under the boot of the dictator Batista, no list of the schools, hospitals, housing, and recreational facilities she had established after the war. There was not even mention of the very park in which the museum sat, Habana's largest, which had sprung from Sánchez's mind. She had considered it so important for city residents to have easy access to nature that she had helped plant a grove of mango trees in Parque Lenin herself. She had not lived to see how they'd grown, but as she placed seedlings in the ground she must have imagined them like the giants that now provided fruit and shade in her hometown at the eastern end of the island.

There was nothing in the one-room museum to tell a visitor those things, or much else about the woman it purported to memorialize. By its silence, history, including the officially sanctioned Fidel Castro version of history, had reduced Celia Sánchez to a pretty face—and not an honest one at that, for all of the gallery's portraits presented her as prettier than she actually had been.

Troubled as always by what the museum did not contain, Celia had exited through the back door into the garden to see the one exhibit that did give her a sense of who the woman had been—a life-sized bronze of Sánchez as she might have appeared in her late thirties. Celia had gazed intently at the statue, then reached out to place a flower at its foot—a rose, rare in Cuba, given to her by the grateful mother of a child patient. It was then, with the suddenness of a TV turned on at top volume in a quiet room, that the silence of the garden seemed to have been shattered.

Habaneras lined the highway, cheering guerrilla fighters as they rolled into the capital. Celia turned to Fidel, sitting next to her atop the tank. A flower was flung from the crowd. He caught the blossom with a high reach, as if it were a baseball, and handed it to her. She could not hear his whisper above the rumble of the tank and cheers of the crowd but read the words on his lips: "Para ti, compañera." Their eyes met and she was embraced by the totality of what they shared: the dreams, struggles, incalculable losses, and this euphoric moment.

Celia Cantú gave a small cry as a thorn on the rose stem pricked her. Her thumb went to her mouth and she sucked at the tiny puncture, extracting herself from something that she had felt, for an instant, she was experiencing.

Of course she had seen Castro's triumphant 1959 arrival into Habana on television countless times; what Cuban had not? That historic film footage was not so different from what had just screened in her mind's eye. Flowers were thrown, but she recalled no picture showing Sánchez and Castro exchanging such an intimate gaze. Indeed, she could not recall seeing Sánchez in the newsreels at all, although as the Revolutionary Armed Forces' first commander, predating even Fidel, she must have been there.

Celia closed her eyes and tried to see the thirty-eight-year-old Sánchez as she would have appeared beside Castro when the tanks rumbled into Habana. No image came. The scene burned into her senses, even after the hallucination had passed, was from Sánchez's point of view. Or was it her own? With absolute clarity, Celia recalled looking directly into golden-brown eyes that for a split second were looking into her own, sharing every emotional nuance.

Worried by what the incident might imply about her mental health—for it bore some resemblance to a hallucination she had had about a year earlier—she turned to leave. For a long moment she stared at the door leading back into the museum. Was she was coming or going? Hadn't she just been here? Or was that another year? She stood there treading time as one treads water when unsure of how deep the bottom is.

"Compañera? Are you all right?"

With difficulty, Celia brought the man who had spoken into focus. He was staring at her with consternation.

"I know you," he said. "You come every year."

She did not know him and wondered, running fingers through her hair the way one sometimes does when trying to wake up, if she was still hallucinating. Then she noticed that he carried a rake and guessed that he was the museum's gardener.

"Yes. I just came to see . . ." She gestured toward the bronze of Sánchez.

"Of course. Did you know her?"

"No." At his look of disappointment, she added, "But my mother did. She was in the sierra with Raúl. And Celia, of course, with Fidel. I did meet her once but I was very young. All I understood was that she was called Celia too. That I was named for her."

The gardener scrutinized her. "You have the same eyes."

It was the sort of thing her father would have said, had in fact said. Only he had meant her mother's eyes, not those of Celia Sánchez.

Celia Cantú smiled. "Brown?"

The gardener ignored her teasing tone. "Tender," he said reverently. "She had the capacity to feel the pain of others. That was why she embraced the Revolution."

He continued to look at her as fathers do when they are assessing the worthiness of their offspring. "And you? Are you a good communist?"

He must be an old revolutionary himself, Celia thought. They grew up in such serious times. She shrugged. "I'm a good doctor."

The answer seemed to satisfy him. She smiled goodbye and took the path around the building, back to the parking lot. He followed her, walking rather too close. Perhaps he was not convinced that she really was okay. Celia was not entirely convinced herself, but she affected the purposeful stride that on normal days carried her up and down hospital corridors.

With egalitarian good manners, he did not try to open the car door for her. Celia slid in, nodded goodbye, and drove away. Just before she turned the corner she glanced in the rear-view mirror and saw that he was still staring after her—a small, muscular man in his seventies who had grown up in an era that she, barely thirty-five, seemed compelled to reinvent.

By the shortest route it was a mere kilometre to the restaurant, but she chose a more meandering route through Parque Lenin, past rowboats on the lake and children flying kites in open fields. She heard in the near distance the toot of a little choo-choo train taking families around the park, and farther away, the whistle of a larger one, which, now that it was late afternoon, would be taking others back to the city. The drive gave her an extra few minutes to consider what had happened back there in the garden, time to wonder why, although it had alarmed her, she felt a lingering sense of exhilaration.

Psychiatry was not Celia's area of expertise, but her medical training told her that whatever tricks her mind had played on her must have sprung from some brief aberration in brain chemistry. She would have to consider the implications of that later, and perhaps seek a second opinion. But now she must hurry, because Luis was waiting, had been waiting for—she was not sure how long.

TWO

LUIS LAGO approved of Las Ruinas' Soviet-inspired architecture. It did not bother him that the restaurant, monstrous in size, with heavy horizontal lines painted dazzling white, seemed as out of place in its wooded setting as a luxury liner in an orange grove. Its weightiness promised the durability of Cuba's colonial construction, while clean lines implied a purity of purpose lacking in edifices of that ostentatious era. But the place *was* expensive. Luis was here only because of the location, and because Celia liked it.

It was his discovery, three years ago, that she bussed out to Parque Lenin every year to visit the Sánchez museum, his offering to drive her, and inviting her to dine at Las Ruinas afterwards, that had led to their engagement. Naturally he would have liked to visit the museum with her, but she made it clear at the onset that she wanted to go alone.

He assured her that he didn't mind waiting at the restaurant. He really didn't mind. It was a small thing and helped fill a void in their relationship—his nagging sense that nothing he had to offer was particularly important to her. He could not fault her courtesy in acknowledging the things he did for her, but he sensed that it was more ritual than need. Celia Cantú asked for nothing.

Consciously he admired her quiet restraint as much as he had detested the voluble emotions flung at him by women with whom he had been involved when he was younger. Yet Celia's self-containment was almost too complete. Luis knew that among family, friends, and co-workers he was most at ease when taking cues from the group. Celia, though, did not signal her desires. She had a kind of emotional opaqueness that left him perpetually unsure of what she wanted, how she felt, or, perhaps, even who she was.

Luis gave a disparaging grunt at that last, stupid thought. They had known each other since childhood. It had always been him watching her, not the other way around, so what could there be to know about her that he didn't know already?

Even as he told himself this, Luis knew he was whistling in the dark. He did not know, for example, what her reaction would be to the letter in his pocket—a letter that he had kept to himself as long as possible.

A trickle of sweat slid down his spine. He moved into the shade of Las Ruinas' cement-heavy portico. Unobtrusively dressed in a short-sleeved guayabera, grey slacks, and black shoes, he went unnoticed by a quince party posing for pictures in the restaurant's flower-filled garden. Although he stood a head taller than most Cuban men, he rarely attracted attention. He had what he jokingly called "a talent for invisibility." It had bothered him when he was a child, especially in the presence of his polar-opposite brother, but later, in politics, it was an asset. His input, never controversial but always thoughtful, was given consideration at the highest levels of government. From the outset he had aimed for an approach that would never be perceived as threatening. A genuine readiness to serve the Revolution in whatever capacity his colleagues deemed most useful had facilitated his rise in the ranks.

Luis watched a man, probably the fifteen-year-old's father, snapping pictures. The man must be forty, which meant that like Luis he had been born soon after the victory of the Revolution and had grown up steeped in its values. But what good had it done? The fool had obviously spent a bundle of money, more likely the money of Miami relatives, to make an extravaganza of what Luis viewed as one of the bourgeoisie's most obnoxious traditions.

The tight fit of the girl's formal gown suggested that it had been purchased elsewhere by someone who remembered her as more slender than she was now. New outfits worn by the brothers, sisters, and cousins who surrounded her to simulate the escorts and attendants of a royal child were likely from Miami relatives too. In return, those who sent the crap would get copies of the photos that the proud father was snapping so feverishly. He probably imagined that the pictures would offer incontrovertible evidence that he had done right by his daughter; proof that although island Cubans lacked certain consumer goods, they had one thing that many Cuban emigrants did not: a close family that included happy, well-adjusted adolescents.

The girl's father noticed Luis only when, trying to get an overview shot of the group, he actually backed into him. The man quickly apologized, then held out the camera. "Would you mind taking one of us all together? You know, with me in it?"

Luis hesitated and then accepted the camera. The man positioned himself next to his daughter, a pouty girl who would have been pretty without the mask of makeup.

"Ready!" The father beamed.

Luis snapped the shutter, only to be greeted by cries of "Aye, no! I had my mouth open!" "My eyes were closed!" "Otro, por favor!"

Luis took one more. He returned the camera with an expression meant to convey that he did not approve of the event or his small part in it.

The man did not seem to notice. He raced back to pose his daughter for other photos, tilting her chin, instructing her to smile. Luis saw that the girl was growing impatient with the mannequin treatment. At last she flopped onto a bench and refused to look up. The father shouted in exasperation. Then, seeing something in her sullen downcast eyes that the camera would translate into modesty, he gave a delighted, "Wait! Perfecto!" and snapped the picture.

Luis turned away, frowning, and saw Celia coming toward him. She was walking fast, almost trotting. The short dark curls, usually so tidy, had the messy look of a woman just up in the morning who only half-combed her hair, and without benefit of a mirror. Her smile was tense and did not reach her eyes.

Before he could ask what was wrong, she burst out, "Sorry I kept you waiting so long, Luis!"

"Long? Why, you haven't been gone an hour!"

She stopped in her tracks and checked her watch, as if she couldn't take his word.

He wondered why she seemed surprised. The museum was not five minutes away. "You didn't stay as long as usual."

"But I—you were frowning," she said faintly. "I thought it was the waiting."

"No. It's that nonsense over there." He jerked his head toward the quince party, which was being rearranged into yet another combination on the broad white steps leading into the restaurant.

Celia glanced toward to the group. "*Pobrecita!*" she exclaimed in a low voice. "Look at the swelling! Those shoes are so tight they have cut off circulation in her feet. And the way the high heels have thrust her pelvis forward; see how it exaggerates the curvature of her spine?"

Luis dropped an arm around Celia's shoulder. "A girl that age ought to be spending the weekend at a campismo with friends, not enduring this, this charade!"

"Thank goodness Liliana didn't want a fiesta de quince," Celia murmured.

"Surely you would not have given her one?"

Celia tensed and Luis immediately regretted the question. Both in tone and phrasing it recalled their major area of conflict: his belief that she was too lenient with her sixteen-year-old niece. Had Celia replied yes to his question they would have quarrelled, and he would have agonized later over how he could have been so inept as to anger this normally even-tempered woman whom he only wanted to please.

But what Celia said, patiently, as if explaining herself to someone who barely knew her, was, "I may not be a communist, Luis, but I am not so bourgeois that I would allow my own flesh and blood to be paraded like a commodity."

The fact that he was a party member and she was not was not an issue between them—or, rather, only became one when he tried to defend some National Assembly decision that annoyed her. But the quinceñero had nothing to do with politics, nothing to do with them, and now of all times he did not want to annoy her. He pulled her close and asked, "Are you hungry?"

"I suppose . . . yes," she replied vaguely, as if food was the last thing on her mind.

They stepped through the ornate door and stopped, waiting for their eyes to adjust from harsh sunlight to the shadowed interior. In contrast to the ultra-modern planes that made up the shell of the building, the interior was graced with the brick ruins of an ancient sugar mill, age-melted into soft irregular shapes. Indirect natural light filtered through spaces left between the walls and roof, revealing tables artfully arranged against crumbling walls overgrown with tropical vegetation.

Luis stood slightly behind Celia when they entered so he could watch her. She was wearing a dress, which she did not often do, giving him a view of bare shoulders and well-muscled calves. She loved Las Ruinas and it thrilled him to make this pleasure possible—not often, but once a year, on the day she chose to visit the Sánchez museum. He had no idea why the restaurant appealed to her. It was out of character for her to crave luxury and she positively detested the ostentatious. But there was no denying that Las Ruinas entranced her. "What is it you like so much about this place?" he asked.

He rarely asked a direct question about her feelings. He had learned better. He had learned that while her answer was never an evasion, neither was it enlightening.

But with the letter in his pocket, the one she did not know about yet, he had a more urgent need than usual to know her true feelings.

"The contrast," she replied thoughtfully. "The modern exterior gives no hint that the inside conceals so much history and mystery and . . . forgotten lives."

The headwaiter approached and they followed him to a table. Luis welcomed the distraction. A discussion of what they would order made it unnecessary for him to ponder her explanation. Although perfectly straightforward, instinct told him that it concealed labyrinths of meaning that he could not even guess.

They spoke little during the meal. Luis thought Celia seemed distracted, and knew for a fact that he was. As they dawdled over dessert, he finally forced himself to tell her what he had put off for two weeks. He spread his hands flat on the table to ensure that they neither shook nor balled into fists and said in what he hoped was a steady voice, "I got a letter. From José."

"José who?" she asked, licking chocolate icing from her fork.

"José, my asshole brother!"

He hadn't meant to raise his voice but he must have because the only other party in the restaurant, the family of the quinceañera, stopped mid-conversation and stared.

"No! De veras?" Celia's expression was one of disbelief, as he supposed his had been when he first realized who the letter was from.

"After ten years of total silence! What the hell does he want?"

"What did he say?" Celia laid her fork on the empty plate carefully, perhaps too carefully, and folded her hands out of sight.

Lowering his voice, Luis muttered, "That he has two daughters. Which I suppose implies a wife. And—get this—he signed himself 'Miami Joe.'"

"Did he say why he was writing?"

Luis's broad, bony shoulders slumped. "The great 'Miami Joe' is coming for a visit. Apparently *without* his family."

He waited for Celia's reaction. When it came he felt stupid for not having known in advance what it would be. Concealing her own feelings, she focused entirely on his. It was exactly what she did dozens of times a day when dealing with children in distress. She reached across the table and enclosed his large cold hands in her small warm ones.

"What was between us was a long time ago, Luis. I am not the woman I was then," she said firmly.

Although unconvinced, Luis clung gratefully to her hand.

THREE

JOE LAGO, driving too fast, swerved the BMW into the drive with practised precision. He loped across a manicured lawn and rang the doorbell. After a long wait he heard the tap-tap of Vera's high heels.

For an instant he took the wide-open door for welcome, then it registered that his ex-wife's posture was one of defiance. She was flaunting the fact that she could open the door as wide as she liked and he couldn't enter—except by invitation, which he was unlikely to get.

He felt a flutter of bewilderment that the same blue eyes that once had the power to attract him from across a crowded room now repelled him like an icy sea, and the small tilted nose he'd found so charming now made him want to slap her. But where would that get him? Joe Lago was a practical man whose pattern was to ignore the past and focus on what he wanted in the moment. He gave Vera his most engaging grin and got right to the point.

"Hi, honey. I'm going to be away for the next few weeks, so I'd like to take the girls out for ice cream or something. It's been quite a while and—"

"No."

Of course it hadn't worked. Countless times had he tried ignoring past conflict and acting as if they were on the best of terms. "Let bygones be bygones" worked well in business, but it had hardly ever worked with Vera. The more he let things slide, the more she elaborated on them until they filled her head and exploded in accusatory shrapnel. If he dodged, she only became more infuriated; understandable, since her intention was to do damage. His best ploy was to play dead, or at least act hurt.

"Have a heart, Vera. You know I've been out of town. I really miss them."

"They don't miss you."

It wasn't the lie so much as the triumph in her voice that caused him to explode. "Bullshit!"

"You can't play father on a drop-in basis, Joe. We agreed—"

"No! You and your fucking lawyer agreed—"

The door closed in his face. For a minute he just stood there, imagining how easy it would be to kick the damned door down. Well, actually not all that easy—not in Gucci loafers. Screw it. He had never let her provoke him to violence before; no point in losing control now.

He strode back to the car. Control was the issue, had been from the beginning. She'd been willing to share his bed, his name, and, of course, his money—but only on her terms. When he thought about it, it astonished him that from the start he had let her call the shots: whether to buy a house, where to buy it, whether to have children, when to have them, what his role as father should be, and now, apparently, whether he'd have any role at all. On the slim chance that she was watching, he turned and gave her the finger.

But the faces peering out the picture window were those of Keri and Amy, his

8

angel-blond daughters. Sheepishly he raised more fingers to convert the "up yours" insult into a wave. Keri, only four, lifted her tiny hand to wave back. Or so he thought but couldn't be sure, for at that moment Vera pulled the girls away from the window.

He got into the BMW and sat there filled with disgust—not for Vera but for himself. He had watched numerous acquaintances go through the same thing, allowing themselves to be pussy-whipped until they fell backwards into the pit of divorce, then flounder there for months or even years while being pelted with crap from the wife's lawyer and, often as not, their own. Although Joe always made the appropriate sympathy noises, he privately considered it their own fault for not playing their cards right. Now he'd been dealt the same cards and, it was fairly obvious, had played them no better.

It seemed incredible to Joe that his life had come to this. "A goddamned daisy-chain of clichés," he muttered.

As quick as the revulsion hit him, it disappeared. His strength was the ability to face things head-on, make fast decisions, and follow through. He was going to turn this around, not tomorrow, not next week, but right now. He had known all along he would have to do it and how it would have to be done. He had to put distance between himself and them—permanent distance. No more phone calls. No more stupid visitation games.

"Walk away," he told himself. "Just fucking walk away."

He could do it. Hell, he had walked away from Celia when he was more or less in love with her. He doubted he had ever loved Vera, although God knows he'd been hot for her. Every inch of her Barbie-doll body, from shiny hair to aerobics-perfected buttocks, had turned him on, and he had gone after her as if she were the best deal in town.

She had hardly been that. But give himself credit; once he'd had it with her insatiable appetite for shopping combined with an all too satiable appetite for sex, and no appetite for it at all unless she'd been pre-sweetened with a gift or promises of extravagances to follow, he had shut her off. And she, of course, had shut him off. He had let her file for divorce, let her think it was all her idea. But he had done his homework. The game plan was perfected in his head before the lawyers were called in: assets tucked away where she couldn't get at them, generous child support, and a generous lump sum for her in exchange for an ironclad agreement to not ask for more, ever. If he hadn't got that she would have had him in court every other month just to maintain an element of control over him. He had outsmarted her and now she was using the last thing she had—the kids.

He had a mental replay of Keri raising her tiny hand to wave and the wistful way she'd looked back over her shoulder as Vera pulled her away from the window. His gut twisted. Sure, they were little dolls, but the reality was that they were not his dolls, they were Vera's, had been from birth. She was the one who chose their clothes, chose their toys, chose their friends. Hell, she even chose their language.

"No Spanish," she had decided when he agreed to pop for a full-time maid. "Miami is a divided city and it is not in the girls' best interest to be taken for Latinas."

So they had got a Haitian housekeeper. Given their fair skin, they certainly would never be taken for Haitians. Half their blood might be Cuban but it didn't show and never would. Vera would see to that.

"American kids," he muttered as he fumbled through his CD selection. He imagined the girls ten years from now, phoning him the way his friends' kids phoned them, to ask for use of the car, or their own car, or money: price tags for affection that would become larger as they grew older.

He dropped *Buena Vista Social Club* into the CD player and cranked the volume up as high as it would go. On impulse, he hit a button and all the car windows slid open. Cuban music blasted across the lawn and crashed against the side of his all-American ex-dream house like a fist.

FOUR

CELIA stepped out of the shower and moved into her bedroom, leaving a trail of wet footprints across the worn tile floor. She stood towelling herself dry, considering the choices offered by her minimalist wardrobe while telling herself that she did not care enough about José Lago's return to dress in any particular way.

She had to go to work later, so could wear the white slacks and smock in which she felt most comfortable. But would that not seem as if she was advertising the fact that she was a doctor? On the other hand, not a dress, definitely not. Since her teens she had not been able to wear a skirt without attracting the admiring glances of men who felt compelled to let her know they thought she had nice legs. She cringed at the thought of José telling her she had a nice anything, especially in front of Luis.

She absently wrapped the towel around herself, wandered into the kitchen, and poured a cup of coffee. Then, remembering that she was on evening shift and would be sipping coffee all night, poured it back into the dented aluminium pot. Celia did not particularly like being alone. She missed her niece during the weeks when she was away at school and more so during a home week like this when Liliana chose to join friends at a beach campismo.

Still wearing only a towel, Celia went out onto the balcony. She sat down in one plastic chair and put her feet up on the other one. The sun, combined with a breeze off the ocean, felt wonderful on bare skin. She looked through the railing at the expanse of wind-ruffled water and listened to the rhythm of wavelets washing ashore across the street and four stories below.

She chose not to think about José, whom she would soon see. Instead, she forced herself to recall the previous weekend with Luis. She had enjoyed being with him, both at the restaurant and later. He was so upset about José's visit that she had gone out of her way to make the rest of the evening pleasant. Because predictability soothed Luis, she had tried to make their lovemaking just that, and knew as his body relaxed that she had succeeded. She had feigned tranquility too, but it had been hard to keep her mind off the hallucination—if a hallucination is what it was, and what other name could there be for an experience so clearly recalled that had no basis in reality? Only later, alone in the privacy of her own bedroom, had she gingerly reviewed the vision.

It resembled one she had had a year earlier, in that it had not lasted more than a second or two. Perhaps the only reason she had retained both was because for those few seconds she had felt so sure of herself, so strong! Was her psyche reaching back into Cuba's glorious revolutionary history in an attempt to claim some of its participants' courage for herself? If so, she thought ruefully, it hadn't been particularly successful, since the feeling had vanished along with the visions.

She noticed that the towel had slid down, exposing her breasts to the sun, and hiked it up to cover skin that had already turned pink. Here on the small balcony of her apartment she saw how her mind had been playing tricks on her. Those things had not happened to her and may not have even happened to Sánchez—at least, not the way she had visioned them. The incidents were hallucinations, dreams, fantasies, or . . .

"Whatever they are they are *not* me," Celia said aloud, and mentally began to list all the reasons why not. She had never been into mysticism. She did not even care for the magic realism of such fine Latin American writers as Isabelle Allende and Gabriel García Marquéz. By temperament and training, she was a rational, scientific-minded person.

Like the good doctor she knew herself to be, Celia prescribed what reason and intuition told her was the best regimen. She must not dwell on sensations that momentarily made her feel as if she had become Celia Sánchez or Celia Sánchez had become her or whatever was going on there. Yet she should try to remember, perhaps write down, the details of each episode. They were, after all, symptoms of something. Meanwhile, she should examine other aspects of her life that might be causing the mental aberrations. Was she under some stress that she was choosing to ignore?

José's imminent arrival popped into her head, but she waved it away as one might a mosquito. Even the most recent hallucination had occurred before Luis broke the news that his brother was returning. Naturally she had grieved when José walked out on her, and had it not been for Franci's support she might well have failed her final medical school exams. But hers was not a profession nor was Cuba a culture that encouraged emotional self-indulgence. In recent years she could honestly say that she had rarely given her former fiancé a thought.

Liliana, at sixteen, was more of a challenge now than she had been when she was a little girl, but Celia had not come up against any parenting issues that could be called stressful. She truly enjoyed Liliana's vivacious personality and had confidence in her niece's innate good sense—discounting, perhaps, her addiction to disco music. Their bond was strengthened by the fact that Liliana looked to Celia as a role model. Even before Liliana's mother died, the child had declared that when she grew up she was not going to be a soldier like Mommy but a doctor like Tía Celia. No, Celia concluded, whatever this glitch in her psyche, it had nothing to do with Liliana.

Work had certainly been difficult in recent months, not so much for the nature of it, which she loved, but because everyone was working longer hours. She knew that toward the end of a shift she simply did not have the same reserves of patience nor could she provide the same quality of counselling to her child patients, their parents, and members of the pediatric staff who looked to her for reassurance and guidance. Celia smiled with faint irony, wondering if her disturbing experiences might be rooted in something as trivial as insufficient sleep.

Or in her relationship with Luis?

Had Celia focused on that, she might have found, if not a causal factor, at least a facet of her life worth examining. But the instant the thought of Luis entered her head she sprang up and moved to the balcony doorway to check the living room clock. *Aye Madre!* He would be here any minute! As if conjured by the thought, Luis's small grey Fiat rounded the corner a block away.

In her bedroom, Celia snatched the first clothes that came to hand. She pulled on jeans and a T-shirt, slipped into sandals, and ran a brush through her hair. Moments later she heard, along with the sounds of everyday living from other apartments in the building, Luis's footsteps coming along the hallway toward her door.

She opened it on the first knock, and said, glancing at her watch, "I suppose you want to be there when he arrives. Shall we go then?"

FIVE

JOE could barely believe he was back in Cuba. But here he was, crossing heat-rippled tarmac over island soil as real as the dinky terminal where the Aerocaribe flight from Cancun had landed. As the bus shuttled passengers to the international terminal to clear immigration and customs, Joe wondered how much of what he had read was true. After the Soviets cut off aid and the Cuban economy hit rock bottom—which was where it was when he left—had the country really pulled itself up by the bootstraps? No mean trick, he conceded, when you have to start by creating the boots—or, in Cuba's case, creating a tourist industry—from scratch. He could not imagine that white sand beaches, which in his youth had been enjoyed by Cubans and a sprinkling of fleshy Russians, now swarmed with foreign tourists. But he had seen the pictures. Would slick magazines like *Islands* and *Conde Naste* lie about a thing like that?

Joe gave no credence to the US media's endless stream of stories about supposed abuses of the 11 million Cubans who remained in their homeland; tales regularly trotted out to explain why 10 per cent of the Cuban population had immigrated to North America. Being one of the 10 per cent, he knew that most were like himself, people more interested in money than politics, simply looking for economic opportunities that didn't exist or weren't permitted on the island. Joe wasn't skeptical by nature, but given the biased reportage about Cuba, common sense dictated that he go see for himself.

He flipped his US passport open in front of the immigration official and waited to be hassled, but all she asked was where he would be staying and how long. He said he would be in Cuba a month and named the hotel he had written on his tourist card. He hoped neither was true. With luck he could check out business possibilities in half that time and expected to stay at his mother's place. She hadn't replied to his letter, but that was probably because he had sent it to Luis, who might not have shown it to her. Joe wasn't worried. Mothers—at least Cuban mothers—didn't know the meaning of rejection.

The customs agent performed a perfunctory search of his luggage, and Joe passed through into the lobby. He found the Havanautos rental agency and waited with growing impatience for the clerk to do the paperwork. It was an annoyance to learn that the Audi he had reserved was not available. He was unapologetically offered a Korean-made Daewoo. Grumbling, he signed the form. Then there was a twenty-minute wait for credit card confirmation. As he waited for the endlessly redialed call to go through, he scanned the lobby. He saw no familiar face nor had he expected one. Even if Luis had a car, which was improbable, the fuel shortage could have prevented him from driving out to the airport. More likely he had chosen to ignore the visit. Not that it mattered. Joe never had waited for his older brother to open doors for him and wasn't about to start now.

Paperwork finally completed, he stepped out into the sweltering heat and looked across to where he was told the car was parked, beyond a row of cassia trees. The Cuban name for those trees came back to him: lluvia de oro. "Rain of gold" could not have been more appropriate, he thought as he paused to watch a shower of yellow blossoms shaken loose by a slight breeze. Then he saw her. She stood in the shade of a cassia tree talking to a man, oblivious to the blossoms drifting around them. Oblivious to him.

From the back, he honestly didn't recognize the tall man in grey polyester trousers and short-sleeved white shirt. But then, it wasn't the man who magnetized his gaze. It was the one person he would never have expected to see here—or to see at all, for that matter. He had thought of Celia briefly on the flight over. He supposed she was married by now with two or three kids. She probably would have put on thirty pounds and switched to matronly skirts that bulged at the belly. It was not an image he cared to cultivate. The image he preferred, although he had blocked it too, was the one he was staring at fifty feet away: the same trim figure she'd had back in med school, clad in the same jeans and T-shirt. He almost expected that when she spotted him her face would darken with the same rage it had held the last time he saw her. But he was wrong about that too. As he drew near he realized that she had already seen him and, for whatever reason, was keeping her expression impassive.

Maybe the guy was her husband—but no, hell, it was his brother, Luis! The everything-is-black-or-white brother who had snarled at him when he was leaving that if he cared a whit for their mother he'd never try to contact them, to spare her painful reminders of having reared a gusano son. Joe knew it wasn't true, but it had offered a convenient rationale for avoiding incessant pleadings for him to come home. The last thing he needed in those first years of near-daily humiliations was the suck of family pulling him back. He had considered re-establishing contact after the kids were born, but it was obvious that Vera's determination to distance them from their Cuban heritage was an in-law war in the offing. Given how soon the marriage turned into a war within, he could think of no good reason to launch another, especially one where he'd be a hostage staked out in the middle and used as a shield against missiles launched from both sides.

Joe instantly saw that whatever his brother had been up to during their decade-long separation had put him on a fast track to middle age. The grey hair was why he hadn't recognized him from the back, that and the way Luis's broad shoulders had hollowed out and become slightly stooped. He might have known that once Luis stopped playing baseball he wouldn't keep himself in shape. Joe had, of course: regular workouts being virtually obligatory in the medical supply business in order to project a healthy image. He was not entirely surprised that Luis had come to meet him, but Celia—why was she here? Maybe she wasn't married? Or had been and was now divorced? Kids? Well, maybe that would be to his advantage. A protective barrier, so to speak. Even as Joe's mind was scrabbling for ways to maintain a safe distance, his gaze never left her face and his feet carried him directly to her. Without so much as a glance at Luis, he dropped his bags and wrapped his arms around her. "Celia! You haven't changed at all!"

She slid out of his embrace and moved close to Luis. "Hola, José. You're alone?"

"All by myself," he said in a tone of hearty good humour more feigned than felt. He turned to his brother and, as Luis had not extended his hand, Joe thumped him on the back. "Luis, man, you're looking great! I can't believe I'm here."

With a resentful glance at Joe's expensive bag, Luis said, "I hope you don't have more luggage. The Fiat is quite small."

"No problem. I got a rental car. Didn't expect you to come all the way out here to meet me." Joe tried to catch his brother's eye, to convey appreciation that he had.

Luis refused to meet his gaze. "It was you who broke off contact, José, not us. As far as Mamá is concerned, we are still a family."

Just what I figured, Joe thought. You told me not to write, I didn't, and you haven't forgiven me for it. Mother will, of course, and Celia's neutral. Or pretending to be. He shifted his gaze to Celia. "How about riding back with me, Celia? Fill me in?"

"You know the way," she snapped.

"No I don't," Joe grinned. "If you recall, I didn't leave by air. I don't think I've ever driven from the airport into the city. I might get lost."

Celia folded her arms. "Maps are sold inside the terminal."

Luis laid his hand on her shoulder. "Go ahead, Celia. Ride with him." To Joe he said, "Mamá and I will be waiting for you."

Joe noted the look that passed between Celia and his brother. Although Luis, tight-jawed, had urged her (given her permission?), she was reluctant. Her eyes remained on his face, warm and worried.

Luis spoke in a low, firm voice. "It's best for you to go with him. Really."

Celia turned to Joe, gaze level and cold. "All right, José. Let's go."

He located the car and she got in, leaving as much space between them as was possible in such a compact vehicle. She gave directions for getting out of the airport complex and onto the highway. "The quickest route is the Primer Anillio, the freeway that circles the city."

"Quicker to where?"

"Habana del Este, where I live. You can drop me off, then zip through the tunnel and take the Malecón to Vedado."

"Mother still lives in Vedado? In the same apartment?"

"Naturally."

The way she said it reminded Joe that spending one's entire life in the same home was the norm in Cuba; something he had completely lost sight of in the States, where frequent moves were expected of everyone. A sudden image of his diminutive mother in the apartment where he had grown up gave him the first pang of nostalgia.

"How is she?"

"The same." Celia paused. "It is a shame that you came alone. Seeing your children would have meant a lot to her."

Joe took a deep breath. Might as well get it over with, he decided, and told her about the divorce. "I had a good lawyer," he explained. "He worked out a deal where support payments go straight from my account to hers. That way I don't have to have personal contact with her or the girls. I figured that was best—a clean break, you know?"

Celia said nothing. They drove in silence, except for Celia's indication of the entrance onto Primer Anillo, and a few kilometres later, one leading onto the Vía Monumental. After a lengthy silence, Joe asked, "Did you stay in medicine?"

"Sí. Pediatricas. I work there." She pointed to a large hospital, and at the same time indicated the Habana del Este exit. He followed her directions along the edge of an apartment complex that sprawled over several blocks and along a waterfront street. Four-storey apartment buildings faced the sea, separated from the rocky shoreline by the street and a strip of windblown weeds. Celia indicated her building and he pulled to the curb. It was one of the older buildings in the complex, probably built by the original micro-brigaders back in the 1960s. Some windows still had the original wooden slat shutters. Quite a few were broken or hanging awry.

Without looking at him, Celia said, "How sad."

Assuming she meant the divorce, Joe said, "That's life. Nowadays anyway. Hell, even Fidel got divorced. And there was that long custody battle for his son."

"But not his daughter."

Joe shrugged. "If she was his daughter,"

"I don't understand how a father could walk away from his little girls."

Joe realized that it was that, not the divorce, she had meant when she said it was sad. He muttered, "Fidel never jumped through hoops to see his."

"If she was his."

Joe noticed with mild amusement that Celia had switched sides, but he was tired of the conversation. "Yeah, well, when it gets to be a hassle, what's the point?" He looked up at the building, which was as bleak as modern function-over-form architecture could make. Although some nearby buildings had recently been painted, hers was a mouldering grey. "This is it? Which apartment?"

She pointed to the top floor. "The one with red geraniums on the balcony."

"Looks like a Miami slum. Public housing gone to seed."

"Oh? Since when do the Yanquis put low-cost housing on waterfront property?"

He thought of Miami's bleak, crime-ridden public housing and conceded the point. "You do have a good view. Prime location."

"Wasted on the working class?" she asked sarcastically.

Joe laughed. He had remembered her face and figure but had forgotten that quick ironic wit. "Are you trying to pick a fight? Forget it. Let me take you to dinner."

"I am working this evening," she said and promptly got out of the car.

He caught up to her on the sidewalk. "I'll pick you up at the hospital after work."

"No, thanks. I always ride my bike."

"At night?"

Her eyes flashed contemptuous. "Día, noche, no importa. Habana no es Miami."

"You *are* trying to pick a fight. And I'm warning you, you'd better lay off or I'm going to kiss you." Joe tried to slip his arms around her, but she peeled out of his embrace even quicker than she had at the airport and stalked up the sidewalk.

"Wait!" Joe moved to mitigate her annoyance. Or her pretended annoyance. In his experience women were never all that upset to discover that a man found them attractive. "Just one question?"

Celia stopped and half-turned, warily.

"A personal one. Do you live alone?"

"No. Carolina's daughter, Liliana, lives with me."

"Don't tell me that crazy sister of yours made a career of the army and dumped her kid on you!"

"Carolina was with the Cuban armed forces in Angola. With her husband. They were both killed there." Celia's voice was low and unemotional, but there was something in her eyes that said that she liked slapping him in the face with such harsh news, that it served him right for being flippant on subjects he knew nothing about.

Joe had a fleeting image of Celia's vivacious older sister, so full of bold laughter at parties and equally bold indignation at anything she perceived as a social injustice; that pretty, busty body lying in the mud of some distant battlefield. He promptly erased the image and did what he did best: focused on the moment, on the living woman a few feet away. "Oh Celia! That must've been terrible for you."

"Sí, terrible."

Images of Carolina must have been in her head too because there was a pained silence before she added, "But raising Liliana has been a blessing. She is sixteen already."

"You're not married, though? No children of your own?"

She gave him a cool, altogether knowing look. "No more personal questions from you, old friend. You have been gone too long."

She turned and walked away, this time not looking back.

SIX

RATHER than returning to the Vía Monumental for the twenty-minute drive to his mother's apartment, Joe followed the waterfront street a little farther, then veered off onto a dirt track that wound through a brushy area. Sandy paths leading down to the beach were imprinted with bicycle tracks, evidence that the undeveloped area was as much an unofficial playground now as it had been when he and Luis were kids.

Although he had felt prepared for a family reunion on the flight over, Celia's being at the airport had thrown him off balance. He needed a drink and time to put it into perspective. A few kilometres from Celia's place, the dirt track terminated at the parking lot of El Castillo de los Tres Reyes del Morro. Joe had never been to El Morro when the fort wasn't overrun with students on field trips. Maybe it was still like that during school hours, but now, nearing sunset, only foreign tourists milled about.

Joe parked the car, crossed a drawbridge over the moat, and circled around to the side of the fort that faced the harbour. How many times had pirates passed this way to storm and sometimes burn Habana? How many times had he and Luis re-enacted those battles, sometimes casting themselves as defenders of the city, sometimes as the pirates?

In ancient times a chain running from fort to fort, this side of the harbour mouth to the other side, was raised at nightfall to keep out pirate ships. How much could such a span have weighed in sixteenth-century iron? How many slaves would it have taken to raise and lower that clanking monster? Fewer, certainly, than the thousands it had taken to build this and all the other forts surrounding Habana's harbour, not to mention the city wall that alone had taken two hundred years to construct. One thing for sure, he and Luis had never imagined themselves as slaves. He had got a taste of slavery, at least in its modern sweatshop manifestation, only after immigration to the States.

As a boy wielding a wooden sword, Joe had been oblivious to the spectacular view of Habana's skyline across the harbour, and he was more or less oblivious to it now. He ordered a mojito from the bar and leaned on the stone balustrade to watch the sunset, placing as much distance as possible between himself and a group of German tourists. Shutting out their guttural voices, Joe reviewed his plans, a review necessary because Celia's coming to meet him at the airport had the potential to undermine his focus.

The basic plan, he assured himself, was untouched. He knew exactly which government agencies he would visit, could guesstimate how many calls would be required to establish solid contacts, and how much schmoozing with those contacts would be needed to set the stage. The part he hadn't worked out was Celia because she had played no part in his decision to return to the island. It had been a business decision, personal only to the extent that he wanted to put some physical distance between himself and his ex-wife. If he wasn't going to be given access to the kids, then, by God, Vera wasn't going to find him all that accessible either.

But Celia's being at the airport, not to mention how she felt in his arms, caught him off guard. Who would have guessed that at thirty-five she'd look the way she had at twenty-five? As he leaned against the stone wall, the pressure of an erection made him acutely aware of something that, if not exactly in his mind, was certainly in his blood.

A purely biological reaction, he told himself. After all, it had been what—nine months?—since he'd had a woman. Of course there had been opportunities, both with women he had fooled around with before the divorce and ones he had met since. But something in the way Vera got her hooks into him, then extracted several pounds of flesh had put him off "nice" women. And with Dade County's huge HIV-infected population, a guy would have to be a whole lot more desperate than he was to screw a prostitute, even with so-called safe-sex precautions.

Celia, though, was another story. Given Cuba's nationwide testing program and her being a doctor, she'd be safe. Sexually, anyway. But what about entanglement? Non-capitalistic society be damned, nobody was going to lay that lady for free. Not that it had cost him all that much before. But it almost had. He had almost stayed in Cuba because of her. And probably would have if he hadn't believed until the very last minute that her anger would cool and she would go with him.

As the setting sun transformed white cloud streamers into streaks of magenta, Joe shifted uncomfortably. He wanted to walk away, to drive straight to his mother's house and follow all the plans he'd made, the way he always followed his plans, without looking right or left or making things any more complicated than necessary. Embarrassment, though, kept him glued to the stone balustrade, concealing his projected feelings from the tourists. But not from himself.

Okay, so he *had* paid a price when he walked out on Celia. But that was because he had let himself get addicted to her sweet compliance, underscored by the incredible pent-up passion of a virgin in love with her first lover. Given a decade of lovers and water under the bridge since then, such emotional traps were unlikely to snare him now. But what if she was one of those Cubans whose allegiance to the Revolution had not lasted; one of those who, having collected a free education in the field of their choice, resented working for chicken feed and longed to fly the coop? What if she got the idea that he ought to facilitate her move to the United States in exchange for a tumble in the hay?

He savoured the last swallow of rum and played with the scenario. It wasn't entirely unattractive. If she chose to follow him to Miami, as she had refused to do back then, he might acquire a safe sexual partner with no sticky commitment to monogamy or lifelong support. Assuming, of course, there weren't complications. Joe's thoughts flashed briefly back to Vera, and his erection wilted of its own accord.

That's the kicker, he thought as he headed back across the parking lot to his rental car. Keep your eye out for complications.

SEVEN

LUIS stood at the window watching the play of sunlight until it ceased to filter through the leaves of ancient trees that formed a canopy over the street. Softer tones of sunset touched the old houses with a rosy glow. Then sunset faded to dusk and he no longer saw the street. What he saw was Celia and José alone in her apartment, his hands on her there as quickly as they had been on her in the airport, but touching places far more intimate. Luis fought an urge to retch.

It was exactly as he had known it would be, from the moment he first learned of his brother's intended return. Yet he had resisted, as one naturally resists pain, and would go on resisting until the end. Grown men don't puke and they don't cry. They pick up the goddamned phone and act.

The telephone rang three, four, five times—longer than it should take Celia to get to it from anywhere in her small apartment. The receiver was halfway back to its cradle when Luis heard her breathless, "Hola?"

In a choked voice, he said, "Celia? Ask José if he is coming for supper or if we should go ahead and eat."

The surprise in her voice was genuine. "Why, he left long ago!"

"You mean . . . he isn't there?"

Her voice took on an edge of annoyance. "Look, I only let him bring me home because you insisted. I certainly did not invite him in."

Abashed, Luis stuttered, "Yes, but, well, I thought he was coming straight here."

"So did I. But he didn't say and I did not ask. Look, I have to go or I will be late for work. I was already out in the hall when the telephone rang. You barely caught me."

"Oh, sorry. I suppose he will turn up eventually."

"I'm sure he will. Chau."

"Hasta luego, mi amor." But she had already hung up.

Luis held the receiver a moment longer, reinventing images of Celia. Now he saw her alone in the apartment, changing into hospital whites and crepe-soled shoes. He saw her going out the door, swiftly down the stairs, getting onto her bicycle for the short ride to the hospital. And José?

"*José!*" His mother screamed in a voice that might have been proclaiming the Second Coming of Christ. "Mi hijo!"

Luis dropped the receiver back into the cradle and turned in time to see José lift their tiny mother off her feet in an all-encompassing hug.

"I knew you'd come back! I told Luis—didn't I tell you, Luis? He will come back!" Without turning to Luis for confirmation, Alma shouted to neighbours, "My son José! At last! He is here!"

The scene, which Luis had seen played out in other families countless times, sickened him. Why did Cubans always treat visiting gusano relatives like returning heroes? What was so heroic about abandoning your country? Once, after observing

21

a neighbour behaving exactly as Alma was now, he had asked his mother those questions. With patient superiority Alma had replied, "You have no children, Luis. You cannot understand what it is like to lose one."

That was one of the times, one of many times, when she had said, with tears glinting in dark eyes that seemed too large for her tiny face, "My José will come back. I know he will."

Luis could not fathom his mother's unconditional love any more than he could challenge her tears, but neither had he changed his opinion of those who welcomed rogue relatives with open arms. He believed that most families were more excited by the expectation of lavish gifts than by the visit itself. That would not apply to Alma, of course. She was like himself in that respect: largely indifferent to material things.

Luis stood unobtrusively in the background as José, still locked in Alma's embrace, grinned self-consciously and waved to neighbours who peered from windows, doorways, and balconies up and down the street. Although the old mansions had been constructed with an eye to privacy, subsequent transformation into apartments ensured that their wide marble steps and decorative balconies provided everyone in the neighbourhood with ringside seats, so to speak, to everyone else's life.

When Alma finally dragged José inside, she left the door wide open. Luis knew that this evening and for as long as his brother remained, curious neighbours would be dropping by to say hello to get a look at the local boy turned Yanqui. He turned to get a better look himself.

José stood blinking at what had once been the main salon of a lavish colonial home. Prior to their family's tenancy, the spacious room had been converted into an apartment; the main part a living-dining area, with a narrow strip at the back walled off to form a minuscule kitchen. Down one side a somewhat wider strip had been partitioned into two bedrooms and a bathroom. Only the fourteen-foot-high frescoed ceilings, with fleshy cherubs entwined in faded banners, remained as an incongruous reminder of former grandeur.

"I can't believe it!" José exclaimed. "This place looks exactly the same! I swear, even the plastic flowers!"

Luis had forced his face into a welcoming grin, but that remark set his teeth so on edge that the smile more closely resembled a sneer. Before he could compose a rejoinder, a neighbour's child skipped in carrying a chipped enamel cup.

"Tía Alma, Mamí wants to borrow some cooking oil."

"By the stove, María. I'll pour it." From the kitchen Alma called, "Put your bags there in your old room, José. Luis, did you make space for his things in the wardrobe?"

José raised his eyebrows at Luis. "You still live here? With Mamá?"

"Why not?" Luis snapped. "You know what a housing shortage we have in Habana."

"Well, yeah. But you being in government, I would've thought—"

"That I would use my position to get put ahead on the housing list? Thereby depriving someone else of a place to live? No, José. *I* would not do that. Nor would my compañeros." Pursing his lips, Luis waved his hand toward the bedroom they had shared for the first twenty-odd years of their lives. "Help yourself."

The little girl headed for the door, her face puckered with the effort of not spilling the oil. Alma called after her, "Ask your mamí if she found any tomatoes at the agromercado."

José continued to stand in the middle of the room, eyes moving from one well-worn object to the other. He motioned to a small statuette of the Virgin. "That's new, though. Since the Pope's visit?"

"No, no! I have had it for years. You don't remember? It used to be in my bedroom." Alma placed serving dishes filled with steaming food on the already-set table and cast an accusatory glance at Luis. "Always I have been a good Catholic."

María skipped in with a tomato for Alma and slipped out again, this time daring a shy smile at José, who absently ran a hand across her dark hair.

"And what's your reward, Mamá?" José winked at Luis. "Two sons—one a godless communist the other a godless capitalist."

Luis snickered. One quality he had always appreciated in his brother was José's use of humour to shield both of them from Alma's scoldings. They had never been allies—José was too self-centred for that—but he had a way of linking them in remarks like the one he had just made that allowed Luis to feel, at times, that they were on the same side. No sooner had the warm memory surfaced than the corners of Luis's mouth turned down. Alliances of convenience, he thought contemptuously. The only kind José understood.

"I pray for you both." Alma placed the plate with sliced tomato on the table with a sharp thwack that said *she* wasn't amused. "Come. Dinner is ready."

José walked to the door of the bedroom. Without asking which bed might be Luis's, he heaved his bags onto the one he had occupied before leaving home. Through the open door, Luis saw him glance around and imagined a sneer at the room's smallness.

It didn't seem that small after you left, he thought grimly. But if you stay long, it is going to get very small indeed.

José moved from bedroom to bathroom—the only bathroom—squeezed narrowly between his room and his mother's.

Luis tried to stop himself from seeing the apartment—the only home *he* had ever known—the way he imagined his brother now saw it. But it was no use. How many bathrooms, he wondered, did "Miami Joe" have in his house?

As José slid into what had always been his place at the table, Luis mumbled, "Guess the place seems kind of small to you now."

"It's bigger than my apartment," José said. "The one I moved into after the divorce."

"Divorce?" Alma looked stricken.

"Sorry, Mamá, but that's the way it is. In America, anyway."

Luis watched his mother trying to cover her disappointment by plying first José's plate, then his, then her own with food. The news jolted him too but with mixed emotions: sorry for his mother's sake, yet pleased that José had not returned with a triumphant entourage of wife and children. Somewhere beneath those feelings was yet another one that left Luis shaken: fear of the unknown. Not yet identified for what it was, he did his best to suppress it. Yet it rose up in his gut and spread out like the hood of a cobra: the knowledge that just as his brother's leaving had changed everything, so would his return.

Luis put down his fork and reached for the only defence he could think of: a better understanding of what he was up against. "So, José. What brings you back?"

"Business." José wiggled his eyebrows comically and lowered his voice to suggest shady dealings. "Pharmaceuticals." Then added seriously, "Basic medical supplies."

José reached across the table and caught Alma's hand that had lain limp on the table since mention of the divorce. "Plus I wanted to see my mamá, to ask her pardon for being such a neglectful son."

Alma slapped his hand away. "*Perdón, no!* A good paddling is what you deserve." But she smiled and began eating.

Luis felt a simmering resentment at the ease with which José charmed their mother, and fished for a question that would show him in a less favourable light. "Did you finish medical school?"

José dug into his food and, mouth full, shook his head. When he was able to speak again, he said, "Couldn't afford it."

"Naturally. Not in the States," Luis observed smugly.

If José noticed the smugness he didn't show it. He replied cheerfully, "But you know how it is: one door closes, another opens. I've done well; my company's still growing."

"And you have some notion of expanding into Cuba."

"That's the plan," José mumbled from behind another mouthful of rice and beans.

"No chance. We are not ready to travel that road."

"We?" The expressive eyebrows shot up. "*You* may not be a capitalist, Luis, but the Cuban government is cutting business deals right, left, and centre."

"With Europeans and the Chinese, sure. With Yanquis, never," Luis informed him coldly. Then added, as honesty compelled him to do, "Except for essential foodstuffs."

José waved his fork dismissively. "Food now, medical supplies tomorrow. Eventually all Cuba's essentials will come from the United States. It's only natural—"

José broke off up when a hip-swinging woman in her early twenties walked in without knocking. She flashed a neighbourly smile at Luis and one of bold curiosity at José. Motioning to the cooking pot she carried, she spoke to Alma. "I ran out of kerosene. My rice needs another ten minutes."

Alma waved her to the kitchen. "Leave it, Yvonne. I'll bring it over when it's done."

Luis poked irritably at his food. "Cuba does not need US pharmaceuticals! Ours are vastly superior. But for the damned blockade, we would be producing plenty!"

"Hey, I don't support the embargo. Most Americans don't. As soon as Fidel kicks off—"

"Damn you Miami gusanos!" Luis shouted. "Like maggots, just waiting—"

Yvonne came out of the kitchen and headed for the door. "Gracias, Alma." She cast a mischievous glance at them as she passed. "I see your sons get along well."

"Just like old times," Alma called after her in a cheery voice. But when Alma looked at her quarrelling boys, now men, her eyes were sad. "Never a meal in peace," she said quietly so that only they heard.

Luis was immediately ashamed for having let his temper get the best of him so quickly over—nothing, really. "Perdón, Mamá."

He thought José ought to have apologised to her too, but José was looking at him. "I didn't mean to set you off, Luis. So what're you up to these days?"

Luis was considering how he wanted to answer that question when Alma spoke. "Luis is the fourth-highest-ranking official in the energy department. A very important post. He has been a member of the National Assembly for five years."

"Holy shit!" José exclaimed, giving Luis the satisfaction of seeing his younger brother look genuinely impressed. "What is Cuba's energy outlook? I hear it's pretty bleak."

"Only because of the blockade. Once our oil reserves are developed—"

"Cuba has oil reserves?"

"We do. And unlimited solar potential. Of course, being cut off from US technology has delayed our solar development." He gave José an accusing look. "I guess you heard that US State Department refused to grant its own scientists visas to attend the most recent international conference held in Habana on solar energy."

"Yeah, but that's going to change." José glanced around the shabbily furnished apartment and back at his mother. "It's bound to be for the better."

Alma tilted her head, thinking this over. Luis had a general sense of his mother's politics but could not guess how she might feel about what her younger son had just said.

After a moment of silence, Alma spoke heavily, with the certainty of a person who has lived through political upheaval. "The only good change is slow change."

Two children, one black, one brown, bounded in. The younger boy was holding his arm, crying. The older one, a self-assured ten-year-old, took charge. "Where is Doctora Celia?" he demanded. "David hurt his arm."

"She is not here at the moment," Luis told him. "Let me see."

David held up a chocolate-coloured arm for Luis's inspection.

"Can you wiggle your fingers?" Luis asked.

The boy wiggled his fingers, flapped his hand, then waved his whole arm up and down. "Maybe it's okay now," the child conceded.

Luis suppressed a smile. "Seems to be. But if it keeps hurting, perhaps you should walk over to the clinic and have the nurse look at."

"*Sí, sí, gracias!*" they shouted in unison and bounded out.

"Celia still visits?" José addressed the question to Alma.

"Claro. That girl is like a daughter to me."

"Did she ever marry?" The question appeared casual, but Luis wasn't fooled for a second. Por Dios, how he wished he could answer that in the affirmative!

Alma sighed. "Not yet."

"Maybe she's still pining for me." José grinned.

Luis guffawed. "What an egotist you are, José!"

Then Alma delivered what Luis appreciated as the *coup de grâce*. "Celia's engaged. Didn't she tell you?"

José looked abashed. "No, she didn't."

"To Luis. Since two years ago."

José's open-mouthed astonishment gave Luis enormous satisfaction. He had been momentarily put out to find that Celia had not told José herself, but now he was glad she hadn't. It was worth anything to have this moment of triumph.

Suddenly José burst out laughing.

"What is so funny?" Luis demanded.

José shook his head. "Just—life, I guess. Always ready with the curve balls."

Alma replenished their plates with more black beans and rice. "I'm sorry there's no meat. Do you still like moros y cristianos?"

"Love 'em," José assured her. "I've cut way back on meat anyway."

He gave Luis a long, speculative gaze across the table. "Tell you what," José said finally. "I'm going to Varadero Friday next. Come along, you and Celia. I'll treat you to lunch."

"Celia will be in Santiago that weekend for a medical conference."

"Okay, then. Just you and me." José reached across the table and smacked Luis on the biceps. "We'll celebrate you winning the hand of my fair maiden."

Alma beamed, and Luis felt a surge of anticipation. It was an emotion he recognized from his youth when José—for it had always been José—came up with a plan of adventure and included him. But Luis had other reasons to look forward to this particular outing. Varadero more than anyplace reflected the economic miracle the Cuban government had wrought, while displaying the natural beauty of the island. The resort fairly flaunted what José had lost when he chose to abandon them. As for the timing, that too was perfect. Given that Celia had to be away, it would be only the two of them, not the triangle it had been all through their childhood, with him in one invisible corner.

EIGHT

CELIA pedalled toward her apartment, bone tired. She had caught herself treating an asthmatic child brought into emergency with an emotion that was dangerously close to apathy. She fully intended to complain to Luis again about the scheduling. Not that he had anything to do with it, but he *was* in a position to let other officials know how doctors felt. She smiled grimly. On the other hand, his being aware of how cranky she got when working long hours might be why he had not called all week; he did not want to listen to her whine. At least she had tomorrow off, and if he did call—

Just as she turned up the walk to her building the electricity went off, plunging the whole area into darkness. Partly due to an embargo that prevented Cuba from getting the petroleum needed to generate electricity, partly because so much of what was generated was utilized by resorts, and partly because old power plants were being shut down with increasing frequency for repairs, rolling blackouts had become a regular nuisance.

As Celia reached for the doorknob, a hand touched her back. She jumped, not frightened but startled. A bouquet of three large sunflowers was thrust in front of her.

"*Aye, Luis!* You surprised me!"

"Perdón, mi amor. I thought you saw me. Before the lights went out."

"I didn't, no. I think I was half asleep already."

Two boys came crashing out the door of the apartment building. "Doctora Celia!" the older boy exclaimed. "We're going for candles. Can we borrow your bicycle?"

Celia handed the bike over to the boy. "Put it away when you get back, please."

"Claro, Doctora." He pedalled off with the smaller child behind him, standing on the spikes that protrude from the back axle of the Chinese-made bike.

Celia looked down at the flowers. They glowed pale yellow in the moonlight. "Gracias, Luis. Es una occasión especial?"

"The anniversary of our engagement. Celia, you must set a date!"

Celia sagged against the door frame. "Ay, Luis! How can you ask at a time like this? I am exhausted! These twelve-hour shifts—"

"It's not my fault longer shifts are more efficient!"

Celia could count on one hand the number of times in her life she had lost her temper. And this was about to be one of them.

"Efficient for who?" she exploded. "The bureaucrat who draws up our schedule? How would you like to be the patient operated on by a doctor who has been on her feet for ten hours? It is not as if Cuba has a shortage of doctors! Or nurses or restroom attendants. Yet we're all on these damned double shifts just to save on transportation costs. Surely you and your National Assembly comrades see how stupid that is!"

"I will not argue politics. Just set a date, any date! I can't go on like this!"

Celia heard the desperation in his voice. Had she not been so tired she probably would have responded. As it was, it took all the willpower she could muster to bring her temper under control. "I told you before, Luis. I do not know. Not then and not now. Especially not now!"

He slumped forward as if hit from behind. "Because José is back, right?"

Suddenly the lights came on. Disco music spilled down on them from the balcony of Celia's apartment four floors above.

Luis grimaced. "Liliana must be home." He laid a hand on Celia's arm. "Can we go somewhere?"

"I *am* going somewhere. To bed. To sleep. Goodnight, Luis."

Seeing the desperate hope in his eyes, so like the eyes of hurting children and frightened parents she spent her day reassuring, she weakened just a little. "Thanks for the flowers. It will be wonderful waking up to them in the morning."

She stepped inside and for a moment stood at the bottom of the stairs, gathering strength for the climb to her fourth-floor apartment. Even more than the tiredness, she felt a sense of weakness. The encounter with Luis—not his need but her own conciliatory words—had drained her.

The lights went out again and simultaneously the door crashed open to admit the boys who had gone for candles.

"Careful!" she warned, just in time to prevent them from bumping into her.

"You want a candle?" asked the younger child as the older one manoeuvred the bike through the darkness and into its customary parking place under the stairwell.

"No, gracias. I have some. Share them with the families on your floor."

They bounded past her, a bit recklessly, she thought, given that it was pitch-black in the stairwell. She followed slowly. Living on the top floor was a great way to keep in shape, but oh, what she would not have given for a ground-floor apartment tonight!

By the time she reached the fourth level the electricity had come on again. As she walked along the corridor to her own apartment she noted the absence of disco music. Liliana must have gone to bed. She glanced at her watch. It was not yet ten. Stepping inside the apartment, she saw light coming from under the girl's bedroom door and called, "Hola, Liliana."

Getting no reply, she put her head into Liliana's room. Liliana was in bed, wild dark curls splayed across her pillow, a textbook propped on her chest. She had not turned off her music after all but was wearing headphones. She slipped them off and smiled up at her aunt.

"You're late. Tío Luis came by." She glanced at the flowers in Celia's hand. "Did he wait for you downstairs?"

"Yes. Pretty, aren't they?" Celia reached down to stroke Liliana's tumble of brown curls, a longer, wilder version of Celia's own, and so like those of the girl's now-dead mother. "Where did you get the CD player and headphones?"

"From a friend." Liliana held up the chemistry book. "Want a bedtime story?"

Celia laughed. "That would put me to sleep for sure." She touched the girl's cheek. "Did you have a nice time at Playa Jibacoa?"

"Claro. I love that campismo. Have you ever stayed there?"

"Your mother and I and Luis and all our friends went there often," Celia replied. "The swimming pool was brand new then. Is it still nice?"

"Terrific. The caretaker lives close by. His kids let us ride their horses."

"Sounds fun." She bent to kiss the girl's forehead. "See you in the morning."

"Not if you sleep in." Liliana nestled the headset into her dark curls again.

"Oh, right." Celia had forgotten that this was the last day of the pre-university students' monthly week off. Liliana would be leaving early the next morning to return to boarding school. "In three weeks, then."

She fell asleep almost immediately and could not have said, when she awoke, how long she had been sleeping. Or where she was waking to, and why there should be so many ghostlike people moving around in the shuttered dimness of a sickroom.

Fidel looked so tired, so very tired. If she was in her sixtieth, her last year of life, that made him what? Fifty-five? "You are young! You must go on!" she wanted to cry. But it was only a thought, a ragged intake of breath. He knelt by the bed and took both her hands in both of his; not callused now as they were that long time ago in the mountains, but soft, the hands of a man for whom everything was done but thinking, speaking, deciding. She did not want this clinging to her hand like a child clutching something fragile, something about to break. She wanted him to fling himself on her as he has done so many times in the past, not minding that her body was so much smaller than his or that his boots were dirtying the sheets. She wanted to tell him this, or better, show him, for had she not always had to show him? "Like this, my love. This is what I need. This is what you need. This is what our nation needs." But she had no breath. Not even enough to whisper "Yes," when he promised, "Our work will go on. The Cuba our people build will be your Cuba, Celia. Yours."

Celia Cantú jerked up, gasping for breath. There was no man beside her bed, no ghostly figures lurking in the shadows. It was moonlight, not daylight dimmed by the drawn blinds of a sickroom, that had found its way into her bedroom. By the time her breathing returned to normal, she knew that it was not a dream, at least, not the kind she was used to. It was another attempt by her unconscious to take her back to a time she never knew. The same clarity of mind and strength of purpose she had felt in previous visions had infused her, but in this one the body had run its course. She herself was healthy as a horse, yet for the duration of tonight's episode she had felt, as surely as Celia Sánchez had felt, the swift approach of a stone-hard end of time.

NINE

JOE knocked three times before the door opened. Celia stood there in bare feet and an oversized T-shirt, which, he recalled, was what she had always worn to bed— although not for long, once he got there. She was half-asleep, dark curls deliciously dishevelled.

"Sorry if I woke you. But, geez, it's nearly noon!"

"It is?" she asked groggily and turned away, rubbing her eyes.

Joe stepped inside, glad to be out of the dingy hallway that to him appeared not to have been repainted in years.

"What do you want?" Celia demanded, backing away.

"Let's go shopping." He beamed.

"Shopping?" She echoed the word as she had never heard it.

"Come on. I'll make coffee while you get dressed."

He crossed the small living-dining area to the kitchenette and opened first one then the other door of the single cupboard. It seemed impossibly bare for a functioning household.

Celia pushed him aside with undisguised annoyance. "Get out of here. I will make my own coffee."

Joe's impulse was to run his hand up under the thigh-length T-shirt to where he knew for a fact there would be no panties. But he was no fool. He backed out of the kitchen and sat down at the small table. Medical literature might be full of PMS studies, but in his experience, female moodiness was a morning thing. He'd never figured out if it was physical or emotional or, for that matter, if there was any difference, given how readily hurting women became excessively emotional and emotional women developed physical symptoms. All he knew was that until that pre-breakfast prickliness passed, a man who valued his body parts did not put them in harm's way by standing too close.

Celia filled a dented aluminium percolator with water and ground coffee, slammed it on the stove, and lit the gas burner. "Shopping for what?"

"Everything. I don't think Mamá has bought a single thing for herself or the house since I left ten years ago."

As he spoke, Joe looked around the living room. In contrast to the public areas of the building, the apartment was clean almost to the point of sterility and freshened by a sea breeze blowing in through open jalousie windows. Apart from the ugly grey-topped Formica table at which he sat, the room held a sagging sofa facing a small TV set, one wooden rocking chair, a side table upon which was an old-style black phone and a cheap blue vase filled with three big sunflowers, and a bookshelf with a shockingly worn collection. Some of the volumes he recognized as dating back to college.

He was not aware that Celia had come out of the kitchen until she spoke. Voice harsh with scorn, she said, "Por Dios, José. You *have* become a Yanqui."

Normally Joe didn't mind being called a Yankee; on the contrary, he was proud of it. But coming from her, and in that tone of voice! "What's that supposed to mean?" he asked in the aggrieved manner of one wrongly accused.

"The way you sit there judging the quality of our lives by how much or how little we have. That is how it is done up north, no? *Stuff* is joy. *No* stuff is misery."

"Ah, Celia—"

"Cubans have not much stuff, so it follows that we must be miserable."

"I never said that!" he protested. "It's just, well, there was Mamá this morning, squeezing fresh orange juice with her arthritic hands and sending over to the neighbours to borrow toilet paper. Toilet paper, for Chrissake! How can things be that bad?"

"Things are not 'that bad.' They are far better than they were when you left."

"Yeah, but Mamá says this change to the dollar economy has been brutal. Her pension is in pesos and Luis's salary is in pesos and pesos don't buy a damned thing anymore."

"True." Celia thumped a cup of coffee on the table in front of him. "And if her dear son had been sending her as little as fifty US dollars per month, she could have been living like a queen all this time."

Joe held up his hands in a gesture of surrender. "Okay! So I've been a jerk. But believe me, it wasn't easy to get by over there. Now that I am in a position to help, I want to make it up to her; I really do. Come with me, Celia. Help me pick out the things she really needs. Groceries, clothes, household items, whatever. You can decide."

"You want her to have all the stuff your Miami family had?" she mocked. "The one that fell apart?"

Once again Joe was reminded of how on the mark her laser-sharp retorts could be, and how they had always surprised him, given her essentially compliant nature. But he wasn't offended. On the contrary, he enjoyed the challenge. If there was one thing he knew, it was how to disarm an angry woman. Lowering his eyes like a chastised puppy, he said softly, "I never said possessions make families happy. But with people who're already happy, I don't see how a few presents can hurt. I mean, that is the Cuban way, isn't it? Sharing?"

He took a sip of the coffee, and although he had long since begun to drink coffee black, like an American, he smiled. "You remembered just how much sugar I like."

His looked up in time to see her anger turn to red-faced embarrassment. Without a word, she picked up her cup and marched into the bedroom. A dresser drawer slammed, and there was the sound of water running in the bathroom. Moments later she emerged dressed as she had been at the airport, in jeans, T-shirt, and sandals.

"*Vamos*," she snapped.

He leapt ahead of her to open the door. She ignored the pseudo-servile gesture, turning back for the sunflowers. Joe wondered why she chose to bring them but didn't ask. He had got what he came for.

A handful of commercial billboards along the Vía Monumental jolted him; certainly there had been nothing like that when he lived here. Supposedly there were dollar stores selling consumer goods all over the island now. However, from what he had seen so far, Habana still had fewer commercial venues than you would find in a heavily restricted residential neighbourhood in the States.

He drove through the tunnel under the Bahía de Habana and followed the Malecón. It was thronged with midday traffic made up of late-model rentals and pre-1960 cars that had become a Cuban symbol. Cyclists and pedicabs crowded a bike lane along the seawall. In some places waves splashed up and over, leaving sidewalk, bike lane, and the right side of the street drenched in salt spray.

They passed a plaza hung with strange bird-looking metal sculptures, new to him yet somehow familiar. Ah yes, he'd seen it on TV. This was where they'd held the largest of many mass rallies to demand the return of the child Elián. According to network news, half a million Cubans had turned up to demand that the five-year-old, whom the mother had opted to take to Florida in a small boat, be returned to his father. The mother had died en route and Miami relatives had fought sending the boy home. Media coverage at the time made it appear as if all Cuban Americans were in favour of keeping the kid in the States, but privately Joe was pleased when US courts ruled against the relatives and allowed the boy to return to Cuba with his dad. A girl, maybe not. But damn it all, a boy belonged with his papá.

Joe glanced over at Celia, who had not spoken since they left the apartment. "Where's the nearest shopping centre?"

"Turn here," she said abruptly.

He swerved into the left lane and headed down Avenida de los Presidentes until she directed him to turn right on La Rampa. He did as he was told, although he recalled that the commercial part of La Rampa was the other way, nearer the Malecón.

Celia appeared to have her mind on other things, as her fingertips lightly caressed the petals of a sunflower. "Who's the bouquet for?" he asked.

She gave no sign of having heard. Joe thought, uneasily, It's as if she's not here.

"Celia!" he said more loudly.

"What?"

"I asked you, what are the flowers for?"

"Her grave."

"Whose?" To his exasperation, a bus had stopped ahead, making it impossible to pass or to escape the noxious exhaust.

"Celia Sánchez."

Surprised, he asked, "Why her?"

"Is there something wrong with remembering her?" she asked testily. "Or does one have to have a beard to be a hero of the Revolution?"

He thought, What's wrong is that I thought we were going shopping. But all he said was, "Nothing. It's just—"

"Fidel would never have survived in the mountains without her. Let alone the next twenty years. *She* was the one who got things done." Celia's voice dropped so that he barely heard the last sentence. "If I could be like her . . ."

Joe laughed aloud. "You? Like her?"

Celia gave him a poisonous look. "What is so funny?"

"She must've been hard as nails. A commander in the rebel army—"

"She was *more* than a commander. A true leader! But hard? No! Not before the war, or during, or after! It was to her the people always turned when they needed help. She was the very soul of the Revolution!"

Celia's declaration reminded Joe that the woman he considered little more than one of Fidel's paramours was honoured in Cuba as the island's equivalent of the Blessed Virgin. Having read several published-elsewhere histories of the Cuban Revolution, he felt confident in stating, "History doesn't seem to remember her that way."

"You think *she* wanted any credit?" Celia cried passionately. "She devoted her entire life to making things better for ordinary people on this island. At least we have *that* in common!"

Although he could not have said why, the subject made Joe uncomfortable. But at least he now knew where they were going. "I take it she's buried at Cementerio Colón?"

They were nearing the big midtown cemetery that dated back to colonial times and contained some of the world's most unusual memorials. If they could find a parking place, dropping the flowers off shouldn't take long. She'd owe him for the favour, which might make her a little less fractious.

They had played in the cemetery as children, he and Luis and Celia and Carolina and other kids, delighting in the more outrageous statuary. A favourite had been the tomb of an old lady, who, for her love of dominoes, had been memorialized with a slab in the form of a giant marble domino. Luis, who took baseball seriously, always paid homage to the life-sized statue of a muscular baseball player, naked to the waist. Celia, Joe recalled, spent a considerable amount of time puzzling over why the families of plane crash victims felt it appropriate to top their tombs with marble aircraft zooming toward infinity.

As they walked along the cemetery's shady paths he felt Celia slip into a mellow mood. She even smiled and nudged him to draw his attention to the statue that had always given them the giggles when they were kids, a larger-than-life hermaphrodite angel.

"Celia's tomb is farther back, in the Armed Forces mausoleum," she told him.

"You have to wonder why El Lider Maximo chose her, when he could have had anybody," Joe mused.

"Not anybody. His wife left him."

"True. When a man gets jailed for trying to overthrow the resident dictator, I guess you can't blame his wife if she figures he hasn't got much of a future." Joe recalled something he had read and snickered. "Did you know that the first woman Fidel got involved with after his divorce—not counting that one-night stand with Natty Revuelta that she claimed gave them a daughter—was a Mexican debutante?"

Celia gave him a disbelieving look. "How would you know that?"

"It was in a book written by an American. He discusses the women in Fidel's life."

The skepticism in Celia's voice turned to disgust. "Don't you find that distasteful? Pawing through people's personal lives just because they happen to be public figures?"

"I don't see anything wrong with it. It sheds light on the man."

"And the woman?"

"Sure. Not that anybody cares who she was. Just some eighteen-year-old he fell for when he was living in México. She broke it off. Apparently Fidel came calling one day and found her by the pool in a bikini and went right out and bought her a one-piece suit. She probably lost interest in her dashing revolutionary when he turned out to be more fashion-conservative than her mother."

"I have never heard anything about it."

"Because they don't have tabloids here. Anyway, that must've burned him out on the young and restless, because a year later he was back in Cuba, shacked up with Sánchez, who was what—five years older than him?"

"*Shacked up?*" Celia flung the phrase back at him as if it were a personal insult. "Is that how you see a relationship that lasted twenty-three years?"

"Sánchez certainly wasn't the only woman in Fidel's life," Joe countered.

"She was the one he loved," Celia said, as if that settled it.

Suppressing a skeptical retort, Joe dropped behind Celia and ran his eyes over her firm buttocks. "I can see that. She was about your age when they met. She might've been kind of cute in a bikini too."

Celia either second-guessed his intention or remembered the habit because as his hand moved to pat her on the behind, she deftly caught it and flung it aside.

"Or maybe he was looking for something more in a woman."

Joe grinned. "Like brains? Could be. Smart women always turn *me* on."

Celia gave him an exasperated look and picked up her pace. Near the back of the cemetery she turned into an open-air mausoleum reserved for the Revolution's most notable military leaders. Joe would have laid bets that if Sánchez wasn't the only woman whose remains were interred in this company, she was one of very few.

Marble vaults lined the mausoleum to a height of about two metres. Celia stopped before one with no name, its polished white surface interrupted only by the number of the vault and a bronze handle. Stuck through the handle was a bouquet of wilted red roses. Celia removed them and inserted the sunflowers.

It struck Joe as unseemly that a final resting place would be without an identifying name, even if it was that of the president's mistress. "If Fidel thought so much of her, why the unmarked vault?"

Celia shrugged. "Everybody who cares knows where it is."

"Still, you wonder why."

She half-turned so that her clean brown-skinned features were profiled against the white marble. In a husky smoker's voice he did not recognize, Celia said, "She wanted it this way."

TEN

CELIA was aware of José chattering cheerfully beside her as they walked back to the car. She may have made appropriate responses, but the visit to the cemetery had left her feeling oddly alone. She paid no attention to which way he drove when they left the parking lot and did not notice her surroundings until they drove past the sentry post at the end of Calle 11. Looking out the car window, she saw a soldier in the kiosk. The soldier frowned. Celia remembered him from when she had last passed this way; remembered because that was the instance of her first hallucination.

It had been a Sunday afternoon. She and Liliana had lunched at the Lagos. Afterwards Alma and Liliana went across the street to visit a neighbour. Luis wanted to use their few minutes of privacy for lovemaking. Celia, while not saying no outright, had been nervous, fearing that they had not enough time and might be interrupted. Luis had become annoyed with her. Not verbally abusive—he was never that—but stonily silent.

Celia, feeling both guilty and resentful, had gone out for a walk.

About twenty blocks from the Lago apartment she had passed by the street where Celia Sánchez lived during the last two decades of her life. The apartment Sánchez once inhabited was not visible because of the big trees lining the sidewalk, but gazing toward it, Celia had imagined herself inside, looking out the window through a screen of leaves.

She had of course been in Sánchez's apartment, but only once, as a child. Perhaps she had even looked out the window, although she could not recall doing so. In any case, what happened in her head just then was not as an incident remembered. She had felt herself in the apartment, looking down . . .

The jeep barely stopped at the curb before long legs were thrust out, a nod of dismissal to the driver, his athletic stride across the sidewalk, a quick glance up at the window, at her—these details telling her he would stay the night; that they would wait, together, for the invasion. Despite his having been awake almost forty-eight hours, despite the morning's long oratory at the funeral of those killed in Saturday's bombing raid on Ciudad Libertad, they would not sleep but would lie in each other's arms until the call came. They would not speak of those who died yesterday or the ones who would die tomorrow, but of how that battle would be waged—her throat tightened at the thought—without her by his side. While he ensured that the main invasion force did not establish a beachhead—he believed it would be at the Bahía de Cochinos but was not certain enough to go there yet—she must remain in Habana, at Punto Uno, so close to where Saturday's bombs fell, to coordinate the defence of the rest of the island. This she knew already, and what assurances he would need of her before he left. She turned at the sound of footsteps as familiar as her own and moved toward the door.

Celia had unconsciously turned, as if about to walk down the tree-lined street toward Sánchez's apartment. That had brought a soldier out of the kiosk.

"No pase!" he said brusquely, even as he gave a nod of permission to another pedestrian, a man pushing a pram.

Celia, having grown up nearby, was not surprised. She knew that only residents were allowed on the short street. No explanation had ever been given to the public, but the rumour was that it remained a restricted area because even now, twenty-some years after Sánchez's death, Fidel often spent hours alone in the apartment that had been hers.

Looking past the soldier to the leaf-laden trees that screened the building from view, Celia had said, "You can't see Celia Sánchez's apartment from here."

"No," he said, without turning around. "Move on, please."

"Those trees must be at least fifty years old. They never prune them, do they?"

"I wouldn't know," he said and gestured with one finger, like a traffic cop, for her to continue on in the way she had originally been going.

She had complied, of course. Her attempt to engage him in conversation had not been meant as resistance. She respected the Cuban military, without which she did not believe Cuba could have remained as independent as it was. She was only trying to fasten on some solid detail that she could legitimately claim to remember from the one time she had been in that apartment—something to explain away a vision that had occurred in broad daylight when, as far as she could tell, she was in full control of all her faculties.

But she could not, so she had hoarded the hallucination, secretly bringing it to the surface when she was alone at night. On the pretext of trying to understand it, she had in fact tried to relive it. Although she remembered the details, as she remembered details of the two more recent ones, she had been unable to evoke the accompanying sensation: that of she herself, but not herself, a participant.

"Weird," she murmured and started when José spoke.

"What's weird?"

She thought, Weird I forgot you were here. But what she said was, "Roaming around Vedado like we did ten years ago, as if nothing has changed."

"Nobody had a car then. Or if they did, no gas. I'd call that a change."

"Cuba has barely enough gasoline now," Celia said tartly. "Not enough to be wasting it in aimless driving. I thought you wanted to go shopping."

José grinned. "I was waiting for you to direct me to one of the new malls."

"The closest is Juan Carlos II, on Avenida Salvador Allende."

José made a U-turn and headed back through the residential area toward Centro Habana. When they passed Calle 11 again, Celia looked in the direction of Sánchez's apartment but felt nothing, magical or otherwise.

ELEVEN

JOE was amazed how, once they reached the crowded Juan Carlos II shopping plaza, Celia seemed like a different woman. Or, rather, she became the quiet, task-oriented woman he remembered from college and as he imagined she now was at work. After two hours, she stuffed his list into her shoulder bag and said, "That should do it."

"Good. Let's grab some lunch." Joe had in mind taking her to a good restaurant, possibly the one next to that old fort on Río Almendres. Back when they were dating they couldn't have afforded a cup of coffee there. Celia probably still couldn't. But before he could propose Restaurante 1840, as he now remembered the snobbish eatery was called, she motioned him into a hole-in-the-wall diner. He was too hungry to protest.

They ordered pizza, although Joe should have known better, life in the States having taught him, if nothing else, how extraordinarily inferior Cuban pizza was. It arrived shortly, two plate-sized slabs of hot baked dough gooey with tomato sauce and melted cheese. He did not voice his opinion aloud, though, and was pleased to see Celia eating with gusto.

When she finished, she took the shopping list from her purse and began ticking off items. "Cooking oil, toilet paper, laundry soap, bed linens, towels, toaster, blender, rice cooker, juicer. I have no idea where she is going to put all these small appliances, and with the rolling blackouts . . ." She shook her head.

Joe visualized his mother's minuscule kitchen and shrugged. Cuba's energy shortages and finding places to put things weren't his problems. "She'll manage."

"I suppose." Celia signalled to the waitress for water.

Joe watched her lips curl around the rim of the glass as she tilted it back and drank. Perhaps it was the sensuality of her parted lips that impelled him to ask, "You aren't seriously planning to marry Luis?"

Celia set the glass on the table with a smack and picked up the list. "The shoes she will have to shop for herself. I think we have everything else."

"If you were, you wouldn't have gone two years without setting a date."

Celia flashed him a venomous look. "Is that what he told you?"

"No, but that's how I wrecked my own marriage." Joe reached for her hand, but she snatched it back and confined it in her lap, out of sight and reach.

"By not rushing into it? Ha ha."

"By not marrying the woman I really loved."

"Loved?" Her voice dripped with sarcasm. "The one you walked out on? You seem to have forgotten—"

"Hey, you broke it off!"

"When you waved your emigration documents in my face!"

"And you slammed the door in mine!"

"Don't you think it hurt—?"

"Hurt me when you wouldn't let me explain! And along with the rest of them,

37

called me a gusano! You never gave me a chance, Celia! I planned to come back!"

Simultaneously both became aware that other diners were listening to their exchange, small smiles denoting embarrassment or perhaps sympathy.

Celia lowered her voice. "Well, now you're back. And I have news for you, Miami Joe. I am not the starry-eyed student I was then."

"Ooo-kay." Joe dropped his voice to match hers but refused to retreat from her cold stare. "So tell me, Dr. Cantú, who are you?"

Celia blushed. He could not know what caused the blush, but it crossed his mind that it might be because she was a woman hungry for something more than Cuban pizza.

As hungry, he hoped, as she had been back then. Not that she had been an easy lay, but once he taught her what her body was for, that resistance he found so stimulating had turned into something he *thought* was the girl's total addiction to high-voltage sex. How she had managed to go cold turkey when he invited her to come with him to Miami he'd never understand, but one thing he was certain of was that she must be half-starved now to have accepted his plodding brother as a replacement.

When Celia didn't answer, Joe offered his own scenario, couched in more tactful terms. "Don't you think we might enjoy finding out who we are right now?" He smiled with confident hope. "I'm game if you are, Doctor."

Celia sighed. "This is a waste of time, José. Even if things could go back to where they were, we would be right back where we were. You are not going to stay in Cuba, and nothing could induce me to move to the States."

Joe recognized this as the first time she had bared her feelings to him since his return. He was on the verge of responding with something like never-say-never, but she was already gathering up parcels to leave. Joe dropped a bill on the table that included a tip as big as their check and followed her out.

At the car he asked if she wanted to go anywhere else. She said no, she had to get home. She remained silent for most of the ride back. Once, she started to say something but didn't. Not until they were nearing her apartment did she come out with what was on her mind—or close enough that Joe picked up on it.

Glancing at the purchases on the back seat, she said, "Alma will feel a lot better about these things if she thinks you picked them out by yourself."

"And Luis will feel a lot better if he doesn't know we spent the afternoon together."

"Sí." From the corner of his eye he saw her lips compress. "Not that you give a damn about how he feels."

"Not particularly," he acknowledged candidly. "But if it matters to you, my lips are sealed."

Celia looked miserable. Joe knew, and she probably did as well, that even in keeping something as insignificant as an afternoon of shopping secret, they had formed an alliance that shut Luis out.

It was all Joe could do to keep from smiling. Celia, by insisting that there was zero possibility of renewing their relationship, had thrown up a barrier that made it unnecessary to court her and would prevent him from becoming distracted from the business matters that had brought him back to Cuba. At the same time, he did not believe that all the passion they had once set alight in each other had been reduced to cold ash. He could relax, blow on the coals as opportunity presented itself, and deal with the resulting sparks according to his mood.

What Joe didn't recognize in himself, but felt somewhere below the belt, was that it was not the woman but the chase that fired his jets.

Like a child stacking and restacking bright coloured blocks, Joe spent the drive back to his mother's apartment playing with images of the varied and subtle ways he would pursue Celia. Not once did he form a mental picture of what the aftermath of a successful seduction would mean for her, his brother, or even himself.

TWELVE

LUIS looked out across the yellow-flowering thorn bushes, beyond which lay glittering blue ocean. The dividing line between land and water was not beach but jagged black rock. The view helped reduce the tension caused by José's driving. Despite having already been ticketed once since they left Habana for failing to slow to the posted limit in a construction zone, he continued to drive over the speed limit. Luis must remember to mention the ticket to Celia when she got back from Santiago—a subtle reminder of José's lack of concern for the safety of pedestrians and cyclists.

They were about twenty kilometres from Varadero when he saw the hitchhiker, a trim figure flaunted in tight white shorts and a red-and-white striped top that exposed her midriff. From a distance Luis registered only the head of lush brown curls whipping in the breeze of passing cars. José whistled appreciatively as they flashed by.

In the same instant, Luis saw the girl's face. "Stop!" he shouted.

At José's startled look, Luis repeated, "Stop! Pull over!"

José braked and swerved onto the grassy shoulder. Before the car stopped rolling, Luis was out and striding back to the girl. Without a word he grabbed her by the wrist and dragged her to the car, ignoring shrieks that he was hurting her arm. He opened the door and shoved her roughly into the back seat.

"*Puta!*" he hissed.

"Christ, Luis, take it easy!" José protested. "She's just a kid!"

"Kid my ass!" Luis muttered, getting back in beside José. "Let's go."

The girl's whimpering edged toward sobs. "I was just going to the beach!"

"Liar!"

"I'm not lying! Please, Tío Luis! Let me explain!"

"Tío?" José's eyes left the road long enough to give his brother a look of incredulity. "Who is this kid, Luis?"

The whimpering ceased abruptly. "I am *not* a kid," Liliana informed him indignantly. "And he's not my real uncle. Just my aunt's fiancé."

José's head swivelled around to stare at their back-seat passenger. "You're Liliana? I don't believe it!"

"Watch out!" Luis yelled, grabbing the armrest.

José swerved around a tourist-filled mini-bus barely in time to avoid a collision. To Luis's relief, he slowed down to the actual speed limit. Keeping his eyes on the road, José said over his shoulder, "Last time I saw you, you were barely out of diapers!"

Liliana instantly metamorphosed from a child in fear of punishment into a flippant adolescent. "Well, believe it. Because I *am* Liliana. *And* out of diapers. Who are *you?*"

"My brother, José." Luis was surprised. "Didn't Celia tell you he was here?"

"Tía Celia's old fiancé? The one who ran out on her? No! She didn't say a word! She *never* talks about you!"

"That's nice to know," José responded dryly.

"Where are you going?" Liliana tried to catch José's eye in the rear-view mirror.

"Where were *you* going?" Luis demanded. "You're supposed to be at school!"

"Just to the beach. But I'd rather go with you. Por favor, Tío Luis?"

Luis noted with satisfaction that she had addressed the question to him. She seemed to have got the message that even though José was driving, he, Luis, was the one she was going to have to deal with.

"In that ridiculous outfit? Absolutely not. You can wait in the car."

"Ah, come on," José intervened. "It's not that bad."

"It's a disgrace! She'll be taken for a jinetera."

"A jinetera?"

"A hustler. Or a hooker," Liliana informed him in an exaggeratedly bored voice.

"I *know* what it means," José retorted. He glanced at Luis for further explanation. "What's the problem?"

"They want to keep us off our own beaches," Liliana pouted.

"Luis? Have they segregated Varadero again?"

"Don't be absurd," Luis snapped. "You know the Revolution opened all beaches to all Cubans. Didn't we spend our share of weekends here? And still do, when Celia and Alma *and* Liliana," he added pointedly, "choose to make the drive. The government is cracking down on prostitution, that's all. Especially young ones. If the police see us with a girl dressed like this we could spend the next hour answering questions. We'll be lucky if they don't give us a hard time at the toll booth."

José made an expansive gesture. "So I'll buy her a dress."

"Miami-brand discipline for a child who skips school?" Luis sneered.

José caught Liliana's eye in the rear-view mirror and winked. "Okay, a T-shirt."

Was it ever thus? Luis thought despairingly. Five minutes with any woman, any age, and my goddamned brother has her eating out of his hand.

As they slowed for the toll booth, Luis wondered if he would have to flash his credentials to avoid being questioned. He glanced back at Liliana and saw that she had curled up on the seat, covered herself with Joe's jacket, and was pretending to be asleep. The toll booth attendant either didn't see her or took her for a relative of the men in the front seat. The effective way she concealed her provocative outfit caused Luis to wonder if she had used a similar guise to slip into Varadero with other men.

Luis stared morosely out the window until they crossed the high bridge at the entrance to Varadero. Pride revived his spirit as the resort came into view. Its modern buildings rivalled any in the Caribbean, and the well-paved streets were filled with late-model cars and shiny hotel shuttle busses. "Take this exit," Luis indicated. "The autopista along the bay now runs all the way to the end of the peninsula."

"Where are we going?" Liliana asked, sliding forward to breathe on José's neck.

"Luis claims things have changed since I was here last," José said over his shoulder. "Let's drive out as far as the campismo and cruise back to town from there."

"There's no campismo anymore," Liliana informed him. "But they're talking about making a tent campground for tourists in Parque Ecológica."

"Parque Ecológia?" José echoed. "What's that?"

"The area around Playa Calaveras and on out to the tip of the peninsula," Luis clarified. "For environmental reasons it was left in native vegetation. It was necessary to eliminate the campismo to make room for another resort."

"The beach has been developed that far out?" José asked in disbelief. "Why, that's got to be twenty miles!"

"All developed." Luis smirked, basking in José's astonishment at what the government had accomplished in the past decade. "Like Cancun. Only we did it better."

José slowed the car to a crawl. Luis swelled with pride as his brother, with mumbling amazement, read aloud from signs advertising scuba diving, deep-sea fishing, sailboating, hang-gliding, windsurfing, river rafting, kayaking, catamaran rides, glass-bottomed boats trips, yacht excursions to nearby islands, even swimming with dolphins. Joe's head swung from side to side as he gawked at manicured grounds rolling off toward hotels lining the beach on their left and whistled at the sleek sailboats, big trimarans, and sporty catamarans berthed at a marina on their right.

Luis's gaze followed his brother's across the deep blue waters of the Bahía de Cárdenas. They and their friends had come here often when they were Liliana's age. Weekending at the now-vanished campismo on the beach side of the peninsula, more than once they had danced until dawn, then hiked over to the bay side to watch the sunrise. Luis glanced at José, wondering if he remembered the camaraderie of those mornings.

As if responding to the thought, José pointed. "See those rocks out there, Liliana? Can't tell you how many times we"—here he punched Luis lightly on the shoulder—"sat right there and watched the sunrise. Celia too," he added, with a nostalgic edge that caused Luis to remember images of the two of them together that he had tried to forget.

They passed the caves, and as they entered Parque Ecológica, José sped up. Luis could not recall his brother ever showing an interest in human or natural history. It had taken Celia's prodding, on one of those campismo weekends, to get them to visit the Cueva de Ambrosia to see its small pre-Columbian drawings. José had pronounced them "boring." Years later, again at Celia's request, Luis had taken Liliana to see them. He smiled grimly, remembering that Liliana had used exactly the same word.

When they reached the end of the peninsula, José screeched to a stop at the entrance to Marina Gaviotas. "I see this is still under military control." He motioned to a yacht being hosed down. "Officer recreation?"

"Not necessarily," Luis explained. "The military is involved in tourism too. Especially things that require air and water transport. They have the equipment, so why not? No reason for boats and planes to sit idle when they could be bringing in hard currency by providing services for tourists. That boat is used for deep-sea fishing trips."

"I'm starving," Liliana piped from the back seat. "Can we stop for lunch somewhere?"

"You bet." José made a U-turn and headed back to town. In central Varadero he parked at the curb near a sidewalk vendor selling T-shirts. Passing a twenty-dollar bill to Liliana, he said, "Okay, kid, go get something cute. And decent."

"Gracias, Tío!" Liliana jumped out and, forgetting the care required to balance on five-inch platform shoes, stumbled and fell.

Luis and José simultaneously opened their car doors, but Liliana regained her footing with the agility of a cat and laughed to let them know it was no big deal.

"Hey," José called and motioned her back to the car. He handed her another twenty and said, "Get yourself a pair of sandals too."

Liliana rewarded him with a brilliant smile and avoided looking at Luis, whose face registered disgust and other emotions that his gut told him were equally poisonous. Didn't José know he had just handed the girl as much as Luis's or Celia's monthly salary?

While Liliana mingled with sunburned tourists at the T-shirt racks, José sat tapping his fingers on the steering wheel. Finally he said, "I've always wanted to eat at Al Capone's beach house—you know, the one they turned into a restaurant. I don't remember where it is. Is it any good?"

"It's that way." Luis pointed farther along the beach. He suspected that José had not forgotten where it was but was merely trying to find out if Luis ever ate there. He *had* eaten at La Casa de Al once, along with other National Assembly members. No need to explain the circumstances. His personal inability to pay for a meal there was none of José's business. "It is overpriced but pleasant. People go there mainly for atmosphere."

José flashed a grin. "Or to pretend for an hour that they're part of the mobster set."

"If they can afford to eat there regularly they probably are," Luis shot back.

Liliana returned wearing a big blue T-shirt that concealed her tartish clothes. Back in the car, she traded the platform shoes for a pair of thongs. The T-shirt probably cost ten dollars, and the thongs at most two, but Liliana did not, Luis noticed, offer José any change from the forty dollars he had given her.

La Casa de Al, set somewhat apart from its neighbours, was built of natural stone in a linear style that gave almost every room a view onto the sea. In Capone's days there was only the old gangster's beach house at this end of the peninsula, more private and more heavily guarded than the DuPont mansion on the other side of town. In recent years two hotels had been built down this way, but Capone's house still stood apart. It had an unobtrusive quality that Luis admired.

Entering the restaurant, Luis was satisfied that Liliana looked decent; a trifle casual, but this was, after all, a resort town, and she was only a child. Liliana promptly excused herself to go to the restroom. She returned with her face scrubbed clean, looking every inch the wholesome teenager.

Gazing around the dining room, she bubbled, "This place is amazing! I've always wanted to come here. Imagine what it was like when Al Capone and his gangster friends sat around deciding who they were going to snuff out next!"

"Probably not so different from gangster get-togethers nowadays," José said, declining drinks and pointing to a selection on the menu so that the waiter had to lean over his shoulder to see his choice.

"Like the Miami Cubans planning their next futile attempt to assassinate Fidel?"

cracked Luis. "The same for me," he said to the waiter, without knowing which entrée his brother had ordered.

"Me too." Liliana piped. "It's so sweet of you to bring us here, Tío Joe!" And to Luis, with a modest flutter of eyelashes, "Thanks for letting me come along, Tío Luis."

Luis said nothing. He wasn't going to spoil the outing by pressing the issue of her truant behaviour, but neither did he want her to think it was forgotten.

She turned wide eyes on José. "Have you ever been to one of those meetings?"

"There are a few of us who don't move in those circles. Actually quite a few," José glanced at Luis, "who want *productive* relations with Cuba."

Luis did not respond to that overture either but sat quietly as Liliana plied José with questions about Miami, questions that he answered without recourse to modesty. Yes, Miami's beaches were nicer than Habana's. Yes, Miami had more hotels than all of Cuba and lots of famous people came there; anyone with the dough could stay in those hotels and attend the celebrity performances. Yes, there were hoards of wealthy people in Miami and even ordinary people lived in houses as nice as this one, although not right on the beach. It was true that there were blocks of side-by-each shops, including Calle Ocho, which was almost entirely Cuban. It was also true that there were hundreds of shopping complexes bigger than Habana's Juan Carlos II mall, and there was absolutely nothing one might want that couldn't be bought in Miami.

Liliana drank it in with the wonder of a child being offered a first-hand report from Fantasyland. When José grew bored with the chatter—which was long after Luis had grown bored with it—he turned his attention to their immediate surroundings. "You'd have thought a Mafiosa like Al Capone would have built something more grandiose, like the DuPont place. Or else something more fortresslike."

"He had this whole section of the beach to himself," Luis commented dryly. "With security blocking off the road and the beach from a kilometre or more back, I suppose he could sit out on the terrace without worrying too much about assassination."

"Everyplace in Miami must be this nice," Liliana said with a wistful sigh. "Don't you just love living there?"

"I miss my friends and family here in Cuba," José replied.

The answer surprised Luis. That was the last thing he would have expected José to say, even if it was true, which seemed highly unlikely.

Liliana, though, took the remark at face value. "I know I'd miss my family." She looked from one to the other. "You're a lot alike, you know that? Tía Celia always said you were."

José arched an eyebrow. "I thought you said she never talked about me."

Luis grimaced. Physical resemblance was hard to deny, but that Celia had characterized them as similar in any other way was, well, hurtful.

"Alike? How?"

Liliana, sharp little vixen that she was, again looked from one to the other, giving them time to realize that they had spoken the words in perfect unison.

"Tía Celia," she began primly, like a child reciting catechism, "said that you're both 'true believers.'"

Luis glanced at José, who seemed equally baffled by the characterization.

Liliana pointed a pink-enamelled forefinger at Luis. "She said that *you* think the government ought to make all the rules, like the church did in the old days. And you'd get to be one of its rule-makers."

She put two fingers together, pistol fashion, and aimed at José. "And she said *you* went to the States because you believed in freewheeling capitalism and had fantasies about being one of its high rollers."

José rolled his eyes at Luis. "Is this how Cuban teenagers talk nowadays?"

"Only the bright ones," Liliana quipped, reverting to the flippant tone that Luis abhorred and Celia so readily tolerated. "Can we go for a walk on the beach after lunch?"

"Sure," José said.

Luis glanced at José. He had seen very little of his brother in the week he had been back and had supposed he had business to conduct in Varadero today. He found it hard to believe José had planned the day with its attendant expenses just for the two of them. But as José appeared to have no other commitments, Luis was forced to conclude his brother had actually planned to spend the day with him alone—and would have had it not been for their unexpected encounter with Liliana.

An uneasiness tugged at Luis. It had to do with a lifelong and generally futile attempt to resist his younger brother's charm. To forgive the abandonment, which seemed to be what José was after, was undesirable but possible. To forgive unnamed injuries that Luis's gut told him would be inflicted by this breezy return was incomprehensible. But where his brother was concerned, had he ever had a choice?

José saw the check coming and handed the waiter a credit card before he reached the table. Luis waited for the waiter to reject it, but after studying it carefully, he seemed to find it acceptable. José, he realized, must have known that credit cards issued by US banks were not acceptable and had got one issued elsewhere. It caused Luis to wonder how long José had been planning his return to Cuba.

When the receipt was brought for José's signature, Liliana leaned across and thanked him with a kiss on the cheek. Her timing, Luis noted, allowed her a glimpse of the bill's total, which José had casually shielded from Luis's gaze.

They left the car in the restaurant parking lot and went directly out the back door onto the beach. José paused for a long look at the house. "Beautiful stonework. And what a location. I wouldn't mind owning that place."

There's a difference between us, Luis mused. I see something I like and think, That's nice. What José likes he imagines owning. Well, in this case it's more mine than his because La Casa de Al belongs to Cuba, and I am Cuban and he is not.

They walked along the cleanly raked beach, nearly empty in the mid-afternoon heat. Luis felt tensions being dissolved by the combination of hazy sunshine, a cool sea breeze, and the gentle rhythm of wavelets lapping the sand. He and José walked at the same pace, something they had started doing in adolescence, as soon as both had got their full growth and their legs were equally long. Liliana raced ahead of them and was soon out of sight.

"Celia certainly has her hands full with that little package," José remarked. "Lucky she has you and Mamá."

"That is one of Cuba's strengths. A value system that puts family ahead of everything. But with tourism and this transition to the dollar economy, I don't know." Luis shook his head.

"Can't keep 'em out down on the farm after they've seen Paree. Or should I say, 'out in the cane field after they've seen Varadero?'"

"Probably not. It's hard on the country, though. So many of our best and brightest, well-educated, multilingual kids being seduced by the glitter of places like this."

"So how do you stop it?"

"That," Luis replied with a deep sigh, "is a subject of endless debate."

José pointed. Liliana was no longer on the beach but above them on the grounds of a large hotel. A band was playing poolside. Waving her arms in time to a salsa beat, she made exaggerated motions for them to come up. Luis felt some trepidation as they climbed the beach stairs of what he knew was a resort complex open only to registered guests. But he took his cue from José, who seemed perfectly at ease.

By the time they reached the pool area Liliana had disappeared. She wasn't watching the band, nor in the crush of semi-nude men and women, most of them kilos overweight, clustered at the bar. Luis and José walked around the pool to where a larger crowd, likewise dressed in beach attire that exposed large areas of pale skin, moved in time with the music. With laughter that suggested alcoholic excess, couples cut in, switched partners, and called challenges to each other as they danced. Luis squinted into the noisy crowd. She had to be here somewhere.

Suddenly Liliana appeared, gyrating to the music. "Come dance with me!" She held out her arms to include them both. "Don't give me that stiff look, Tío Luis. I know what a good dancer you are! Come on, Tío Joe. If you don't know how, Tío Luis can teach you."

The brothers looked at each other, grinned wolfishly, and moved in unison to dance with their niece. Liliana whirled and clapped her hands, her own daring egged on by José's uninhibited, inventive style. At first Luis danced a bit apart, getting a feel for the music. Then he moved in to claim Liliana with a repertoire of steps that his brother couldn't begin to match.

But José hung in there and gave Liliana a twirl or two when Luis passed her to him. Liliana played her role perfectly, so well, in fact, that Luis later wondered if she had sensed their competitiveness and deliberately set them up.

Whatever she might have guessed, one thing she could not fail to have noticed was that he, Luis, was the better dancer. It was him the crowd fell back to watch and applaud. The dance floor was one arena where he had never, not ever, played second fiddle to his brother.

THIRTEEN

CELIA scanned the crowd as the train, with a shrieking of brakes and a rattling of couplings, pulled into the Santiago station. Franci and Philip always insisted on meeting her and were always here, no matter how late the train. Today, thankfully, it was on time.

Celia and Franci had been best friends for twenty years, dating back to the time when, as coltish teenagers, they took a mutual pledge to stop chasing boys and make the grades necessary to get accepted into medical school. They frequently defaulted on the boy-chasing part, and if José had not left for the States when he did, Celia's pledge might not have been enough to keep her focused on a medical career. Ultimately Celia's academic achievements outshone Franci's, but Franci's love life fared better. Soon after graduation she had married Philip Morceau, then a young naval officer, now a harbour pilot responsible for moving great ships through the dangerously narrow entrance to Santiago's harbour. Celia always stayed with them when she came to Santiago de Cuba, just as Franci stayed with her when she came to Habana.

Celia spotted them immediately. Even in Cuba, where mixed-race couples were commonplace, they stood out. Philip, close to two metres tall, cut a striking figure in the dark blue uniform. Franci was not much taller than Celia, but she had a style—high heels and a towering Afro hairdo—that gave her the appearance of being as tall as her husband.

Hugs and kisses exchanged, Celia was soon tucked into the back seat of their Fiat. As Philip manoeuvred smoothly through Santiago's chaotic traffic of cars, trucks, buses, bicycles, pedicabs, pedestrians, and horse-drawn carriages, Franci turned half-around to talk to Celia. "Good the train was on time. That gives you plenty of time for breakfast and a shower before heading over to the campus. How's Liliana?"

"Healthy as can be, making good grades, lots of friends. I could not ask for more," Celia told her proudly.

"And Luis?" Philip asked.

"Pretty high at the moment. Geology reports from the offshore area near Santa Cruz del Norte definitely show petroleum deposits."

"Wouldn't that just make Cuba's future!" Philip exulted.

"How are Las Madres?" Celia asked.

Franci and Philip looked at each other, rolled their eyes, and laughed. *Las Madres* was a term they had adopted when they decided to invite their widowed mothers to live with them. The original idea was that the mothers would share a suite above the garage, but that proved unworkable from the start. The move had to be delayed until they could construct a tiny, one-room cottage in the backyard. Franci's mother had opted for the cottage, leaving Philip's to rule the roost above the garage.

Observing her friends from the back seat, Celia felt a twinge of envy for Philip and Franci's intimate laughter. Did the humour derive from their closeness, or were they close because they had the capacity to turn often-stressful situations into private jokes?

Franci laid her arm across the seat, fingertips touching and caressing Philip's shoulder, and said, "You go first."

"*My* mother," Philip began, "has been reincarnated as a French-Cuban version of Scarlett O'Hara." He and Franci chuckled in unison.

"How is that?" Celia had read *Gone with the Wind*; in fact, she and Franci read it together in their teens. She could not picture Philip's wizened mother with her overpowdered face and pixie cap of dyed red hair in any way resembling its heroine.

"She is given to recalling the 'gracious days' when our family owned a coffee plantation in Guantánamo Province."

"Wasn't that a while ago?" Celia asked. "Like, uh—"

"Two hundred years ago," Philip cut in. "But the way she talks, one would think she grew up in a plantation culture instead of a Guantánamo barrio. You know, I studied French in college but we never spoke a word of it at home. Now she affects a French accent, and if you let her, she'll bore you out of your gourd talking about la culture française."

"And servants," Franci added. "She keeps reminding me that they had more than two hundred slaves."

"No!" Celia gasped. "Surely she realizes—"

"That my ancestors *were* slaves? Apparently not." Again Franci and Philip reached out to each other with sympathetic laughter.

"Then there is *my* mother." Franci turned to look at Celia. "She has become a serious, and I might add much respected, Espiritista."

"Santería?" Celia surmised.

"Naturally. And since she weighs nearly one hundred and forty kilos, you can imagine what a figure she cuts in one of those long white priestess dresses."

Bemused, Celia said, "And you were hoping they would become friends."

"Oh, they have," Philip assured her. "They do have separate social lives, and in their own circles they run each other down unmercifully. But they spend hours of every day together and form a united front—against us."

"It's the baby thing." Franci sighed and Celia saw that she found this less amusing. "It's so bad I've told them that if they keep bringing it up, Philip and I will move out."

"They do know . . . ?" Celia delicately left the sentence dangling.

Philip finished it for her. "That we can't have kids? Listen, those two know only what they want to know. They've been given the same medical information we have. We even had Franci's gynecologist explain it to them. You think it did any good? My mother implies that it's because I'm not the macho my father and grandfathers were—overlooking the fact that I myself am an only child. Franci's mother thinks it's all a matter of praying to the right fertility goddess—or possibly our conversion to Santería."

They pulled into the driveway. As if materializing for a Santería ceremony,

Franci's massive mother sailed toward them in a billowing white lace dress. A blue turban, wrapped African-style, added almost a foot to her height. The whole effect might have been awe-inspiring were it not for the comic touch of a live chicken tucked under one arm.

"Would I be right to surmise that that chicken is not long for this world?" Celia murmured.

"Good guess," Franci replied and called, "Hola, Mamá. Look who's here."

Philip opened the back door for Celia and took her bag. "It's been an ongoing battle to keep her from filling the backyard with chickens," he muttered. "So she buys them live, one at a time, and sneaks it into the cottage until it's needed for ceremonial purposes. We are not supposed to know, of course."

Laughing, Celia called out, "Buenos días, Tía Yolanda." She approached Franci's mother on the opposite side from the clucking chicken and stood on tiptoe to brush a kiss across her espresso-coloured cheek. Normally the old lady was garrulous, but apparently she had more serious matters to attend to this morning, or possibly some trepidation at having been caught with a contraband chicken. She murmured a welcome to Celia and moved majestically down the sidewalk toward the bus stop.

Franci paused under a vine-covered portico from which dangled lavender blossoms. One flower lay decoratively atop her frothy hair. Although the Afro style had gone out of fashion decades ago, Franci's poise was such that on her it looked as avant-garde as tomorrow. She motioned Celia into the house. "Come."

Celia followed her into a living room ringed with family photographs. Several were from their wedding. One showed Franci's beautiful black hair brushing Philip's blond crew-cut as they bent to cut the wedding cake. Another caught them as they descended the church steps. One of Franci's smooth dark arms was linked through the white sleeve of his dress uniform, the other lifted to fling her bouquet to her bridesmaids. What the picture did not show, but Celia remembered vividly, was how deliberately Franci had aimed it toward her, and how, with equal determination, she had refused to reach for it, still being too raw from José's abandonment to participate in the fantasy of someday finding her own perfect mate.

"You know where your room is," Franci called over her shoulder as she headed for the kitchen. Celia did, but tossed bag and briefcase onto the sofa and followed them into the kitchen. Franci put on the coffee. When Philip went to take eggs from the refrigerator, Franci leaned past him for the milk, rubbing one well-endowed breast provocatively against his arm.

"Phe-leep! Franc-ee!" The high-pitched decibels of Renée Morceau rippled through the open kitchen window like an opera singer's aria. "Is the café ready?"

Celia looked in the direction of the voice in time to see Philip's mother retreat back into her apartment over the garage. Surprised that she had not come down to join them, Celia asked, "Is your mother ill?"

"No," Philip sighed. "It's her latest manifestation of the Scarlett O'Hara syndrome. She wants morning coffee served in bed."

Franci hacked off a piece of bread and placed it, along with a dish of guayaba marmalade, on a tray. She added the requested coffee and a large bowl of sugar.

"It's not that I mind taking it up to her," she said in a tone that suggested that she did. "It's the way she always says, 'Franci, ma chérie! I didn't expect *you* to bring it up.' As if I might have sent one of our non-existent servants!"

Philip reached for the tray. "I'll take it."

"No, you go ahead with the omelettes."

"Let me." Celia lifted the tray with a firmness that caused both to relinquish their hold on it. "I want to say hello anyway."

"Good idea," Philip said. "But tell her you can't stay; breakfast will be waiting."

"Shall I call her tía like always?" Celia asked. "Or should it be madame?"

"Oh, these days it's definitely madame," Franci clarified. "But still tía for my mother. That will make them both feel superior."

Celia climbed the steps to the apartment over the garage. The old lady, hearing her pause outside the door, called, "Entrez."

Celia stepped into the room and saw Philip's mother propped against the headboard of a large bed, her bottle-bright hair vivid as a child's orange crayon against a pillowcase printed with pink rosebuds. "Bonjour, Madame."

"Celia, ma chérie! Tu parles la langue de mon père!" Renée Morceau responded in such an atrocious accent that Celia almost laughed aloud.

"A few words," Celia acknowledged, placing the tray before her. She brushed the woman's cheek with her own, noticing, as she did so, that only one side of the wrinkled face had received the dubious benefits of heavy-handed powdering. "I am sorry I can't stay, but breakfast is ready downstairs."

"Go, go." Renée Morceau already had knife in hand and was attacking the bread and jam. "We shall chat later, n'est-ce pas?"

Celia slid into her chair at the kitchen table. Philip eased a perfect fresh-herb omelette onto her plate. "Um!" Celia murmured appreciatively. "You can deny your French heritage all you want, Philip, but you did not get your flair for elegant cuisine from the Cubans."

"Didn't I tell you that's why I married him?" Franci poured coffee all around. "As soon as I found out he liked to cook but didn't know how to make rice and beans." Again the shared laughter at what had to be an old joke between them.

Philip divided the second omelette and slid one half onto each of his and Franci's plates with a practised air that suggested this was their breakfast routine. Philip ate quickly, saying apologetically, "Sorry, but duty calls."

Guilty for her dawdling, Celia pushed another bite of omelette into her mouth and washed it down with a swallow of orange juice.

"Take your time," Franci admonished. "Philip is in a hurry, not us. When you're finished you can take a shower and I'll drive you to the campus."

"It's so close," Celia protested. "I can walk there easier than Philip can walk to work."

"I don't walk!" Philip crossed the living room to where a shiny Flying Pigeon bicycle was parked. Striking a pose beside it, he told Celia, "I *fly*."

When he had gone out, Celia and Franci relaxed over a second cup of coffee. "Does he always bike to work?" Celia asked.

"Except when it rains," Franci said proudly. "And what it's done for his body! Maybe you noticed? He's got the buns of a twenty-year-old."

"And if I had noticed, would I tell you?" Celia teased. "You think I have forgotten the time you threatened to run one of my A-cup bras up the flag pole if I kept flirting with some creep you had a crush on?"

Laughter filled the kitchen like sunshine as they reached across the table and clasped hands, needing that physical contact to reflect an emotional closeness that had survived loves serious and false, found and lost. For a few minutes it seemed like old times, their discussing the physical attributes of whatever boy or man had turned up their hormonal thermostats. In the old days such an opening would have been followed by interminable analyses of attendant emotional issues. But Franci and Philip did not appear to have any issues, and Celia was reluctant to mention her noticeably long engagement to Luis. Celia could tell that Franci expected it, but when nothing was forthcoming, she tactfully changed the subject.

"What is your presentation on this time?"

"The damaging effects of second-hand smoke on the respiratory system of small children, infants in particular. And government avoidance of the issue."

"Madre de Dios! Are you looking for sainthood as a martyr, or what?"

"I doubt it will come to that," Celia protested with an uneasy smile. "We have plenty of data. Somebody has to go public with it."

"If you say so." Franci rose and began clearing the table. "Go take your shower. I can already smell you, and the pressure you'll be under in that lecture hall will have you sweating like a horse. No, leave the dishes; I'll have them done by the time you're dressed. I hope you brought something cool?"

"A summer dress my mother would have approved of," Celia said primly, heading for the bathroom.

"It's going to be a scorcher," Franci yelled through the bathroom door. "Forget the stockings. In fact, forget your underwear too."

"Neither of our mothers would approve of that," Celia called back. "And mine I hope will be watching. Guardian angel with a flaming sword, waiting to strike down anybody who gives me a hard time."

Once on the medical school campus they went their separate ways, Franci to her office, Celia to the auditorium where the conference was being held. She slid into the front-row seat reserved for speakers just as the first one was adjusting his microphone.

Celia listened attentively to statistics that confirmed that broken bones and serious head injuries were becoming increasingly frequent as more bicycles competed with more cars. The only fault she found with the doctor's approach to his subject was that he neglected to note that the prevention of such injuries was more a matter of public policy than medicine: helmets, safety classes, more bike lanes, and hard dividers on existing bike lanes. They all cost money, of course. But surely the cost of prevention compared to the cost of treating such injuries was worth mentioning?

Next was a presentation by a doctor whom Celia knew slightly. It was on the subject of non-drug alternatives that could be substituted for drugs not easy to obtain because of the embargo. The results of a study that showed that hyperactivity could often be brought under control by a combination of physical exercise and massage therapy gave Celia a ripple of satisfaction. For the past five years she had been prescribing just that for children suffering from any disorder that she suspected might result from or be exacerbated by tension.

The next presenter, as if fearing that too much focus on children's health problems might lead to negative publicity, rehashed studies showing Cuba's children to be among the healthiest on earth. The statistics were well known and had repeatedly been verified by the World Health Organization. Celia allowed her mind to drift. Or rather, it drifted of its own accord, to a plan she had begun to formulate on the train ride. Her attention snapped back when her name was called.

She moved to the podium and presented the results of her own study on what she believed to be the most prevalent health issue presently facing Cuban children: asthma. The assembled pediatricians listened politely. Given the number of asthmatic children they were treating, they hardly needed her review of the statistics to tell them how serious a problem it was. "Asthma and most other respiratory ailments in children are aggravated by, if not precipitated by, smoking parents," she summarized.

When Celia could see that they were in comfortable agreement, heads nodding, she dropped her bombshell: "Government policies exacerbate the problem."

There was a rustle of unease as she went on to make points no one could deny. Cuba was a smoking culture. Tobacco was a major generator of foreign exchange and something for which Cuba was famous. But which was more important—healthy sales or healthy children? When she completed her presentation of the data, Celia concluded, "I agree with our colleague, Dr. Caicedo. Without an adequate supply of drugs to alleviate the symptoms of certain illnesses, we must place heavier emphasis on prevention. The government has demonstrated its concern by raising taxes on cigarettes, causing many Cubans to cut back on smoking. But is it not the government's responsibility, and ours, to educate parents on the harmful effects of second-hand smoke, particularly as it relates to their children's respiratory problems?"

Letting the question hang in the air, Celia picked up her notes to indicate the conclusion of her presentation. The discomfort of the audience was palpable. All of the previous speakers had been peppered with questions, but for Celia, there were none. She waited a long minute, then said, "Gracias para su atención" and left the stage.

The schedule indicated a lunch break so Celia did not return to her seat but followed the audience out of the auditorium. Doors to the dining hall were not yet open, but coffee urns had been set up in the lobby. Perhaps, she thought, it was too personal an issue. Smokers, who included at least half of the doctors present, were embarrassed to speak up and non-smokers were reluctant to pose questions for fear of offending their smoking colleagues. Perhaps they would find it easier to discuss the issue in private.

Celia took a cup of coffee and moved to a quiet corner. No one approached her. By the time she had finished the coffee, the lobby was blue with cigarette smoke.

Impatience welled up in her. She wanted to shout, Shame on you for resting on the laurels of what our health system has accomplished and flaunting statistics to prove that our children are the world's healthiest! Children are not statistics and some of ours are *not* healthy! Why are we not discussing what we can do for *them*?

Celia did not shout, of course. She remained silent, and alone, in her semi-quiet corner. But she knew what she was going to do. She just had not known until this moment that she definitely was going to do it. She flung her paper cup into a trash container and headed across the medical school campus to Franci's office.

The door, bronze-plated to identify it as the office of Dr. Franchesca Cumba, head of the school's psychiatric department, stood ajar. Celia paused, again undecided. If she was going to seek professional help, who better than Franci? But Franci would only tell her what she already knew: that the hallucinations were being generated by her own subconscious and she needed to pay attention to what they were trying to tell her.

Twice Celia put her hand on the door to push it open, and twice hesitated. Two other things gnawed at her. First, that she did not want to be seen as "not normal" by her best friend, and second, barely admitted to herself, she was not sure she wanted the hallucinations to go away—at least, not yet. Disturbing though they were, she felt that they were leading her. But where? Into an imaginary past, which might be another way of saying into lunacy? Or toward something unknown but infinitely tantalizing? Quickly, before she could be immobilized by indecisiveness, Celia pushed open the door.

Franci peered around a pile of books on her cluttered desk. "Well, how did it go?"

"Marvellous. When we broke for lunch they filed out, smoked up all their cigarettes, and pelted me with the empty cartons."

"Lucky you didn't suggest they give up tomatoes." Franci's forced humour matched Celia's, but her eyes were worried. "Ready for lunch?"

"I—" Celia shook her head. "No." This was going to be harder than she thought. The plaque on the door reminded her that Franci held a responsible position at the medical school. She felt uneasy about confessing that she was about to play hooky from a conference she was attending at state expense.

"No, what?" When Celia remained silent, Franci took off her reading glasses and gave her the once-over. "Well? Are you going to tell me or do I have to guess?"

Celia doubted that Franci could guess, but the possibility alarmed her. So she did something that by her own ethics was despicable. Without lying, she told a truth that would throw Franci completely off the scent. "José is back."

Franci tilted back in her chair, causing it to squeak alarmingly. "Ah. You didn't mention that this morning."

"I—I am really confused. With Liliana and work and, well, you know." Celia took a deep breath, as if about to go off a high dive. Which in a way, she was. "I need a time-out. I want to skip the rest of the conference and go spend a day or two in the mountains. Maybe take a bus up to El Saltón or somewhere like that."

El Saltón was a rustic mountain resort about two hours from Santiago, a place Celia knew because Philip and Franci had taken her there on a previous visit.

Celia could see disappointment written all over Franci's face. "Are you sure you don't want to talk about it? It's not like we've ever kept secrets from each other." Her eyes were warm, inviting trust.

"Of course I want to talk to you about it," Celia agreed quickly. "It's just that right now I am at a loss. How can I know what I feel when I have had no time *to* feel?" Her voice took on a pleading note. "I am simply desperate for some solitude, Franci."

Franci responded instantly to the pleading. With wisdom gleaned from a decade of psychiatric experience, not to mention her essentially practical nature, she took charge of the situation with an alacrity that left Celia speechless.

Franci stirred in her handbag and extracted a ring of keys. She took the one to the Fiat from it and thrust it into Celia's hand. "Get ready to roll, girl. You're out of here. Oh, and since you'll have to stop by the house to change and pick up your bag, grab whatever you want for lunch. If you're not hungry yet, you will be, so take something," Franci came around the desk and wrapped Celia in a strong embrace. "It will be okay, mi hermana. What your instinct is telling you to do is exactly what you should be doing. I'm just glad you got here before all those feelings you're repressing blew up in your face."

"So am I," Celia whispered. One thing she had not considered was that what she was hiding might, as Franci had put it, blow up in her face. The very thought filled her with dread. "It never would have come to this if I could have got some down time."

Franci smiled wisely. "Down time is all normal people usually need to get things sorted out in their head—or heart, as the case may be."

Celia hugged Franci long and hard. "Down time and a friend like you," she murmured, knowing as she said it that she was not making full use of what Franci had to offer as a friend. Nor could she any longer consider herself a "normal" person.

FOURTEEN

CELIA felt comfortable in the borrowed Fiat, or as comfortable as she ever felt at the wheel, given how infrequently she drove. Except for the colour, it was exactly the same as Luis's car, which was the one vehicle she did drive from time to time. She took Avenida de las Américas out of the city and curved along the Carretera Central into the foothills of the Sierra Maestra. She had been this way twice before, once on the weekend trip to El Saltón with Franci and Philip three years earlier and once on a school field trip to visit historical sites when she was eleven or twelve years old.

The historical sites were still there. From a long way off she saw the Basílica de Nuestra Señora del Cobre, where a four-hundred-year-old effigy of Cuba's patron saint, the Virgen de Caridad, resided. The church itself was overshadowed by a monstrous slag heap from copper mines that had been in operation since the days when Hernan Cortéz was governor of the province. She passed El Cobre without stopping and farther along took no notice of historic markers indicating where men and women of previous generations had died fighting for the island's independence from Spain.

Three times she passed turnoffs to El Saltón, but she did not take any of them. The mountains of the Sierra Maestra remained in the distance as she continued along the main highway through rolling ranch lands and citrus groves.

She stopped just past Palma Soriano to buy a string of mandarins from a roadside vendor, a small man with sun-dried skin. He took the coins she poured into his hand with a beatific smile and waved her on with the ancient formality of vaya con Dios still common among older-generation rural people.

Celia glanced at the gas gauge and saw that she would need to fill up in Bayamo. Recalling its shady main square, she briefly considered spending the night there. In Bayamo she had one close friend who, like Franci, dated back to childhood. Joaquín had followed in his father's footsteps, first as a member of the national fencing team and now, with a speciality in sports medicine, as one of its doctors. Joaquín's father and Celia's had died together in the 1976 plane crash that had claimed the lives of the entire Cuban fencing team as it was returning victorious from the Pan American games in Venezuela. Joaquín's dad had been one of the coaches, Celia's merely a civil servant travelling with the team to deal with visas, hotel reservations, and the like. Luis Posada Carriles, a Cuban expatriate working with the CIA, had been arrested in Venezuela and charged with the bombing that downed the airliner. Posada spent nine years in a Venezuelan jail before anti-Castro Cubans in Miami bribed him out. He had immediately returned to the CIA fold, working for Oliver North on the Contra resupply operation. Celia and Joaquín followed Posada's well-publicized career as a government-backed terrorist up until the bombing of several Habana hotels in 1997. At about that time, Celia, having recently assumed the responsibility for Liliana's care, recognized the debilitating nature of her hatred for the man and determined to put him out of her mind.

Driving along a near-empty highway lined with citrus groves, her hands lightly atop the steering wheel peeling a mandarin, thoughts of the tragedy that killed her father brushed her mind but she did not allow them to alight. Instead she thought of her father. For the first time, she realized his resemblance to Luis: a tall yet unobtrusive bureaucrat deeply dedicated to the political aims of the Revolution. Celia recalled him holding her, then a pre-schooler, in his arms as he danced to music from a crackling radio. As far as she could remember, it was only when her father danced that he became playful and revealed his natural athleticism. In that way Luis was very much like him. Except for being danced around a crowded living room in her father's arms, Celia's memories of him were indistinct, with no recollection of his features apart from those preserved in a few faded photographs her mother had left her.

By the time Celia reached Bayamo, she knew that she would not visit Joaquín. For one thing, it would be impossible for them to *not* discuss the deaths of their fathers and the fortunes of Luis Posada Carriles. Celia did not want that—not now or ever again. Furthermore, if it was the comfort of old friends she was seeking, she might as well have stayed in Santiago, for she could not have done better than Franci and Philip.

She pulled into a gas station. While an attendant filled the tank, Celia walked next door to a rental car agency and looked at a road map. She had a vague notion of driving on to Manzanillo to see a street that had been turned into a memorial to Celia Sánchez, but as soon as she looked at the map, she knew she was not going to Manzanillo. Realization of her actual destination hit her with such force that she could not believe she had not known it all along.

She cleared Bayamo traffic and headed southwest, still skirting the Sierra Maestra but moving ever closer to its rugged terrain. At Bartolomé Masó, the road turned due south and Cuba's highest mountains loomed before her. Within minutes she was surrounded by steep slopes covered with royal palms. Their straight white trunks took on a pink tinge that matched rose-coloured clouds floating in the afterglow of a sun just set. Celia would have liked to stop and take in more of the scenery, but night was just minutes away and she did not want to be driving this winding road in the dark. The Fiat complained strenuously at the precipitous climb. She slowed down, geared down, and kept climbing.

One car passed her, its door bearing the emblem of the provincial department of agriculture. It pulled into Villa Santo Domingo just ahead of her and a lone man got out. There were only a few cars in the parking lot.

Celia had changed into shorts in steamy Santiago. As she followed the khaki-clad driver of the other car to the reception desk, the cool mountain air caused her legs to prickle with goosebumps. The desk was not precisely indoors, but was set back under an overhanging apartment—the manager's, she presumed—to protect it from the weather. Two polished wooden rocking chairs sat on either side of the unwalled reception area, inviting guests to relax and chat. The clerk, a trim young man with crew-cut hair and military bearing, greeted the man ahead of her familiarly and slid a registration card across the desk. "Bruno! What brings you back? Not another outbreak, I hope!"

"No, just a routine inspection. Can't take chances with something capable of destroying the entire coffee industry."

"But we got a clean bill of health over a year ago!" the clerk protested.

"I know. Like I said, it's just a routine inspection."

Celia understood that they were talking about a coffee pest that had hit the area, so serious that La Comandancia de La Plata had been closed to visitors and the entire mountain region quarantined for two years. The media had made much of it at the time, but there had been little follow-up.

The man named Bruno passed the registration form back to the clerk and turned to smile at Celia. "Up for the weekend?"

Celia ignored the question and asked, "Did they ever find out the origin of the . . ." She hesitated, unable to recall whether it had been a beetle, a moth, fungus, or what. She settled on "the pest?"

The agricultural inspector leaned on the counter, a little too obviously sizing her up. "It wasn't a CIA plot, like swine fever, if that's what you're asking."

"There was some talk of that," Celia said, a touch defensively.

"Well, naturally. Given all the documented incidents we have of US bio-terrorism, that's the first thing the *lay* public would think." His emphasis made it clear that he did not share the lay public's ignorance. "But this had nothing to do with the CIA. The coffee bore was in Jamaica, barely one hundred kilometres from here. It didn't even need a human carrier; it could come in on birds. Just a question of time."

"I see." Celia moved up to the desk in hopes that the clerk would provide her with a registration form to end a conversation that was benign enough but had overtones calculated to impress that she did not much like. Instead, the clerk extended the discussion by joining in.

"But we were prepared, weren't we, Bruno?"

"Totally. The campesinos in this area were all trained to identify it, so when it arrived they knew exactly what to do. We had traps, and in no time our researchers had developed effective bio-control methods. But vigilant farmers, and the education to know what they were seeing when they saw it, those were the main weapons. The minute they spotted an infected bush, they burned it."

Traps, Celia thought. So it must have been a beetle. Or perhaps a moth. She did not ask for clarification. Instead, she asked the clerk, "You do have a room, don't you?"

He frowned, as if the question was a difficult one. "Just you?"

"Yes, please."

"For how many nights?"

"One."

He consulted a list. "We have two buses coming in tomorrow; we'll be completely full. But tonight, no problem."

"Perfect," Celia said quickly. "The trail up to La Comandancia will be open?"

"Oh yes."

At last he produced the registration form. She filled it out quickly, paid for the room, and held out her hand for the key.

"I'll show you to your cabaña," the clerk said.

Celia smiled and kept her hand out. "That is not necessary."

Reluctantly he handed over the key. "Are you sure?"

"Quite sure," Celia said, supposing that cottages would be numbered and she could easily find the one with a number to match the number on her key.

"See you later," the agricultural inspector said with hope. His eyes climbed her bare legs like beetles. Or moths. "In the bar, maybe?"

She balanced a noncommittal reply that might be mistaken for encouragement against the rudeness of no reply and opted for rude. Apparently to no avail. As she took her bag from the car, she realized with a sinking heart that he had taken a step or two toward her, probably intending to accompany her to her cottage on the pretense of looking for his own.

Just then the clerk whom she had so firmly dismissed walked out and reached for the bag. "Permit me," he said. "The path is rough and the light is not very good."

Whether he was aware of the other man's intentions and did not approve or did not want to miss an opportunity for a tip Celia did not know, but she relinquished the case with relief. The other man, seeing that she would be accompanied, headed in the opposite direction toward the bar. Celia gave the clerk a grateful smile and fell in behind him.

They followed a rough sidewalk lined with sword ferns and mariposa flowers, past small citrus trees and large mahogany trees with orchids and bromeliads clinging to their trunks. Celia could hear but not see a stream gurgling somewhere below.

"How far is it to the village?" she asked for the sake of conversation.

"Just across the river. Follow the lower road to where the bridge was."

"Was?"

"It was destroyed by a hurricane. We don't get much wind here, but rain turned the river into a torrent. It's back to normal now, though. You can cross on the stones. There's a museum over there if you're interested."

They arrived at the cottage assigned to her and she handed him the key. He opened the door and flipped on the light.

"How far is it to the Comandancia trail head?" she asked.

"Five kilometres. You can drive that far and leave your car in the parking lot. But you must first stop at the park office for a guide. It opens at eight."

"Gracias." He accepted the tip with a polite nod and was gone.

Celia looked about the rustic room. They could call it a villa if they wanted, but it was barely above a campismo. In fact, she was almost certain it had been constructed for groups of young campers and other Cubans who still came by the busload to visit one of the most sacred sites of the Revolution. The only improvement that she could see was the installation of a window air conditioner, which seemed absurd in view of the altitude and shady surroundings. The temperature was very pleasant. She wound the jalousied window open and stood listening to the gurgle of the river. A mosquito flew lazily in between the glass slats and landed on her cheek. She swatted it, only to feel the bite of another on her ankle.

"So much for fresh air," she sighed, winding the window shut again. She would mention to Luis the inappropriateness of air conditioners in areas where temperatures were moderate. Screens would be perfectly adequate, and night sounds were infinitely preferable to the hum of an air conditioner.

As much to wash away thoughts of Luis as to rid herself of road dust, she stripped and showered. The water was not hot so she did not linger. She dried herself hard with a thin towel and jumped into bed nude and shivering.

In a few minutes she had warmed up enough to reach for her case and extract the sandwich she had made at Franci's. Poor Bruno, she thought, sitting alone in a dreary bar waiting for her to come in so he might have someone for company during dinner. She did not exactly feel sorry for him, but in a way it was kind of sad. Sad that there were so many times when words were not appropriate and body language was not enough.

She got up and brushed her teeth, then crawled back into bed. Warm and fed, she felt utterly peaceful. Oddly, she also felt keyed up. Her emotions carried a current of excitement, but it was not the kind that generates tension. It was anticipation. Somehow, by luck or intuition, she had come to the right place. She was nearly at the epicentre, where it had all begun. If she was to find clues as to why her psyche had become entangled with what she imagined to be that of Celia Sánchez, might it not be here?

Eyes open in the darkness, she tried to recall historical accounts—or, more accurately, historical footnotes. For several minutes thoughts flowed in a logical, linear channel. Then, like a river in flood, her mind overflowed its banks and began sweeping up images without regard for source: books she had read, fragments from stories her mother had told her, half-listened-to conversations, and details that could not have been known or remembered by anyone except the woman her subconscious was shadowing.

It was not at the Comandancia that Sánchez and Castro had met. It was months earlier, near Manzanillo, *beard so scraggly, younger than I expected, never seen eyes so bright, double-bright in the half-light of dawn.* Sánchez had gone to let him know that Matthews, the reporter from *The New York Times*, had arrived. Who had told her that story—her mother perhaps, who had got it from Vílma? How Fidel had stayed out in the farmer's field with Sánchez and other rebel leaders *twenty-one hours of talk talk talk he understands everything organizes nothing; no matter, I can continue with that while they follow him he knows what must be done* while Matthews cooled his heels in a peasant's shack *palm fronds like black cutouts in a sky white with stars, sleepy, sleeping, Frank País next to Fidel, Fidel next to me, Haydée and Armando together, Raúl and Vilma, Faustino, Guillermo, my people my family.*

Sánchez had gone back to Manzanillo to expand her network, had smuggled more weapons and supplies to the guerrillas, and brought in more journalists. There was the CBS television crew she and Haydée took in two months later and stayed on, right through the battle of Uvero. *Oh God the blood I spilled to kill who can say and what would my father say? When does killing to save my country become blood on my hands?* It was after that battle, needing a permanent base for a field hospital, that Sánchez had found the perfect hideaway. While Castro kept engaging Batista's troops, moving from place to place, she remained at La Plata to oversee construction of the Comandancia. *Look, Fidel, how hidden the buildings will be beneath the trees, how the land falls away on all sides; with one hundred soldiers you can stop ten thousand of theirs without such losses as we suffered at Uvero yes, you will have hundreds more I promise!*

Sánchez returned to Manzanillo and in two months had recruited enough soldiers to double those under Fidel's command, Celia's mother among them. *Thank God for my women where would we be without them? Shooting, sewing, nursing as needed how can men be so inept at taking care of themselves how can he command an army when he suffers such toothaches?*

Sánchez had gone to Santiago next, recruiting and fundraising until Batista's henchmen started closing in. Then she returned to the sierra, this time to stay. *Springtime, the smell of gunpowder, the smell of blood, splintered trees toppled amongst alpine flowers, eardrums aching long after the bombs, silence.*

Sensations more powerful than facts stormed Celia's body, making it impossible for her to attach actual dates, places, and events to Sánchez's time in these mountains. How much did she know anyway? The history of the Revolution was the history of *los barbudos*, "the bearded ones," men's big histories recounted in big books. Sánchez's story, what little of it had been written, was told only in children's books. She herself was given a copy of *Celia Nuestra y de las Flores* for her ninth birthday and in high school had read *Celia, La Flor Más Autóctona de la Revolución*, but what had those sanitized tales told her of the real woman?

Celia tossed fretfully, tangling the sheets and swatting at the odd mosquito. Why was it never stated that Sánchez began armed struggle in the sierra five years before Fidel arrived? Why wasn't she celebrated for having found the *Granma's* twelve bedraggled survivors and gotten them to safe houses, thereby saving them from being murdered like the other sixty Fidel had brought from México? Why was it never explained that she had decided that Fidel would command her troops, seasoned fighters who knew the sierra, so she could return to the city to recruit more, raise funds, and buy the weapons they needed? Why was it never acknowledged that it was Sánchez who chose the site of the Comandancia, brought Fidel there, supervised the construction, and integrated women into the rebel force? Why was it not said, simply, that in that time and place, Celia Sánchez had the most workable ideas as well as the final word on almost everything?

Celia's mother had known this. So had all the others who'd served with them in the sierra. During gatherings of old compañeros in their home when she was a child, Celia had heard them speak admiringly of Fidel as their courageous commander but of Sánchez as the decision-maker and infallible strategist who guided him and inspired them. This was what they had witnessed during those years in the sierra. Yet not a word of that made it into those children's books or into any of the museums that memorialized her. Like those portraits at Parque Lenin, history had preserved her in honey, as la flor autóctona, the sweet native flower.

Not a flower, Celia thought as she drifted into sleep. A woman who knew exactly what she wanted. If I find the woman, I will find . . .

FIFTEEN

CELIA woke from dreamless sleep to a darkness that felt familiar. She knew without looking at her watch that it was near dawn. She dressed quickly, not in the shorts she had taken off the night before but in the jeans she had worn on the train and a white shirt she had bought for Liliana that Liliana had not cared for so it had ended up in her closet. She double-knotted the shoestrings of her runners, and out of habit stuck a pen and notepad in the pocket of her shirt.

She hoped, as she started the car, that the sound would not disturb anyone. As there was only one road leading uphill, it should be easy to find the trail head. The important thing was to get past the park entrance before the staff came to work. She was only planning to do what dozens of tourists did daily; the difference being, she did not want to be accompanied.

She had barely cleared the villa when she came to a barricade, several sawed-off tree stumps rolled into the road to block traffic. The small building on the left would be the park office where visitors were expected to pick up a guide. At this hour, though, it was as dark. Celia swerved around the tree stumps and continued up the road. It was even more steeply pitched than the one she had come in on. It ended abruptly in a parking lot that, according to a large sign, was nine hundred and fifty metres above sea level. No wonder the Fiat had grumbled so. In five kilometres it had climbed more than seven hundred metres!

As Celia turned into the parking lot her headlights picked out a small sign made of wooden arrows that pointed toward trails leading off in various directions. Pico Turquino she recognized; all Cubans knew it to be their island's highest peak. La Placitas and Humanities she could imagine; tiny mountain hamlets of four or five families, accessed by trails rather than roads. The bottom arrow read *La Comandancia*.

She parked the car and from her bag took a pencil-sized flashlight she always carried because one could count on electricity going off just about anywhere in Cuba at any time. It was nearing sunrise and should have been light, but massive thunderclouds kept it, if not quite pitch-dark, then close enough.

The trail leading to La Comandancia was on the opposite side of the road from the parking lot. She followed it into a forest of ancient mahogany trees, each one bearded with long grey strands of Spanish moss. A wire gate barred the path. Swinging her light along the wire, she saw that there was a person-sized gap in the fence at the end of the gate. She squeezed through.

For a short distance the path was more or less level, smooth and easy to follow. Then it became less even. Where it pitched up or down, rain runoff had turned it into a trench just the width of the trail, sometimes ankle-deep, sometimes knee-deep. Rocks rolled treacherously underfoot.

It was not yet sunrise but getting light when she reached what appeared to be an uninhabited farmhouse. As she approached she saw a large thatched-roofed, open-sided room and guessed that it served as a visitor's rest stop. The trail seemed to end there, but she was sure it did not. She switched off the flashlight to save batteries and instinctively turned right. Once around the old farmhouse she saw that the trail dipped into a small rivulet, then continued upward.

Occasionally the heavy forest of mahogany and strangler figs fell away, giving breathtaking views across a labyrinth of deep ravines that sliced between the most rugged mountains she had ever seen. Everything seemed familiar, and at the same time astonishing. Celia had not known that such wild areas still existed in Cuba.

Red light spilled across the landscape with startling brightness. Turning to look back, she saw that the sun was a red ball balanced in a narrow slot of clear sky between earth and leaden clouds. As it moved upward and behind the thunderheads, it became half a sun, then none. The landscape faded back into shades of grey, although lighter than before. Celia turned to continue uphill and gasped. While she was watching the sunrise, a man was watching her.

"Compañera," he said sternly. "It is prohibited for visitors to walk this trail without a guide. Didn't you see the sign at the park entrance?"

"I—it was dark. There was no one there." Celia's distress was not feigned. To have come so far, only to be stopped! Her knees, already shaky from the climb, seemed to give out entirely. She leaned against a boulder and finding it not adequate support simply sat down.

The man knelt beside her. Higher up the trail, looming above her, he had seemed tall. In reality he was a small man, scarcely as tall as herself.

His face registered concern at her sudden collapse. "Are you all right?"

"Yes. I—I just need to rest a bit."

"No hurry," he said. "I will wait with you. You were going to La Comandancia?"

As if the trail led anywhere else, she thought, but nodded politely. "I have never been there, and this morning—this is my only chance."

"I see. Unfortunately the guides do not arrive until eight."

It occurred to her that it would be better to go with him than not to get there at all. "But you are here."

"Well, yes. But I am not a guide."

"Are you from Santo Domingo?"

"I am. Did you visit the museum?"

"No, not yet."

"It was my home. Before the war."

"Really?" She gave him a second look. "You were here then?"

"I was born here. Already ten years old when the war reached this area. The soldiers forced us out of our home, that house where the museum is now."

Celia was shocked. "The rebels did that?"

The man laughed at her confusion. "The rebels? No! Batista's troops. Our house was a very nice one. Four rooms. The commander, he had his men cut a hole in the floor, right through the strong boards my grandfather had shaped by his own hand from trees such as these." He flung out his arm to indicate the forested slope.

"More than two metres square this hole was, and two metres deep. He had them lower a bed into the hole, my parents' bed it was, and he got in that bed and stayed there night and day. That's what kind of coward he was. He said he had migraines and perhaps he did, but I think it was his cowardliness that made him sick. That and the terrible things he did. He had a terror of a mortar attack on the house so he hid in that hole while his troops perished and messengers brought him word of one defeat after another."

"You were here!" Celia was so thrilled by this human connection to the past that her disappointment was momentarily forgotten.

"Yes. I was a guerrilla."

"Surely you are not that old!"

"I told you. I was ten years old when the rebel army made their headquarters here." He jutted his chin toward the Comandancia. "I *was* one of them."

Perhaps taking Celia's silence for skepticism, which in fact it was, he went on to give details that, Celia suspected, he had recounted many times. "All the men in the village were already with Fidel. Or dead," he added gravely. "My papá, because he protested when Batista's men put us out of our house, he was shot. And others."

He paused for emotion or dramatic effect, then continued. "There were only a few old men, and they were closely watched. The women, too, for by that time it was known that there were women with the guerrillas. It often fell to children to be the rebels' eyes and ears. It was easy for us. One minute we would be skipping stones in the stream or gathering firewood for our mother, and the next minute we would have slipped away to carry a message or food or whatever there was to be carried to La Comandancia."

"My mother was one of them," Celia said suddenly. In fact, her mother had spent most of the war in the Oriente, under Raúl's command. But she had been recruited by Celia Sánchez and was brought here first for a month of training before being sent with others to the Second Front in the Sierra Cristal.

"She was a rebel soldier?"

"Yes. And a nurse."

"Where is she now?"

"Dead, I'm afraid."

"Killed in the war?"

"No. Cancer. She was a very heavy smoker."

The man nodded, as if Celia had just provided a detail that authenticated her claim to having had a warrior mother. "One of the city girls."

"From Pilón, yes. How did you know?"

"All of those women who came from the city to fight with Fidel were smokers. As a child, this was something I had not seen before, women smoking. But those women from the city, they all did."

"Do they now? Your women, I mean. Do they smoke?"

He thought about it for what seemed like a long time, long enough for Celia to realize that he must be visualizing the faces of all the women in his community.

"Some," he said finally. "Those who have gone to live in town, they come back smoking. Because they have money, you see."

"And the men?" Celia asked, although she knew the answer. "Did they smoke then? And do they now?"

He looked at her with surprise. "Of course. Smoking is a man's thing, no?"

As if to prove his point, and to acknowledge that she was an outsider, an urbanite, he took a packet of cigarettes from his shirt pocket, shook one out, and offered it to her.

Celia smiled and shook her head. "No thanks. Smoking kills women."

He lit a cigarette for himself and smoked a moment in silence, studying her. "Your mother," he said.

"Yes. And Celia Sánchez."

"It probably kills men too," he conceded. "But we must all die of something, no?"

Tears sprang unexpectedly to Celia's eyes. Frank and José País shot by Santiago police. Able, Boris, Mario, Che, all tortured, all murdered. Camilio disappeared on a solo flight to Camagüey. Joaquín's father and her own flung into eternity by a terrorist's bomb. Haydée by her own hand. Then Carolina and her husband . . .

The man must have supposed the tears to be for her mother, for he suddenly said, "She was your mother. You have a right to see where she fought for us."

"Gracias, compañero!" Celia jumped to her feet.

"Are you sure you can make the rest of climb?"

"Oh, definitely! I just needed to rest."

"We are almost there. To the first building." He turned and climbed so rapidly that almost immediately she fell behind. Suddenly he stopped beside a tiny thatch-roofed hut. When she caught up to him, panting, he grinned and said, "It doesn't look like a hospital, does it?"

It certainly did not, nor did Celia think it ever could have been. The place where her mother received her battlefield training had to have been more than this dirt-floored hovel or they could not have cared for as many wounded as they did.

"Not the main hospital; it is up there." He waved toward the densely forested mountainside above them. "This was where Che saw sick people from the area, the non-combatants. Most had never been to a doctor before. Che was the first to come to this part of the sierra. He treated everyone."

"What kinds of illnesses?" Celia asked, peering into the tiny hut with interest.

"Everything. Many suffered from toothaches. That's why we called this the dentist's place."

"The guerrillas had a dentist?" Celia asked in surprise.

"Eventually, yes. But not in the beginning. Che wasn't a dentist himself, but he could pull teeth. See this?" The man pulled back a gum to reveal a missing upper tooth halfway back in his mouth. "Che took it out. When I was eleven."

Celia shook her head wonderingly. "I am a children's doctor and cannot imagine having to work under such conditions. Or pulling a child's tooth. How brave you were!"

"At times one must be brave. Of necessity." He glanced up at the sky, and as he did so, a large raindrop struck his nose. By the time he had wiped it away, she, too, was feeling drops.

"You want to get back," she said. "You were on your way home."

"True," he admitted. "The trail is more difficult in the rain."

"Could I stay? The guides will be here soon, no?"

He hesitated, clearly torn between wanting to get home and wanting to give her the gift of time in a place that he must presume was as sacred to her as it was to him.

"I could sit there." Celia pointed to the hut. "And just wait. And remember."

In one way or another, she, or perhaps her mother's service to the Revolution, had earned his trust. "All right," he said. "But wait for a guide. Farther up there are many trails. You could get lost." He glanced again at the lowering sky. "Do not try to walk back alone. The trail is slippery when it is wet, very dangerous."

"Gracias," she said, offering him her hand.

He barely touched her fingers. "Que te vaya bien, compañera," he said and was gone, swift as a forest animal, down the path and out of sight.

SIXTEEN

AS soon as he disappeared from view, she crossed the clearing and again entered thick forest. Other buildings appeared among the trees. One seemed to fit what she could remember of her mother's description of the hospital. Another she thought might have been where the women's brigade lived. Then the sense of familiarity vanished, and she was lost. She wandered for short distances along various trails, always choosing those that led higher up the mountain.

Suddenly she came upon a stairway made of earth held into place by rough logs. It climbed the mountainside for at least a hundred steps, yet was hidden, arched over by hibiscus bushes larger than any she had ever seen. Reaching to two or three metres, stalks so slender that they could not bear the weight of their own height, they flopped over, forming a tunnel through which the steps ascended the mountainside.

Celia climbed rapidly, her previous confusion erased by exhilaration. At the top of the steps, just to the left, would be the cookhouse with a tree growing up through the roof. *Do not cut the trees*, she heard herself saying. *If we protect the trees they will protect us.* Celia peered inside, to where the floorboards had been sawed short to allow the forked trunk of a huge jagüay to pass into and through the room. One fork, the larger one, was dead and half-rotted away. The smaller fork continued on through the roof, its spreading boughs still green with leaves, concealing the cookhouse from the air.

Celia did not linger in the cookhouse but followed a trail that her feet seemed to know. A thatch-roofed cottage came into view. The side from which she approached was ground level, but at the back it perched on stilts, high above a steeply sloping hillside.

She paused. On her left, against a vertical bluff hung with tropical vegetation, was a rough wooden bench. *Fidel's place to sit, think, write, talk.* On the opposite side of the narrow trail the land fell away so that the view—a view that seemed as familiar to Celia as the one from her apartment balcony, was into the tops of plants that grew tall in a forest such as this: the twisted upper trunk of a great mahogany tree, and a hibiscus that would have been ten metres tall, had it stood upright instead of arching like a rainbow with the weight of green leaves and red blossoms.

Celia faced the cottage. There was no door, just a plain plank wall barely two metres high, overhung by the thatched roof. She studied the wall, momentarily confused. Not about where she was; she knew exactly where she was. But confused about how one entered because in her mind's eye she saw that room from the inside, open to the forest.

Without forethought, she knelt, felt for the bottom of the wall, and lifted. It was heavy but came up easily, a section about six feet square. Of course; that was how it had been designed: to lock down at night and be raised like an awning by day. She looked around for a long stick to prop it open but saw nothing she could use, so she slipped inside and lowered the wooden flap behind her.

The sense of familiarity was so strong that it took everything she had to keep herself in herself. A few times in the past two years she had felt herself slipping through cracks into the past, but here she was surrounded by past. She could swallow it whole—or be swallowed by it.

"No time travelling," she said aloud, or almost aloud. She was whispering because whispering was what they had been trained to do. Batista's men were loud; the rebels were not. No one spoke above a whisper here, ever.

"But that was then," she told herself, trying to raise her voice, which again came out as a whisper. "This is now. I am now."

Perhaps because she asserted it with such firmness, the room did not claim her. It was a kitchen, not even three metres across. From where she stood she could reach the skinny built-in cupboard on one wall and the rough wooden table on the other. Directly in front of her was a small gas refrigerator, and next to it an open doorway.

In four steps Celia crossed the kitchen and stepped out onto the balcony. She touched a narrow, L-shaped bar built into the railing of the deck. "See?" she whispered. "If this was then it would be covered with her papers, or cleared to make room for their té. But there's nothing here, has been nothing here, for the whole of my life."

The view from the balcony was idyllic. The forest-and-fern-covered slope fell away to a stream with small waterfalls dropping from one bath-sized pool to the next. A steep narrow stairway led partway down, a stairway not fastened to the deck but leaning against it; built, she knew, to provide easy access to the stream for drinking water and bathing—yet movable, so that if danger threatened from that direction, it could be pushed away in an instant.

There was a flash of lightning followed by a thunderclap so close that she nearly jumped out of her skin. Rain, which until then had been scattered drops, came down in a gush. Celia dived inside the house and stood there laughing, breathless. All I need is time, she thought. If I can stay here long enough, it will all come together; I know it will.

As her eyes adjusted to the murky light of the kitchen, she saw that her sneakers had left muddy tracks across the rough wooden floor. Celia pulled off her shoes and socks and walked barefoot to the hut's one other room.

The bedroom was dark. The only light came from the kitchen, which itself was dim with the big wall flap closed. The bedroom would not have been dark if the wooden flaps on each of three walls had not been closed. Had they been propped open, awning style, as they were designed, the effect would have been that of an unwalled tree house.

The room held only a double bed—a bed that, with two people curled tightly together, would not have seemed small. She crouched next to the bed and, pushing back the plastic covering it, stroked the coarse off-white sheet. A musty scent filled her nostrils, but it was overridden by another, more animal smell: that of the two warm bodies who had shared this intimate space.

"Forty-five years ago you were here," she whispered and waited for whatever it was she needed to know about forty-five years ago and now.

Out in the kitchen, she heard the flap lift and the rushing sound of rain driven by wind. The sound persisted for a few seconds. The person entering was looking, as she had looked, for something to prop it open. Finding nothing, the flap closed again, shutting out the wind and darkening the room. Celia waited for the sound of footsteps, but there were none. For a moment she did not move, but remained on her knees, clutching the rough-woven sheet. She tried to stay where she was, who she was. It was no use.

She rose and walked to the door of the bedroom. He was kneeling, unlacing a boot. He pulled it off and, one white foot bare and gleaming, went to work on the second boot. It and the sock were sopping wet, as if he had walked through the creek or stepped in a puddle. He sat down like a child and grasped the boot with both hands to wiggle it off his foot.

As it slid free his eyes flickered to his left, to where she stood, then travelled slowly upward from her feet to her face. For several seconds he sat completely motionless, boot and sock suspended in mid-air, dripping. Then, with extreme quietness, he set the boot on the floor. He dropped the sock beside it and stood up.

Celia moved to him and with her sleeve blotted the wetness from his forehead. She ran her hands down the sides of his face, wiping away droplets of rain clinging to his beard. Her fingers moved lower to undo the buttons of his shirt. It was very wet.

She smiled up at his surprise. *You expected me to be at the hospital or meeting with my commanders. But I am here. We are alone. No one, friend or foe, is coming through that rain. It is a torrent, a wall. We are inside a fortress made of water.*

She turned and walked into the bedroom. Although she could not hear his bare feet moving silently behind her, she knew he was there. At the bed she paused and waited for him to grasp what her body was telling him. *My decision, your command; take it, feel your power. It means nothing to me.*

His fingers, light as feathers, stroked down her arms. She unbuttoned her shirt and he peeled it back over her shoulders. When she started unzipping her jeans his hands left her shoulders. She knew without turning around that he was doing the same.

Her jeans were tight. She got them and the panties only to her hips, then sat down on the bed to wiggle them off. He knelt on the floor, took each pant leg in turn, and pulled until her legs were free and bare.

They did not stare at each other; little good it would have done anyway in the shuttered, storm-darkened room. It was all by feel. When his damp, warm-skinned weight lay full against her, *it was wonderful soundless as it always is, and swift as it must be. But too quick, oh!* She bit her lip to keep from crying out, knowing that he would not, had never, left her like this.

She felt the discipline of his body as it resisted the urge to melt into her own heat, maintaining the rhythm until she came, gasping. Almost immediately she pushed to roll him off her. He clasped her shoulders, resisting.

Why do you always do that? She pushed again. He gave way to the pressure and rolled onto his back. In the same motion she rolled on top of him, felt his body shudder and relax.

See? This is what you need, as much or more than the sex; your back protected by the bed, the floor, the earth itself, my body a shield against what might come at you front on—my body and the rain, which for this moment in time, guards us both.

They slept.

SEVENTEEN

CELIA could not have said whether she felt the man's body beneath her first, or first opened her eyes to the darkened room. She took it that she was in some kind of hallucination, but the physical reality of the body, its musky maleness, caused her to hold her breath in terror. Who was this person? Who was she? Where was she?

The where answered itself first, as she recognized not so much the room as the sound of the rain. It had slackened some but was still pelting down. Without moving her head, for fear of disturbing she knew not who, her eyes roved frantically, looking for clues as to whether this was or was not a hallucination.

The man, whose hands rested lightly on the small of her back, must have sensed her wakefulness because he slid them higher and tightened his embrace. The movement panicked Celia. As swift as a bird taking wing, she was off of him and into a sitting position on the side of the bed. She would have been gone entirely, with or without her clothes—probably without because she had not yet figured out where they were. But his movement was almost as quick as hers, quick enough to catch her by the wrist.

"Hey!" he said softly. "Don't go."

Celia sat, trembling. "Who are you?"

"*Now* you ask," he said in a teasing voice. "I'll tell you if you'll tell me."

Then something, perhaps tension in the wrist he was holding, must have caused him to realize how frightened she was. He immediately released her, rose from the bed, and reached for his pants. She looked for her own, but he was between her and them, between her and the door. She remained perched on the side of the bed. His pants were at her feet. When he picked them up, they brushed against her leg.

"Your clothes are soaking wet!" she said in surprise.

"Well, yeah. It's raining out there." He glanced around, perhaps looking for his underpants. Not seeing them, he pulled on his jeans.

"Is that where you came from? Out there?" she whispered.

Seemingly oblivious to the fact that his crotch was no more than a foot from her face, he unselfconsciously slipped his hand between penis and pants to avoid pinching as he pulled up the zipper. "Well, yeah. I work here. Where did *you* come from?"

Perhaps he sensed that his standing tall, quizzing her like that, was increasing her fear because he sat down cross-legged on the floor, looked up at her, and asked in soft-voiced wonder, "And why did you come to me the way you did?"

"I thought you were . . . someone else," Celia whispered.

He gave a quirky, self-mocking smile. "Funny. For a second I thought you were somebody else."

"Who?" Celia whispered, not wanting to know and afraid she already did.

"When Fidel lived here he had this companion, Celia Sánchez. I'm sure you've seen pictures of her. In most of them she's wearing pants, and a man's shirt, with papers sticking out of the pockets."

"Notes," Celia whispered. "Things Fidel needed to remember or wanted done. She did all the follow-up."

"Oh. I didn't know that. Anyway, there you were, in the doorway of what used to be their bedroom. In pants, with something sticking out of your shirt pocket. It was so weird! For a second I thought you were her ghost."

Celia began to cry, not sniffling but great, wracking sobs.

"I'm sorry!" He reached to comfort her but she fell to the side, arms crossed on her chest as if to shield herself. He drew back. "I didn't mean to upset you!"

"I don't know what happened," she sobbed.

"Nothing. At least, nothing to cry about."

"You don't understand!" For the first time, her voice rose above a whisper.

"No, but—"

"I am becoming interchangeable with her!"

"With who?"

"Celia Sánchez."

"I don't get it."

"Before only a few seconds and only in my head. Never with someone else!" Until now. Now she had not only come into Sánchez's space; she had come into the woman, or the woman into her, in a way that seemed not only psychological but physical.

Celia wiped her eyes and looked at the man, this time, looked carefully, a sort of last-ditch attempt to ascertain whether he was real. He was about her age, perhaps younger. The short, untrimmed beard made it hard to tell. His feet were bare, as was his chest, which was almost hairless. All he wore were the wet jeans, which were mud-caked about the ankles.

She registered the fact that he had made no threatening moves toward her. In fact, he was not moving at all. There was about him a rather amazing stillness. She supposed his eyes were brown but could not tell for sure in the dim light. His head tilted slightly to one side in a posture of thoughtful attention. When she lay still except for a spasmodic jerking of her chest, he spoke in a conversational tone.

"I spend most of my time observing animals in the wild. Sometimes they come to me, sit on my foot, or perch on my head. Mice have even climbed into my pocket. I don't know why they do it. But it's kind of nice."

"Nice for *you*," Celia sniffed. "But for me to take that kind of risk is—" She paused, not knowing how to characterize what she had done. Finally she said. "Over the edge."

"Maybe you should see a doctor," he said gently.

Celia laughed hysterically. "I *am* a doctor. Dr. Celia Cantú. I have just come from a conference in Santiago." She gripped the fabric beneath her head and, realizing it was her own shirt, sat up and jerked it on. "That is where I am supposed to be right now!"

She tried to button the shirt but could not; her fingers were trembling too hard.

He leaned forward, began a button below the one she was unable to fasten and worked his way down, closing the shirt button by button with deft movements that did not cause pressure against her skin.

"And what does Dr. Cantú think?"

"I have no idea! There have been only a few incidents. The pattern is . . . unclear."

As she spoke, Celia was looking about for the rest of her clothes. The man rocked to one side and pulled something white from beneath him. Her panties.

"Sorry," he said. "I didn't know I was sitting on them. Now they're wet too."

Celia stood quickly and, turning slightly aside so that her crotch wasn't directly in front of his face, pulled them on.

He handed her jeans to her. "So what's the problem with this fantasy?"

"I am not the kind of person who goes around fantasizing!" Celia snapped, feeling more herself once she had her pants on. "Forgetting who I am. Jumping into bed with—" The enormity of what she had done struck her full force, and to her dismay, she began to cry again. "It's inexplicable!" she gasped.

He shrugged. "Isn't everything?"

She choked back the new round of sobs. "Everything?"

"That's how I see it." He made a palms-up gesture. "For example, why does a rain-soaked biologist who's been mucking about in the bush since before dawn walk through the door into the oldest fantasy on earth?"

"What fantasy?"

"You know. The one where the woodsman takes shelter from a storm in an abandoned cottage and finds a woman with a sweet warm body waiting for him."

Celia blushed but said nothing. What was there to say?

His eyes slanted with humour. "Was that magic? A miracle? Or just one of life's beautiful surprises?"

She made no attempt to answer and he made no attempt to touch her as she edged past him. Once out in the kitchen where there was more light, she felt better. The rain had become a drizzle. Her shoes lay just inside the doorway to the balcony. She sat down to put them on.

He came out of the bedroom buttoning his shirt. "Know what that is?" he asked, pointing to the floor near where she sat.

She glanced down, saw the trap door, and in her mind's eye, the darkness beyond. "An escape route," she whispered.

"Yeah," he said. "The tunnel caved in long ago, but that's where it was, with a stash of emergency supplies in case the place got surrounded and they had to make a quick getaway."

"Celia Sánchez designed this place," she said, her voice again coming out so low as to be almost a whisper. "This one and all the others up here."

"That's what I heard," he said easily.

She stood but did not move toward the place where a section of the wall could be lifted to let her out onto the trail because he had sat down there and was putting on his boots. When the last one was laced and tied, he rose and faced her. His eyes were so full of question that she felt compelled to ask, "What?"

"If you were Celia Sánchez when I came in, who was I?"

"I don't know," she whispered. "Who were you?"

He did not answer. He looked at her a moment longer, the question still in his eyes, then lifted the large wooden flap. Holding it up so she could pass under it and out onto the trail, he said, "I'll walk you down."

"That is not necessary," she said quickly. "The guides will be here any minute."

"Not likely. After a storm like this they'll wait a couple of hours. They may not come at all. It's not safe for you to go alone."

The man on the trail had said that too, and she remembered the promise she had given him, that she would not go down alone. Still she hesitated. "They were expecting tourists. Surely they will want to come, now that the rain has stopped." She stated what she hoped was the obvious, and waited to see if he would contradict her.

He merely shrugged. "They might this afternoon. Once the sun comes out things dry pretty quick. Most visitors are just as happy to hang out in the bar, eat, and maybe wander down to the museum."

He turned and headed along the trail toward the cookhouse. Celia saw that he was not going to force her to go with him, and because of that, she followed. When they came to the long stairway down the mountainside, arched over with hibiscus bushes, she said, "Celia Sánchez planted these hibiscus. To camouflage the steps from the air."

"Makes sense. Mar de Pacífico—that's what they call them around here—grows fast." He waited for her to come down the steps to where he was, but when he saw that she had stopped, obviously not wanting to come any closer, he continued on past the hospital and down the mountain, more or less the way she had come.

They had descended almost halfway when he stopped and pointed. "See that bohio?"

"The one in the trees?" It was a small thatched-roof cabin a short distance from the main trail, accessed by an almost-invisible footpath. Celia had not noticed it on her way up. "What about it?"

"A brilliant biologist lives there. Miguel Ortega Ramos. He has just published a study on fauna in the Reserva Sierra del Rosario. Which, as you probably know, was Cuba's first UNESCO-sanctioned biosphere reserve. For the next two years he will be working here in the Gran Parque Nacional Sierra Maestra." His eyes, light brown and flecked with gold, were just slightly mischievous. "This biologist and Dr. Cantú would very much like to meet."

"Would they?" Celia tried to smile, but her face was tight with fear. "Why?"

"Because they are both scientists, and naturally curious. They'd like to compare their shadow selves with their ordinary everyday selves, to see which is most real. Or magical."

Celia considered his words, liked his words. They were rational. At the same time they admitted to the possibility of the irrational, which she did not want to accept but had no choice, since irrational appeared to be part of what she had become.

"Maybe another time," she said at last.

"Why not now?"

She wondered what his scientific conclusion about her would be if she said, "Because in my medical opinion, I'm certifiably crazy, that's why!" Of course she did not say that. Instead, she replied with evasive honesty, "Celia Sánchez comes and goes as she pleases. Celia Cantú has obligations and some very unsettled personal relationships."

He stood there a second or two longer, smiling wistfully, then continued walking. He did not speak again until they reached the car park. Her vehicle was still the only one in the lot.

"See?" he said. "Nobody has even thought of climbing to the Comandancia yet."

She fumbled in the pocket of her pants. For one panicky moment she thought she had lost the keys. Then she remembered that Franci had given her only the single key and she had put it in the watch pocket of her jeans. She fished it out and opened the car door. She was halfway into the vehicle when she realized that once inside, if she slammed the door, she would be slamming it in his face. Half in, half out, she paused to say goodbye. Goodbye, she thought wryly, was the least you could say to somebody with whom you had just made love.

"Adios," she said.

"Come back when you can. Will you?"

"I don't know."

She slid behind the wheel and closed the door between them. He stood gazing at her through the rain-streaked window. She saw his lips move.

She rolled down the window. "What?"

"Don't be afraid."

Despite her disappointment that the visit had resolved nothing, but had taken her further along a psychological path at least as slippery as the mountain trail they had just traversed, she forced a smile. "You may not be afraid of ghosts, Miguel Ortega Ramos, but I am."

He laid his arm along the top of the rolled-down window and leaned toward her. Speaking so close to her cheek that she could feel the warmth of his breath, he said, "Even if it's not her ghost? Just one of your own?"

Celia tilted her head away from him. The engine was already running. He drew back. She pulled away, the question unanswered.

EIGHTEEN

BECAUSE of the rain, which slackened but never entirely stopped, it took the better part of the day to drive back to Santiago. The steady hum of the car's engine as she motored along a mostly empty highway might not have been the idyllic retreat Celia had envisioned yesterday—was it only yesterday?—but it provided the solitude she needed.

Alone in the car, the first order of the day was to regain her composure. She found a single mandarin rolling about on the seat beside her and ate it, which helped. Then, in as analytical a frame of mind as she could muster, she reviewed what had transpired.

Miguel Ortega Ramos seemed like an ordinary man, and a rather decent one at that. He had walked in on her in the middle of one of her hallucinations and she had incorporated him into it. He was real; her interpretation was not. She saw how the nature of his work, the quiet observation of wildlife, accepting unexplained animal behaviour rather than trying to interfere with it, would have predisposed him to go along with her. Oh yes, it was easy to explain his motivations—a lot easier than to explain her own!

But what had he meant about it being one of her ghosts? If she had not been so anxious to get away she might have asked; she was sorry now that she had not. Oh well. The answer could hardly have been enlightening, since she did not believe in ghosts, spiritual visitations, or anything of that ilk. Not for the first time, she felt the injustice of having to put up with something that she had never done anything to encourage.

She grimaced. True, she had never done anything to encourage the paranormal, but she had definitely done something to entice a total stranger into bed for what was possibly the best sexual experience of her entire life. The mere thought of it caused her body to tingle in a way that was both delicious and alarming. Mostly alarming, because therein lay what might well be another clue to the tangled mess her psyche had become.

A sexual need? Was she, Celia Cantú, so hungry for a certain kind of intimacy, not merely sexual but definitely including the sexual, that she was trying to extract it from a historical love affair that she was certain had been characterized by an all-levels, all-encompassing intimacy?

Celia ran through what she knew or thought she knew of Sánchez and Castro's relationship, trying to recall what she had read, what she had heard from contemporaries like her mother who had known them as a couple, and what she herself had created, first on a purely psychological level and now, it appeared, on a physical level.

Many pieces were missing but she knew enough to conclude that the Sánchez-Castro relationship had been one between two people whose core beliefs, determination to change Cuba, and drive to action were so completely shared as to make them of one mind. That, combined with very different but complementary abilities, would have given them an extraordinary closeness. Toss in mutual respect and, very probably, a powerful physical attraction, and there you had it: an intellectual, emotional, and physical connection rarely achieved in real life.

Again Celia's body quivered with memory of the intensity that had ignited it during those moments of what seemed a total, all-levels connection. Simultaneously and against her will, her mind produced an image of the quiet lovemaking she and Luis shared—if *shared* was the right word. Guiltily, she recalled how frequently she only went through the motions, not faking climax (well, not often, anyway) but not entirely there either. Had it been like that with José? She distrusted her memory, but she thought not. They had been so young, the attraction so physical. But that was just the point, wasn't it? She had related to José on one level, to Luis on another, but on other levels, to neither. In truth, no intimacy she had ever known had come remotely close to being complete.

Of course not, she thought irritably. The whole notion of such a relationship was a fantasy, a fairy tale to encourage women to buckle under to the demands of domesticity and child-rearing, and men to give their lives over to support of same. She was not prepared to say that close relationships did not exist—after all, she had the example of Franci and Philip. But she entertained such romantic expectations for herself no more than she entertained expectations of winning a Nobel Prize for medicine.

Yet some part of her was more than entertaining romantic fantasies. Part of her seemed determined to turn fantasy into reality. Was that what Miguel had meant by "one of your own ghosts"? Was some suppressed part of her psyche beginning to assert itself? If so, she was not at all sure she wanted to face it. The last thing she cared to discover was that at the core of her being lay a thirty-five-year-old bimbo ready to go off the deep end in pursuit of a phantom "perfect love."

She turned her attention to the traffic, which was heavier on that part of the Carretera Central that dropped out of the mountains down to sea-level Santiago. She followed the boulevard past Lecuy's heroic statue of Antonio Maceo on a rearing horse, the Bronze Titan's arm outstretched in a Vamonos! gesture to battalions of independence fighters who now existed merely as a blur in the nation's collective memory.

Santiago was a city of memorials to fallen heroes—Frank País, Abel Santamaría, José Martí, Carlos Manuel de Céspedes, and only God knew how many others. But a memorial to Celia Sánchez? Maybe, somewhere in the city. Celia had never heard of it and hoped it did not exist. Men made war, and for that some were remembered. If that was what it took to inspire memorials, better not to have one. Sánchez did have memorials in Manzanillo, Media Luna, and Pilón, plus that bronze tucked away behind the museum in Parque Lenin. But those were for her life, not for taking part in some slaughter. They were for a woman whose courage she desperately wished she had.

NINETEEN

CELIA drove down Avenida de las Américas and past the medical school without a twinge of guilt for having cut out of the conference. She turned off the boulevard into a quiet suburban neighbourhood. It was early evening. Seeing no car in the Morceau driveway, she wondered if they might have gone out. Then she realized that she was driving the family car and smiled. Of course they would be at home.

Celia knocked on the front door. Getting no answer, she pushed it open and called, "Franci? Philip? Anybody home?"

Silence. Celia could see through the living room to the kitchen. No one was there. Maybe they were out back with the mothers. Or in the bedroom enjoying a pre-dinner intimacy? Celia hesitated. Should she knock again? Or go say hello to the mothers, to give Philip and Franci time to finish whatever they were up to? Just then Franci came from the hallway into the living room.

"Celia? I thought I heard you."

Still Celia hesitated. Franci's voice had a hoarse quality, as it did when she had been crying.

"Don't just stand there, Girl! Come on in!" Franci reached down to flip on a table lamp. In the second her face bent low to the lamp, Celia saw that she had indeed been crying. Franci straightened up and headed for the kitchen. Celia followed.

"Where is Philip?"

"Working. A Venezuelan ship had to be piloted in this afternoon. He won't be home till near midnight." As she talked, Franci kept her back to Celia. "He made some great bouillabaisse before he left. We had it for lunch. I thought I'd heat it up for our supper, if that's okay with you?"

Celia walked over and leaned around to look into her friend's face. "Franci, did you and Philip have a fight?"

"No way!" Franci lit the gas burner under the pot. "Why do you ask?"

"I have never known you to spend a Saturday evening in tears. Not even when a date stood you up."

"Oh that. It's nothing. Las Madres just got to me. Again. What do you want to drink?" She opened the fridge and pulled out a pitcher of orange juice. "How about this? Squeezed with Mami's own sacred hands."

"Perfect."

Franci brought the juice and two glasses to the table and filled one for each of them. Celia suddenly felt famished. No wonder. All she had eaten that day was one small mandarin. She took a long, grateful swallow. "Um. Delicious."

"Nice moustache you've got there." Franci leaned across the table to wipe a skim of orange from Celia's upper lip.

"So what is going on with the mothers?" Celia asked.

"The damned baby thing again." Franci sighed heavily. "They gang up on me. Not when Philip's around, but when they catch me alone. It's getting so bad that I find excuses to stay at the office when he's working late, to avoid having to deal with them. If I hadn't been expecting you, I would have gone there today when he left for the harbour."

"Gang up on you how?"

"Oh, they're creative geniuses, those two." Franci rose and crossed the kitchen to the stove. She tested the temperature of the bouillabaisse and finding it satisfactory, filled bowls for herself and Celia. Celia carried them to the table. Franci placed bread on the table between them. Celia could barely wait until Franci was in her seat before starting to eat. She could not remember ever being so hungry. She was about to say something about how good the food was when Franci spoke again.

"Today it was my mother who made the first pass. She came in with this vile potion that smelled like ditch water mixed with horse pee and wanted me to drink it. According to her it was a foolproof fertility enhancer. I'm sure it was. It would have enhanced the fertility of every amoeba in my gut." Franci took a sip of the bouillabaisse broth but without showing real interest in the food.

"She made you drink it?" Celia asked, tearing off a hunk of bread.

"Oh, I got rid of the crap. Getting rid of her was the hard part. She couldn't just hand it to me. She had to give me a half-hour dissertation on how fertile all my siblings have been, and all her siblings, and well, I know she's just trying to reassure herself that it's not *her* fault. All the same, it makes me crazy."

Franci gave up trying to eat. She leaned back in her chair and went on. "She finally leaves and I'm just pouring the crap down the drain when *his* mother comes in. That's another thing that drives me crazy. The redhead can get all the way down the stairs from the garage and into the house and be right behind me and I won't have heard a sound, not a sound! I can't tell you how many times I've turned around and found her standing there and nearly had a heart attack. I've begged her not to do it, even yelled at her. But it doesn't do any good." Franci stopped talking and sat there looking sullen.

Celia motioned to Franci's bowl. "Eat. It's wonderful."

Franci smiled. "Yeah. He is, isn't he?" She picked a shrimp out by the tail and nibbled at it. "Philip's mother catches me dumping the stuff down the drain and knows exactly what it is—that's how I know they colluded. They always do. She puts her arms around me and says, in that fake French accent she's affected lately, 'Ma chérie, I don't blame you a bit. It is not *your* fault. Phee-leep, he just needs more encouragement, n'est-ce pas? Perhaps you have a little something, you know, like they sell in the boutique at Hotel Santiago? A little something for the boudoir? In lace, maybe, or black silk?'"

"No!" Celia, in process of swallowing a spoonful of soup, sputtered with laughter, sending droplets across the table.

"Damn, Celia! Don't be such a slob!" Franci howled, but she started laughing too. "Have you seen that sex-tease stuff they sell in the boutiques of all the big hotels? Net stockings, nippleless bras, crotchless panties, all at the most outrageous prices! Those Italians pigs who come to Cuba for a sex holiday snap it up for their prostitutes."

"Naughty, naughty!" Celia wagged a finger at her. "Mustn't be racist."

"Right." Franci got up to get a butter knife. "I should have said *male* pigs. Wouldn't want to sound *racist* when I meant to be *sexist*."

"So what did you buy?" Celia teased. "Crotchless panties or a nippleless bra?"

Franci stood hands on hips, half indignant, half laughing. "I wish you could have seen her, Celia. Twitching her little behind and batting her eyes." Franci twitched and batted her own in a parody of a sexy come-on and mimicked her mother-in-law. "'Les hommes, they find such things très alluring, n'est-ce pas?'"

Franci flopped back in her chair and began smearing butter on her bread. "I felt like telling her, 'Maman, this girl goes to bed in her very own silky black ass, and your son has never failed to find that alluring.'"

Celia, doubled over in laughter at Franci's demonstration and commentary, finally was able to gasp, "Oh Franci! I am sorry. I know this is not funny for you."

"Well, actually it is. Afterwards. It's just that any joke you have to put up with over and over gets old. And annoying.'"

"What *is* the baby issue?" Celia asked.

Franci looked at her in surprise, almost hurt. "Why, you know I can't—"

"Oh of course! I meant—" Celia interrupted quickly. "Well, *having* a baby is not the only way to get one. So I just wondered . . ." Celia let her voice trail off, suddenly aware of how tactless it was to ask such a question when Franci was already feeling raw. "I'm sorry."

"No, that's okay. You're right, there are other issues, and they're no secret. Not between Philip and me anyway." Franci gazed out the window to where children could be heard, but not seen, playing in the street. "He was ready for kids ten years ago, or even five years ago. But now, well, he's older than me, you know. He's almost forty-five. He thinks he's too old to cope with an infant."

"Oh." Celia regretted having asked. Philip and Franci were her ideal couple. She did not want to know that they had something so serious dividing them.

"That's his reason," Franci went on. "But I have my reasons too."

Celia looked up in surprise. "Your reason for what?"

"For not wanting kids." At Celia's questioning look, she stabbed the butter knife toward the garage apartment and backyard cottage. "Them. They'd criticize everything I did. It would be bad enough for me. But for the child, can you imagine? They'd be on that baby like vultures on roadkill. Then there would be the religious wars, with each of them determined to induct it into her particular religion, holy water, chicken blood, who knows what?"

Morosely, Franci munched her buttered bread. "Philip and I went into this mother arrangement with our eyes open. We knew they'd be taking more and more of our time as they got older. Having them nearby we could see them often, but in shorter segments, and not have to waste all that time running back and forth."

"And you thought they would be company for each other."

"Yes, and it worked out just the way we hoped. Also, Philip and I figured out in advance what they were likely to do that could divide us, and came up with strategies to defend ourselves. But you can't teach an infant or toddler to defend itself against manipulative love. Not to mention competitive love, which theirs surely would be."

Franci began clearing the table. "The only way would be if I quit my job and stayed home to protect the poor kid." She stopped, dishes in hand, dark eyes wide with unshed tears. "The honest truth is, much as I want a child, I don't want one enough to give up my career."

Celia carried their glasses to the sink and put her arms around Franci. "Have I told you lately what a wise, intelligent, thoughtful woman you are?"

"Well, not *lately*," Franci conceded. "But compliments sound more sincere when you space them out. Now tell me, did you get a hot shower at El Saltón last night?"

"Well, no. The water was not hot, and it was not El Saltón. As soon as I get myself in and out of one here, I'll tell you where I went. But you take yours first. I'll do the dishes."

"No!" Franci blocked the sink with her body. "I already took a shower. This afternoon, after I finished 'alluring' Philip." She gave Celia a push. "Go! I wash two bowls, two spoons, and two glasses while you wash one you. Then we'll meet in my bedroom for a pyjama party, and you will tell me all about what you've been up to for the past thirty hours."

Standing in the shower, Celia again argued with herself over whether to tell Franci about the hallucinations. It would have been hard enough before. Now she could not imagine trying to explain it, even to her best friend—or maybe especially to her best friend. Franci would want to link the Camandancia episode to Celia's mother and urge her to examine that relationship. It might look relevant but Celia was certain it was not. That was the trouble with using your best friend as a shrink, she thought with a wry smile. Not only does she know you too well; you know her too well and know in advance exactly what she'd say.

So no, she would not go there. Not on this trip anyway. Franci's domestic problems had completely extracted her from her own hallucinatory world and its spillover into real life. She would think of something personal to tell Franci; after all, that was a cardinal rule of female friendship: confidences must be repaid with confidences. But it would *not* be about Celia Sánchez and Fidel Castro, much less about Celia Cantú and a bearded stranger named Miguel Ortega Ramos.

TWENTY

CELIA found Franci sitting up against the headboard of her king-sized bed. "Very alluring," she purred, batting her eyes at Franci's oversized white T-shirt decorated with nautical signal flags.

"You bet." Franci grinned, passing Celia a pillow. "Anytime I get, um, you know, I just signal the Navy."

Celia climbed onto the bed next to Franci and adjusted the pillow. Countless hours of their adolescence and college years had been spent like this, backs against the headboard of one or the other's bed, Celia's sun-browned legs stretched out alongside Franci's longer, darker ones, sharing secrets and using each other as sounding board and morale booster. They still got together two or three times a year, but hardly ever one on one anymore.

"What a treat!" Celia murmured. Even though she had more to conceal from Franci now than before, she felt less tense.

"So where *did* you spend the night?" Franci asked.

"In Santo Domingo. This morning I hiked up to La Comandancia de La Plata."

"You're kidding! You drove all that way? What on earth for? Wasn't it raining? It poured here."

Celia ignored the question about the rain. Rain, at least *that* rain, felt too intimate to discuss. Instead she said, "I intended to go to El Saltón, but it felt good to be driving so I kept going. Around Bayamo I started thinking about Joaquín, which started me thinking about my father. And thinking about him started me thinking about my mother."

"And that took you to La Comandancia?" Franci surmised.

"I guess. I knew she was recruited by Celia Sánchez; they talked about it that one time my mother took me to visit her. And Mamá was proud of the fact that she got her medic training from Che. But since she spent most of the war under Raúl's command in the Oriente, and that was where she met my father, their war stories were all about what happened there. Especially the casualties they suffered in the bombing raids. Veterans were forever telling Carolina and me how our mother's nursing saved their life."

Celia scratched a mosquito bite on her ankle. "Those old duffs could get so angry, just recounting how Batista's bombers were allowed to run raids from the US base in Guantánamo." Celia paused and glanced at Franci. "You know what I mean? They were the wounded, yet it was the politics of the situation they relived. Only Mamá talked about the human tragedies."

Franci nodded sagely. "It's a gender thing. And an experience thing. Bombs would have made the men feel helpless. The aftermath, bloody as it was, would have made nurses like your mom feel competent, even powerful."

"I suppose so. Anyway, because of that I always associated her with the Oriente and never thought much about the month she spent at La Comandancia."

"So how was it?"

"Good. On the walk up I met a man who was there at the same time, although he was just a child and didn't remember her."

Celia paused and deliberately directed Franci's attention away from the Comandancia. "Do you remember her, Franci?"

"Sure! Not that kids take much notice of their friends' parents. But later, when we were in college. Remember the time we took the train to visit her in the hospice?"

"I still feel guilty that I didn't spend more time with her at the end." Celia continued, scratching the mosquito bite until it bled.

"Stop scratching," Franci commanded. "I've told you before you must not feel guilty about that. I have counselled terminal patients. Some are depressed, some are angry, some are resigned. But *all* say the most difficult part of dying is watching the anguish of people they love. It only adds to their suffering."

When Celia did not respond, Franci continued. "Your mother could have spent her last year in a Habana hospital. Or at home, for that matter. She was the one who asked to be sent to a hospice in the country."

Celia nodded. "She loved horses. She said she wanted to be where she could look out the window and see them anytime."

"So that old hacienda was perfect. I don't think the government could have found a better use for it. I liked the way they let horses graze on lawn."

Celia smiled. "She used to ask for extra sugar, not in her coffee but on the side. She fed it to the horses out the window."

"It was perfect," Franci repeated. "Close enough to Habana that she could call you and Carolina when she felt well enough, but far enough away that you couldn't visit every day and she didn't have to watch you watching her deteriorate."

"I suppose," Celia sighed. "That last visit, remember how we sat on the end of her bed and massaged her feet?"

"And she started telling us about a lover who used to massage her feet. Oh yeah, I definitely remember that!"

"And that got her talking about all the lovers she had had since my father died."

"Ay! The look on your face!" Franci chuckled. "You didn't have a clue."

Celia shook her head. "I told Carolina later, and she was as astounded as I was. Old compañeros from the war were always dropping by, often staying overnight, before and after my father's death. Even after she got sick. It never crossed my mind that some of them had been her lovers. Although I should have figured it out. She lived fourteen years after Papá passed away. That is a very long time to sleep alone."

"She was in good form that day," Franci smiled. "I remember her saying, 'Men are like horses. They are bigger than you and stronger than you and you can't make them do anything. You can only make them *want* to.'"

Celia giggled. "The man-horse advice I remember was, 'Never trust a horse or a man until you have observed the beast long enough to understand its basic nature. Not just in tranquil times but how it behaves when it is thwarted or frightened.'"

"Gosh, yes!" Franci exclaimed. "What did we know about horses?"

"What did we know about *men?*" Celia shot back. "I never told her I was involved with José, but I think she knew. Not from anything she said then, but later." Celia gazed pensively into the past. "I sneaked back after visiting hours, to be alone with her."

"I know. I woke up and you weren't there and I knew you'd gone to her room."

"I climbed in the window. She was already awake. As soon as I threw my leg over the sill, she whispered, 'Quick, Celia, so they don't catch us!'"

Celia drew her knees up and rested her chin on them. "I crawled into bed with her and we just held each other for a long time. I told her what a good mother she had been."

"What a gift," Franci sighed. "That must have meant everything to her."

Celia turned her gaze to Franci. "What she said was, 'I never worried too much about being a good mother or a good wife or a good nurse or a good revolutionary. But I have tried to be a good person.' I asked how I could be a good person too. She said, 'Think hard about what matters most to you. When you think you know what it is, do it. Or defend it. *Be strong.* Don't let other people decide for you.'"

There was a long silence. Then Franci said, "Is that why you didn't drop out of med school and go to the States with José?"

"That jerk!" Celia exclaimed, surprised that after such a long time her anger could flare so hotly. "Remember how he burst into our room yelling, 'Let's go, girl! Sunday morning we're off this goddamned island for good!' Did he really think I would throw away four years in medical school just like that?" She snapped her fingers.

Franci laughed. "I remember you started beating him in the face with a rolled-up term paper that you'd spent about twenty hours typing. And when he backed out and was trying to shield himself behind the door but leave it open enough to talk to you, you threw everything in the apartment at him." Franci got up and went to a bookcase in the corner of the room that held, among other things, old textbooks. She picked one ragged volume and held it up. "You know what book this is?"

"How can I tell? It has no cover."

"It has no cover because *you* threw it at José Lago and broke the spine."

"I never knew that!" Celia exclaimed. "If you had told me, I would have—"

Franci shook her head. "You were in bad shape, hermana. When José walked out on you, a ripped-up textbook was the least of your problems." She put the book back on the shelf and turned to Celia. "And now he's here again. What are you going to do?"

Celia shrugged. "José Lago is not my problem anymore."

Franci gave her a suspicious look. Belatedly, Celia remembered that José's return was the excuse she had given for needing some alone time, and backtracked. "I did need time to think about it. Mostly about Luis. José being here is harder on him than on me."

"You could marry Luis." Franci picked up a hairbrush and began fluffing her Afro. "Not that I'm suggesting—"

"Then don't," Celia said tightly.

"So José being back *has* changed things."

"No! But, well—" Celia took a deep breath. "José aside, I doubt that I am ever going to be ready to marry Luis. If I could find a kind way of breaking it off with him—"

"Get real, Celia. There's no 'kind' way to dump a guy. Especially if the dump coincides with the appearance of an ex-lover."

"I know that," Celia said sulkily, the sulk apparently being part of the regression into adolescent mode.

"I can't believe you'd be such a knucklehead as to take José back after—!"

"Hey! You're a certified shrink!" Celia shrieked. "You are supposed to listen attentively and act sympathetic, not call your patient a knucklehead!"

"You are a knucklehead if you—"

"Honestly, Franci, what do you take me for?"

"Uh . . . a woman who hasn't got her feelings sorted out?"

"About José I do. He is the same manipulative macho he was back then."

"But sexy?" Franci probed wickedly.

"Okay. Sexy. But for your information, I am not sex-starved. Just because he has a permanent hard-on—"

"Always did," Franci reminded her.

"—does not mean he is going to turn my head."

"Did before."

"Then I probably *was* sex-starved." Celia smiled ruefully. "Just not as lucky as you with whom I picked to meet the need."

Franci sighed luxuriously. "I am lucky, aren't I? I can't imagine life without Philip. He's more than my playmate; he's my anchor."

"Luis is a good friend," Celia said thoughtfully. "But Liliana is my anchor. I can't imagine life without *her*."

For a moment both were silent, studying their side-by-side toenails, Franci's polished silver, Celia's unpainted.

"Well, Doctor, what is your diagnosis?" Celia queried, wondering whether Franci had an inkling of any of the things she had *not* said.

"My diagnosis?" Franci glanced over at her and smiled. "I think you're right. José Lago is not going to knock you loopy this time."

"Maybe I already am loopy," Celia flipped, again giving Franci an opening to mention any aberration she might have noticed.

"Nope. You're grounded, girl. Looks like we both got lucky. Not in the same ways, but each in a very good way."

"You mean you got the best man, I got the best child?"

"Just our luck. Not 100 per cent but pretty damned good."

"Listen," Celia teased. "I'll share my child if you'll share your—"

"In your dreams!" Franci howled.

Celia stood up and yawned. "Okay, I shall dream about it. But I must say, Doctor, your bedside manner leaves something to be desired. First you criticize the men in my life, then monopolize the one you claim is the best ever."

"Finders keepers." Franci tossed out the cliché they had used as teenagers when one got asked out by a guy whom both found attractive. She pointed her hairbrush at Celia and added, "But think about those Lago boys, okay?"

"Think what?"

"If you want one of them to be the man in your life, fine. If you don't—well, you know running away won't help."

"Franci! Who said I was running away?"

"Okay, okay. So you're standing your ground. You are not going to let either of them push you into something. Promise?"

Celia grinned. "Stand my ground. Don't let them push me around. Sure. I can do that."

"Good." Franci smiled, but her eyes remained serious. "Because what I really think is that there's more than you want to admit going on. In here." She patted her chest.

Celia nodded. "The down time helped. I got a lot of things sorted out."

"Good start, but keep at it. All any woman can get *completely* sorted in a single day is the week's laundry."

"Ha!" Celia kissed Franci on the cheek and headed for the door. "If you think I can get my laundry sorted in one day, that's because you don't live with a teenager."

TWENTY-ONE

CELIA recalled that remark without amusement when she entered her apartment the next day. It was strewn with clothes, most of which looked in need of washing. The table was littered with dirty dishes.

"Liliana?" There was no answer.

Celia collected the dishes and carried them to the kitchen. Sink and counter were similarly cluttered, forcing her to stack dirty dishes atop ones already there. She ran a glassful of water and poured it over a wilted African violet. Then ran another for herself and drank deeply.

She went back into the living room and surveyed the chaos. Liliana had left for school only a week ago and should have been there still, as the pre-university students were on a twenty-four-day class schedule, followed by six or seven days at home. Had Liliana come home because she was ill? If so, it had not affected her appetite. There was a scattering of plantain chips around the sofa, as if she had lain there watching television while she ate. And where was she now? Had she got better and gone out? Or got worse and gone to a neighbour's apartment rather than lie here alone? Probably the former, because if she had been really sick she would have called Alma, and Alma would be here looking after her.

Celia found her own bedroom as neat as she had left it. She and Liliana had meticulous regard for each other's privacy. Not once in all the years Liliana had lived with her had she borrowed a garment, prowled a drawer, or used Celia's cosmetics without asking permission. She dropped her bag on the bed and was deciding whether to call Alma or check with neighbours first when the apartment door banged open.

"Tía Celia?" Liliana called.

"In here," Celia called back.

Liliana rushed in and gave Celia a strong warm hug. "I'm so glad you're home! How was Santiago?"

In the few seconds she and Liliana held each other, Celia felt health and vitality radiating from the young body and from herself a responding surge of affection. She pushed back Liliana's dark brown curls and openly examined her niece. Her eyes sparkled. She was anything but sick. So why wasn't she at school? Celia might have asked but preferred to wait and let Liliana explain, as she was sure she would.

"The conference was fine, and I enjoyed seeing Franci and Philip. I am tired, though. The train broke down twice so the trip took hours longer than it should have."

Liliana sprawled across Celia's bed and looked her up and down. "You don't look tired. You look like—did you get a haircut or something?"

"No." Celia felt suddenly self-conscious. "Like what?"

"I don't know. Younger."

Liliana's intuitive recognition of something Celia felt but had assumed did not show caused her to catch her breath. She covered it with a laugh. "I doubt I got much younger in four days. What about you? What have you been up to?"

"You won't believe it when I tell you. You are going to flip out."

Celia flopped across the bed next to her niece. "Go ahead," she challenged. "I have not had a good flip-out all day."

Liliana smirked. "I went to Varadero with your two fiancés."

"Liliana, I only have one."

Liliana held up two pink-tipped fingers and pointed to them as if teaching a pre-schooler to add. "One past, one present, which makes *two*. And I had lunch at La Casa de Al with *both* of them."

"La Casa de Al?" Celia was shocked.

"Tío Joe paid. The check was more than Tío Luis makes in a month!"

"Ay! That José!" Celia exclaimed indignantly.

"And he bought me a T-shirt. Wanna see?"

Before Celia could reply, Liliana was off the bed and into her own room. Celia waited uneasily. It was no surprise that José would have played the big spender. But why was Liliana with them? Luis, in telling her he planned to go to Varadero with his brother, had not said anything about taking her along.

"And *then*," Liliana called from the next room, "we went dancing."

"They took you *dancing*?" Celia cried. "Where?"

"I knew you'd be jealous." Liliana's voice wafted from her room in a sing-song tease. "At SuperClub Puntarena. There was this great band playing poolside, and you should have seen them go at it. Tío Luis is an awesome dancer, you know. The kind other dancers stop to watch." There was a pause, and Liliana called, "But Tío Joe is more fun."

Celia stood abruptly, opened her travel case, and began flinging things into various bureau drawers. All good fun, she told herself, but what she felt was closer to anger. What might have kindled that emotion she could not have said. Certainly not jealousy. Perhaps it was the image of her adorable niece gyrating on a dance floor encircled not by teenaged peers but by lecherous, half-drunk foreigners—not to mention two men old enough to be her father who were not altogether immune to lechery themselves.

"Ta da!" Liliana pranced into the room, snapping fingers and jerking her body to a rhythm only she could hear.

"Stand still," Celia laughed. "Let me read it."

Liliana stopped and stuck out her chest. Overlaying Liliana's firm young breasts was the face of a member of the Cuban women's volleyball team. Celia read the caption: "She walks like a girl, she runs like a girl, she serves balls at one hundred kilometres per hour like a girl."

"You little minx!" Celia laughed.

"Like it?" Liliana moved to the mirror to admire herself. "I picked it out myself."

"Cute. But I intend to have a word with your 'uncles' about appropriate outings for a girl your age. Not to mention taking you out of school."

Instantly the oomph went out of Liliana's posture. "Please don't," she said in a small voice. "Tío Luis is already mad at me."

Such mood swings were not unusual for Liliana. The needy little girl she had been when she came to live with Celia eight years earlier had gradually evolved into a sassy adolescent. However, in the blink of an eye the adolescent could, and often did, retreat into the child. Celia actually liked both. She felt tender toward the child and thought the sauciness boded well for Liliana's future independence. Liliana had always insisted that she wanted to grow up to be "just like Tía Celia," but Celia hoped that she would be different in some ways: less compliant, less easily manipulated. What she looked for in Liliana, and was just beginning to glimpse below the sass, was the independent spirit and courage of the girl's mother. Those qualities could cost a person's life, perhaps had cost Carolina hers. But they were qualities that could also save one's life. They were qualities Celia wished she had more of, and treasured when they surfaced in Liliana.

However, Liliana's impudence often put her and Luis at odds. He submitted to discipline and believed he was a better man for it. He did not understand Celia's tolerance for her niece's increasing independence, manifested in occasional disobedience. Celia was absolutely certain he would not have pulled Liliana out of school to go to Varadero.

"How did you happen to go to Varadero with them anyway?" she asked in a neutral voice.

Liliana fell onto the bed as gloomy as if expecting to be condemned to a lifetime of house arrest. "I didn't exactly go *with* them. I was on my way there when they picked me up."

Celia turned away and began refolding already-folded underwear in her bureau drawer. Liliana always talked more openly when she wasn't being questioned. This time it was a full minute before she continued, a pause that Celia found ominous.

"Tío Luis got so mad I thought he was going to hit me. He said when we got there I'd have to wait in the car, but . . ." Her voice trailed off.

"They invited you to lunch, bought you a T-shirt, and took you dancing," Celia finished with just a hint of irony. What she was thinking was, *They* did not do that. Damned José did that. When I get my hands on him!

Liliana watched her anxiously. "Please, Tía, don't be mad."

With effort, Celia kept the irritation out of her voice. "I'm not."

She stood there a moment longer, looking at the folded underwear. Three pairs of white cotton panties, three white bras. The spartan intimate apparel of a nun. "I am going to take a shower," she said finally. "Would you wash those dirty dishes in the sink?"

"Claro," Liliana said in a small voice.

Celia closed the bureau drawer and set the travel case in the closet. She stripped down to bra and panties and went into the bathroom. There she took them off, to be washed in the shower. It was a habit she had developed during the Special Period when underwear could not be replaced, having disappeared from regular Cuban stores and for a time being available only in stores requiring dollars, which she did not have.

She stepped into the shower, the first since the one she had taken at Franci's to remove the scent of Miguel's lovemaking. She had not wanted to take that shower, had not wanted to lose that smell. But it had been necessary; otherwise Franci surely would have noticed. Now, too, the hot shower was a necessity, not to wash away evidence of past passion but to wash away tension caused by a feeling of imminent danger.

Not danger, she corrected herself. Just something to be dealt with. Liliana might have been exaggerating, but if Luis was as angry as she said, it would not have been for hitchhiking, which was common among Cubans of all ages. It would have been for cutting class and—Varadero? What was that all about?

Celia turned up the temperature of the shower and absorbed its stinging heat as if to cleanse herself to the bone. To the brain. Above all, she must be clear-minded. No matter how many calming possibilities suggested themselves, she was pretty sure that whatever Liliana had done was no casual indiscretion. She must have crossed some kind of line. She turned off the water in time to hear Liliana call out, "Come in."

The clatter of dishes revealed that Liliana was still in the kitchen and had not come out to greet whoever was at the door.

"If you've come to rat on me," Liliana yelled to the visitor, "don't bother. I've already told Tía Celia everything."

Then Luis's voice. "That you cut class to go to Varadero? How you were dressed?"

Celia did not take time to dry off but pulled on a terrycloth robe and hurried out to interpose herself between them. "Hello, Luis." She kissed him lightly on the lips.

"Did she?" he asked. "Tell you what she did the minute your back was turned?"

"I got the gist of it," Celia equivocated. "I will have a talk with her."

"There's *nothing* to talk about." Liliana called from the kitchen, emphasizing her point with the slam of pot against metal pot. She had taken off the new T-shirt before starting on the dishes and changed back into the white shorts and red-striped top she had been wearing when she first came in. Perhaps it was seeing so much of that perfect figure exposed that gave Celia her first glimpse of looming disaster.

In her mind's eye she saw Liliana not as a little girl clad in shorts racing about the neighbourhood with other children, but the way she had seen dozens of young women dressed, in very similar outfits but somehow less innocent: clothing that flaunted their youth, their beauty, their health, their sexual availability. She had seen them hitching along the highway, seen them hanging around Playas del Este, seen them on the heavily touristed sidewalks of Habana Vieja. And she had seen no small number of those still young enough to be classed as children in her own hospital. The unwanted knowledge that flooded her senses, combined with Luis's interference and Liliana's arrogant dismissal, caused Celia to lose her temper.

"Liliana!" she spoke sharply. "Come here."

Liliana pulled the plug on the dishwater but did not exactly "come here." She stopped in the kitchen door, crossed her arms, and rolled her eyes.

"Do you have any idea how many girls are contracting sexually transmitted diseases?" Celia demanded hotly. "Here! In Cuba, which up to now has one of the lowest rates of HIV-AIDS in the world! Now tourists are bringing it in and—"

Liliana dropped her mouth open in mock astonishment. "Gosh, Dr. Cantú, I thought a person couldn't get AIDS from toilet seats. You think I might've caught it from a *car seat*?"

Luis, who had looked on with a stern but pleased expression while Celia lectured her niece, weighed in. "Cut the sarcasm, Liliana! If you won't listen to Celia—"

"You'll have me put in a re-education camp?" Liliana challenged. "Forget it! Tía Celia is my madrina and she won't let you."

Celia felt her emotions turn topsy-turvy. How had Luis and Liliana got to the point of confrontation before *she* even knew the details of what had happened? Even as the question raced through her mind, Celia guessed the answer. This was meant to be a showdown and each wanted her on their side. She would have to reassure both that their concerns would be heard and considered. But before she could speak to defuse the situation, Luis went too far.

"The law is the law!" he shouted. "Celia may not have any say in the matter!"

"Enough!" Celia snapped. "Liliana, if you have finished the dishes, go clean your room."

"I'm going *out*," Liliana shot back. "So you and Fiancé Number Two can have it out." She flounced out the door, but before slamming it, she stuck her head back in for a parting shot. "This is not about *me*, you know."

Sounds from elsewhere in the building could be heard, but the space around them seemed unnaturally quiet. Celia pulled a chair out from the dinette table and sat down. Luis moved behind her and hesitantly began massaging her shoulders.

"Long train ride?"

"It was."

"I guess from now on it will be necessary to leave her with Mamá and me when you are away. That is, unless you and I—"

"Did you and José really take her dancing at one of those glitzy hotels?"

Luis's hands paused on her shoulders, then began to massage again, weakly. "More a case of her taking us. I can tell you, Celia, it was not the first time she had been there. She knows her way around and how to get into places she is not supposed to be. I looked into it. At this point, six months in a re-education camp would be the best thing for her."

Celia drew the terrycloth robe more closely around her. "I don't believe that. If she was skipping school regularly, her grades would show it."

Luis's hands dropped away from her shoulders and he moved around the table to face her. "No, Celia. Because she is smart enough to do both. I checked her attendance. Since January, her record shows several absences on days you were out of town. We picked her up just outside Varadero. Go through her things and you will understand."

"I would never do that!" Celia gasped.

"Because you don't want to know," Luis accused.

"She will tell me. She did tell me!"

"Did she?" It wasn't a question; it was a sneer. Luis strode into Liliana's bedroom. Celia heard drawers being yanked open. Seconds later he dumped an armful of clothing—if it could be called clothing—on the table in front of her.

It was cruel and tangible proof of the jinitera images Celia had banished from her imagination: spiked heels, platform shoes, lycra shorts, see-through blouses, frilly underwear, expensive imported cosmetics.

"Tell me *you* bought this crap. All available, as you well know, *only* for dollars."

Behind her, Celia heard the apartment door ease open. "Tía Celia, Tío Luis, I'm sorr—" Mid-syllable, the contrite voice changed to a banshee wail. "You've been snooping in my room! Gone through all my stuff!"

Celia turned and looked at her niece. In a voice so neutral she might have been commenting on the unwashed dishes, she said, "I think you owe us an explanation, Liliana."

"Go to hell, both of you!" Liliana screamed, backing out.

Luis was after her in a flash. Liliana fled down the stairs. Celia moved to the door in time to see him catch her on the landing. He only held her by one wrist. With the other hand, Liliana beat on his chest and would have hit him in the face had he not blocked her wild blows. She shrieked incoherently. He held on, doggedly and silent.

Liliana gasped for breath, and in that splinter of silence, Celia's words carried clearly. "Let her go, Luis. Liliana, come here."

He instantly released his grip, probably assuming Liliana would respond to the authority in Celia's voice as he had. Instead, she raced down the stairs. There was a short silence, followed by the sound of apartment doors easing shut as neighbours who had peeked out to see what was going on understood that whatever it was, it was over.

"Oh my," Luis said wretchedly, trudging up from the landing. "What a mess."

"Never mind. I can deal with her when she comes back." Celia did not add, But only if you are not here. What she said was, "I need time to think. I need to be alone."

Luis stopped halfway down the hallway and stared. "You mean you don't—"

"I am very tired," Celia said. She closed the apartment door quietly and leaned against it. It was a minute, perhaps two, before she heard Luis's footsteps retreating down the stairs.

The stillness that followed felt like the cessation of a storm. Celia knew better. This was the eye of a hurricane, those few still hours before the howling would begin anew. This storm, the path of which could not be charted, would cut a swath of devastation through all their lives.

TWENTY-TWO

JOE managed to feign steadiness long enough to convey to his guests, government officials and potential business partners, that he had had a jolly good time at the cabaret. Only when the last one had been seen to his car or poured into a taxi did he drop the act and admit befuddlement. Where the hell had he left his own car? Not the BMW, which he greatly missed, but the damned Daewoo.

He spotted it near the end of the block. As he walked unsteadily toward it, he realized that a woman was shadowing him. He turned to size her up. She had thin legs, thin hips, full breasts, and full lips. Not bad.

"Amigo," she murmured. "Could you give a girl a lift?"

He considered it, then remembered his agenda. "Chica, if I didn't have an early meeting—" He fumbled the key into the lock of the car door.

She stood close to him, breathing warmth onto his neck. But as he struggled to open the car door, she backed away. "I see."

Joe was not seeing all that well himself, not even the damned car door, which he was having trouble unlocking. By the time he got it open the woman had walked on. He was surprised that she had been so easy to shake off. Maybe she wasn't a prostitute, just an employee at the club hoping for a lift home? He looked down the street in the direction she had gone but she was already out of sight.

For a moment he sat in the driver's seat wondering if he was too drunk to drive to Pinar del Río. Should he go back to his mother's apartment? But no, he reasoned. He was barely a mile from the Habana-Pinar freeway, which at this time of night would be empty of traffic. It was no more than a two-hour drive to Pinar. He could still get half a night's sleep. That plus a shower and he'd be plenty sharp for his morning meeting.

"Aren't you going to say hello?"

The voice, coming from directly behind him, caused him to jump violently. He jerked around and found himself facing Liliana, smiling with sleepy sweetness.

"What the hell are *you* doing here?"

"You left the car unlocked. If I hadn't come along somebody might've stolen something. Aren't you glad to see me?"

"Not particularly. How did you know I was here?"

"I'm psychic." She smiled mysteriously, enjoying her little secret. "The car *was* unlocked."

Confusing as the situation was, Joe knew that this was not a product of his personal alcoholic-induced confusion. On that he was quite clear. "Look, I haven't got time to take you home. I'll put you in a taxi."

"No!" Liliana's shrill voice struck his eardrums like a sharp object. "Tío Luis wants to send me to a stinking re-education camp. Him and Tía Celia." She began to sob.

"All right, all right!" Anything to shut her up. "Just—let me think."

"Tía Alma said you were going to Pinar after the show. Can I come along? Please? Just for tonight?"

There were other courses of action he might have taken, which later he would wish he had taken. But in his befuddled state, Liliana's suggestion had the appeal of simplicity. "Okay," he said. "But I don't want to talk. Stay back there. Go to sleep."

He wasn't sure why he told her to stay in the back seat. Partly, he supposed, because he didn't want her to notice how drunk he was. Partly because he knew that in his impaired condition he would drive more safely without the distraction of her chatter. And partly because, given the sexual vibes he'd seen her giving off at that poolside dance in Varadero, he didn't entirely trust her. Joe Lago did not like complications in his life. Driving to Pinar alone was the simple, uncomplicated thing he had planned to do after the Tropicana show and what he wanted to do right now. If she was willing to pretend she wasn't there, fine. Otherwise . . .

But she did exactly as he asked. She either slept or faked sleep all the way to Pinar del Río.

Joe very much doubted that things were as bad as she claimed. On the other hand, she must be pretty desperate to be so compliant. When they reached the hotel, she walked quietly in with him like a sleepy child. While he registered, she wandered off to the far side of the lobby and pretended to be interested in the birds in a small aviary.

"A room with twin beds," he told the clerk. That, too, he would later recognize as bad judgment, but tired and unsober as he was, the idea of sex so far from his mind and the nearness of sleep so tantalizing, it simply didn't occur to him to put her in a separate room. The clerk may have thought that they were father and daughter, or perhaps client and hustler. Joe didn't know, didn't care. He just wanted to hit the sack so as not to lose what few hours of rest were possible between now and his morning meeting with the mayor of Pinar.

The small room was not luxurious, but it was the best Pinar had to offer. Liliana sat down on one of the twin beds and bounced with real or feigned enthusiasm.

"Nice! I like your lifestyle, Tío Joe."

She was wearing the same white shorts and red-and-white striped top she'd been wearing the day they found her hitching to Varadero, and carried nothing, not even a purse. It must've been quite a blow-up, he thought, for her to walk out empty-handed. He glanced at his watch and reached for the phone.

"Two AM. I should have called Celia before we left Habana."

"Oh no! You'll wake her up!" Liliana said quickly. "She has to be at work at six. She said she didn't get any sleep at all on the train last night."

"She's bound to be worried."

"No! I told you. She kicked me out! She's *really* mad at me!"

Joe sighed. "I assume there was a reason."

"Well, yeah. Her and Tío Luis went through my room and found, you know. Stuff. And went ballistic."

"What kind of stuff?"

"Just clothes. From the dollar stores."

"I see. And where did *you* get dollars?"

Liliana drew her legs up, folded her hands across her knees, and lay her cheek on her hands. Eyes dancing like a child confessing a prank that she expects will incite admiration, she said, "Oh, sometimes I go to Varadero. And go dancing, like I did with you and Tío Luis. Guys buy me things."

Joe clicked his tongue with disgust.

"It's not like I go up to their rooms," she protested. "All the shops are off the lobby. And they have such neat stuff!"

Joe averted his gaze from the view she was offering him of lace panties peeking from beneath the drawn-up cuffs of her shorts, the panties no doubt part of the "neat stuff" she had picked up with some schmuck's dollars. "Let me get this straight. You dance with them, they take you shopping, then you say, 'Adios, amigo' and go home?"

"More or less," she said nonchalantly. "I say I've got to go to the restroom. And I don't come back."

Joe gave her a contemptuous look. "A real propio, aren't you?"

"What's wrong with being a flirt?" she demanded indignantly. "At least I don't act like a puta!"

"For your information, that's exactly how some whores act." Joe hung his jacket in the closet and headed for the bathroom.

"Well, if you want me to—"

He closed the door on her words and called, loud enough for her to hear, "All I want you to do is go to sleep. And let me get some."

When he came out she appeared to be asleep. He fell into bed and, if his ex-wife's complaints were to be believed, was soon snoring.

How long he slept he had no idea, nor did he have any idea where he was when he emerged into semiconsciousness, only that the erection was real and *not* self-induced. A hand was stroking his penis through the sheet. He opened his eyes. The window drapes, not quite closed in the centre, let enough light into the room to see Liliana perched on the bed beside him. Joe rolled violently to the opposite side of the bed and jumped up, taking the sheet with him. The signals being fed to his brain were jumbled but one was clear: bad situation, a trap.

Liliana was around the bed in a flash, pressing her body full-length against his. "Hold me," she murmured. "Can't you feel how cold I am? I'm shivering."

"Take the goddamned blanket," he said through clenched teeth.

By way of an answer she moved her hips in a way which, to his dismay, incited his penis to remain at the ready.

"What the hell are you doing?" He tried to back up in the narrow space between bed and wall, but there was no farther back to go.

"*I'm* not doing anything." She giggled. "You're the one getting all excited. We could share the blanket."

The indignity of being wrapped in a sheet, his body in non-compliance, and cornered by a manipulative female infuriated Joe. "We're not going to share a god-damned thing, not even this room if you don't get your ass back in your own goddamned bed!" he snarled, shoving her away, hard.

Liliana stumbled backward, crumpled to the floor, and began sobbing.

"Get up," Joe ordered. "And into your own bed. Now."

She rose and shuffled toward her bed, sobs becoming more heart-wrenching with each step. She dropped down beside the bed and buried her face in the coverlet like a child saying prayers. "I'm sorry, Tío." Her words came out muffled, between sobs. "It's just that I'm so scared."

"I'll bet," Joe muttered. He double-wrapped the sheet around his lower body, relieved to see that the embarrassing erection had wilted. Obviously there was no going back to sleep, not while she was bawling like a four-year-old.

He sighed. "All right, kid, let's have it. What's going on? Are you pregnant?"

"No!" Liliana choked, looking up at him through lashes glued together by tears. "I thought *you'd* understand, that's all."

"Oh I understand all right." He gave her a look of undisguised disgust.

"Why are you looking at me like that?" she sniffled. "Just because I want to be free, like you are? You live in a place where everybody has loads of beautiful clothes and everything. Why do I have to be stuck on this stupid island the rest of my life?"

Joe blinked, trying to compute her out-of-the-blue revelation. The last thing in the world he would have expected was any similarity between Liliana's aspirations and his own, present or past. He walked to the closet and rummaged through a pocket. He came back with a packet of candy and held it out to Liliana.

"Lifesaver?"

Still sniffling, she peeled one off and popped it into her mouth. For a moment she studied the package. He knew she was deciding whether to politely hand it back or pretend he had given her the whole thing. Sadly, she handed it back. "You know something, Tío? We don't even have Lifesavers in Cuba."

"Don't they have everything in the dollar stores?" he asked, returning the Lifesavers to his jacket pocket.

"Yeah, but you know what it takes to get dollars."

He stood in the middle of the room, looking as stern and fatherly as possible for a man wrapped in a bedsheet. "Luis says you speak French, and are studying English. You could get a job in the tourist industry."

"Sure. Waiting tables. Waiting for dollar tips. Is that what I ought to aspire to?"

Joe shrugged. "I thought you aspired to becoming a doctor. Mamá says you have been talking about it since you were a little kid."

Liliana was silent for a moment, sucking on the candy. Finally she said, "Claro. I'd like to be a doctor. But in Cuba? Tía Celia is jefe de sala, with I don't know how many doctors under her, and she only makes six hundred pesos a month. That's about thirty US dollars. Tío Luis is way up the ladder in government; he'll probably be an adviser to the next president. And he doesn't even make that much."

Joe sat down on his bed. "There's more to life than money," he said heavily.

Liliana gave him a sardonic glance. "Like *love*? Is that why you left Tía Celia? And went to Florida and made all that money?"

Joe was no longer drunk or sleepy. He was just tired. And depressed. Maybe that accounted for what he said next, something he had never told another living soul. "For your information, my life in Miami has been a living hell."

Liliana climbed onto her own bed, pulled the sheet up over her bare legs, and stared at him in complete disbelief. "How could it be?"

"Oh, having to work two or three jobs just to survive. Exploited by Cuban Americans. Hated by blacks. Treated like scum by whites." He bit down on the Lifesaver, but its sweetness was not enough to counter the sour taste in his mouth.

"If it was so bad, why did you stay?"

"Why does any immigrant stay? To make money. And I did. Five years ago. No more shit jobs." He paused and muttered, "Just a shit home life. And now no home life."

"Don't you live in a big house, like . . . ?" She waited for him to fill in the details.

"Like you've seen in magazines? No. I live in a rented apartment half the size of my mother's. I could afford better. I could afford a house in a good neighbourhood. Had a house in a good neighbourhood. But that was just one more fuck-over."

He could almost hear the sound of tinkling glass as Liliana's picture of his Stateside life shattered. Minutes passed before she spoke again.

"Did you come back to marry my tía?"

"It never crossed my mind."

"But are you going to?"

His answer, when it came, surprised even him. "It's out of the question. I got nothing she wants."

Again there was a silence, until Liliana's voice floated across to him, cool and confidential. "She wants me to be happy. Take me to Miami with you. Please?"

"And what would you do in Miami?"

"I could help you in your business. Be a mule. Nobody would ever suspect me."

He was so startled by her implication that he switched on the bedside lamp to get a better look at her face. "You think I'm a drug dealer? Where'd you get that idea?"

Liliana shrugged. "I'm not the only one who thinks so."

"Luis? He told you that?"

"Not exactly, but the way he said it . . ."

"You mean"—Joe raised an eyebrow and mimicked in a skeptical voice— "*pharmaceuticals*?"

"Yeah," Liliana agreed. "Like that."

When Joe said nothing, just sat there, chagrined, she asked, "You're not a narco-traficanto? You honestly got rich without dealing drugs?"

Joe generally tried to avoid lying, so he dodged the question with an obvious truth. "Everybody takes some stupid risks when they're young. But if they've got half a brain they don't *keep* taking chances."

Liliana didn't pursue the subject, being less interested in his past than in her own future. "Or I could work for your company. You wouldn't even have to pay me."

"If I didn't pay you, where would you get the money to buy all that cool stuff you want? Takes dollars to shop in Miami too, you know."

"Oh yeah." She lay back on the pillow, no longer a tart but the very image of an alert, intelligent teenager. "I'd think of something."

"I'll bet. Like doing in Miami what you're trying to do here. There you could drive Celia and me both crazy."

Liliana sat up. "No! I promise! Just get me there and I will never cause you or Tía Celia one minute of trouble, ever." Her face was wretched with hope and despair. "Please, Tío Joe! If you don't help me, who will?"

Beyond Liliana, dawn light filtered through the crack where the two halves of the drapes did not meet. Joe looked past the girl, not to this breaking dawn but to one ten years past, to a sky turning from pearl to blue over the Straits of Florida as he waited for the boat that would take him to the magic Land of All.

"God," he groaned. "It's daylight already."

He got out of bed, located his shaving kit and garment bag, and went into the bathroom. He shaved before showering, as he always did, to avoid the hassle of a steamed-up mirror. On what was meant to be the last stroke of the razor, he nicked himself.

"Fuck." While pressuring the nick to stop the bleeding, he studied his reflection. A shower, coffee, breakfast, would erase most of the tiredness. But something else . . . He studied his face a little longer. Sadness?

Well, shit. Liliana had a problem. Celia had a problem. He, Joe Lago, did not have a problem or one damn thing to be sad about. All his life he had known that the key to happiness was not letting other people's problems become his own.

In the shower he did not think about what he had learned in the course of the night's unexpected revelations. However, by the time he got dressed he knew one thing: he might help the kid. Not because it was easy, which it would be, and not to solve what she imagined were her problems. If he decided to do it, it would be for the sole purpose of solving his own. And as yet, he didn't think he had any.

He came out and found Liliana lying in bed, awake. He ignored her hopeful take-me-with-you look. "I'm going to a meeting," he announced. "You stay here." He pointed to the floor for emphasis. "I mean *right here*. Call room service if you get hungry. And call Celia. Tell her where you are and that I will have you home by noon."

When he got back three hours later, Liliana was sitting on her bed watching CNN, the remains of a room service breakfast on the nightstand. He flipped off the TV.

"Let's go. Did you call Celia?"

"Yes, Tío. I called Tía Alma too." She looked genuinely contrite. "You were right. They were worried."

There was virtually no conversation on the two-hour drive back to Habana. Liliana spoke only once, just before they reached Habana del Este.

"Are you going to tell Tía Celia?"

"You said you called her. Didn't you tell her where you were?"

"I mean about . . ." Her voice trailed off miserably.

Joe knew he wouldn't, but felt she deserved a little suspense. So he said nothing. Not until he pulled up in front of the apartment did he glance over at her and answer the question. "No. There's no need to tell anyone."

"Gracias, Tío." She got out and wiggled her fingers in a child's wave. "Bye-bye."

He nodded and pulled away. In the rear-view mirror he saw her standing there, looking after him like an abandoned puppy.

TWENTY-THREE

LUIS could not believe that Liliana was not in the apartment. She had told both Alma and Celia that José would have her home by noon. It was now twelve noon. Luis was here, Liliana was not. Had she been with anyone other than José, Luis would have assumed an ordinary delay. José, though, had always had a thing about promptness. He liked to prove that he could control his life to the extent of predicting exactly what time he would be at a particular place. It made him furious when something beyond his control prevented it—and he always called.

Luis phoned from Celia's apartment, first Alma, then Celia, having her paged at the hospital. Neither had heard from Liliana since the morning call, and both told him more or less the same thing. "For heaven's sake, Luis, it's only a few minutes past twelve. They'll turn up."

Alma's assurance had been consoling, Celia's curt. She seemed to regret having agreed to his coming to talk to Liliana. Actually, that was not quite what she had agreed to. When Luis insisted, she had suggested that he take Liliana for a walk on the beach.

"Keep things light," she had advised. "Liliana does not respond well to scolding." It would be more helpful, she suggested, to find out exactly how Liliana had ended up in Pinar with José. "That is something I will want to know before deciding on a course of discipline."

Now, on the telephone, Celia was saying, "There is no reason for you to wait around, Luis. This is not the best time for a talk anyway. There are some things I would like to discuss with her myself before the whole family gets involved."

Luis gave a noncommittal response and hung up. As if the whole family is not already involved, he thought bitterly. She just doesn't want *me* involved. Fine. Soon it will be out of my hands *and* hers.

But Liliana, it seemed, was out of everybody's hands. The social workers left within the hour. They had more pressing problems than a teenager who had only stayed out one night and had called to let her guardian know she was with a family friend and would be home soon. Luis drove them back to their office and returned to wait for Celia.

She cycled up just before sunset. He could tell by the set of her mouth that she was not pleased to see him. Instead of coming to the car, she headed directly for the building. He followed her in and waited as she parked her bike. She already had her foot on the first stair when he spoke. "Liliana did not come back."

Celia turned to him, incredulous. "What do you mean? Where is she?"

"I got here at twelve. She and José were not here and they have not been here. José mentioned yesterday that he had a meeting at the American Interest Section, so I called there. It was difficult to find out anything, but I leaned on them a little and finally learned that he had been there for his appointment and then left."

"Left to where?" Celia demanded with an irritation that suggested she thought he was deliberately withholding information from her.

"I do not know. José told Mamá before he went out last night that he was going to Pinar and he would be back today and she could expect him for supper." He took a breath. "And we know from Liliana that she was with him this morning."

Celia's fingers encircled the stair's metal railing, gripping it so tightly that her knuckles were white. Luis laid his hand on hers. "You know how José is about promptness. Maybe he didn't get back in time to bring her home. Maybe he took her with him and had her wait in the car while he did his meetings."

Luis remembered how in Varadero José had objected to leaving Liliana in the car and felt certain that was not what had happened. Even if José had told her to wait, he doubted that Liliana would have stayed put. But the scenario offered Celia hope. He felt her hand beneath his relax a little. "They didn't expect you to be home, Celia, so they would have been in no rush to get here. It's almost suppertime now, and if José told Mamá he would be there, he will. We should wait for them there."

There was no waiting. The Daewoo was parked in front of the house when they arrived. As soon as they stepped into the apartment, Luis knew something was amiss. Alma and José met him and Celia at the door. Two pairs of eyes asked two pairs of eyes the same question: "Where is Liliana?"

Celia looked at José. "I thought she was with you."

José shrugged. "I thought she was with you. Or at your place. That's where I left her."

"You did not!" Luis challenged angrily.

José gave him a glance of dismissal and addressed his response to Celia. "I dropped her off out front, a little before twelve."

For a long silent moment the four of them stood there in the once-elegant, now-truncated room with cherubs peering down at them from the dim recesses of the ceiling.

"Are you sure of the time?" Celia asked quietly.

"Yep," José responded promptly. "I had an appointment at the American Interest Section at twelve. I checked my watch while she was getting out of the car and had fifteen minutes. I figured I could just make it."

They all looked at Luis. Luis looked at his feet. José's explanation made him feel as if he had been caught out in a lie. Yet he had told the absolute truth. All he could do was tell it again. "I got there at twelve sharp. She was not there."

"How did she happen to be with you in Pinar in the first place?" Celia asked.

"She was in the car when I came out of the Tropicana. I don't how she knew I was there."

"I told her," Alma said. "She called about eight o'clock and asked where you were."

Celia looked back at José. "Why did you not bring her home last night?"

José spread his hands in a gesture of helplessness that Luis judged to be totally fraudulent. "I was in a hurry. It was late and I wanted to get some sleep. I just thought—"

"Thought it would be okay for a sixteen-year-old girl to spend the night in a hotel with a man she barely knows, without her family knowing?" Luis exploded.

Luis barely had time to register the movement before José had him by the collar. "Goddamn it, Luis. If you want to make an accusation, how about we step outside so Mother's apartment doesn't get trashed when I kick the shit out of you!"

"*Hijos! Por favor!*" Alma shrieked.

José released Luis's collar and stepped back. Luis glanced at Celia to see her reaction. Alma had her hand over her mouth, but Celia's eyes were fixed on José as if nothing had happened. "So at 11:45 you let her out in front of the apartment. Did you see her go inside?"

"No," José replied. "She was standing on the sidewalk."

"On the sidewalk," Celia repeated. "The one along the street or the one leading to the apartment? Was she headed for the building?"

"Now that you mention it—" José hesitated, and Luis had the satisfaction of seeing that he, too, felt caught out, as if he had given inaccurate information and now had to backtrack. "I think she might have stepped off the curb. Like she was going across to the beach."

There was another long silence. All four of them looked away. Luis supposed that each was seeing a variation of the same scene: Liliana walking across the street and down the path to the waterfront. Perhaps she had wandered off along the shore. To the harbour? Or the other way, toward Cojímar?

"Possibly," Alma said hesitantly, "she was across the street when you arrived, Luis. Might she have seen the social workers? If they were in uniform, she might have been frightened and—"

Alma got no further. Celia spun on Luis so fast that for a second he thought she was going to physically attack him. "*What* social workers?" she hissed.

"He didn't tell you?" Alma asked in surprise.

"You said you were going to talk to her! Nothing about the authorities!"

"Oh shit," José said under his breath.

Luis didn't need that, his brother's favourite expression when he wanted to convey the opinion that he, Luis, had screwed up. He was already aware of it. Nothing to do now but to stand his ground, even though the ground, already quaking, would be crumbling beneath him before this day was done.

Luis stared the woman he loved straight in the eyes and said, "I didn't tell you because you would not have agreed, Celia."

"Re-education camp? No! Never!"

"Come on," he pleaded. "You are a doctor! You know what happens to girls like her once they start!"

"You were going to have her taken away!"

Celia's voice held a pitch of fury that Luis had never suspected she could call forth, although later it occurred to him that this was probably the kind of rage she had turned on José when he told her he was emigrating to the States.

Luis's own voice, although not entirely steady, remained measured and reasonable. "Six months in the mountains, tree-planting or whatever, is exactly—"

"Without consulting me!" Celia shrieked.

"Because you are against it," Luis raised his voice. "And you are absolutely wrong!"

He was vaguely aware that Alma, behind the hands covering her face, was crying. He also registered that José had walked to the couch and sat down, distancing himself from the conflict, from the family. As if he wasn't into both up to his turncoat ears.

Celia pointed a finger at Luis's chin in a way that made him glad it was not a gun. "Liliana is not your child. She's mine!"

Still Luis did not flinch. "She is Cuba's child, Celia. The care of our youth is a collective responsibility."

"You frighten my child into running away and think you can absolve yourself with clichés about 'collective responsibility'?" she cried.

It was her putting the entire blame on him that caused Luis to lose it. He shouted, "All right, *I* had a responsibility! Don't you think your niece's behaviour reflects on me?"

"Why on you?"

"Because, damn it, you're my fiancée!"

As suddenly as Celia's voice had raised, it dropped, stone hard. "Not anymore."

"Celia, dearest, no!" Alma cried.

The slam of the door was the answer to everything, spoken and unspoken. José started after her but Alma, closer to the exit, got there first and blocked his way.

"She doesn't need us now." Alma shook her head so hard that the tears streaming down her age-spotted cheeks flew off in all directions. "She needs her child."

"She needs a way home," José protested. "The car—"

Luis moved to the window. Nightfall was near. The street was crowded with people coming home from work, some walking, some in pedicabs, some getting off a bus at the corner. Small children were hanging on front porches to greet their parents while older kids tried unsuccessfully to confine their energetic games to the sidewalk.

"She doesn't need a car either," Luis said. "She just boarded a bus."

TWENTY-FOUR

CELIA got off the bus in Habana del Este and cut across the housing complex, taking the shortest route to her building. She walked swiftly at first, but as the apartment came into view her steps slowed. The jalousied windows were open as they almost always were to catch the breeze. The rooms beyond were dark.

The ache in Celia's heart suffused her body so completely that climbing the three flights of stairs to the apartment was as difficult as if she were an invalid. As she reached her own level she encountered two boys, Federico, who was one of those who had borrowed her bicycle to go for candles, and Tomás, who lived in the apartment next to Celia's. They were racing in the hallway but skidded to a stop when she appeared and shouted, "Hola, Doctora."

"Hello, boys." She took a deep breath and asked, "Have either of you seen Liliana this afternoon?"

"Isn't she in school?" Federico asked.

"I—don't think so," Celia said, hoping he didn't hear the catch in her throat.

Tomás peered at her keenly. "Is she still mad at you?"

The question jolted Celia like an electric shock, but she instantly realized that he, along with everyone else on their floor, would have heard Liliana's shrieking outburst at Luis the evening before.

"I hope not," Celia said simply. "But she isn't home yet. Would you boys mind asking the other people in the building if they've seen her today?"

"Ask who?" Federico queried.

"Everyone. Every apartment."

The boys looked at each other, their eyes sparkling with excitement at being given such a responsibility. "We'll start on the ground floor," Federico decided. "And ask everybody."

"If they're home," Tomás agreed, and they were off.

Celia let herself into her own apartment and went from living room to Liliana's bedroom to her own bedroom to the bathroom to the kitchen and back to the living room, looking for the child she already knew was not there.

The revealing clothes Luis had found in Liliana's room still lay on the table. Celia was as loath to touch them as if they were poisonous—which in sense they were. With a shudder she swept them up, carried them into Liliana's room, and dropped them on the bed. Dresser drawers still hung ajar from Luis's ransacking. From them he had taken these things that bore no relation to a schoolgirl's life or to any Liliana she knew.

Celia sat down on the bed and stared at the pile of inappropriate clothes, baubles, and cosmetics, guestimating costs. By the standards of any Cuban, let alone an unemployed student, the total was staggering. Gifts from foreigners? With or without sexual favours? Luis said her attendance record showed absences since January. And what about the week at home each month, when Liliana often spent a day or two at a time at a campismo (so she said) with her friends?

The awareness that there had to have been occasions when Liliana lied to her cut like a knife. The knife became two-edged with the realization that her blind trust had made it easy for Liliana to deceive her without resorting to lies. Celia recalled Liliana lying in bed, the headphones of a portable CD player nestled in her hair. "Where did you get that?" Celia had asked, and Liliana had replied, easily, "From a friend." Such an innocent response, now so ominous. Celia pushed the trashy clothes away and looked around the room. To which girl did it belong? The one who bought and wore such things for reasons she could not yet bear to contemplate? Or the one she thought she knew so well, just emerging from childhood?

Seeking traces of the child Liliana had so lately been, Celia's gaze fell on a blue music box, the kind with a key one winds to make the ballerina on the top twirl. Carolina had bought the Belgian-made music box in Angola. It was the last thing she sent to her daughter before she died, and it was Liliana's most treasured possession. Celia picked up the box and idly wound the key. The music did not play, nor did the dancer twirl. She examined it and saw that there was a way to unscrew the bottom in order to get at the mechanism. She unscrewed it, and stared, at first not sure of what she was seeing. The area around the mechanism was tightly packed with—what? With her fingernail, Celia flipped out a greenish bit of paper, many times folded into a small tight square. Money. The bill she smoothed out on the dresser was an American ten. She pried out more, and more, and still more, in all, more than two hundred dollars in ones, fives, tens, and a couple of twenties. Where could Liliana have gotten so many dollars, and for what?

Hardening her emotions in order to free her mind to analyze, Celia considered the likelihood of prostitution. Unless Liliana had more squirrelled away, there wasn't enough here, even including the probable cost of the clothes, to suggest that she had been marketing her body on a regular basis. But irregularly? It was the only possibility she could think of.

Carefully Celia replaced the folded bills and screwed the two halves of the music box back together. The one thing she felt sure of now was that Liliana had not come into the apartment, that she had fled the second time as the first, with nothing except the clothes she was wearing.

Celia rewound her thoughts as she might a videotape, to the moment when Liliana had broken away from Luis's grasp on Sunday afternoon and disappeared down the stairwell. Celia had been distressed by her running off like that but not frightened. Clearly Liliana was only embarrassed at their discovery of her cache of sexy clothes. Celia was certain that she would phone or come home in a matter of hours. And she had phoned, first thing this morning. The only surprise was that instead of calling from a friend's house, she was calling from Pinar del Río.

Celia had not had time to consider the implications of Liliana's choosing José, whom she barely knew, over one of her lifelong friends, but then, what had she had time for? She felt a renewed burst of anger at Luis for having persuaded her to go with him to Alma's place. What if Liliana had called while she was away? Of course she would have known where Celia was if not at home, but given Luis's actions, would she have called the Lagos? Or would she have seen Celia's going there as proof that she supported his decision to call in the youth authorities?

If Liliana had gone to the home of a friend, most of whom lived in the same housing complex, their parents would insist that she call—or would call themselves to let Celia know Liliana was there. Although there were more than one hundred thousand people in this and other buildings in the huge Habana del Este apartment complex, Celia was well known and well liked. Some she knew better than others, liked better than others. But there were none whom she did not trust to do the responsible thing when it came to a child; none who would let a parent worry needlessly. The trouble was that she had not remained in the apartment until the call came.

A call did come, a little before nine o'clock. It was Tomás's mother, Marianna, calling from down the hall. "Celia?" she greeted her. "Tomás and Federico just got back from asking people in the building if they'd seen Liliana today. I wish I'd known. I could have saved them the trouble."

"You saw her? This afternoon?" Celia's heart leapt with joy.

"Yes. I was just coming from the bicycle bus stop with my little one. I saw Liliana across the street and waved, but I don't think she saw me. I know she's supposed to be at school this week and at first I thought maybe she wasn't feeling well and was on her way over to the hospital to see you. But she didn't go through the underpass." Marianna stopped speaking, the way a person will sometimes do when they know you don't want to hear what they're about to say.

"Was she headed for the bus stop?" Celia prompted.

"No. She was walking up the ramp onto the Vía Blanca."

"Are you sure it was Liliana?"

"Oh yes. She was wearing the same white shorts and that red-and-white striped halter top she had on yesterday when she . . . when I saw her out in the hall."

Of course, Marianna, hearing Liliana screaming at Luis in the hall the evening before, would have been one of those whose doors opened to see what was going on. Celia saw in her mind's eye what the neighbours had seen, and at the same time, saw Liliana, dressed in shorts and tiny top, walking up onto the Vía Blanca, headed for—Varadero? Or maybe somewhere closer, like Playas del Este? Or the campismo at Jibacoa, hoping to meet up with friends there?

"Thanks, Marianna," Celia murmured. "I'm sure I'll hear from her shortly. I'm just upset that . . . that she didn't go to school today."

"I can imagine." Marianna sounded genuinely sympathetically. "They're a handful at that age. My oldest is only twelve and I'm ready to pack him off to boarding school already."

They hung up. Celia, still in her hospital whites, did not change, shower, or eat. She sat down next to the phone, listening with preternatural attentiveness to sounds from elsewhere in the building. Little by little the building grew quiet, until at last all she could hear was the silence of her own apartment. The telephone did not ring.

Around midnight she called the hospital and said she would not be at work in the morning, that she was ill. She did not have to elaborate. The tone of her voice was enough to elicit commiseration from the person who took the message, and no further questions. Then she lay down on the sofa to wait.

TWENTY-FIVE

JOE stayed at the Casa de la Trova listening to acoustic music until the place closed. Had a jinetera accosted him as he left he would have gone home with her to avoid returning to his mother's place. But none did, so he drove back to Vedado.

The whole situation angered and depressed him. It hadn't been that easy to disengage from his Cuban family in the first place, and it had cost him a year and a small fortune to disengage from his American family. Yet back in Cuba not ten days and already he was up to his eyeballs in a family drama in which, without even auditioning, he had landed a leading role.

He blamed Luis, and Liliana, of course. At the same time he felt guilty. Or no, not guilty. What he felt was *trapped*. Once on a trip to Los Angeles he had visited the tar pits in Hancock Park, had seen mock-ups of mastodons and sabre-toothed tigers stuck in the tar that lay beneath what appeared to be a pool of water. In the Page museum he had marvelled at the bones of once-powerful creatures pried from the tar that had held them fast to and beyond death. That's what family is like, he thought grimly. Something that seems to offer sustenance and turns out to be a fucking tar pit.

He pulled up to the wrought-iron fence in front of his mother's place and got out to unlock the gate. There was a garage, or what had been a garage back in the 1920s when the mansion was built and horseless carriages were the newest toys of the rich. Luis's car could have fit into the garage had it not been converted into an apartment for another family long ago. As it was, Luis parked in the postage-stamp-sized front yard. By moving aside Alma's potted plants, they had made room to squeeze the rented Daewoo in next to the Fiat.

Joe had to pull up till the bumper touched the house in order to get the gate locked behind. A pointless gesture. Petty thieves—and there was no shortage of those in Habana these days—could easily scale the iron pickets and take hubcaps or whatever they fancied from either car. Luis said they never had. Neighbours watched out for each other in Cuba. Whether you liked being watched or not, it definitely cut down on theft.

Light shone through the living room window. Somebody was still up. To avoid going in, Joe took a slow walk along the tree-lined street where he had spent the first twenty-four years of his life. All of the old homes were two-storey, designed by architects who tacked on balconies, turrets, towers, friezes, and ornaments without apparent concern for cost or utility. Not one had been painted in his lifetime.

They had once been honest-to-God mansions. Even in their decrepit state they had dignity. In the right hands, all that former grandeur could be reclaimed. Joe picked out the house on the street he liked best and played with the fantasy of restoring statuary and stained glass windows, replacing broken tiles, painting it top to bottom, and landscaping the yard. Or hiring other people to do it for him.

He stumbled over a bit of sidewalk pushed up by the roots of a great old tree and cursed. Neither the sidewalks nor the grassy strip alongside them were maintained. Private yards were just as bad. He could understand the lack of paint; the embargo made it hard to get, and what little became available was expensive. But what was it with Cubans that they couldn't be bothered to plant a lawn, put in flowers, and trim their hedges? Small as front yards were, most were untended patches of bare dirt, grass gone wild, or weeds, the latter sometimes so high that they obscured the one gardening passion Cubans had: potted plants.

It wasn't that Joe himself had any interest in gardening. Right after his arrival in Miami he had worked briefly as a below-minimum-wage gardener's helper, running a leaf blower until he thought he'd lose his hearing. However, once he got past dead-end jobs and had a home of his own, he had never touched a lawn mower or a gardening tool.

"Leave it to the peons," he had told Vera sharply, and she did, employing ethnic gardeners every bit as low-paid as he had been. He'd done it; now it was their turn. Maybe that was how island Cubans felt; like they'd done their time as peasants, fought the Revolution to put an end to grubbing in the dirt, and weren't about to go back to it even for the sake of neighbourhood beautification.

Standing under the dim streetlight, Joe smiled sardonically at the direction his fantasies had taken him: boy returns to hometown, restores classy mansion, and lives a life of elegance and refinement in old neighbourhood. As if such a thing was possible in Cuba. What you got when you came home to Cuba was just what he was getting: a cream pie mess of family responsibility right in the face.

Besides, he had already made his choice as to cultures, opting for one where other people's problems did not so easily become his. In Miami you could die a lingering death in your apartment, your suburban home, or your walled estate, and if you didn't have live-in family or live-in servants, few would notice and even fewer would care. That kind of disconnect between people made Joe uneasy, but it was vastly less complicated than the overshared quality of Cuban life.

He consoled himself with the reminder that he'd probably have things wound up here in a few days. All he had to do was skate on the surface a little longer, pretending concern but staying uninvolved. The tricky part was to not break through the thin ice, beneath which lay all that emotional tar.

He trudged up the broad marble steps and pushed open the door to that portion of the old mansion that his family had called home since before he was born. Luis sat on the sofa in a circle of lamplight. He looked drained, as if he had been crying. Muffled sounds from Alma's bedroom said she hadn't gone dry yet. If there was any way Joe could've decently got the hell out of there, he would have. Of course there wasn't.

Joe dropped into a rocker. "So. Any idea where the little shit might've gone?"

Luis seemed shocked but pleased with the way he had characterized Liliana.

"Varadero, I suppose. Or some other resort."

Joe nodded. "I suppose Celia will have notified the police by now."

Luis gave him a startled look. "The police? Why?"

"Well, missing kid, isn't that what you do?"

"Man! You forget you're back in Cuba? We don't criminalize our kids. This is a matter for social services."

Joe tried to remember any kids he had known growing up who got into serious trouble, but only recalled ones who'd been called on the carpet by neighbourhood watch groups for failing to show up for some "voluntary" community service, and getting assigned more of same. "But well, you said Varadero. Guys on the lookout for a babe, her being a minor—that must be a crime."

"For the foreigner, sure. Any neighbour seeing a foreigner going into a private home with what looked like an underaged girl would call the police. And if the police thought a kid was involved, they'd show up with a social worker. Same thing if a hotel employee saw some jerk trying to sneak an underaged girl into his room."

Remembering the ease with which he had taken Liliana into Hotel Pinar del Río, Joe raised an eyebrow. Luis quickly amended, "Of course, there's the odd hotel employee who'll accept a bribe to look the other way."

"Or just doesn't want the hassle," Joe added.

Luis nodded, a little reluctantly. "But people can lose their jobs over shit like that. It all goes back to when the island first opened up to tourism in, well, just about the time you left. Before we could turn around there were charters from Spain, Italy, México, and God knows where else, to joint-venture resorts managed by the foreign partner. Whole planeloads coming for sex! And to tell the truth, we were a little slow on the uptake. Fidel especially. He thinks the younger generation is God's gift to Cuba and wouldn't believe kids raised with Che as their model would sell their bodies."

Joe snorted. "They didn't have any trouble believing it in Miami. I was barely off the boat when I started seeing articles about how Castro was turning the whole island into a giant brothel and—"

"—depositing all the money in a Swiss bank account," Luis cut in. "Total crap, of course, but it was a wakeup call he—well, all of us—needed. The minister of tourism was thrown out on his ear and in my opinion should've done jail time. The court ruled that there was no evidence that he knew about the resorts being used for sex tourism, but if he didn't know he should have. Either way, he disgraced himself and his country."

"But it's still an issue, right? Didn't you say that day we went to Varadero that the authorities were on the lookout for girls like Liliana?"

"Oh sure. But laws are in place now and police have the authority to stop couples on the street when they think prostitution is involved. Preventive policing, they call it, and I'm all for it. They'd ask for her ID card, and if she was underage she'd be handed over to social services. Which," he added bitterly, "is exactly what I was trying to do when I brought the youth authorities to pick her up."

Joe refrained from reminding his brother where *that* had got them and offered a more hopeful scenario. "You know, bro, we're assuming she headed for Varadero, but maybe she's just holed up at a friend's house. The way we used to go to Joaquín's place when we thought Mother was keeping us on too short a leash."

"Any neighbour would have called Celia by now, and she would have called Mamá." Luis spoke with a certainty that Joe knew was justified.

"What about family?"

"Family? We're all they've got. You know that."

Joe did know that, but until Luis said it, it hadn't registered. Close as the two families had been when they were growing up, they were separate entities; Alma Lago and her sons; Kristina Cantú and her daughters. He supposed that with the death of most of the Cantús, Celia and Liliana had folded into the Lago family. Or had they?

"How come Celia moved out of this neighbourhood?"

"She was working in Habana del Este and didn't want to commute." Luis paused. "At least that's what she said. Personally, I think she couldn't stand living here after all the others in her family died. Except Liliana, of course."

"Pretty grim," Joe agreed.

"It was the year after you left that her mother was diagnosed with cancer and went into a hospice. Then Carolina and her husband were killed, leaving Celia alone with Liliana. Celia said the place was too big for just the two of them and traded it for the apartment she has now. We have stayed close, though. This is the first time . . ." His voice trailed off.

Joe rose and gave Luis's shoulder a squeeze. "Rough patches with teens, comes with the territory. We just need to figure out how we can help Celia till it blows over."

As he stripped for bed, Joe wondered why he'd said "we." What he had meant to say was "how *you* can help her." Not that he necessarily considered Celia his brother's woman. But he certainly considered Liliana to be Luis and Celia's problem.

TWENTY-SIX

CELIA paced all night, around the apartment, out onto the balcony, back inside to stare at the silent telephone. She was frantic to find Liliana, to physically *search* for her. But she had no idea where to start and it made no sense anyway. Since Liliana knew where to find her, reason insisted she stay put. She would, as long as she could bear the inaction.

Toward morning Celia stopped prowling the apartment. She went out onto the balcony and sat waiting for daylight. Soon after sunrise the street filled with people. Those who worked nearby either walked or biked to work. Others strolled toward bus stops.

By eight the morning rush was over. Primary school children clad in red-and-white uniforms and secondary school children in gold skirts and white blouses had been absorbed into neighbourhood schools. There were no children in the fifteen- to eighteen-year-old range, of course; pre-university students in their blue-and-navy uniforms and technical school students in tan-and-brown outfits had left for their boarding schools a week earlier.

Celia had often wondered who felt the greatest relief: parents seeing teenagers off to boarding school or teens escaping from close parental scrutiny into peer groups that were like a second family. And conversely, who was most delighted to see whom when they returned: children not quite as ready to be free of family as they had appeared three weeks earlier or parents who all during that time had felt the same aching absence for their almost-grown children that she now felt for Liliana.

When the last child had disappeared from the street and Celia was sure that the school secretary would be in her office, she telephoned.

Emily Solana was a thin woman with a small voice pitched high by the tension in her vocal chords. "Good morning, Dr. Cantú," she chirped. "I was just about to call you. How is our Liliana?"

"She—" Celia paused. She had been clinging so hard to the hope that Liliana would be there that she had not prepared an answer. Only when Emily asked did she realize that she was not ready to spill out the whole story. "—will not be in for a few days," Celia finished lamely. "I plan to stop by later. To discuss the situation."

She had almost said "with Compañera Campos" but held back the name of the woman who headed the pre-university program. On several visits to the school she had observed that the large black director had a tendency to bully her frail white secretary. She did not know whether it was racial, personal, or merely a matter of the one physically overpowering the other, but it grated on her nerves. To have said that she specifically needed to speak to the director without responding to Emily's expression of concern would have implied that she was too lowly to warrant a confidence. The truth was that whenever possible Celia dealt with the secretary rather than the overbearing director.

"We can talk then, Emily. When I have more time," she promised.

"Of course, Dr. Cantú," Emily said quickly.

Celia wanted to hang up before the secretary could ask questions but realized that she did need more from her.

"Emily," she said hesitantly, "in case Liliana does show up at school, be sure she calls me. Or better yet, you call. Please?"

"Why, certainly!" The secretary's voice carried pleasure at being entrusted with this small service, but at the same time confusion. "Is she not—?"

"Excuse me, please, Emily. I have to go. We can talk later."

Celia was about to return to the balcony when the telephone rang.

"Hello?"

"Celia, it's me, Alma."

Celia did not have the heart to hang up on the older woman, but neither was there anything to say. When she said nothing, Alma asked, "No news?"

"Nothing," Celia whispered.

"You're not going to work today?"

"No. I—if you don't mind, let's not tie up the line. In case she calls."

"I am praying for her," Alma said. "For all of us." At Celia's continued silence, she said sadly, "Adios," with heavy emphasis on the *dios*.

The telephone continued to ring throughout the day. Most of the calls were from the hospital, colleagues wanting information or guidance. Was it okay to let a mother take her child home from hospital early? A test had been inconclusive; should a different type be run? They had run out of a particular drug; what substitute would she prefer her patients be given? Celia answered each question and cut all extraneous conversation short. There were afternoon calls from both José and Luis, but she hung up on them. After each call she returned to the balcony and sat there, waiting.

She strained her eyes to see to the end of the street in each direction, as if catching a glimpse of the spot where Liliana disappeared from sight—had anyone been watching her flight—might cause her to reappear. The day had turned foggy.

Or maybe it was her mind. She felt that she had known such waiting before, must have, because she knew in her bones that this first phase was the easiest. However anxious, it was filled with moment-to-moment hope.

Was that a boat on the waves or only a piece of driftwood? How much longer could she keep the trucks waiting on the beach when every hour, every moment, increased the risk of their being discovered by Batista's soldiers? Where was the Granma? *How long could it take to motor from México to Cuba? How could there have been a miscalculation of this magnitude?*

Celia came back from wherever she had been, into the reality of Liliana's absence. She went inside and pulled a decades-old textbook from the bookcase. She knew the story her emotions had revisited but could not recall why the boat had been late, why instead of making landfall where Celia Sánchez waited with trucks to transport the rebels to safe houses, it had not reached Cuba until two days later.

The book offered no real explanation, only said that the *Granma* had got lost and made "landfall" (a nice euphemism for running aground, she thought) at a place that forced the rebels to struggle to shore through a kilometre or more of mangroves.

Celia did not want to read on, but she did: how the eighty-two men lost most of their supplies and weapons as they made their way through the swamp in chest-deep water. Their difficult march inland was described too, but here it was necessary for Celia to fill in details that the textbook's authors had found too un-heroic to include: how the hungry men chewed sugarcane to sustain themselves as they marched, and how, within hours, Batista's army was closing in, following a trail of discarded cane pulp. The book did go into detail about the Alegría de Pío battle that most had not survived: some shot, some burned alive in the cane field in which they had taken cover, some captured and tortured to death. Only Fidel, Raúl, Che, Camilo, and eight others had escaped.

Celia flung the book aside, unable to read further, unable to think further. The waiting was driving her crazy. Or, she grimaced, driving her more crazy. From one moment to the next, she could not keep track of whether she was Celia Cantú waiting for her niece or Celia Sánchez waiting for Fidel. In both states, the whole of her being cried out against the waiting, the utter helplessness of her predicament.

She had not eaten since—when? She could not remember. She knew she should eat to keep up her strength, yet felt relieved when she looked into the refrigerator and found it bare. Liliana, she recalled, had been at home on the weekend and had eaten whatever was there. On Monday Celia had not made the weekly trip to bakery, farmers' market, and ration store; thus the cupboard was as bare as the fridge. She left the kitchen and resumed pacing the apartment. Finally she fell across her bed. "Oh Liliana," she whispered. "Please call!"

She awoke in the heat of the afternoon, drenched in sweat. Something had wakened her but she was not sure what. She listened intently and heard footsteps in the hallway. They were going away from her apartment. She went to the door. The person she had heard in the hall was already out of sight, but it was easy to guess who had been there. At her feet sat a cardboard box that smelled strongly of fresh-cooked food.

Celia carried the box inside and put it on the table, then went to the balcony and looked down on the street. José's rental car was at the curb. Alma came into view, walking slowly, shoulders bent in a way that made her seem older than her sixty-three years. It was not that Celia lacked sympathy for the woman who had been like a mother to her since her own mother's death. It was just that, drained as she was by worry and waiting, she had nothing to offer.

Celia returned to the kitchen and opened the cardboard box. It contained a thermos of soup, a dozen cartons of fruit juices, and a pot of black beans and white rice. She put the moros y cristianos in the refrigerator and poured some of the soup into a bowl. She wondered where the thermos had come from; it was not a household item Alma would have had, or would have had use for. She suspected José had bought it. She felt sure of it when, reaching for a carton of juice, she saw that they were all mango. José knew she preferred natural fruit juices to soda, and must have remembered that mango was her favourite. Luis might have known too, but he would not have been able to buy the brand or, at any rate, not so many cartons, which cost two Yanqui dollars each.

Once Celia had eaten the soup and drank most of a carton of juice, she felt better. More importantly, the chemistry of grief abated sufficiently for her to focus on the problem at hand. It was now late Tuesday afternoon, thirty hours since José had dropped Liliana off outside the apartment. Where was she?

She had not gone to Alma's because Luis, the person from whom she was fleeing, lived there. If she had gone to a friend's house, why had the parents of that friend not called? Celia was certain that none would put up a child for more than a day without letting the family know—and even more certain that none would let a child skip school. But Liliana was not at school. What was at school were her attendance records and a list of classmates. There were students there who did not live in Habana del Este and some friends Celia had not met. But the school was at least two hours away by bus, and the office would be closed already. So that would have to wait for morning.

Celia also needed to speak to her supervisor at the hospital. She could not very well go roaming about the countryside while claiming to be sick. Mentally, she made a short list: hospital, see supervisor. School, see director. Find Liliana's friends outside this complex, whoever they are. Celia felt fairly sure that families of Liliana's classmates from other areas would be as unlikely to support truancy as those in their own neighbourhood. So who did that leave? Older, non-school-aged friends? Strangers?

Celia's heart skipped a beat. By an act of will, she blocked further speculation. She also blocked out two potentially helpful facts: that Luis had high-level contacts and could cast a net farther and faster than she could, and José had a car that could take her wherever she wanted to go quicker than the bus.

However sensible Celia tried to be, her anger at the two of them burned with such irrational intensity that there was just no way she was about to ask either for anything.

TWENTY-SEVEN

LUIS struggled to get through the day. Serious things were afoot at work, not on the surface but leading up to changes he suspected would involve him. What they were he did not know and at the moment did not care. His mind was too muddled with negative emotions about how he had failed Celia—and she him.

When he got home he saw that Alma was not in much better shape, but he lacked what it took to help her. José, who could have cheered her, was avoiding the apartment as if its occupants were inflicted by something contagious. Alma said he had called to let her know he would not be home for supper. That was his style, all right. When things get tough, disappear.

As soon as she cleaned up after supper, Alma, instead of turning on the television to watch her favourite Brazilian soap opera, went to her room. Luis did not feel like television either, nor like sitting out on the porch talking with neighbours as he often did in the cool of the evening. He took a shower and wondered where José was. Probably shacked up with a whore. Luis forced himself to visualize exactly that, mainly as a means of keeping Celia out of the picture. He had allowed himself to imagine his brother fucking her once and was not about to knife himself in the gut like that again. He willed himself to picture Celia alone, hurt, angry, and frightened. If only he could help her! Towel wrapped around his waist, he sprawled across his bed, sobbing. Not from his eyes but, it seemed, from all his internal organs.

He heard the front door open and close and footsteps to the bathroom. Ten minutes later José entered the bedroom. He undressed without turning on the light. Luis did not move, but José must have sensed he was awake because he asked, "You talk to Celia today?"

"I tried. She hung up on me."

"Me too."

"Really?" Luis was ashamed that her having also hung up on José made him feel better, but it did.

"Don't let it get you down. Things will get sorted out."

If Luis had not been in so much pain he would have laughed. His brother the divorced man assuring him that this was a temporary problem? His brother who had lost this very same woman? A wave of hopelessness as uncontrollable as retching forced out questions that were driving him loco. "How is that going to happen when she refuses to speak to me? How can anything get sorted out when we are so different?"

José lay down and pulled the sheet up over his lanky body. "Naturally you're different. You're male. She's female."

Luis snorted, something between laughter and derision. "What a help that is, hermano. You ought to become a couples counsellor."

That elicited a chuckle from José, but when he spoke, Luis could tell that he had been thinking about the break-up, and maybe had some ideas about why it had happened. He did not want advice from his brother, but he needed it.

"You think it's you and her?" José asked. "Or is it the kid?"

"What difference does it make? It comes to the same thing."

"I don't think so." In the dark, Luis saw José prop himself on one elbow and turn toward him. "Liliana's away at pre-university three weeks out of four. Another year and a half and she'll be in university at the other end of the island. At least that's what Mamá told me. She said Liliana wants to go to the med school in Santiago rather than here in Habana."

"Assuming she comes back."

"That's a given. When she does, let Celia handle her however she wants. If you don't get in her face about it again, it'll blow over."

Luis knew his brother was offering valuable advice—or it might have been valuable if he had heard it, and taken it, six months ago. Now it was too late. He shook his head.

José misunderstood and elaborated. "Either that or Celia sees for herself that comportment camp is the best option. Because you're right, Liliana is out of control."

Luis felt a rush of gratitude toward José for seeing the situation his way. That may have been what gave him the courage to speak a truth he had always refused to admit. "There is more to it than that. The real problem is us. Celia and me."

José dropped back onto the pillow and stared at the ceiling. "Meaning what?"

Luis did not have to search for words to explain. He had thought about it too many times, rationalized it away only to have it come back looking exactly the same.

"I am a team person. A 'committee mind-set type,' Celia calls me when she is annoyed. I believe in working together as a group. You know, for the common good."

"Maybe this particular 'group decision' should have included Celia. And Liliana," José said with heavy irony.

Luis sat up and pounded on his thighs. "Damn it, José, I tried! Liliana ran out on us and Celia wouldn't discuss it. She always does that! I have no idea what goes on in her head!"

José sighed. "So why do you want to marry her?"

"I love her!" Luis leaned forward, trying to see his brother's eyes in the darkness. "What else, José? What else is there?"

José turned his head toward Luis and said, without sarcasm, "I guess you have to have something she wants."

Luis moaned. "She won't take it! How do I get her to take what I have to give?"

José gave a short humourless laugh. "If only I knew."

Luis dropped back onto the pillow feeling oddly comforted. For once his know-it-all brother did not know how to make things turn out the way he wanted either.

TWENTY-EIGHT

CELIA hoped to see the hospital director, Angel Leyva, first thing in the morning and get a leave of absence starting immediately. However, when she reached work she learned that Dr. Leyva was meeting with other hospital directors in Habana and would not return until afternoon. To make matters worse, the pediatrics unit was short a doctor; if she left, it would be short two. So, consoling herself with the knowledge that Liliana knew her number at the hospital by heart, she forced family matters to the back of her mind and went to work.

She did not stop for lunch. By three in the afternoon the overload of patients had been dealt with; there was only one more child to see. It was a seven-year-old boy with a boil on his back that needed lancing. Celia made reassuring noises as she prepped him, then, with a deft movement, lanced the boil. The same instant that puss squirted from the boil, the telephone rang in the adjacent office. Celia turned sharply, and as she did so her right hand jerked upward, slicing a small vein just where her wrist joined the heel of her left hand. She managed to get her thumb on it with enough pressure to stop the gush of blood, but not before the child had been splashed and, imagining the blood to be his own, set up a howl.

"Call another doctor," Celia instructed the nurse tersely. As the nurse obeyed, Celia distracted the child by showing him her cut. Then the nurse was back with a younger doctor in tow, who, casting a puzzled look at Celia, dressed the boy's lanced boil. Celia understood the look. It took considerable carelessness to cut oneself while performing such minor surgery. She had never done it before, not even as a medical school student.

The nurse tugged at her, trying to get her to a sink to sterilize the wound, but Celia pulled away and rushed into the outer office. Her secretary, not realizing there was anything amiss, held up the phone, "Dr. Cantú, do you want to take—"

Celia snatched the telephone and held it to her ear, oblivious to blood dribbling down her arm. "Hello?"

"Celia? It's me, Luis. Have you heard—"

"No," Celia snapped, hating the voice that was not Liliana's. "I have not heard. And unless you have, do not call again." She slammed the telephone down and went to the sink where she relinquished her wrist to a nurse who sterilized and bandaged it. She was shaking.

"Maybe you'd better—" the nurse began with a diffident murmur.

"I know." Celia forced a smile. "I should quit for the day. I am obviously— clumsy." She turned to the secretary. "Yvette, do you know if Dr. Leyva is back yet?"

The secretary started to shake her head, then smiled and pointed out the window to the parking lot. "Oh look. There he comes now."

As the director approached from down the hall, he registered surprise to find Celia waiting outside his office door. Dr. Leyva was not often surprised. For the administrator of such a large facility, he was astonishingly aware of what was going on in the hospital at any given time. "Dr. Cantú? Did you want to see me?"

"Please, Doctor, if you can spare the time," Celia said.

Angel Leyva was a small man, about the same height as Celia. When he bent his head to unlock the door, she noticed that his thick wavy hair, salt-and-pepper grey when she started working at the hospital seven years ago, was now salt white. It had happened so gradually that until this moment, she had not noticed.

Leyva led her into the office, motioned her to a chair, and slid into his own. He leaned forward, elbows on a wooden desk that was so battered it might have come through the Revolution. That seemed unlikely, though, as this hospital had not existed then, but had been constructed later, specifically to serve the east-bay populations of Habana del Este, Cojímar, and Casablanca.

"You have been unwell?" He looked at her expectantly, with a flicker of his eyes toward the bandaged wrist.

"It's nothing," Celia said in response to his glance at her wrist. "Just a nick. And no. I was not sick yesterday, Dr. Leyva. I need time off. To attend to a personal matter."

"Do you have a date in mind?" His voice was mild, but a subtle change in his grey eyes told Celia that it was not going to be an automatic yes.

"Now. Today. It is urgent." She looked down in an attempt to conceal her anxiety.

"Given the long hours everyone is already working, you must know how difficult it will be to accommodate your request on such short notice. With the current shortage of doctors—"

Celia's head snapped up. "Since when," she asked tersely, "does Cuba have a shortage of doctors?"

"Since thousands have left medicine to work in tourism."

Celia was aware that doctors from this very hospital had left to work as hotel managers, taxi drivers, even waiters. It simply had not occurred to her what the cumulative effect had been. "A real shortage?" she asked stupidly.

"Not by world standards. But by Cuban standards, yes. A huge number have switched to tourism."

"To earn dollars," she said bitterly.

Leyva gave a slight shrug. "It's not only individuals who want dollars. Cuba needs foreign exchange too. So it must be tolerated."

From the flatness in his voice, Celia realized that he was not expressing his opinion but repeating the reason he had been given for why doctors, trained by the government at no small expense, had been allowed to switch to a non-medical field.

Celia shifted in her seat, anxious to have this discussion over, get her leave approved, and be gone. "There are plenty of programs to train people for the hospitality industry. Half the young people—" A sudden flooding image of Liliana and her friends sprawled around the apartment discussing the advantages of going into tourism caused Celia's words to die in her throat. She could not continue.

"Yes, but it takes time. Most doctors are already multilingual; that is what made them so—" He paused, searching for the right word. "Desirable." He attempted a smile. "But the worst is over. The tourism schools are graduating a lot of young people now. A new law is about to go into effect, prohibiting doctors and teachers from wasting their training like that. By the end of the year, perhaps." He leaned back in his chair and looked at Celia in a way that she recognized as diagnostic. "The long hours are burning you out, is that it?"

She took a deep breath. "No." Please, she begged silently. Don't make me explain.

The white-haired man behind the desk, who appearance-wise could easily have played the role of family doctor in a television drama, fastened his unrelenting grey eyes on her. Of course he was going to make her explain.

"My niece, the one who lives with me. She has disappeared."

"Disappeared?" Leyva spoke the word as if it were not part of the Cuban vocabulary. In fact it was not—not in the context Celia was using it. The nearest thing to a child disappearing was an occasional Elían-type situation, where one parent bundled up their offspring and went abroad. Even then there were always family members who knew exactly where the child had gone and with whom. Children never disappeared into thin air, as Liliana seemed to have done.

"She did not go to school Monday, Tuesday, or today." Celia spoke rapidly. "She has not called. None of her friends' parents have called. She is not with relatives."

"Have you contacted social services?"

"No. I—I am going to take time off. To look for her. I know her better than they do and, well, they have other children to deal with, don't they? I have only her."

She did not mention, but he surely knew, the bureaucratic hassles that would be involved if the youth authorities were brought in. How counselling would be required for both of them once Liliana was located and, depending on what mischief she was into when they found her, she might very well be sent to a re-education camp. That last, the possibility of Liliana being removed from her care, Celia did not believe would be best for Liliana. Or bearable for her.

Leyva's eyes changed again. To what, a sadder grey? Could a colour be sad? Celia waited for his response, wondering if she looked as desperate as she felt. But he was no longer looking at her.

His eyes had strayed to a photo on the desk. Celia could not see the picture from where she sat but she had seen it before. It had been there when he first interviewed her. She had seen it again each time he had summoned her to inform her of a promotion—promotions that had been rapid because so many Cuban doctors had left to practise abroad. Or to go into tourism. The picture was not always in the same place or at the same angle, but changed, as if he often picked it up to study it. It was a snapshot of two teenaged girls, arm in arm, waving gaily to the person with the camera.

"A week?" he said. "And you will return to work sooner if it takes less time?"

"Of course," Celia said with quick relief.

"Is there anything we can do to help?"

"The switchboard. If Liliana calls I would want to know. Day or night."

"I shall speak to the head operator personally," Leyva said. "We will make sure all the operators are on the lookout for her call."

Celia stood up and reached across the desk to shake his hand. It was warm and had that quality that some hands have—more often the hands of lay people than medical professionals—of imparting comfort through touch. "Thank you, Doctor."

She was already at the door when he cleared his throat, indicating that he had something else to say. She turned and saw that whatever it was, it was not easy for him.

"Do you know . . . that is, did she ever speak of leaving Cuba?"

The question stunned Celia, but her answer came swift and sure. "No. Never."

TWENTY-NINE

JOE walked into the apartment to find Alma kneeling in front of the statue of the Virgin. She crossed herself, rose, and said brusquely, "Dinner's ready. Luis is working late. He said we should go ahead and eat without him."

"Good. I'm hungry. Smells delicious." Actually Joe was more tired than hungry. Had he been alone he would have skipped dinner. But it was a small deception that cheered his mother and cost him nothing. "I don't suppose Celia called?"

"She did, to thank us for the food. She still hasn't heard from Liliana."

Joe might have made nothing-to-worry-about noises, but given what he knew about the kid, he wasn't going to put on that much of an act. The meal passed in silence.

After dinner Joe said he was going for a walk. He never walked in Miami, not during the day because it was so bloody hot, and not at night because it was so bloody dangerous. But it seemed natural here, especially in this neighbourhood, with its old trees and half-uprooted sidewalks. He walked beyond the neighbourhood and a few blocks farther, to the Habana Libre Hotel. He checked the venue but nothing appealed to him. Then on to Hotel Nacional, but there was nothing of interest there either. He had an overpriced beer and left.

The problem wasn't the entertainment. He just wasn't in the right frame of mind. Not until he got back to his own street and had circled the block twice to avoid going into the house did he realize why he was so bothered by the sombre atmosphere. It used to be like that when his father was alive.

Alma, prior to retirement, had been an ambulance driver. One of her first emergency calls, when she was barely nineteen years old, was to El Encanto, a Habana department store blown up by terrorists. One of the wounded Alma scraped off the sidewalk that day was Lázaro Lago. Five days after hauling young Lázaro and other injured shoppers to the hospital, Alma was providing the same service to Bay of Pigs casualties. Months later, when Lázaro was released from hospital, he came to thank her. Although he had not recovered from his injuries and never would, he began courting her. Within the year they were married. They rarely talked about the occasion of their meeting, and when they did, the focus was on the romantic aspect, not the gory details. Lázaro Lago lived a dozen years longer. By then most had forgotten, if they ever knew, how his body got broken in the first place.

By contrast, everyone knew how the Cantú girls' father died. The entire nation was reminded, every October 6, how on that day in 1976 its national fencing team, plus coaches and other passengers, had been blown out of the sky by a terrorist's bomb, the tragic voice of the co-pilot as preserved on the flight recorder while the plane was plummeting toward the sea being replayed again and again. The story was particularly relevant to this neighbourhood because two of those passengers—Celia's father and their friend Joaquín's father—lived on the street.

Joe stared at the house that had triggered the memory, where Joaquín's family had once lived. Like the house in which he and Luis had grown up, it was an old mansion that had long since been divided into apartments. A bluish light in the living room window indicated that the family inside was watching television. It was the blue light that brought back the memory.

Joe had been about seventeen at the time. After hanging around with the Cantú girls all his life, mostly lusting after Carolina, who was two years older and only made jokes when he hit on her, he had just begun to notice her younger, shyer sister. That night he followed Celia over to Joaquín's house to watch a rerun of televised testimony by an ex-CIA operative, Philip Agee. Joe wasn't much interested, but it seemed a small price to pay for a little touchy-feely in the dark on the way home.

Joe assumed there would be something in the program about the bomb planted on the plane that killed the Cantú girls' father, and so there was. However, Agee's testimony also covered the department store explosion that had broken his own father. Agee claimed that what blew El Encanto to smithereens was dynamite that CIA operatives had stuffed into dolls in the store's stockroom. A few days later, when Joe had time to assimilate it, he realized that this was what made his mother and Kristina Cantú so tight. It wasn't just that they were widows, but that they had been widowed by similarly irrational (or purely evil) acts.

Standing there in the dark, looking up at a window that glowed with pale blue light, it occurred to Joe that Agee's testimony on television that night, which confirmed what Cuban security forces and some international tribunals had been saying all along, had been a defining moment for all of them. Naturally it hadn't seemed that at the time. After all, they were just a bunch of horny teenagers sprawled on a hardwood floor in front of the TV, munching plantain chips that Joaquín's mother had fried for them.

Joaquín had picked up a rapier and leapt about the room making lightning thrusts at empty air, punctuating each jab with "*Pendejo!*" and "Take that, *caca!*" He had inherited his father's quick reflexes and was already competing at a high level, but it was when he started using fencing to vent his anger at the subhumans who had killed his father that he vaulted onto the Cuban Olympic team. For a while he and Celia were obsessed with all that crap, using every scrap of news they could get their hands on to feed their anger. Lucky for Celia that she and Franci were so tight. Franci was always telling Celia to let it go and more than once got into it with Joaquín for bringing it up in every conversation.

Thinking of Franci, Joe smiled and absently scratched his crotch. He had had his eye on her too, but whenever he tried to put a move on her she brushed him off as if he was a gnat. That night he had been sitting on the floor next to Celia, with Franci sprawled on the other side of him. The program over, Franci leaned on her elbow and mused on the psychology of the criminals, wondering if there was any way to prevent people from developing into the type of perverts who had done the things Agee described in his testimony. Her Afro brushed Joe's arm, causing parts of his anatomy to tingle. Joe, wondering if he might make out better if he ditched Celia and walked Franci home, had surreptitiously slipped a hand up the back of her sweater.

Franci sat up, looked deep into his eyes, and said, "Please, José, try not to be a prick at a time like this."

Luis, the oldest in the group, had adopted a certain grim seriousness, causing him to look like a hardline Cuban patriot of the bureaucratic stripe, as their father had been and Luis would later become. He had just begun attending Communist Party meetings and might have mouthed some Marxist cliché about the inherent corruptness of capitalism. Or maybe he hadn't said anything. Luis often didn't. In that respect he was like a religious person who doesn't go in for proselytizing. He believed deeply and practised his beliefs but rarely talked about them.

As Luis brooded, Franci mused aloud, and Joaquín leapt about the room imaginarily skewering the men who had murdered his father, Celia and Carolina had sat holding hands, speaking in low voices. Then Carolina had said, to the room at large, "I shall join the army." And Celia said, "I would rather be a doctor."

As for himself, that very evening Joe made up his mind to get the hell out of Cuba by any means possible. Whatever his life turned out to be, he sure as hell didn't want it to be a permanent target for the guys with the biggest bombs.

THIRTY

CELIA reached Liliana's school just before noon. She stepped off the bus into sweltering heat and walked across a grassy expanse toward the administration building. A once-gracious country house, it had, like many others, been confiscated when its owner left Cuba. Two-storey additions, constructed later, winged out on either side. The wings compromised the architectural integrity of the original Spanish-style hacienda but made it more functional as a school. Verandas ran the length of each wing. Classrooms were on the ground level. Dorm rooms were on the second floor, boys in one wing, girls in the other.

A pretty chestnut filly with a white blaze down her face grazed on the lawn, reminding Celia of the horses that had kept the grass down at the cancer hospice where her mother spent the last months of her life. As Celia approached the horse, it threw up its head and eyed her with an ears-forward alertness that suggested it might welcome a startling move as an excuse to go galloping across the grass. Celia reached out to touch the velvet muzzle. The filly quivered its upper lip against her palm and, finding it empty, went back to grazing.

Celia entered the director's office just as Compañera Campos was preparing to go out. A grimace of displeasure at having her departure delayed was quickly replaced by an insincere, "How nice to see you, Dr. Cantú. How can we help you?"

However, to make it clear that she was leaving, the director strode from her office into the reception room clutching a large plastic handbag. Celia knew that it was lunchtime, and got right to the point.

"As you know, Compañera Campos, my niece, Liliana, has been absent this week. I understand that she has missed other days as well."

"Well, yes. Her asthma . . . ?" Campos left Celia to finish the statement.

Celia hoped that the shock she felt was not reflected on her face. Liliana did not have asthma. She *had* suffered from it as a small child, when she was living in a household where mother, father, grandmother, and most of their friends smoked more or less continuously. The asthma was one reason why, after Liliana's parents and her own mother died, Celia decided to move to the beach. She thought living in a smoke-free apartment cooled by a fresh offshore breeze might help. And it did. Liliana had not shown symptoms of asthma in at least six years.

It took Celia only a second to realize that Liliana knew how to fake an asthma attack and must occasionally have used it as an excuse to explain short absences.

"I want to go over her attendance record," Celia said. "I would like a copy of every month back to September."

The director's face took on an offended look, as if Celia had asked her to give up her lunch hour to run the copy machine herself. Celia ignored it and launched into the little speech she had prepared on the bus ride out. "Liliana has been missing from home for three days. I need to talk to her friends. Of course I know the ones in our neighbourhood but there are others I have not met. So I would like a list of students in her class, as well as the addresses of any older and younger friends."

This second request seemed to cheer the school director enormously. Celia guessed that it pleased Campos because it was one she could legitimately refuse.

"I'm so sorry, Dr. Cantú. Sorry to hear about Liliana and sorry we can't provide you with the names and addresses of other students. Such information can be released only to family members. And to the authorities, of course. I'm sure, as a doctor, you understand that."

Campos held the hard plastic pocketbook against her ample belly like a shield, giving Celia the impression that in any moment she would withdraw a dagger from behind it and thrust. Which, in a manner of speaking, she did.

"Now, if you were to send out a social worker, Dr. Cantú, or Liliana's doctor—"

"I *am* her doctor," Celia snapped. "And social workers are aware of the situation. I prefer to deal with it myself."

Even as she said it, she saw it was no use. Campos leaned toward her, attempting to intimidate Celia with her bulk as Celia had often seen her intimidate the secretary. "I assure you, we are ready do everything possible to assist you. But without a formal request from the proper authorities, our hands are tied. Completely tied." She beamed at Celia. "I'm sorry to run off, but unfortunately," she glanced at her watch, which showed five minutes past twelve, "I have another appointment. If you had called first, perhaps—"

"Then I will just take copies of Liliana's attendance records." Celia folded her arms and fixed the larger woman with a gaze that she had perfected specifically to gain the compliance of recalcitrant patients. "But I would not want to keep you, Compañera Campos. Surely your secretary will not mind staying five minutes to run them off."

The director's bosom heaved with the burden of having to settle for half a victory. After a moment of obstinate silence, she turned on Emily.

"Emily!" she snapped in a voice that stabbed the secretary with her own name. "Copy the attendance records of Dr. Cantú's niece."

Emily bounded to the filing cabinet. By the time the director's heavy footsteps had faded down the hall, she had the copy machine humming.

While Emily made copies, Celia stood at the window. Children were flowing out of classrooms and clattering along the verandas. Most headed for the dining hall but a few spilled into the yard. Celia could not have described the pain caused by their joyous kinetic energy. Like the little filly, they seemed to be looking for an excuse to go bucking across the lawn, manes flying. Why was her Liliana not among them?

Emily left the copy machine to refile the originals, fumbling them nervously. "Liliana is not like most girls her age," she confided.

"In what way?" Celia felt her throat constrict with panic at what she might hear.

"She isn't cliquish. She treats everyone the same. That's why she's so popular."

The panic melted into relief, not because Emily's observation was complimentary but because it validated Celia's own judgment. She took the copies Emily thrust at her and automatically flipped through them to be sure they were all there: September, October, November, December, January. She stopped. The next page was not February; it was a list of student names and addresses. She thumbed through several others and saw that this was what she had requested. Quickly she stuffed the papers into her handbag. "Muchas gracias, compañera!"

"I marked a couple of them," Emily whispered.

"Special friends?" Celia asked.

"Mm, I'm not sure. Like I said, Liliana doesn't play favourites. But there is this one boy . . . and Magdalena."

Liliana had mentioned Magdalena but Celia had never met her; as far as she knew, she was just one of the girls in their twenty-bed dorm. "Why Magdalena?"

"Well, you know what she is like."

"Actually, no. Liliana's friends often drop by but I'm usually at work. I don't recall having met this Magdalena. What *is* she like?"

Emily pursed her lips. Celia sensed that she was looking for a way to describe the girl that would not seem unsympathetic. "She is one of those who deliberately excludes herself. Then gets lonely and looks around for someone who won't tease her for being different."

"Is she?" Celia asked. "Different, I mean?"

Emily gave a small laugh. "She tries to be. Mostly she's just difficult."

"You seem to know the students well."

Emily took it for the compliment it was meant to be. "Well, I do live here on the grounds. And I enjoy them. We are not exactly friends—I'm sure none of them think of me that way." She gave a self-depreciating laugh. "Or think of me at all, for that matter. But I love watching them. They are so lively and full of self-assurance."

"That's what I like about working with children too," Celia smiled. "And if I say so myself, Cuba does have good children. Not perfect or perfectly healthy, but I cannot imagine children have it much better anywhere. They are truly treasured, and they know it."

"I agree." Emily nodded. "But different children do different things with their energies. Magdalena, for example. She will go to any lengths to be seen as a rebel."

"Is she from a broken home?" Celia asked, unconsciously falling prey to the stereotypical notion that difficult children are more often from one-parent families.

"Heavens no!" Emily exclaimed. "She has two parents, two sets of grandparents, and two older siblings. All in the tourist industry."

"All?" Celia repeated in surprise.

"The brother and sister are still in training, but that's where they're headed. Her father is a rental car agent and her mother works in a boutique. I don't recall what the grandmothers do, food preparation, I think. One grandfather is a musician. The other one sells cigars. Magdalena goes on and on about the money they make and can't wait to finish school and get her share." Emily shook her head dubiously. "But she is not the kind of girl they hire for those jobs."

"What do you mean?" Celia asked.

"She is not the helpful type. More the look-at-me type."

Celia guessed she knew what Emily meant, but could not imagine such a person as one of Liliana's friends. "Why do you feel that I particularly should talk to her?"

The secretary lowered her voice, "They have been absent on some of the same days. Including last Friday. Magdalena returned on Monday, but when Liliana didn't come to school this week, she presented a note from her mother saying she would need to miss school the rest of the week due to a family emergency." Emily dropped her voice still lower. "Of course it's a forgery, but frankly, she is so disruptive that the director prefers it when she's not here. Then her behaviour is not our problem."

As she spoke, Emily glanced down at Celia's watch.

"Forgive me!" Celia exclaimed. "I am taking up your lunch hour."

"Oh, that doesn't matter," Emily assured her quickly. "But I expect you'll want to catch the one o'clock bus. There isn't another till five."

"I would like to get back," Celia acknowledged. "But I was hoping to talk to the nurse, to ask her about this asthma business. I don't recall receiving any reports."

Emily shook her head. "One of her own children is sick, so she didn't come to work today. I can give you the details." She hesitated and backtracked. "But that wouldn't be very professional, would it?"

"I would be grateful if you did," Celia encouraged. "It would save me a trip."

"Well, it's not certain. That is, there was one occasion when Liliana seemed to have an attack and was allowed to go home. But the second time, the nurse thought, well, she thought it was not as serious as Liliana made it out to be. So she didn't let her go, and the next day Liliana seemed fine. Then last Friday—" She stopped. "Is that the day she disappeared?"

"No," Celia said. "She was at home most of the weekend."

"Well, this past Friday Liliana did not go to the nurse, maybe because she had been turned down before. She left a note that said she had gone home because she felt an attack coming on."

Celia frowned. "I am surprised the nurse didn't call me."

"Well, you are a doctor." Emily looked at Celia as if that explained everything. When she saw that it did not, she clarified. "We have had notes from you in the past, excusing Liliana's absences on account of her asthma. The nurse probably didn't want to appear to be calling your medical opinion into question."

Celia suddenly felt unbearably tired. She knew she should ask to see the notes, but why put herself through that? They were forgeries, and their very existence revealed yet another side to Liliana that she would have to look at squarely. But later. Alone.

"Magdalena's address is here?" She touched her shoulder bag. "And the boy's?"

"Danilo Silva. Such a gorgeous boy!" Emily fingers flew to her mouth and she flushed, as if she had uttered something sexually explicit.

"They are at that age, aren't they?" Celia said, to ease her embarrassment.

"Um, yes." Emily seemed to recover herself. "Please don't think I go around eavesdropping on the students, but my room is at the end. They often stand out back, just under my window, for privacy, you know. They probably forget I'm there."

"I doubt that," Celia smiled. "My guess is that they appreciate your sensitivity. And trust your discretion." She paused and added, "Just as I do."

"Thank you," Emily whispered.

"Thank *you*," Celia put her arms around Emily's thin shoulders, feeling, as she did so, how needy the woman was for physical contact. But Celia's mind was on the boy, whether, if she tried to locate him here at school, she might be thwarted by the director.

Emily must have guessed as much because she pulled away and said, "Danilo goes with our best athletes to work out at the Estadio Panamericano. That will be tomorrow, around four in the afternoon." She paused and said uncertainly, "He did ask Liliana to meet him there."

Celia's heard leapt with possibility. "They're meeting? Are you sure?"

"Um, no. It's just something they were talking about before the last break. I don't know what they decided."

THIRTY-ONE

LUIS drove down Avenida 5 toward the Convention Centre in something of a daze. He knew he was not a particularly flexible person. But a major career change on top of Liliana's disappearance, Celia's walkout, his mother's all-night crying jags, and José being in town, no wonder he had been caught off-guard. He had sat in the meetings, understood what the discussions were about, and correctly identified which actions had got approval from higher up. Or so he thought until the minute a broad smile was directed at him, along with the words, "You, Compañero Lago, are our man!"

The smiler was his own boss three levels removed—minister of the department of energy. The man was not a veteran of the Revolution and dared not imply that he was by wearing a beard. He compensated with a Pancho Villa–style moustache that gave him an eerie likeness to the Mexican bandit. Despite the minister's moustachioed pretensions, Luis liked the guy and felt respected by him. Nevertheless the whole thing caught him unawares. For a good fifteen minutes he could not figure out what was coming down.

The conference had offered plenty of clues in the form of remarks that were essentially self-evident truths, with lots of nodding all around. Luis's professional life had been spent in such meetings so he knew this meant that a decision had been made, probably at a level higher than anyone there. Waiting for what that decision might be, he listened to the head of the energy department state the obvious.

"Meeting Cuba's energy needs is largely a waiting game; waiting to see whether the US succeeds in preventing Venezuela from selling us oil, and waiting to see if Canada will continue investing in oil exploration. But while we wait there is more we can do."

Then his immediate supervisor, a bifocaled engineer, chimed in with what Luis later realized was meant to reassure him that the new position was not a demotion. "Food self-sufficiency is as important to national security as energy. It was fine to focus on export crops as long as we had markets and could get the food we needed from abroad. That has changed. National security now lies in self-sufficiency. That means we must produce the food Cuba needs without infusions of pesticides, herbicides, and chemical fertilizers from abroad. And most of all, without infusions of energy from abroad."

Luis had nodded along with the others and continued to nod when the thread was picked up by Alba Renan, head of the organic agriculture program, whose presence in the meeting had struck him as peculiar from the start.

"The road to sustainable agriculture is now paved," she stated with pride. "Cuba is on it and moving fast. No nation in the world has a program as comprehensive as ours. But while we focus on cloning, bio-pest control research, organic soil enhancement, and small farmers whose production is continuing to break records, we also have to keep our eye on costs, especially energy costs. If we can produce more food and use less energy simultaneously, the benefits to Cuba will be incalculable."

The meeting had continued in that vein for an hour. Everybody's polite agreement with whatever anyone else said was proof that after months of sometimes heated discussions, the moment for an agreed-upon action had come. Then the shoe dropped. The minister announced that he, Luis Lago, was to become the liaison between what, next to tourism and the military, were Cuba's most important ministries: energy and agriculture.

When Luis protested out that he had no background in agriculture, he was quickly informed that agricultural output would not be his responsibility. "See here, Compañero Lago, it's the broader view we want to develop," explained the minister as he twirled one tip of his moustache to a fine point. "To see energy not merely as something we must get access to internationally but as something we can create right here in Cuba. Solar, wind, methane gas, animal traction. Well, animal traction is already pretty far along; probably not much new you can add there." He glanced toward Alba Renan by way of acknowledging her expertise in the area.

Luis turned to her too, as it had just become apparent to him that she was the person in agriculture with whom he would be working most directly. However, his own boss spoke, giving Luis his first clue as to what the new job would entail.

"There will be experts on both sides providing input. What we need is someone to liase with the farmers and the sustainable energy experts and make recommendations to Compañera Renan and myself. That's where you come in, Luis."

Luis still didn't get it. Why wouldn't the experts make recommendations directly up the chain of command, and those responsible select the projects to receive funding? He looked to Renan, who nodded vigorously, causing her straight grey hair, cut to ear length, to swing back and forth.

"That is exactly what we need, Compañero Lago. Liaison with both sides, followed by recommendations to ensure maximum efficiency."

At last Luis understood. Efficiency was not exactly what they were looking for. When a high-level policy decision was taken, cost was rarely the main concern. *Efficiency* was a buzzword for honesty. Luis knew that if he had a reputation for anything, it was for incorruptibility. That was why he had continued to advance in the bureaucracy even after his flaky brother defected to Florida. For the government, the problem was that every farmer and engineer working with alternative energy sources would be trying to gain funding for his or her particular project. What the people at the top wanted was somebody they could trust, who could talk to both sides, or rather listen to both sides, and make recommendations as to where the government's limited resources should be put for maximum results.

Well, maybe they were right, Luis thought as he pulled into the Convention Centre's underground parking structure. He had been sent to attend the international conference on sustainable agriculture not so much because they thought the conference would bring him up to speed on the subject but because it was the best place to begin networking in a segment of the population with whom he would soon be working, and within which he had few contacts. For a few minutes he sat there, still trying to come to terms with the change. He did so, finally, the way he always did: by accepting the direction of his superiors. After all, who was he to question their judgment? Back when he played baseball, hadn't he taken whatever position the coach asked? And hadn't he done equally well at all of them? It was with good reason, he thought with a touch of nostalgic pride, that the coach occasionally called him the team's "secret weapon"—a player they could put in anywhere on a minute's notice and the team would be stronger for it.

A smile flickered and faded from Luis's face. That was then and this was now. He would go home and tell the family that he had been made the liaison between the energy department and agriculture, and his brother would make a joke of it. Alma respected his competence and under normal circumstances would be quick to point out what an asset to the nation he would be in his new position, but these were not normal circumstances. He doubted she could stop sobbing about Liliana's disappearance and his break-up with Celia long enough to register the change. And there was Celia, whom he should have been able to count on above everyone else to say something warm and wise—Celia, who was not there for him now and might never be again.

Luis reached for a large manila envelope on the seat beside him. Hotel Palco was adjacent to the Conference Centre. He would make copies there before heading over to sit in on one of the discussion groups Compañera Alba had marked in the schedule. Later he would drop the copies off at Celia's apartment. Maybe when she saw what he had done she would understand that he cared and could help; that he had something she needed after all. Maybe she would talk to him.

THIRTY-TWO

JOE had discovered Hotel Palco on a drive out to the western suburb of Cubanacán. If he needed concrete evidence that the Cuban government was doing its utmost to make itself attractive to foreign business, Hotel Palco and the adjacent Convention Centre were proof positive. From the minute Joe walked through a glass door and took in the hotel's quietly elegant, no-frills corporate atmosphere, he knew that for the rest of his stay in Habana, the Palco would be his home-away-from-home office. The business centre was quiet, its computers fast. He finished exchanging emails with his Miami office in record time and headed across the lobby to the long-distance office to get a pretty young thing (whose legs he had already checked out) to place a call for him.

He had just reached the bank of elevators when, unbelievably, he saw his brother, Luis, coming toward him. Luis saw him at the same time and stopped dead in his tracks.

"José! What are you doing here?" Luis demanded, as if the sight of Joe disoriented him and caused him to think he was not where he thought he was.

"Using the business centre. What about you?"

"Same thing," Luis said quickly. "Actually, attending a conference. I need to run off a few copies."

"How about lunch? You eaten yet?"

"Well, no, but—"

"Good. I have to make just one phone call. Make your copies and let's meet at the bar. Or the dining room if you'd rather."

"Uh, no." Luis still seemed confused, as if there was too much coming at him at once and he didn't know whether to face it head on or dive for cover. "The bar is fine."

"Sandwich and a beer? Might be just what you need to get you through—did you say a conference?"

"That's right."

"Meet you there in ten minutes."

Ten minutes later Luis was not at the bar but still standing where Joe had left him, staring at a multicoloured parrot in the atrium that kept squawking, "*Aye, Mamacita!*"

Together they walked to the other end of the lobby and took seats at the near-empty bar. Luis waited till Joe ordered a ham-and-cheese sandwich and a beer, then said, "The same."

"What's the conference about?" Joe asked.

"Sustainable agriculture."

"Agriculture?" Joe wasn't sure he'd heard right. "How does that tie into energy?"

During the next thirty minutes he learned more about his brother's professional life than he had ever known or cared to know. Joe recalled their mother mentioning something about Luis holding an important government post, and Liliana had made a remark to that effect too, but he had not taken either seriously. When Luis finished explaining his new role, Joe gave him a congratulatory grin. "Sounds like a promotion."

Luis shrugged. "Maybe, maybe not. You know how it is in Cuba."

"In what sense?"

"Everybody earns about the same, so position is not that important. The real question is whether I have the skills to do what's expected of me. Otherwise I would let the country and my comrades down."

"I guess." Joe washed down the last of his sandwich with a swallow of cold Cristal and decided this was a time to bring Luis up to date on his own plans.

"I'm heading back day after tomorrow," he said.

"To Miami?" Luis's half-eaten sandwich paused in mid-air.

"México first. I've done about all I can do here without getting some critical links nailed down there. But it's been a good visit. I didn't expect to get as much done as I did. Business-wise, things still move like molasses over here." He grinned. "But that's better than no movement."

"Are you—does that mean you will be coming back?"

"Definitely," Joe assured him and then wondered, from the way the oomph seemed to go out of Luis, if that was what he wanted to hear. If it wasn't, well, too damned bad. Joe took another swallow of beer. "I expect to be doing a lot of back and forth. For the good of the pater-land as well as for the good of ye old Miami Joe."

"Oh yeah?" Luis gave him a cynical smile and slid off the bar stool. "I have to go. Is this your treat?" He waved at the empty sandwich plate.

"You bet. Not every day I get to hobnob with one of Cuba's governing elite."

As Luis walked away, it occurred to Joe that while "governing elite" might be an exaggeration, having a close relative well placed in the federal bureaucracy could be an asset once he was actually doing business in Cuba. Only belatedly, after Luis had disappeared down the long hallway leading to the conference centre, did it cross Joe's mind that Luis might have government contacts that could help Celia locate Liliana.

THIRTY-THREE

CELIA arrived home in late afternoon, feeling weak and exhausted. Little wonder, since she had again forgotten to eat. She heated Alma's rice and beans, ate a few bites, and headed for the shower. She stayed under the spray a long time, letting it wash away neck and shoulder tensions. She came from the bathroom nude, drying her hair. Then stopped short. She had the uneasy feeling that someone had been there. She glanced at the door, which she was sure she had locked.

It was locked, and someone had been there. A large manila envelope lay just inside, too fat to have been slid under the door. She carried it into her bedroom, closing the door behind her as if a second door, without a lock, could make her more secure.

She sat down on the bed, tumbled from nights of restless non-sleep, and pulled a sheaf of papers out of the envelope. Her heart caught in her throat when she saw that they were announcements, each with two pictures: one a close-up of Liliana's face, the other of her vamping on the beach in a new swimsuit the family had given her for her sixteenth birthday. At the top was the caption, LILIANA IS MISSING. And below, "If you see her please call . . ." Three numbers were listed: Celia's, Alma's, and Luis's office.

Clipped to the packet of pictures was a note. It read, "Dearest Celia, I have kept some to distribute in Varadero this weekend. Someone is sure to have seen her and will know where she is staying. Love, Luis."

She refolded the note and slipped it back inside the envelope. As she did so, she saw that there were other things inside. She dumped them out. A roll of tape and a key.

She recognized the key at once. It was the one to her apartment that she had given Luis a year ago. He must have sensed her reluctance—perhaps because he'd had to ask three times before she stopped making excuses and gave it to him. Maybe that was also why, as far as she knew, he had used it only twice. He used it the day he brought social workers to talk to Liliana. He had entered the apartment and called Celia at work to let her know the girl was not there. And today. When Celia had not come to the door in response to his quiet knock (because she was in the shower and had not heard it), he must have opened the door to put the packet inside.

Celia held the key in the palm of her hand, all at once knowing things that only added new aches to her heart: what a good, decent man Luis was, that she never should have given him a key to her apartment in the first place, and that she would not likely give it to him, or to any man, ever again.

She fell asleep on the rumpled bed. She woke sometime after dark and for a long time could not get back to sleep. Her anguish lay in the fact that Liliana had not called—not the apartment, not the hospital, not the school, not Alma. The longer she went without calling, the more it suggested that she might be involved in something that she was certain Celia would not tolerate.

Celia had already forced herself to accept what that might be and knew very well what the risks were and were not. If she was with a man she would almost certainly be at a hotel or in a private home licensed by the government to rent rooms, so there would be others nearby if she felt threatened. Unless she contracted HIV, sex with a stranger wasn't going to kill her. But such thoughts did little to ease Celia's mind. She knew from her own medical practice that when children violated the norms of society, they often judged themselves much more harshly than the adults around them. A sense of self-respect could take a very long time to rebuild. And what of Liliana's lack of trust in her? How could she, Celia, regain it when she didn't even understand how it came to be lost?

THIRTY-FOUR

JOE hung about the apartment waiting for Luis to leave for work and various neighbours who popped in to pop out again so he could speak to his mother alone. She was alone now, her back to him, washing dishes. She held a single plate, washing it over and over with an automatic motion as she gazed out the back window into a patio animated by flapping laundry. He did not have to see her face to know that she was thinking about Liliana and that her eyes were probably filled with tears.

"Listen, Mamá. I need to talk to you."

"Talk. I'm listening."

Joe lifted the overwashed plate from her hands and put an arm around her shoulders. "Let the dishes go for now. Come, this is serious. I need some help."

Alma dried her hands and replaced the ratty dishtowel on a cheap metal rack, then let him guide her into the living room. He pushed her into a wooden rocker and pulled up the other one to face her.

"I've got good news and bad news," he said, wiggling his eyebrows in a way that usually made her smile. She did not smile, just sat there, large dark eyes moist and sad.

"The good news is that I'm leaving."

Alma's eyes widened, stricken. Before she could speak, Joe hurried on, "The bad news is, I'm coming back. And the really bad news is, I'm probably going to go back and forth from now on." He caught one of Alma's tiny hands, still damp from the dishwater, and squeezed it. "Think you can handle that?"

Her eyes overflowed. "How can you leave with Liliana still missing?"

Joe shrugged impatiently. "Look, she'll come back when she's good and ready. The one I'm worried about is Celia, who doesn't want our help—obviously, since she blames Luis and me—and doesn't want to call in the authorities, why I don't know."

"Because they could, well, they might . . . send Liliana away," Alma choked.

"Right. So she'll try to find her on her own. I've thought of something that might help. That's what I want to talk to you about. I'm going to buy a car. Today."

Alma gave him a bewildered look. "A car? You can't buy a car just like that."

"Of course I can! I know I can't take it out of the country, but they sell old cars in the street; I've seen them all over. And that's what I want—not an import like Luis's Fiat, and certainly not a piece of junk like that Daewoo I've been driving. I'm going to buy one of the old classics, if I can find one in decent mechanical condition."

Alma began to rock in an agitated way. "How is that going to help?"

"Well, for starters, I won't have to pay an arm and a leg to rent a car every time I come back." Belatedly, Joe realized that he had given his personal financial reason first, before explaining how it might help Celia. To cover his blunder he spoke optimistically, with more assurance than he felt. "But the main reason is that when I fly out tomorrow I plan to leave the car with Celia. She can use it to find Liliana."

Alma nodded, then suddenly tipped forward so that her forehead struck hard against his chest, and sobbed and sobbed. Joe sat still, except for a hand patting her back, until she quieted. Then his mother did as he himself would have done. She marched to the bathroom, washed her face, and came back with her purse, ready to go.

They spent all day wandering up and down the street where cash-strapped car owners displayed antique vehicles that they could not sell for anything close to actual market value. Private owners were not allowed to export their treasures. If he, Joe, had wanted to take one of these cars out of the country it would have been a complicated rigmarole whereby its owner first sold it to the Cuban government for pesos. The government would in turn sell it to him, for dollars, at its actual market value, hundreds of times more than what the original owner had received. Car owners could sell their vehicles within the country but few Cubans had the tens of thousands of dollars a well-maintained pre-1960 classic was worth. However, by selling on the street an owner might get, if not what the car would have fetched on the international market, at least some part of the purchase price in US dollars.

Price didn't matter to Joe. The main thing was something reliable, which was asking a lot from a half-century-old vehicle whose owner wouldn't have been able to dump the kind of money into restoration that antique car buffs did in the States. Still, some of the old cars had been babied in the extreme. Growing up, Joe had known families who knocked out one wall of the house in order to park their precious car in what had been a bedroom.

Joe's mechanical knowledge was limited but not entirely absent. One of the many low-paying jobs he had been forced to take when he first arrived in Miami was in a garage. He hadn't stayed long enough to develop into what the boss wanted: namely, a good mechanic with such limited English that he'd be stuck working there forever at slave wages. As soon as he got the rougher edges smoothed off his English, Joe cleaned the black grease from under his fingernails and vowed never to take any job that turned them that colour again.

Only now, sticking his head under first one ancient hood then another, and being able to identify recently replaced parts from near-dead ones, was he glad for his brief apprenticeship in auto mechanics. Alma stood at his elbow while he checked the engine and kicked the tires. There was no need for her to be there, of course, but he figured it was something to take her mind off problems that she couldn't do anything about. Each car he examined, he'd ask her, "Is it comfortable? Do you think it has been taken care of?" Then, drawing her aside, out of earshot of the seller, he'd ask, "Think we can trust this guy?" As if he couldn't make such a judgment on his own.

A 1959 Chevrolet convertible, canary yellow, particularly took his eye. Alma expressed doubts about a convertible; too easy for thieves to break into, she opined. But after test-driving it and making sure the top went up and down smoothly, Joe bought the classy old boat.

"You drive it home," he told Alma. "I'll follow in the Daewoo."

She protested but he could tell she was pleased. She had always been an excellent driver, rare in a country where not many women did drive. Joe knew that his trusting her with the car was an affirmation of her competence. Under the circumstances, it was the most he could offer by way of consolation.

THIRTY-FIVE

CELIA was out at first light, cycling the small blacktop road that ran east along the coast. There was no traffic as she followed the waterfront past the Pan American stadium and into Cojímar. She rode through the old fishing village without a glance at the bronze bust of Ernest Hemingway; an artifact cast decades earlier from boat fittings donated by all the fishermen who docked in the bay where the writer berthed his boat during the few years he lived in Cuba. Just past Las Terrazas, a bar where Hemingway was alleged to have spent as much time as on his boat, the street pitched steeply upward.

Celia pedalled hard for several blocks and arrived at the top of the hill panting. She stopped to catch her breath. As her heartbeat slowed, so, too, did her sense of the moment. She turned her head slowly to the left and saw the house, a flat-roofed bungalow perched on a corner lot with a lawn that sloped down to the street. How could she have a memory of that house? How could she not? The sense of wretchedness that swept over her, wasn't it reminder enough?

Air thick with smoke from cigarettes and cigars, everyone's nerves jangled from too many cups of coffee, not a hopeful meeting like others they'd had here in the first years after La Revolución, but one of excuses, dissention, denial. Fidel insisting that conditions in the prison could not be so bad; Raúl and Vilma showing no sympathy for the counter-revolutionaries assumed to be confined there; Che merely shrugging when she pointed out that not all the inmates had been convicted of anti-revolutionary activities; indeed, some were merely non-conformists, homosexuals, and the like. Hours she had argued the necessity of closing the umpa detention centres, until at last she had flung testimonials of abuse on the table in front of them all and demanded to know how something like this could be anything other than a betrayal of revolutionary ideals. Only then, when her own capacity to reason had dissolved in rage, did Fidel agree that the camps would be closed. Exhausted and depressed, they fell onto the bed in their clothes, Fidel still feeling so embattled that he would not even remove his boots. He slept but she had not, tormented as she was by images of the shameful incidents recounted in those letters. How she longed for the cottage in Playa Jibacoa where the surf might have lulled her to sleep, rather than this city street with the sound of traffic grinding up the hill. Was that why they never came to this house again?

A car horn startled Celia. She started pedalling again, leaving behind Cojímar, the house, and memories that were not her own.

She cycled through Alamar, said to be the largest public housing development in the world. There were clusters of people at the bus stops and children heading to school, some on foot, some perched on the crossbar or back rack of a parent's bike. Then she left the high-density Alamar complex, with hip-hop music competing from open apartment windows even at that early hour, and entered the quieter ambience of Tarará.

Of the Playas del Este communities she knew Tarará best. She had worked briefly at a hospital devoted entirely to child victims of Chernobyl. Children rotated through to have their permanently damaged health partially restored by eye operations, skin grafts, treatment for their many cancers, therapies enhanced by sunny hours lolling on the sand and playing in gentle surf. The hospital was directly on the beach, so even children too unwell to go out had the soothing sound and visual effects of the water. Celia had learned a great deal while working there but it had been heartbreaking too, some days filling her with a sadness that she knew was not an emotion she should be carrying home to recently orphaned Liliana. Thus she had been relieved when she finished her residency and received a permanent assignment to the hospital in Habana del Este.

The next beach community, Santa María, was where the touristy part of Playas de Este began. With stops to leave a notice about Liliana at every beachfront hotel, it took most of the morning to reach Guanabo, the last little town in the strip. There she turned around and began working her way back along the other side of the street. A little after one, tired and hungry, she pushed her bike across a footbridge to a tiny island called Mi Cayito, which floated in Laguna Itabo.

She ordered a sandwich and went to the restroom to wash up. When she came out, some young men were pushing together several tables for their group. Celia listened discretely to their conversation, from which she deduced that some were Cuban, some foreign, and all gay. By the time she finished lunch they were on a second round of drinks. Screwing up her courage, she approached the table. "Excuse me," she said softly, holding a notice out to the man nearest her. "Have you seen this girl in the past week?"

The man peered at the pictures. "Darling, lots of cuties like this hang out on the Playas del Este, but this one—" He shook his head and passed it to the man next to him.

The second man, a Cuban with black hair close-cropped in the back and tumbling like a pony's forelock in front, barely glanced at the pictures of Liliana before passing the notice on with a snicker. "Sorry. Not my type."

As if to compensate for their companion's insensitivity, the others studied the pictures closely. Each in turn shook his head. The last man at the table, a golden-skinned hunk with the easy confidence of those born beautiful, squeezed Celia's hand as he passed the flyer back to her. "Don't fret, Mamacita. Your little Barbie will find her way home. With or without a Ken doll."

Celia murmured thanks and headed for the cashier. Leaving a notice there, she biked back to Cojímar and the Estadio Pan Americano.

In front of the stadium, metal sculptures depicting athletes engaged in boxing, volleyball, and other sports at which Cuba excelled were arranged around a fountain. Celia had intended to wait there, but the fountain was dry and the sun very hot, so she moved to the other side of the stadium where she could wait in the shade of a red-blossomed flame tree.

The stadium was barely a kilometre from her apartment, but she had only been inside twice. The first time was soon after its construction for the 1991 Pan American games, when José had wangled a job as an usher during one of the track events and sneaked her in. Five years later, Joaquín had invited her and Liliana there to watch a fencing match. Between major events it was used to train promising Cuban athletes.

It was late afternoon, the hottest part of the day, but pleasant in the shade. There were acres of open space between the stadium and the ocean. Here, as across the street from her apartment, the land along the waterfront was covered in low natural vegetation that gave an unobstructed view of the sea. The breeze was kicking up whitecaps but traffic on the Vía Monumental drowned out the sounds of the surf. She wondered if she was too late; if the bus had passed by already. Even as she wondered, she looked up to see it grinding to a stop to let off a dozen boys and girls.

Their fitness was apparent even from a distance. Instead of walking, they jogged toward the stadium. Several recognized Celia and called out, "Hola, Doctora Cantú."

"Buenas tardes," Celia responded. "Have any of you seen Liliana this week?"

Their blank looks gave her the reply she did not want, even before they opened their mouths in a babble of answers in the negative, followed by questions.

"She has gone missing," Celia said brusquely. "Please call me if you hear from her. Oh, and which of you is Danilo?"

Several hands lifted to point toward three boys who had peeled off the main group, headed toward the underpass beneath the Vía Monumental.

"Doesn't he work out here at the stadium?"

"Sometimes," said one boy, hopping around throwing punches at an imaginary opponent as he spoke. "But he's a cyclist. The team meets at the Velódromo."

"Gracias." Celia swung onto her bike, waved to the group, and pedalled off to catch the boys before they reached the underpass.

As she rode up behind them she called out, "Danilo?"

They all turned and stopped as she stopped. By the way two of them looked at the third boy, she knew he was Danilo. She probably would have picked him out anyway. He was slightly built, the dark blue slacks of his school uniform concealing what must have been well-muscled legs. But it was his face that told Celia why Emily had used the word *gorgeous* to describe this particular boy. His eyes were a penetrating green, framed by the longest, blackest lashes Celia had ever seen on a boy.

She put out her hand. "Buenas tardes. I am Celia Cantú. Liliana's aunt."

"Encantado," he said shyly and shook her hand with a grip as solid as if he were squeezing the handlebars of a bike. "How is she?"

"I don't know," Celia said.

Behind him, the other boys exchanged a glance. One said, "Catch you at the gym, Danilo." They nodded politely to Celia and were gone. Danilo stared at her.

"What do you mean? Is she in hospital or something?"

"She has gone missing," Celia said.

"Missing?" He responded to the word with a dubious look.

"I thought you might have seen her. That you might be meeting her here."

"Oh." Danilo looked down, embarrassed. "I guess she told you I asked her to. I thought she might, not today but when school lets out. She invited me—well, sort of invited me—to come to dinner at your place." He glanced up quickly. "If it was okay with you. She said she'd ask. But then she didn't come to school this week. I figured she was sick, and, well, it wasn't definite anyway. Just an idea."

Celia said nothing, knowing that in silence people often reveal more than they intended, sometimes more than they thought they knew. All Danilo revealed was that he knew even less than she did. "How did she go missing?"

"I don't exactly know. She got caught skipping school on Friday. She thought she was going to be punished and ran off. I think it was unplanned."

The boy looked straight into her eyes, his own filled with the questions that she had hoped he might answer.

"If you were going to look for her," Celia asked, "where would you begin?"

"A friend's place?" Even as he spoke, he shook his head. "But not all week. And you'd know if she was with relatives, right?"

"I would," Celia affirmed. "That is why I am asking around. To find out if she has other friends I have not met."

"I wouldn't know," he said in a tone that suggested he was beginning to feel grilled. He added, almost defiantly, "She never mentioned any other guys."

"I don't think there are any," Celia smiled. "She likes being in a crowd. You know, typical only child, she wishes she had ten brothers and sisters. Or at least some cousins."

"Yeah. That's what she said." He half-turned from her, his body language begging to be released so he could catch up to his friends.

"You had better go," she obliged him. "Gracias, Danilo."

He nodded and spun away from her, only to rotate back to face her. "Is there anything you want me to do?"

"If you hear from her, call me. Or ask her to call. Tell her she is not in trouble. Really." Celia paused. "Do you have her telephone number? My number?"

"Five-five-six, seventy-two hundred?"

"That's right."

"Chau." He turned and jogged off in the direction of the Velódromo. Almost out of earshot, he paused, turned, and yelled, "Ask Magdalena."

Celia raised her arm to wave. "Going there now," she yelled back.

THIRTY-SIX

CELIA stopped next to a waiting taxi parked across the street from Magdalena's house and studied the place. It was a flat-roofed bungalow from the 1950s, surrounded by a chain-length fence. A second storey had been recently added, with an outside stairway. A blue triangle sticker on the front door advertised the fact that the owner was licensed to rent rooms to foreigners.

The upper storey slightly overhung the lower one, creating a covered front porch with two wrought-iron rocking chairs. But they were empty and the place did not look friendly. It looked, Celia thought, like the sort of place where, when you're walking past, a large dog flings itself against the fence, barking furiously and scaring you out of your wits. But she saw no dog or any reason why she should not go to the door. So she did.

The door was opened by a skinny girl with spiked, metallic-orange hair. She held an open bottle of nail polish in one hand, brush in the other. Looking past Celia she said, "Sorry. No rooms. We're full."

"I am not looking for a room," Celia said, wondering why on earth the girl had mistaken her for a foreigner. "I just wanted to talk to you. If you are Magdalena."

"Oh! I saw the taxi and I thought . . ." Magdalena's mouth stayed open but empty, revealing that she had not actually thought anything beyond the fact that the taxi across the street must have brought Celia, which must mean she was a tourist.

"I cycled over." Celia motioned to the bike, which she had leaned against the fence just inside the gate. "I am Liliana's aunt. Celia Cantú." She smiled, waiting for the information to register. "May I come in?"

Magdalena lowered her eyes and carefully screwed the cap back on the nail polish bottle. "Sure."

Celia had never been in a home with so many consumer goods on display. A television, of course, but every Cuban home had that. This set was the largest she had ever seen, with a VCR. There was also a computer, a CD player, and astonishingly large collections of CDs and DVDs. Family photographs and cheap prints in gaudy frames covered the walls. Heavy furniture left barely enough room to move about, and every surface was crowded with knick-knacks.

"Go ahead. Say it." Magdalena had taken a seat on the sofa behind a coffee table littered with cosmetics, including bottles of nail polish in vivid colours. Her posture was casual, even sloppy, meant to convey unconcern. But Celia noticed bright spots on the girl's cheeks that, along with wary eyes, indicated unease if not outright fear.

"Say what?"

"What you're thinking. That we're rich, or have rich relatives in the States, or how lucky we are to have all this." She gave a dismissive wave around the room.

"Actually I was thinking about whether you were going to ask me to sit down."

The spots on Magdalena's cheeks turned a brighter pink. "Claro," she said quickly, jutting her chin at an overstuffed chair. She picked up first one bottle of nail polish, then another, pretending to examine the colours. "So what's with Liliana? How come she wasn't in school this week?"

"That is what I came to ask you."

"How would I know?" Magdalena snapped.

Celia sighed, not at Magdalena's rude retort but at her own ineptness. To a girl already expecting to be accused of something, the question could only have sounded accusatory. She should have approached her as one would any nervous child, turning the focus elsewhere and giving Magdalena time to realize that she intended her no harm.

Celia sat down on a footstool across the coffee table from Magdalena and looked at the array of nail polish. "Which one are you going to use next?" she asked.

"I was thinking black." Magdalena smirked.

Celia picked up the bottle of black. "Will you clean the red you are wearing off first or apply it over top?"

Magdalena studied her nails. "I think I'll put it on over the red."

"Have you ever done designs?"

"Designs? Like what?" For the first time Magdalena looked directly at Celia.

"Oh, a dot or a diamond or something."

Magdalena frowned at her bright red nails. "I'm not that good an artist."

"My friends and I used to put tape on our fingernails with tiny cut-outs, so you could get a two-coloured design. Like, if you were to cut a diamond in a piece of tape and stick it on your fingernail, then paint over it with black, when it dried, you'd pull off the tape and there would be a black diamond in the middle of your red fingernail."

Magdalena dark eyes sparkled, then went flat. "No tape," she said sourly.

"I have some," Celia said. "In my bicycle basket."

Without waiting for a response, she got up and went out to her bike, returning with the roll of tape. "I had this for posting notices asking if anyone has seen Liliana," she explained. "But none of the hotels would allow it. Most of them said they would show the notice to their employees, though. Do you have nail scissors?"

Magdalena produced a pair of scissors and watched as Celia snipped off a small piece of tape and cut a tiny circle out of the middle of it. She handed it to Magdalena, who pressed the tape onto the nail of her forefinger. Then, with black polish, painted over it. Celia noticed that the high colour on her cheeks had faded to a more normal pink.

"Think it'll work?" Magdalena asked, staring fixedly at the newly painted nail.

"If you wait till it dries. I used to get impatient and pulled the tape off too soon. If you do that, it smears."

"How come Liliana doesn't know how to do it?" Magdalena asked, suddenly suspicious.

"I guess I never thought to show her. She mostly uses clear or pale pink. Designs show up best with bright colours."

Magdalena slid to the end of the sofa and held the painted nail in front of a fan. After a minute or two she touched it, and deciding it was dry enough, pulled off the tape. "Cool!" she exclaimed, holding the finger for Celia to see. "Can you do other designs?"

"One of my friends used to do stars," Celia said, thinking of Franci's beautifully manicured nails spangled with stars. "But all I ever learned to do were diamonds and dots and hearts." Celia snipped off a fresh piece of tape and cut a tiny heart-shaped hole in it.

This time Magdalena held out her hand for Celia to apply the patch. The small gesture told her that despite Magdalena's prickly behaviour, she was no different from most Cuban children in that she automatically anticipated kindness from adults. Celia had wondered, given the family's apparent focus on material acquisitions, whether they might have neglected their youngest child. But Magdalena's quickness to trust made it obvious that the attention of affectionate adults was something she took for granted.

Celia stuck the tape on Magdalena's pinkie finger and chose a pearl polish to go over it. "The more contrast, the better it shows up," she explained. "Neutral colour over a bright one, or vice-versa."

Again Magdalena dried the freshly painted nail in front of the fan, peeled off the tape, and leaned back on the sofa to admire the results. "You're right. The more contrast the better." She pointed to the red nail with its tiny pearl-coloured heart. "Liliana would like this one."

Knowing that Liliana would like that one, that she had never thought to show her, and now she wasn't here to do this silly girl-thing with them, caused tears to spring to Celia's eyes. Maybe Magdalena saw them, or sensed the sadness in Celia's silence, because she said, "Lili likes living with you, you know."

Celia recognized it for the indirect compliment it was intended to be, but it only deepened her pain. "I thought so. Until she disappeared. She was afraid, you know."

"Yeah."

A single word, yet it told Celia that Magdalena *had* seen Liliana. The question was when and where. "I was not going to punish her for skipping school on Friday," Celia said. "She makes good grades, so if she needed a break, no harm done. She might be a better student for it."

Magdalena gave a snort of humourless laughter. "I wish my parents felt that way. But they're more like the guy Liliana calls Uncle Luis. Your fiancé." A sly look crept into the girl's eyes. "Or one of them, right?"

"Actually not." Celia murmured.

"Not?" Magdalena's voice echoed surprise. "You dumped him for his brother? Lili said she wished you would but she figured not a chance."

"No," Celia said. Without really thinking about it she laid herself open, using her own angst to lure the girl in. "I broke up with Luis because he frightened Liliana. By threatening to send her to a re-education camp. That was why she ran away."

Whatever Magdalena knew about Liliana, her astonished expression showed that she had not known this. "Ran away? Like, where to?"

Before Celia could answer that she did not know, Magdalena said an entirely unexpected thing. "This Uncle Joe guy—did he take her back to Miami?"

A decade of medical practice had taught Celia to conceal surprise from her patients. She needed every bit of it now to maintain a neutral expression as the bombshell Magdalena had just dropped exploded in her mind.

"Liliana barely knows her 'Uncle Joe,'" she said quietly, reviewing their relationship more for herself than for Magdalena. "They met on Friday. She saw him again on Sunday evening. He brought her home Monday noon. That was when she disappeared. He is still here. At his mother's house."

"Oh." Magdalena frowned, then tried to justify her assumption. "When I stopped by to see her on Saturday, she was talking about it."

"About—going to the States with him?" Celia's voice trembled.

"Well, just kidding around." The wariness returned to Magdalena's voice.

Feigning nonchalance, Celia picked up a bottle of pale pink polish. "May I?"

"Sure," Magdalena said. "But let me shape them first." She fished for an emery board in her manicure kit. "I don't mean to hurt your feelings, but your nails are a mess."

"I guess they are," Celia said meekly and held out her hand. She waited until Magdalena was engrossed in the manicure before asking, "Do you know why Liliana went to Varadero alone in the first place? On Friday."

"You won't tell my parents?"

"No, I promise."

"We planned to go together. Only my dad didn't work that day. I told him I was sick, that's why I'd come home from school. But he stayed home all day, and since I was supposed to be sick, I couldn't get out of the house. Lili hung around awhile, then decided to go to Varadero alone. I guess that's when she met up with your fiancés."

"But you talked to her later," Celia pressed, thinking, Otherwise she would not have been able to tell you that José was here and Luis was angry with her for having skipped school. "Was she upset?"

"Totally bummed out. I couldn't talk her into going back to Varadero with me on Saturday, or to Playa Jibacoa. That bummed *me* out because I'd been stuck here at home all day on Friday. So when she decided to stay home Saturday, I went without *her*."

"Did you see her Sunday?"

Magdalena gave the nails a quick once-over with the emery board and blew away the dust. "She came by Sunday evening but I wasn't back yet. She was trying to call this 'Uncle Joe,' or at least find out where he was. Or so my sister said. By the time I got here she was gone."

"And you have not heard from her since?"

Magdalena shook her head. "No. And school was the pits without her. That's why I only stayed two days, then came home. I figured this time I *could* get out of the house, and if I could touch base with Liliana; I mean, I thought she might be sick, or—" She paused and frowned at the pale pink polish Celia had selected. "Wouldn't you like something brighter?"

"You pick a colour."

Celia grimaced when the girl selected hot pink. But what did it matter? The polish remover she would have to buy later was a small price to pay for information she could not get anywhere else. "Where do you stay when you overnight in Varadero?"

"We've never done that," Magdalena said quickly. "We go during the day, for the beach and, well, dancing too. But we try to be back at the campismo by dark because that's where our friends are. There's this one boy Liliana's pretty sprung on."

"Danilo," Celia supplied. "But I'm not sure Liliana wants him to know that yet."

Magdalena chuckled. "Yeah. She's cool that way. More than me."

"More than me too," Celia said, thinking not so much of Liliana's coolness toward Danilo as all the things Liliana had coolly kept from her. "But Danilo has not heard from her."

Magdalena, focused on painting Celia's nails, frowned but said nothing. Celia had the impression that she was thinking about who Liliana might have called or why she might not have called anyone. She waited, but when the girl spoke all she said was, "It's quick-dry polish. Only takes a couple minutes. You want something to drink?"

"Water?" Celia stood and waved her hands in the air to dry the gaudy polish. "Then I had better be going."

Magdalena disappeared and returned with a glass of water. "Has *anybody* heard from Liliana this week?"

Celia drained the water and handed the glass back. "Not so far as I know." She hesitated and threw out one last question that she could only hope Magdalena would answer honestly. "Do you think she could be staying with friends in Varadero?"

Magdalena snorted. "What friends? Tourists don't stick around and the guys who work there are only interested in foreign chicas."

"What about in the city? Might she have gone there?"

Magdalena looked dubious. "Anytime I mentioned hanging out on the Malecón, she never wanted to. Lili's more of a beach person. Besides, Varadero is closer to Playa Jibacoa. Hitching, it only takes an hour or two to get back."

Celia looked at her hands. "Thanks for the manicure. Next time I'll do yours."

Magdalena stared into space, holding the empty glass as if she had not heard. Only when Celia headed for the door did she say, "She must've called somebody."

Celia turned to stare at her. "Like who?"

"Like me. But she didn't. Or she did, but that was Sunday. You said she disappeared on Monday." Magdalena followed Celia down the sidewalk and opened the gate for her to push the bicycle through. "The thing is, Liliana's not a loner. To not call anybody, well, that just isn't like her."

"I know," Celia said softly. "That is exactly why I am worried."

She brushed Magdalena's cheek with a kiss and rode into the gathering dusk.

THIRTY-SEVEN

JOE swore under his breath and jammed the key in the ignition. If he waited much longer he'd miss the plane. It didn't help to know it was his own fault; that if he had called first Celia would have been here. Or maybe she wouldn't have been. But at least he would have known beforehand and made other arrangements. Now he'd have to leave the car in the airport parking lot where, security or no, it might get stripped. No, that wouldn't do. Better phone Luis from the airport and ask him and Alma to come pick it up.

He glanced into the rear-view mirror and, seeing no traffic, pulled into the street. Then registered what he *had* seen—a woman rounding the corner on a bicycle. He slammed on the brakes. It was too much to hope for, but as the cyclist drew closer, he saw that it was Celia. He pulled to the curb and got out.

The studied way she looked past him left the impression that she would have ridden right by if he hadn't been standing in the middle of the walk leading up to her building. She had no choice but to stop.

He spoke quickly. "Put the bike away. I need you to drive me to the airport. Hurry. I'm already late."

Her hostile expression was replaced by bewilderment. "Where is the rental car?"

"I turned it in when I bought this one." He gestured toward the '59 Chevy convertible.

"Bought it?" she echoed. Then, with what appeared to be a resurgence of anger, she wheeled the bike past him. "So you are staying."

"No, I'm leaving." He opened the door so she could park the bike in its usual place. When she turned around he was at the foot of the stairway with a look he hoped made it clear that no damned way was she going up before she'd heard what he had to say. "But I'll be back and forth a lot. So I bought the car. Which I'm leaving with you."

"No."

"Yes. Because you know damned well that if she was in the neighbourhood, you'd have heard by now. You need the car to look for her."

"I have no gasoline ration."

"There's gas money in the glove box. And don't give me any crap about not using it, not if you want to find her."

Joe did not consider himself a particularly sensitive person, nor did he aspire to be. But with Celia standing as she was, close enough to be kissed if he had dared, he could smell the witch's brew of pain, anger, confusion, and despair roiling in her. He had smelt it before, but he knew a little more about women now than he had then. This time she wasn't going to scald him with it.

"Come," he said firmly. "We go now or I miss my plane."

He clasped her arm but she brushed it off, turned, and walked ahead of him out to the car. With barely a glance at the vehicle, she slid into the seat like an exhausted child.

On the drive to the airport, he babbled about the business connections he'd made, why he needed to go to México City and Miami to keep things moving, and how this would be his pattern from now on. When her silence made it plain that she was not interested, he switched to the subject of Luis's new position and wondered aloud whether it was a step up the bureaucratic ladder. Celia's continued silence made it fairly obvious that she either had no opinion or did not care.

Joe guessed that she was burnt out from worry about Liliana. The car would make a big difference, not in terms of finding Liliana, but in allowing Celia to move around enough to feel that she was doing something until the brat decided to come home. Girls might disappear in the States but not here. Although Liliana hadn't mentioned having a boyfriend, he guessed she did. That was probably where she was and where she would stay, shacked up until their first lovers' quarrel. Then she would head home, knowing she faced little if any disciplinary action—especially if she came back pregnant.

He pulled up in front of the international terminal, a recent gift from the Canadian government. Its modernity reassured him in the same way Hotel Palco reassured him. First Worldness might be spotty on the island now but it was bound to spread. And he, Joe Lago, was going to be part of that spread. He glanced at his watch. "Ninety minutes. Plenty of time."

He reached across to squeeze Celia's hand. "Don't leave anything of value in the glove box overnight. In case the car gets broken into. Contact info for a mechanic is in there too, in case you have—" He almost said "an accident" but changed it to "mechanical problems."

He was just beginning to get thoroughly spooked by her silence, by the lack of anything that could properly be termed a response, when the hand that lay limp in his own suddenly tightened into a finger-snapping grip.

"José, did Liliana say anything to you about wanting to go to the United States?"

The way she said it reminded him of a woman who had once asked him if her husband was having an affair. Voice and eyes said that she already knew the answer and suspected he knew, that if he denied it she'd be sure he was lying and if he confirmed it, she would be devastated.

Joe disentangled his hand from Celia's and got out. "Yeah," he said gruffly as he grabbed his bags from the back seat. "She did."

"Do you think she found a way to go?"

"No. In fact, I'd be damned certain she didn't."

"How can you be sure?"

"Because she didn't have a clue how to go about it. No passport. No visa. No contacts. No money."

"If she had those things, do you think she would? Just go, without a goodbye?"

Joe tightened his grip on his luggage. "Ask her that, Celia. When you find her."

He bent down and kissed her hard on the mouth, but quickly, not giving himself time to feel whether her response was one of receptiveness or rejection.

THIRTY-EIGHT

CELIA did not know, returning from the airport, which made her most uncomfortable—driving the heavy old Chevrolet, so different from Luis's tiny Fiat, or driving a car that belonged to José Lago. But by sunrise on Saturday morning, as she headed east on the Vía Blanca, she had adjusted. She could not deny that a car would make it easier to search for Liliana, nor could she deny that Liliana had been roaming at least as far as Varadero.

She shied away from the thought of going to Varadero, as Luis had said in his note that he was going to put up notices there on Saturday and she did not want to risk running into him. Besides, Magdalena had said that even when they went there, they returned to the Jibacoa campismo at night. The campismo, then, was where she would start, and Saturday would be a good day. Besides the teens who hung out at campismos during their monthly week off, there were frequent school outings to the beach, so some students from Liliana's school would likely be there.

Celia felt that Liliana was near the water, although she had no idea why. Maybe it was the simple fact that Liliana loved the ocean. That was one reason why Magdalena's mention of Liliana wanting to go to Miami had upset her so badly. However, the more Celia thought about it the more convinced she was that the conversation between Liliana and Magdalena had been in the nature of girlish fantasies like, "Don't you wish we could go to Paris?" or "How about Canada? Wouldn't you love to see snow?" The idea of going to Miami was merely a notion cast up by the thrill of meeting her infamous Tío Joe. Celia believed José was correct in saying that Liliana did not know how to go about it—which meant she had not *seriously* considered it.

At least, Celia thought that was what she believed. What she knew for a fact was that Liliana had concealed thoughts *and* actions of which she would never have imagined her capable. Was a desire to leave Cuba really one of them?

From Celia's apartment, Playa Jibacoa's Campismo El Abra was only an hour's drive. Some of the cabañas were probably occupied with kids who had come the night before, but they were not up yet. The only person about was a gardener, grumbling as he bent down to pick up a gum wrapper. He straightened when he heard her footsteps crunching behind him on the leaf-strewn path.

"Good morning." Celia smiled. "You begin work early."

He acknowledged that it was early and asked if he could help. She showed the pictures of Liliana and asked if he had seen her recently.

"Not since last week, but I know her. Likes horses, she does. Her and that girl, the one with orange hair. They often go over to my place." He waved toward a cottage barely visible on a distant hillside. "My kids take them riding."

Celia smiled. "Liliana told me how much she enjoys that. She likes your family."

The man beamed. "Not a big family like when I grew up. Twelve we were. Me, I only got four. But four is enough, don't you agree? The younger generation stops at two, one even. That's better, I think. Times change. An island can only support so many."

Once the gardener told her that he hadn't seen Liliana recently, Celia excused herself and headed for the cafetería. There she went through the ritual of passing around the flyer and listening politely to responses that told her nothing.

On the way out of the dining room she stopped by the pool, a large one that she remembered from when it was new and she and her pre-university friends came here. She was standing there, staring into the still-empty pool and into her own past, when she heard her name shrieked in a high-pitched girl's voice. "Dr. Cantú! Celia!"

She looked up and saw that a school bus had pulled in. Teenagers were piling off and swarming toward pool and cafetería. She would have given years off her life to have that voice belong to Liliana. Of course it did not. Magdalena sprinted toward her.

"Look!" Magdalena flashed ten red-nailed fingers in her face, each glistening with a tiny white heart. "Aren't they wild? Everyone wanted to know how I did it, but I wouldn't tell. It's going to be my secret—mine and yours and Lili's, okay?"

A boy's voice spoke from behind Celia. "I thought they grew like that naturally, Magdalena. Like your hair." Celia turned and saw Danilo, who was pulling off his jeans to reveal a swimsuit underneath. He gave Celia a shy glance. "Heard anything from Liliana?"

"No," Celia said. "Have either of you?"

They both shook their head. Magdalena said, "I phoned about a hundred people and asked on the bus too. Nobody has seen her since she left school Friday morning."

"Same here," said Danilo. He started to walk away, then stopped and asked, "Does she know anybody with a boat?"

"A boat? Where?" Celia asked blankly.

"I don't know." He looked at Magdalena.

"Not that I know of," Celia replied nervously. "Why do you ask?"

Danilo shrugged. "One of the guys said you"—he jerked his chin at Magdalena—"and her were talking about going out on somebody's boat."

Magdalena coloured but answered straightforwardly. "It was just an idea. We thought we might find somebody who'd take us out."

"Do you know anybody who might?" Celia asked, trying to keep the alarm she felt from creeping into her voice.

"No. It was just, if we ever met somebody, we'd ask, that's all."

"Yeah," Danilo said, giving Magdalena a look of barely concealed contempt. To Celia he said, "Chau, Doctora" and dove into the pool.

"He doesn't like me," Magdalena said matter-of-factly.

"Because sometimes Liliana goes with you to Varadero rather than coming here? Maybe he is jealous."

"Probably. Not of me but of the guys she meets there. Especially if she met one who had a boat." She grinned. "Like a young Hemingway. But without the beard."

"Hm. Yes," Celia replied noncommittally.

"Lili said she has a friend, a friend of yours, I guess, in Santiago who operates big boats. If she ends up in med school in Santiago, maybe he'll take us out."

"Maybe," Celia agreed cautiously, not at all sure that Philip could authorize a joy ride on one of the ships he piloted into the harbour. She suspected that Magdalena was only trying to confirm that Liliana actually knew a ship's captain.

Someone from the other side of the pool called Magdalena's name. "Gotta go," she said abruptly. "Tell Lili to call me when she gets back."

Celia prowled the campismo grounds a while longer, questioning other students and staff. When she passed the pool again, Magdalena was executing a cannonball off the diving board, deliberately splashing a group of boys. Predictably, they yelled and grabbed her. Then, perhaps because Celia was watching, the boys released her. Their playfulness contrasted so sharply with Celia's despair that it hardly seemed real.

She was about to walk away when Magdalena shouted, "Dr. C! Wait!"

"I thought of something," Magdalena announced as she came paddling to the edge of the pool. "Where Lili might have gone."

Suddenly breathless with hope, Celia extended a hand and pulled Magdalena up onto the cement next to her.

Magdalena's eyes swept the group of young people in and around the pool in a way that caused Celia to think she was checking to see who might be watching—and would not have been displeased to discover that everyone was. However, only a few glanced their way, so Magdalena turned to Celia, whose full attention she had, and confided, "Once when we were hitching to Varadero a couple of Yanquis offered to take us to Playa Girón." She giggled. "Why do Americans always want go to the Bay of Pigs? You'd think they'd want to avoid it."

"Did you go with them?"

Magdalena shook her head. "Lili wanted to because she had never been. Plus the guys promised to rent snorkelling equipment for us. But"—she shrugged—"they were jerks. We decided to wait and hook up with some backpackers. They usually head for Trinidad. I've been both places," she said proudly. "Trinidad is definitely more fun. It has beaches *and* discos."

"I have heard that," Celia said weakly. "Do you know any, uh, backpackers?"

"We met some in Playas del Este. Canadians, from Quebec. They wanted us to go to Trinidad with them. But when we said we didn't have bus fare"—Magdalena's mouth turned down at the corners—"they didn't offer to buy tickets for us."

Celia picked up one of Magdalena's hands and studied the scarlet fingernails with their painstakingly applied white hearts. "So what do you think, Magdalena? If Liliana met the right person, might she have gone to Trinidad? Or to Playa Girón?"

"I didn't *think* she would go without me. But she did go to Varadero by herself last Friday. I guess if she met somebody she liked, and he offered to pay her way . . ." The thin shoulders shrugged to indicate nonchalance, but Celia saw hurt in Magdalena's eyes.

She wished she could reassure the girl that nobody was more loyal than Liliana, that surely she had not intentionally walked out on friends and family. But how could Celia offer such reassurances? The alternative not to having done it deliberately was that someone had forced her to do it, a possibility that here in Cuba was simply inconceivable.

Leaving the campismo, Celia headed west on the beach road. A kilometre along, she parked in the shade of a sea grape tree and walked down to the beach. Small private cottages lined this section of Jibacoa beach. She walked not knowing which house, only that when she reached it, she would know: *a place from another time, where she had been held and loved and strong because she gave all that to someone who gave it back to her. She wanted that intelligence at her command now, not his or hers but the force that both had become when they sat in this cottage, walked on this beach, talked and talked and talked of plans for a better Cuba, one where everyone would have enough and children, above all, would be safe.*

Celia stopped in front of a small bungalow built of natural stone and surrounded by twisted, wind-shaped trees. A woman with short brown curls like Celia's own sat on the porch in a wooden rocking chair painted red. She watched Celia and rocked.

Celia said, "Where is Fidel?"

The woman rocked and watched her for a long time. Finally she said, "Fidel doesn't come here anymore. I don't think he's been here in twenty-five years."

THIRTY-NINE

LUIS squinted into mid-morning sun as he drove toward Varadero. Never in his life had he felt such blind fury.

The rage had begun to build last night after José left for the airport. Alma kept nattering about how wonderful it was that he could go out and buy a car just like that, and how generous it was for him to leave it with Celia. Luis kept his annoyance to himself, knowing his mother needed to believe that the car was the magic carpet that would bring Liliana home. However, when she kept repeating the same things at breakfast he was tempted to tell her that the damned car was not endowed with magic powers, and José had never in his life done something for someone without a eye to what was in it for him. Luis didn't have to think twice—in fact, he didn't want to think once—about how his big-spender brother expected this little act of so-called generosity to be repaid.

Besides, the car was irrelevant. In Luis's opinion, the only thing that was going to bring about Liliana's return was if a social worker, alerted to her walk on the wild side, caught sight of her and physically brought her home. But of course, what did a pile of Xeroxed notices, for which he had paid half a month's salary, mean next to a canary-yellow convertible?

He had arrived at Celia's apartment as early as he dared, planning to wait until she appeared on the balcony with her morning coffee. He felt sure she would agree to go with him to Varadero to distribute the notices. They could talk on the way and get things sorted out. But that was not how it went because when he arrived she was already gone. At least the car was gone. Luis wasted fifteen minutes driving around the neighbourhood trying to discover whether she might have left it parked somewhere other than outside her own building. But he saw no sign of it so had headed for Varadero alone.

On a whim, he decided to whip off the Vía Blanca at Playa Jibacoa to leave one of the posters at an all-inclusive resort there, plus one at the campismo where Liliana often spent weekends—or claimed she did.

He was stopped at the gated entrance to SuperClub Saturno. He produced identification and waited an insultingly long time while the guard spoke to his supervisor on the phone. Then the guard had the temerity to ask exactly he wanted to see the head of security about. "That's between your superior and myself," Luis snapped and walked past the guard in a huff.

A paunchy man wearing a badge that identified him as head of security for the resort met him just outside the ornate lobby door. Luis got the distinct impression that his intention was to conceal—although whether to conceal something in the hotel from him or to conceal him from guests who might be miffed to see a Cuban in their exclusive midst, he did not know. He treated the security boss the same way he had treated the guard, demanding to see the manager, then demanding to see *him* in private.

In the manager's office he produced a notice with Liliana pictures on it. After being assured that there was no one on the premises who looked anything like her, Luis instructed him to post it in the lobby. The manager appeared reluctant but muttered that he would take care of it.

From SuperClub Saturno it was only three kilometres to the campismo. Being Saturday morning, the place was swarming with kids. No one was in the office so Luis walked to the cafetería, some distance away on the other side of the pool.

Unlike the hotel, which had seemed like alien territory, the campismo was, or had once been, his turf. Disco music played at ear-splitting volume through giant amplifiers was different from what they had played on smaller speakers twenty years ago. But twenty years ago any one of the skinny boys performing attention-getting stunts off the diving board might have been him, with Celia one of the girls shrieking in the pool. Even more strongly than nostalgia, Luis felt pride. What a good thing the Revolution had done, creating rural camps like this for Cuban youth! One had only to see these healthy bodies and listen to their carefree laughter to know that.

When he entered the cafeteria, he was stunned to see a notice about Liliana on the wall behind the cashier. The swell of pride in his chest popped like a balloon. "When was that posted?" he demanded with none of the preliminary courtesies the cashier's smile said she expected.

"About an hour ago. By her aunt," the cashier stammered. "Do you know her?"

"I am her fiancé. That is, her aunt's fiancé." The abruptness sprang from unbearable frustration. Had he not wasted time looking for the dammed car in Habana del Este he might have caught up to Celia here!

"Number One or Number Two?" asked a girl's voice behind him.

Luis turned to see a truly revolting-looking teenager, orange hair smeared with some kind of goop that allowed it to be shaped into spikes. Her ears were punctured with more holes and dangling more baubles than he would have imagined possible. She fiddled at them with fingernails so pointed that they looked like claws.

"Excuse me?"

"Are you her aunt's formerly dumped fiancé or the recently dumped one?"

Luis had never in his entire forty years heard any Cuban teenager speak to an adult in such an insulting way. The girl's tone of voice was shocking. What she said left him gasping like a fish. What in God's name had Celia done? Come out to this campismo and here among a bunch of rowdy kids spilled every detail of their personal relationship? What could have impelled her to do such a thing?

He literally could not answer. Walking away, he heard the girl say to the cashier, "He must be Number Two. Number One's supposed to be really good-looking."

Luis stumbled past the pool and across the grounds to his car. Ten minutes later, back on the Vía Blanca, he was still shaking.

FORTY

CELIA'S reaction to Magdalena's revelations was not entirely rational. Rational would have been to drive from the campismo on to Varadero and search for Liliana there; either that or go home and wait for her to call. But she could not bear to spend another day waiting by the telephone, and should she encounter Luis in Varadero, she doubted she could swallow her anger and show the gratitude he deserved. The two places Magdalena had named tugged her like magnets: Playa Girón and Trinidad. They were what—three, four hours away?

Thus, instead of turning west toward Habana, she turned east. She left the Vía Blanca at Matanzas and angled southeast toward Playa Girón. Soon the hilly landscape levelled out into mile after mile of citrus groves. South of that she entered the Parque Nacional Ciénaga de Zapata, a great wild swamp cut in half by the Bahía de Cochinos.

The highway was lined with memorials to Cubans who had died during what North Americans called the Bay of Pigs invasion and Cubans called la victoria. The small cement monuments were mute reminders of how many had fallen and, if one stopped to read the inscriptions, how very young most of them were. The shame of it, Celia thought sadly, was that it had been a war of Cubans against Cubans; wealthy ones who had lost their holdings following the Revolution against poor ones who had gained, among other things, hope for a better life. But as in any war, many of the poor had not lived to enjoy that better life, had not lived past this brief, bloody struggle.

They had not even lived to see how complete the victory had been, how after La Victoria most of the captured invaders—some 1,175 men—were traded back to the United States for 53 million dollars' worth of medicines and food, thereby saving the lives of countless other Cubans. Celia smiled at the sheer audacity of the ransom demanded, and was certain, although no one had ever said so, that it had been Celia Sánchez's idea.

She was on that part of the highway that closely followed the eastern shore of the bay when she passed a familiar place. Campismo Victoria de Girón was a row of cement block cottages strung along a beach that alternated white sand and sharp black rock called diente de perro—"dogs' teeth." As a Young Pioneer, Celia once spent a holiday here. There had not been enough snorkelling equipment to go around, so they had taken turns donning masks and diving into the crystal water to see a barnacle-covered landing craft, remnant of a brief but decisive battle that ensured that she was born into this Cuba, not some other.

At Villa Playa Girón, Celia asked the manager to circulate the notice among hotel employees. He looked uneasy but agreed to do it. Walking through the lobby to the pool area, Celia saw what may have accounted for his uneasiness. The Cuban women among the guests may have been vanguardia, model workers here on a government-paid holiday, but their youthful beauty and the fact that they were with much older foreigners suggested otherwise. She thought it likely that the hotel was in violation of a law that prohibited Cubans and foreigners from sharing a hotel room unless they had documents showing they were married. Celia's gaze moved from one guest to another as she made her way down to the beach but saw no familiar face.

Guests were lodged in individual cottages lined along the beach for about a kilometre. Celia pulled off her sandals and walked west along the smooth sand. There were not many people on the beach, and the lounge chairs in front of each cottage stood empty. Most seemed to have forsaken sunbathing in favour of the cool interior of their air-conditioned cottage. By the time Celia reached the last cottage her feet felt blistered from the hot sand. Discouraged and feeling foolish for having imagined she could find Liliana by searching resort to resort like this, she walked to the water's edge. Her gaze fastened on the horizon, but not really on the horizon, for what she saw was an invisible island just beyond the curve of the earth. She sat down at the edge of the gentle surf and wiggled her toes in the warm water.

Her legs dangled over the side of the dock, feet cooled by the dark as it swirls in and out with the tide. Behind her, in the island's only house, the prime minister's wife had put her infant to bed and, somewhat slowly grasping the fact that her husband and Fidel were more focused on each other than on her, she had retired. Celia would not have been surprised if the men had talked all night, for they got on well, but perhaps Pierre felt a need to attend to his young wife, because soon after she retired he excused himself. Fidel had gone to speak to the crew about the following day's activities, a spear-fishing trip to a favourite spot near the mouth of the Bahía de Cochinos. Now the house was quiet. For the first time in the prime minister's week-long visit, she had stolen a few moments alone. Alone until she heard the creak of the dock under bare feet. He wrapped his arms around her waist. She waited for him to speak, to indicate what was uppermost in his mind.

"Well, what do you think? Will Canada stand with us?"

"It won't join the blockade, no. Trudeau is too proud to let the United States dictate Canada's foreign policy."

"He has a social conscience."

"And a flirtatious wife." She paused. "Was it wise to tell her she has the most beautiful eyes you have ever seen?"

His breath was warm in her hair, his voice teasing. "What else can one say to a woman who looks only to see herself reflected in the eyes of a man? It's not as if she's an intellectual. Besides, it will please her husband to think I find her beautiful."

Celia did not respond to that, but thought, It pleases you too that she should be flattered by your flattery, although I know you better, know well what kind of woman you find beautiful. Just as you know I am untroubled by your roving, as long as it doesn't compromise La Revolución. And know, too, that my question was not prompted by jealousy, that being an emotion impossible between two people as transparent to each other as we are and as bonded by common purpose. I may be right, though, in feeling that it was unwise to flirt with her under her husband's nose. Then again, you may be right, that it was just the right touch to give them a romantic evening, and Cuba a stronger ally.

The silence between them was long, not broken until he pressed close behind her and whispered, "Quita la ropa." Then dove into the water.

She glanced toward the house and up at the moon. It was a sliver of silver, low in the sky, not casting enough light to make her visible to the sentry at the door of the cottage. If Fidel wanted her to swim with him in the nude, he would have given orders that no one should follow him down to the dock. She removed her shirt, untied the wrap-around skirt, and stepped out of her underwear.

Fidel had not yet surfaced, although it had been more than a minute. Nineteen years together and she still had not got used to the length of time he could remain underwater. It always alarmed her, perhaps more so tonight because the prime minister's visit had been so tiring. Fidel, though, was pleased with himself, confident that he had established a genuine rapport with Trudeau. No wonder he was treating himself to the luxury of this midnight swim. She dove. The dark water parted with a flash of blue-white phosphorescence. She surfaced and treaded water.

Long-fingered hands grasped her ankles, slid upward on her legs and, holding her hips, turned her to face him. She revised what she had just told herself about his need to unwind. He had not been stressed by the social demands of a visit from a head of state; for him the week had been exhilarating. It was she who found social rituals tension-generating, more exhausting by far than a pack-laden march through the sierra. This midnight swim in caressing warm water, beneath his caressing hands, the lovemaking that would melt away the vertical crease between her eyes and relax every knotted muscle in her body—this was not for him. It was his gift to her.

"Please, do you want to buy a fish?"

Before she could surface from her hallucination, Celia was surrounded by children. She rubbed her eyes as the dream was replaced by an even more hallucinatory image: that of a large silver fish, held up and flopping just inches from her face.

"I—no. No fish."

One of the children, a boy of about twelve, turned to look across the water in the direction Celia had been staring. "Were you trying to see Fidel's island? You can't, not from here. It's too far. You'd need a power boat. Or a sea kayak."

The children fell into an instant debate as to whether Cayo Piedra, although beyond the horizon, was within swimming or rowing distance.

One wiry boy puffed out his small chest. "I could swim there if I had fins."

The others laughed. The boy who had made the preposterous claim laughed too. Celia smiled and ran her fingers through his brown curls. Sure you could, she thought. Just like I could get there in my head. All it takes is being a little crazy.

"Why do you want to sell the fish?" she asked.

"To get money to buy candy," the smallest girl informed her.

"Why not take it to your mother so she can cook it for supper?"

The children's enthusiastic smiles faded. A plump black girl with a streak of red in her otherwise dark hair was quick to invent a criticism-proof answer. "One fish isn't enough for all our mothers. If we sell it we can buy enough candy to share all around."

"We'll give you a piece," the smallest girl promised, putting her sandy hand in Celia's.

Celia was so touched by the children's sweetness that she almost gave in. She nodded to let them know she approved of their plan to share, at the same time suggesting an alternative. "Candy is easier to share than a fish. But if no one buys it, maybe one of your mothers can cook it in a soup and another mother can bring an onion and another one a potato, and some cabbage. If everybody adds something, then there might be enough to share, yes?"

"Okay!" they chorused and raced off down the beach, splashing in and out of the surf like a flock of brown-legged sea birds.

Celia watched them out of sight, then walked back to the hotel. It was tiredness, she told herself. She had been driving what—four hours? Well, maybe not that long, and maybe she was not that tired. But it had to be more than mere proximity to someplace Celia Sánchez had been that caused her to let go of mind to the point that it went wandering like that!

What she suspected, and was reasonably sure any psychiatrist she revealed herself to would tell her, was that she was fabricating fantasies out of forgotten memories—not of her own experience but things she had heard or read. She had never been anywhere near Cayo Piedra, had never even seen a picture of it other than as a dot on the map, and was sure she had not been thinking about it when she walked down the beach. But it was common knowledge that Fidel often took visiting dignitaries there. With little security in attendance, they dined informally on fresh fish and lobster. Prime Minister Trudeau and his wife, Margaret, had in fact visited Cuba with their infant son, probably about the time she herself started to school. Had they been taken to Cayo Piedra? Had the visit been discussed in class, considered of interest to small children because of the Trudeau baby over whom Fidel had made such a fuss? Was that where her psyche had got the material to foment—or *ferment*—this absurdly personal vision?

A gust of wind blew sand into her eyes, causing them to sting and probably redden too. And didn't it serve her right! She was supposed to be searching for Liliana, not lolling on the beach. She had gone in search of "the real Celia" once, she reminded herself, and ended up at the Comandancia mired in more unreality than before. That was *not* what this trip was about and she was *not* going to let it happen again!

She almost ran back to the hotel and arrived hot and panting. She again scanned the crowded pool area, then went into the restroom to wash up. Next she called Alma, the hospital, and the school. All reported the same absence of news. She told no one where she was, just said she would call again the following day.

FORTY-ONE

LUIS had never been a repressive bureaucrat. In fact, he had gone to great pains to become precisely the opposite—unobtrusive, soft-spoken, and helpful—a true servant of the people. If asked for self-criticism, he would have said that perhaps he took his work too seriously and lacked a sense of humour. He rarely smiled.

He certainly was not smiling when he arrived in Varadero. Anybody who had dealings with Luis that day might well have described him as exactly the kind of official he had always tried not to be. For the first time ever he used his high-ranking position to intimidate others. He might not be the richer brother or the better-looking one but, by God, he was somebody in his own country. Although he was not conscious of it, he wanted to see that fact reflected in the face of everyone who crossed his path.

He crested the overpass leading into Varadero and for once did not mellow with pride at its traffic-thronged streets and big hotels. He drove directly to SuperClub Puntarena, the resort at the end of Varadero closest to the mainland, where Liliana had lured him and José into dancing. He knew that only registered guests were allowed on the premises, but when the guard came out of the kiosk with the intention of stopping him, Luis flashed an ID card and kept walking. When the hapless guard hurried after him to get a better look at the card, Luis coolly folded it back into his wallet and snapped, "Call the head of security and the manager. I want to meet with them immediately."

Luis's air of authority was not feigned. He had a job to do and he would do it. The notices would be circulated, Liliana would be found, and she would be sent to a re-education camp for as long as it took her to learn to behave. She could bloody well forget about hanging out with disrespectful, pointy-haired kids like that girl at the campismo.

The security chief greeted him at the door and led him to the manager's office. There was no point in asking whether Liliana was there, as they would certainly deny it. Hotel staff well knew the law against Cubans sharing rooms with foreigners to whom they were not married, and that in the case of an underaged girl, all of them, including the hotel manager and the foreigner, might go to prison.

Luis slapped a picture of Liliana on the manager's desk. "This girl is missing," he snapped. "If she comes here, or even tries to get in, call me immediately and hold her until I arrive." Luis took a pen from his pocket and made a big checkmark next to his own telephone number on the poster.

There were murmurs of willing compliance. Luis acknowledged them with the barest nod and gave both men a meant-to-be-intimidating look. "I know for a fact that she has come here before, via the beach access. So keep your eyes open."

And so it went, hotel after hotel after hotel. It was three-thirty when he reached the last hotel he had time to visit. He had skipped numerous smaller ones, guessing that Liliana would have chosen the larger resorts. At those, not every guest was known to the security staff and she would have found it easy to slip in and mingle—just as she had at SuperClub Puntarena.

The manager of the final hotel on Luis's list was in an empty dining room, filling his plate from a picked-over buffet. Luis waited until he was seated, then approached. The man looked to be about sixty, with thinning grey hair. Because he appeared tired, Luis spoke firmly but not unkindly. He produced Liliana's picture and did not imply, as he had elsewhere, that the management itself might be involved in harbouring a minor.

As the manager looked at the pictures, Luis's eyes unconsciously fastened on the food. The manager glanced up and saw him staring. "Would you care to join me?"

Luis opened his mouth to say no even though his stomach was screaming the opposite. The manager spoke first. "Please. It's on the house. I hate eating alone."

It was common hospitality of the sort Cubans all over the island extended to each other every day of the week. Yet because this was Varadero, where one did not expect generosity, or because he himself had been so ungenerous with everyone he had met that day, or because he was so in need of simple kindness, Luis felt his eyes moisten. It was all he could do to choke out, "Gracias, compañero."

When he returned to the table, his plate heaped with roast pork, chicken, lobster, rice, potatoes, and buttered rolls, the manager was gazing at Liliana's picture.

"They drive me crazy," he said, not seeming to notice or care how much food Luis had piled onto his plate. "They chat up guests on the beach and every time you turn your back they slip in." He studied the picture of Liliana in a swimsuit. "Good you brought this one. They often show up wearing just this, nothing else, and mingle with guests around the pool."

Luis nodded. "I know. I caught this very girl doing that."

The manager glanced briefly at Luis, and Luis knew he was wondering whether the girl might be a relative. Luis was not ready to admit how close he was, or had been, to becoming a relative. But the need to confide in someone upon whom he could count for sympathy was irresistible.

"I tried to persuade the family to put her in a re-education camp. But it is hard for families to accept that *their* child is up to this sort of thing. And now she is missing."

"Making our jobs just that much harder."

"Just that much harder," Luis repeated. The very admission of what a hard day this had been allowed him to feel his own exhaustion. Both men ate quietly, hungrily. Neither spoke again until their plates were empty. The manager signalled a waiter, who brought a silver pot.

"Café?" At Luis's nod, the waiter poured coffee for each of them.

"How long have you been in Varadero?" Luis asked, thinking that the man might be new to tourism, which would explain why he had the hospitable ways of an ordinary Cuban.

"Always," the manager smiled. "My name is Jon Madera, by the way."

"Luis Lago." They reached across the table and shook hands. "Always?"

"I was born here. My father worked on the estate that is now Parque Josone."

"Really!" Luis exclaimed. "They say the owner was so fanatical about privacy that he built a tunnel under the road so he could walk to the beach without being seen."

"It's true," Madera smiled. "Although that was well before my time. Back when the whole peninsula was owned by a few rich families."

"You must have seen Varadero through a lot of changes!" Luis sipped his coffee and looked at Madera with interest.

"More than you can imagine. When the Revolution triumphed, I was in secondary school in Habana. I volunteered for the campaign to eradicate literacy. We were sent here for teacher training. My group was housed in Cuatro Palmas."

"Batista's own villa!"

Madera laughed. "If you don't think that wasn't a change! Of course, it was later turned into a tourist hotel. Which it still is."

Luis leaned forward. "I considered going into teaching. Did you like it?"

"Very much. I spent a year in Guantánamo Province, then came back and taught at the Universidad de Matanzas until retirement."

"Then switched to tourism?" Luis prompted.

Madera gave a wry, sideways smile. "Given what happened to the economy in the early nineties, it was that or a gardening co-op. I don't have much of a green thumb, and I do speak English, so . . ." He gave a self-deprecating shrug. "Here I am."

Seeing that his host was about to rise, Luis quickly rose too. "Thanks for the lunch. It hasn't been an easy day. Problems like this—" He gestured toward the flyer.

Madera glanced again at Liliana's pictures. "I understand. Sometimes I wonder if we have done the right thing, going the tourist route. It is contaminating them, you know. It flaunts what they don't have and causes them to overlook what they do."

"I know," Luis agreed. "We all know. In government, that is. It is debated every day. But what can one do?"

"What can one do?" Madera echoed.

Rather than return to the parking lot where he had left the Fiat, Luis walked along the beach until the sand gave way to rough diente de perro. Just before reaching the rocks, he sat down. Little by little, the late afternoon sun turned the hard anger that had fuelled him through the day into something softer, more digestible.

He had often sat here, perhaps in this very spot, back in the days when they had spent weekends at the now-disappeared campismo—he and José and Carolina and Celia and Franci and Joaquín and all the others from their Vedado neighbourhood. Sometimes, tired of chasing each other like puppies across the sand and into the surf, he had walked to this far end of the beach alone. What tired him more than their games was watching girls he liked as they paired off with other boys. Celia had been the last to do it. Perhaps because she seemed more serious than the others, he had fantasized most about her. But of course, it was José who bedded her in the end. The only mercy was that she had not given in to José then, but later, when they were in college and Luis was already at the ministry, involved with work he deemed important.

Having completed what he set out to do that day, Luis no longer needed to think about his appearance. He removed shoes and socks and lay, belly down, on the beach. How often as a boy he had lain just so, imagining the soft warmth beneath him to be Celia's body. Some long time later, it was. Now, again, it was only sand.

FORTY-TWO

CELIA returned to the autopista and stayed on it all the way to Santa Clara, then drove south over the Sierra Escambray, on a road much rougher than she remembered. A previous trip along this route, made with other medical school students, had been to a spa high in cloud forest. It was part of the government's medical tourism program, aimed at giving the students a sense of what Cuba had to offer foreigners.

"A health holiday," their instructor had said. "In return, Cuba gets hard currency and an international reputation for our doctors. Given the necessity of tourism to rebuild our economy, medical tourism will be the cleanest, the least corrupting to our youth."

Being only twenty-something herself, Celia did not understand the reference to tourism as a corrupter of youth. Now, recalling the promise of "clean" tourism, she was saddened that that earnest effort had not earned enough foreign currency, and Cuba was compelled to turn to recreational tourism to keep the economy afloat.

As she drove the last steep bit up to the village of Topes de Collantes, she passed a flock of foreigners in matching blue jogging suits that bore the name "Kurhotel." The spa was now famous for post-operation recovery, as well as for fitness programs to lower blood pressure and reduce the risk of heart attack. She waved as she passed. Whatever these middle-aged foreigners were about, at least they weren't lying around with a drink in one hand and a Cuban girl in the other!

Because she was watching the joggers as they and she climbed the hill toward town, Celia failed to notice that the temperature of the car was also climbing. Only when she came around the curve in front of the massive seven-storey Kurhotel did she glance down and see that the temperature gauge was well into the red. She pulled to the side of the road, wondering what she should do. Regardless of the spa, Topes was like most small Cuban communities in that it had no commercial centre, gas station, or garage.

A boy of ten or so walked slowly by, his gaze caressing the convertible.

"Hola, amigo. Is there a garage in town?" Celia asked him.

He came to the drivers' window. "No, compañera."

"What about a mechanic?"

"For this máquina? Oh sure!" The boy's eyes lighted with anticipation. "Want me to take you to his house?"

"That would be great." Celia opened the passenger door. "What is your name?"

"Simón," he replied, closing the heavy door so delicately that she had to reach across him to slam it harder.

He studied the dashboard gages. "She has overheated," he announced.

"I know. That is why I need a mechanic."

"Don't worry. Obregón will know what to do."

"Is he close by?" Celia fretted. "The engine is awfully hot." What she was really concerned about was whether this Obregón person might live up one of the town's steep hills, which would overheat the car even more. Fortunately, the opposite was true; it was a downhill glide of only a block. Celia parked in front of the small house and started toward the door, but Simón motioned her to follow him around to the back.

"He'll be in the backyard, working," the boy explained.

The area behind the little cinderblock house was grassless but shady. Along the back of the lot was a carport that held four ancient cars. A fifth was in pieces, carefully laid out on the ground next to a man who was hammering on a piece of metal. The hammer paused in mid-air as Celia and the boy came around the corner of the house.

He was near Celia's age and, she couldn't help noticing, astonishingly good-looking. He had the narrow nostrils and high forehead of Spanish lineage, combined with tight black curls and full mouth of African ancestors. His hands were jet black, but that had nothing to do with his heritage; rather, his passion for mechanics. His smile revealed dazzling white teeth.

"Obregón," the boy called out. "The compañera has trouble with her máquina. A '59 Chevy."

He gave Celia a polite nod and asked the boy, "What kind of trouble?"

"She's running hot," Simón replied seriously. "All the way in the red."

"A '59, eh? At her age, you can expect that in the mountains. How long did you drive it after the needle hit the red?"

Celia turned what was probably a fair shade of red herself. "I am afraid I was not paying attention. I noticed it just as I came into town."

"Let's have a look."

The three of them walked around the house to the car. "Nice máquina, no?" the boy said to the man.

"Very nice," Obregón replied. "How long have you had it?"

"It is not mine," Celia explained. "A friend lent it to me for this trip. I am on my way to Trinidad. What do you suppose the trouble is?"

"Probably a bad fan belt or leak in the radiator. I can't check it till it cools down."

As they spoke, a woman, hugely pregnant, came out onto the front porch. "Won't you come in for coffee?" she invited Celia.

"Actually, I drove from Habana this morning and really need to stretch my legs," Celia replied with an apologetic smile, although in fact, what she wanted to do was walk back to the Kurhotel and leave a notice about Liliana there. There was virtually no chance of her being at the spa, but Celia reasoned that employees here must know hotel employees in nearby cities and could help spread the word. She turned to Obregón. "What if I walk down to the Caburni waterfall? Would that give you enough time?"

"Time to cool so I can take a look. After that, well, it depends what the trouble is. As long as the radiator's not blown I can probably have her running in time to get you to—Trinidad, you said?—by dark."

"It is not very far, is it?"

"Only twenty kilometres, and all downhill." To the boy he said, "Why don't you walk our compañera to the trail head, then come back and help me check the máquina?"

At the Kurhotel, Celia asked Simón to wait outside while she dropped off a flyer. She also phoned the school, the hospital, and Alma, even though it had only been four hours since her last call. They had nothing new to tell her.

When she came out, Simón was waiting to discharge his duty as her guide. Although Celia's thoughts were on Liliana or, more accurately, on her stupidity in having taken off as she did and getting stranded in this remote place, she tried to carry on a conversation with the boy. Simón told her that his father had been a worker at the local coffee processing plant but had recently received a grant of land from the government to grow coffee. "I don't want to be a farmer," he confided. "I'm going to be a mechanic like Obregón. He's the best. Even with one leg."

"One leg?" Celia had noticed that the mechanic walked with a slight limp but had been too preoccupied with the car to wonder about it. "How did that happen?"

"Banditos," Simon replied, using the government's name for counter-revolutionaries who had operated in the area in the early '60s. Celia knew from Luis that the US-supported Contra War had lasted five years and resulted in three times as many casualties as the Bay of Pigs invasion, but as it had taken place before she was born and her own parents weren't involved, she knew little about it.

"Obregon got shot in the leg," the boy explained matter-of-factly. "He doesn't remember it because he was just a baby. I don't know why his leg had to be cut off, but it was." He stopped walking and turned to Celia. "You can see his village—not the real one but a model—in Trinidad at the Museo de la Guerra Contra los Banditos. There is a plane there too. An American bandito plane that got shot down. I went there with my class. We got to go right up and touch it."

Simón stared thoughtfully off across mountains that appeared and disappeared as peaks were alternately highlighted by the afternoon sun and obscured by swirling clouds. "I might be a pilot. Flying a plane would be fun. If it didn't get shot down." He stopped suddenly and pointed. "There's the trail to the river. You get to the rapids first. If you want to see the falls you have to hike a little farther."

Following a trail through pine and eucalyptus forest, it took less than an hour to reach the river. As she stood watching water churn to white as it cascaded over rocks, the sun broke through. Her ears registered the songs of countless birds. Celia sighed deeply and sat down on a large rock.

A tocororo on a nearby branch warbled its distinctive mating call. There followed a few seconds of silence, then, in a flash of red, white, and blue—colours for which reason it had been designated national bird of Cuba—a second tocororo glided to a bush almost within reach. Celia held her breath.

As she watched the birds, seemingly so intent upon each other and so oblivious to her, her abdomen clenched with sexual tension. She remembered Miguel telling her how birds sometimes sat on his foot or perched on his head.

Not a hallucination. Not the imagined words of a man who had been the lover of a woman she was not, but the words of a real man who had bedded her just a week ago. It seemed incredible that Miguel Ortega Ramos had not once crossed her mind since returning to Habana. Could it have been only seven days? Surely it had been the longest week of her life, a week spanned only by this feeling in the pit of her stomach, which for a startling instant made it seem as if his body had just lifted its weight from hers.

Celia sat motionless, absorbed by the brilliant colours of the tocororos, their lilting song, the music of water over stones, and air saturated with the scent of pine and eucalyptus. Her breasts seemed to swell toward the warmth of the sun as, for a brief, unmeasured period of time she allowed herself the solitary pleasure of uncensored physical sensation.

Then the bird flew and she rose, ready to resume her search for Liliana. It wasn't that she had forgotten or lost her sense of urgency. It was simply that there were other things she sought as well—or other chimeras. At the moment Liliana herself seemed unreal—although whether it was the person Liliana seemed to have become or the girl she thought she knew so well who was the illusion, Celia could not tell.

FORTY-THREE

CELIA rolled into Trinidad just as lights were twinkling on. Instantly the car was surrounded by boys on bicycles, all screaming at her to follow them to a casa particular that rented rooms.

"Get away from the car!" she shouted, terrified that she would hit one of them or that one of the bolder boys, riding with one hand on his bike handlebar and one hand on the car, would have an accident. In truth, she needed a guide and would have been grateful for a single nice boy like Simón to give her directions. But how did one deal with twenty or thirty of them at the same time? She had read about problems caused by jineteros in the more heavily touristed towns, but this was the first time she had experienced it. How off-putting it must be for foreigners who did not speak the language! Still, the boys must be earning something from it or there would not have been so many.

"Go away!" Celia yelled at the boys, to no avail. Finally she stopped the car in the middle of the street and shouted in exasperation, "I am not a tourist! I have a friend here. Angelica Salina. Do you know where she lives?"

She did not know Angelica well, knew her only as the mother of Nanita, who had been a college classmate. Years ago Angelica had come to Habana for Nanita's graduation, which coincided with Celia's. The Cantús had put her up for the week she was in the city, and Angelica naturally invited them to visit her. They intended to do that, as Trinidad was only six hours by bus from Habana. In fact, they were planning the trip when Carolina was posted to Angola. Then her mother was diagnosed with cancer, followed by death, followed by news of Carolina's death. By that time Cuba had lost Soviet assistance and gasoline shortages made getting around extraordinarily difficult. For all those reasons the trip had never been made.

There was a moment of babble before one said, "That's Pepe Salina's madrina."

"Where does she live?"

There was another lively discussion, from which one of the smaller boys emerged, yelling, "I know. Follow me!"

Off he went, on a bike so tall that he had to thrust his legs under the crossbar and ride sideways in order to reach the pedals. How he did it on the cobblestone streets Celia could not fathom but it seemed to work for him and he as a guide worked for her. The other boys backed off, no longer aggressive little hustlers but polite helpful teenagers—until the next hapless stranger rolled into town.

She had not called Angelica to let her know she was coming, for fear that it might lead to questions that she preferred not to answer over the telephone to a woman she barely knew. All she wanted was a bed for the night and a chance to see for herself whether Trinidad was the kind of place to which Liliana might have been attracted. Or perhaps—was it too much to hope?—that she might actually find her here.

The boy stopped before what she took to be an enormous house, centuries old. Two tall windows overhung the narrow sidewalk, each with iron bars on the outside and wooden shutters, open wide, on the inside. Massive doors, big enough to drive a truck through, also stood open. "Here," the boy pointed and pedalled off.

As Celia approached the threshold, she saw that the great house was not a house in the modern sense. Four-metre-high stone walls surrounded a large compound. Directly ahead of her was a paved courtyard with three rooms opening off either side. Beyond was a larger, unpaved courtyard. Celia could imagine carriages being driven through these doors in centuries gone by, with horses to be stabled in the back with other livestock.

"Angelica," Celia called. "Are you here?"

A grey-haired woman came from a room toward the back, a kitchen, judging by the pot she held in one hand.

"Que milagro!" Angelica cried, setting the pot aside and rushing to the door. She caught Celia by both hands and gazed at her as if her appearance at the door was in fact a miracle. "Celia Cantú, I can't believe it's you. Why didn't you let us know you were coming? Nanita left only yesterday for Cienfuegos. If she had known you were coming she would have waited! Did you drive from Habana this morning? How is—" She broke off, perhaps remembering that both Celia's mother and sister were dead. "Come. You must be tired. And hungry. You can't have eaten yet."

So it was at the kitchen table that they talked. When Celia asked about the jineteros, Angelica sighed. "They do bother visitors. The tourists complain all the time. But the families who rent rooms—and there are hundreds here in Trinidad—can't advertise. The boys bring them business and get a commission. In a way it's fair because it does make it possible for boys whose families do not own homes to earn dollars too."

Tourism, Celia thought bitterly. Was there any aspect of it that wasn't corrupting? But she said nothing, as Angelica had switched to talk of her children and grandchildren. Celia did not mention Liliana and Angelica did not ask. Perhaps she did not remember, from that single visit so long ago, that Carolina had a little girl.

Around nine o'clock, Angelica said, "You should bring the car inside. There is a lot of theft these days."

Celia didn't grasp what she meant until Angelica began to bustle about the courtyard, moving potted plants and rocking chairs to the side. Then Celia realized that just as horses and buggies were driven into the paved courtyard in the olden days, she was to drive the car inside, securing it for the night behind hacienda walls.

While bringing the car in, Celia heard loud music. "Is there a fiesta going on?"

Angelica cocked her head and listened to raucous sounds that seemed to be coming from everywhere and not in harmony. "Funny. I have become so used to it I hardly notice it anymore. There is a nightclub around the corner, and now a larger one has opened down the block. Both are built amidst the ruins of old colonial buildings. Oh, what a shame that Nanita is not here to show you around!"

"I would like to walk a bit, to see if Trinidad has as much charm as they claim,"

Celia said, hoping Angelica would not offer to come with her, as she was not, as yet, ready to reveal the reason for her visit.

"It is pleasant this time of the evening. Ever so much nicer than during the day, when you can't see the town for the tourists. When I was a girl we always went out walking after dinner. Not alone, of course. That would never have been permitted." She patted Celia on the arm. "But you'll be fine. Thank goodness we don't have much of *that* kind of crime in Cuba."

Once the car was parked in the courtyard and Celia was shown her bedroom, actually Nanita's bedroom, Angelica walked her out to the street and gave her a key to let herself back in. "They play salsa at La Casa de la Música. The clubs feature a folkloric group around eleven, and there is acoustic music at the Casa de la Trova there on the corner."

Celia would have loved nothing better than to sit in the Casa de la Trova and listen to an old maestro make love to his guitar. But there was no point in looking for Liliana there. She walked to the disco nearest Angelica's house.

Inside the club, despite the fact that the place had no roof, the air was thick with tobacco smoke. Squinting into the gloom, she moved around until she had seen everyone in the room, then went down the street to a second, smaller club. The crowd was not as young as she had expected. Rather than young travellers of the sort that Magdalena might have called "backpackers," most of the foreigners appeared middle-aged or even seniors. Youth was represented mainly by Cuban girls, and some young men, who were with, or trying to pick up, foreigners. Celia wondered how many of them came from the housing estate in nearby Casilda where, as in her own apartment complex, there would be schools, clinics, places to hold dances, sports facilities, and easy access to the beach; in short, everything needed for a wholesome life—but where few families would have a dollar income with which to buy consumer goods.

Yet Angelica had said that hundreds of families in Trinidad rented rooms to tourists. Those homes probably contained personal entertainment equipment such as she had seen at Magdalena's and perhaps the kind of cosmetics and clothing that Luis had unearthed in Liliana's room. Was that what drew so many young Cubans to places like the discos where, if they took the fancy of a foreigner, they too might earn dollars? Was it just that—a desire to have new clothes and other consumer items such as friends from dollar-earning families had? Was that what had drawn Liliana?

In the dim, smoky atmosphere of each club, Celia saw more than one girl with a head of dark curls enough like Liliana's to stop her heart. After watching couples gyrate on the dance floor to music at a volume she was sure must be doing permanent damage to everyone's eardrums, Celia left profoundly disturbed. As she trudged back to Angelica's, she no longer found it difficult to imagine Liliana as one of those pretty Cuban girls hanging out at discos for reasons that by no stretch of the imagination could be called wholesome.

It was dark in the windowless, high-ceilinged room when Celia woke, but a thin line of light under the door told her that it was morning. She heard soft sounds from the courtyard, indicating that Angelica was already up. Celia dressed and went out, carrying her shoes in her hand. Angelica, despite her sixty-some years, was wearing jeans and running shoes. She held a large bouquet of flowers and was pushing a bike toward the door. "What beautiful flowers!" Celia exclaimed. "Where are you taking them?"

"Oh, Celia, good morning. I didn't expect you to be up so early. They are for my sister. That is, for her grave. I thought I'd be back before you woke."

Celia stared. For her the death of a sister had always been a deeply personal, unshared thing. It never occurred to her that this woman might be living with a similar loss. "I'll drive you to the cemetery," she said quickly. "It will be easier on the flowers."

"She isn't at the cemetery," Angelica said, but showed acceptance of the offer by leaning her bike against the wall. "She is buried at the old place, where we grew up."

Celia recalled Nanita telling her that her grandfather, one of Trinidad's sugar barons, had owned a plantation that was confiscated by the revolutionary government.

"All the more reason for me to drive you," Celia said, sitting down on a rocking chair to put on her runners.

"Would you like coffee first?"

"No, let's go now, while it's cool and the flowers are fresh."

Bouncing slowly over ancient cobblestones, Celia saw that Trinidad was an exceptionally pretty town, more so than she had realized the night before. Streets and parks were empty at this early hour. The elegant old buildings were still in shadow, but here and there church spires captured and held golden sunshine against a pure blue sky.

"How lucky you are to live in such a lovely town!" Celia exclaimed.

"I like it. My mother also preferred living in town. But my father hated it, and that poisoned it for her. It poisoned him too, in the end, all that hatred."

"You mean after he lost the finca?"

"Sí. Confiscado." Angelica pointed. "Take that road, the one to La Boca."

In another few blocks they were in rolling hill country, the mountains mere purple silhouettes in the distance. Perhaps five kilometres from Trinidad, Angelica spoke again. "That turnoff just ahead. Don't go down the road, though. It's too rough. Park on the highway. We can walk from here."

Celia saw no buildings and wondered how long a walk she was in for. Angelica answered the question she had not ask. "It's not far. You can't see it because it's down in a hollow." She gazed across the gently rolling landscape, thickly covered with bright green thorn bushes that gave the illusion of lushness. "A shame, isn't it?" she murmured.

"What?"

"To have such rich land lying fallow. In my father's day it was sugarcane as far as the eye could see. I don't fault the government for making a mistake. But that it took twenty-five years to realize it!"

"What do you mean?"

"The notion that big farms had to stay big and were better in the hands of the state than individual families. Certainly big farms made some families rich, while those who worked the land were exploited, but under state management they didn't make anybody rich. They still had to have cheap labour, didn't they?"

"Do you think the government realizes now that was a mistake?" Celia asked.

"Obviously. That is why they have started breaking up big farms and giving small parcels to families and co-ops. But first they let this happen." Angelica waved her hand at the rolling land around them, which was lush only with thorn bushes.

"When the Soviets stopped providing farm machinery and fuel, I think Cuban officials sulked, just like my father, hoping somehow they would get back what had been taken away." She gave Celia an ironic smile. "That's men for you. It has taken them all this time to face the fact that they needed to try something new." As Angelica spoke, they were walking along a rutted road. She stopped and pointed. "There is the house."

Nestled in a wooded glen was a long low ranch house with the traditional veranda running along one side. It was smaller than Celia expected, given how wealthy the family was said to have been. "How big was your family?" she asked.

"Twelve children," Angelica replied. "But we never lived here at the same time because we were spread out in age. And there were the townhouses. That was how my father kept a lot of property when the farm was confiscated. The government said from the start that private homes wouldn't be confiscated so Papá gave each of the children a townhouse, either in Trinidad or Cienfuegos. I didn't get one because I remained with my parents. Their house—the one where I am now—became mine after they died."

They descended into the glen and were soon standing at the edge of a small family cemetery with markers dating back to the beginning of the nineteenth century. Angelica moved among them, pointing out various relatives, more than half of whom were children. "So many babies died in those days," she said, kneeling by a gravestone with a 1953 date, the last one buried in the family plot. "Not that my sister was a baby. She was sixteen."

"Younger or older than you?" Celia asked.

"My twin. She died of cholera. A terrible death. It was so contagious no one wanted to nurse her. I alone did that. And promised to bring flowers on her birthday. That was all she asked for at the end."

Celia stood quietly, sharing yet not sharing the loss of a beloved sister. She had thought that nothing could be worse than the pain of being told that the person closest to you in the world had been killed in a purely random way. Now she saw that it might have been worse; that like Angelica, she might have spent days or weeks watching her sister suffer as she slipped away. Yet grief was not an emotion to be compared. Each person, she knew, lived with their own, unmeasurable against any other.

At last Angelica rose to go. Celia looked at the house and back at Angelica.

"Did you want to visit the house?"

Angelica shook her head. "It doesn't mean anything to me. It was my father's home. The place in town, it was more my mother's. And mine."

"So it wasn't so bad for you, the changes that came with the Revolution?" Celia asked as they headed back toward the car.

Angelica walked without answering for a minute or more. Finally she said, "My family was one of the wealthiest in this area. But of twelve children, my father could only afford to send two to university, his two eldest sons. Both live in Miami now and are even richer than our father was. We never hear from them. They hold it against us that we stayed. They think we chose to support the Revolution."

"Did you?" Celia asked.

Angelica looked at her in surprise. "Me? I chose nothing. I was the youngest girl. It fell to me to look after my parents in their old age."

Celia felt foolish for having forgotten that a woman of Angelica's generation would not have had the options she had had. True, there were those like her mother and Alma who had used the chaos of a revolution to break free. But they were ordinary city girls, not shackled by tradition as a girl raised in a wealthy conservative family in the provinces would have been.

Angelica looked out across the wasteland that had once been a great plantation. "I have six children," she said softly. "Boys and girls alike, they *all* went to university."

As they reached the car it occurred to Celia that if this was the dead sister's birthday and she and Angelica were twins, then it was Angelica's birthday as well. Also, they were only a few kilometres from the coast. The resorts on Playa Ancón, where she intended to drop off notices about Liliana, were close by.

"I would like to see the beach resorts," she told Angelica. "Are there many?"

"Two, I think, with another one under construction," Angelica replied. "I haven't been out there in years. I would enjoy the drive."

"How about a birthday breakfast at one of the hotels?"

Angelica looked askance. "I have never even been inside one of them. I'm sure they are frightfully expensive."

"Not for us." Celia gave her a smug smile. "Remember that José Lago I had just broken up with when you visited us?"

"Your mother mentioned him," Angelica recalled. "But I never met the boy."

"He emigrated to the United States. But he came back recently. He lent me this car *and* some money. I am going to use both to take us to breakfast at the beach."

The four-dollar price of the breakfast buffet at Hotel Ancón made it unaffordable for the average Cuban, but Celia supposed it was nothing to José. Recalling how he had flaunted his affluence by taking Liliana and Luis to La Casa de Al for lunch, she determined not to feel guilty for this extravagance. They joined the line of guests and heaped their plates, the morning walk having given them a good appetite. They spoke little until they had eaten their fill and a waiter had come by to refill the coffee cups.

Suddenly Angelica looked up and asked, "Your sister's little girl, she must be in her teens by now. Where is she?"

For a moment Celia sat perfectly still because she had been thinking exactly that: *where is she?*

Celia spent the next half-hour telling Angelica about Liliana, admitting her fear that the girl had either become a jinetera or had hooked up with young foreigners who would only use her while they were vacationing in Cuba. When she finished, Celia sat there feeling as desolate as she had felt at the cemetery thinking about her dead sister.

Angelica reached across the table and took her hand. "Listen, Celia. Children don't get lost in Cuba and they don't disappear, not for more than a short while. Whatever foolish thing Liliana might be doing now, she will come back to the person she loves and trusts. You wait. You'll see. I know I am right about this."

After breakfast, Celia made phone calls to Liliana's school, the hospital, and to Alma, but there was still no news. She left flyers at each of the hotels on Playa Ancón, drove back into Trinidad, and left others at hotels there that Angelica directed her to. She also left copies of the flyer with Angelica, who said she would circulate them among casa owners who rented rooms to foreigners and show them to the boys on bicycles.

"Those boys are as good as palace guards," Angelica assured Celia. "They stop every car that comes to town and meet every passenger who comes by bus. If Liliana sets foot in Trinidad, they'll see her. Once they know we're looking for her, I'm positive they will let me know." Angelica promised that she, too, would watch for Liliana on the streets of Trinidad. Nanita often went dancing so she could keep an eye out for her in the clubs, and Angelica's grandson Pepe, in university in Santa Clara, could watch for her there.

On her way out of town, Celia stopped for gas. Not until the tank had been filled did she know where she was going. Not home, not back to work, and certainly not back to lean on the Lagos. But neither did she want to be alone. Franci she could count on, no matter what. Why return to Habana when she was already halfway to Santiago?

FORTY-FOUR

JOE checked his seat assignment and stopped in the aisle next to a young woman with eye-catching breasts. He preferred an empty seat between himself and the next passenger, but if it must be occupied, better an attractive female than a sweaty male. As he fastened his seat belt, the woman murmured, "Oh no!" in a stricken voice. He saw that she was reading a *People* magazine article about the break-up of a movie-star couple.

The man in the window seat glanced over her head at Joe, their eyes meeting with a sardonic twinkle. The woman shut the magazine and gazed pensively at the barf bag in the seat pocket for a moment before sizing up her seat mates. Joe, being the younger, got her attention. "Hi," she said brightly. "Did you enjoy México? Or are you from there?"

"I'm from Cuba," Joe told her. "And I enjoyed my visit there, yes."

"Cuba?" Her expression hovered between horror and fascination. "Isn't it, like, awfully dangerous? Or illegal, or something?"

Joe grinned. "As far as I know, it's not against the law for Cubans to have their own country. And a woman friend, a doctor in Habana, bikes back and forth to work in the middle of the night, so I guess it's not all that dangerous to live there. Compared to Miami anyway."

While the woman struggled to integrate his reply into her preconceived notions about Cuba, the man in the window seat remarked with interest, "I have heard tourism is booming there. *Travel and Leisure* readers just voted it the best vacation destination in the Caribbean."

"Not surprising," Joe responded. "Cuba always had great beaches, and now it's got a whack of new resorts. I guess some people prefer a place that isn't a Cancun clone."

"I liked Cancun," the woman said defensively. "Besides, it's against the law to go to Cuba, isn't it? I mean, they don't really want us there, do they?"

"It's the United States that forbids travel to Cuba," Joe informed her. "Or, more accurately, limits it. A person has to get State Department permission, which is not given for tourism. Only for political junkets or family visits, things like that."

"And you have family there?" the window-seat passenger surmised.

"A non-issue for me," Joe nodded, not bothering to explain that like most Cuban Americans, he had opted to ignore the embargo. No need to mention any of that to complete strangers who for all he knew might be CIA plants.

The woman sighed. "Did you see Robert Redford in *Havana*? I'd love to visit Havana. Especially if he was there making a movie."

The other man took out his laptop, and Joe, having lost interest in the exposed tops of the woman's breasts, did likewise, callously leaving her to fulfill any emotional needs she might have through empathy with the celebrities featured in *People* magazine.

Joe was surprised when he pushed open the door to his apartment at how crammed it seemed: the long sofa and big recliner facing a forty-eight-inch-TV screen, coffee table and end tables cluttered with books and magazines, a globe, a GPS he hadn't got the hang of yet, the large collection of CDs, a trumpet he had never gotten around to learning to play, the telescope he had used only once, a bag of toys he intended to give to the girls if and when he ever saw them again, an open gym bag with contents pulled out to get at the tennis shoes and racquet he had meant to take to Cuba and decided at the last minute to leave behind, a desk with phone, fax, answering machine, PC, and printer—smaller versions of the ones at the office. He dropped his luggage on the bedroom floor and headed for the kitchenette, where he hoped to—and did—find a cold beer in the refrigerator.

He walked back into the living area and stood for a minute breathing the musty odour of the closed-up apartment, predominately his own stale smells, before flipping on the air conditioner. Then, with something less than enthusiasm, he pushed the New Messages button on the answering machine.

The first words of the first message caused him to choke on his beer. It was what he would discover was one of seven left by Vera, her voice rising with apparent panic on each subsequent call. "Joe, *please* phone the instant you get in. This *is* an emergency and I've *got* to make a decision. You have no *idea* what Keri is going through!"

Joe's stomach did a flip-flop. He hit the automatic dial for Vera's number and waited for what he hoped would be an immediate pickup. It was. However, it was not Vera's voice but Keri's that came over the line.

"Hal-loo," she drawled in her sweet Southern child voice.

"Keri?" Joe tried to modulate his voice and the thudding of his heart. "How you doing, honey?"

"Hi, Daddy!" she exclaimed. "Mommy got me a kitten. It's fuzzy white all over."

"That's great, Keri." Joe's mind was running in circles, trying to figure out what signals he was getting and what ones he had missed. Keri certainly didn't sound sick, but accident or illness was the only thing he could think of that would account for Vera's semi-hysterical tone of voice. "Are you in bed, sweetheart?"

"No, but Fluffy is. She's sleeping on my pillow."

Vera, allowing a *cat* on the bed, when she'd never even allowed one in the house for fear the kids would catch something from it? He hated to brush Keri off, given how long it had been since he'd had a chance to talk to her, but this whole thing was beyond weird. "Could I, uh, speak to Mommy for a minute?"

"Mommy!" the child called, forgetting, as small children often do, to move her mouth away from the receiver before raising her voice to a volume meant to carry to some other part of the house. Joe rubbed his ear as her footsteps pattered down the hall, to be replaced by the quick tap-tap of Vera's heels on the tiles.

"Joe! Thank goodness you're back. Listen, this awful thing—" Vera's tone changed and he heard her calling, "Keri, honey, why don't you go upstairs and check on Fluffy?" Then Vera came back on the line, her voice a tragic whisper. "It's Keri."

"What? Has she had an accident? She sounds okay."

Vera's voice sliced into his eardrum even sharper than Keri's had. "It was *no accident*. And the damage—well, there's just no way to tell. Not until I get her to a specialist."

Once again Joe's blood pressure shot up, and he wanted to yell at Vera that if it was that serious why the hell hadn't she taken Keri to a specialist already? Instead, he asked in as calm a voice as he could muster, "Just tell me what happened, and whatever needs to be done, you know the girls are completely covered for every medical—"

"She's not covered for *this*." Again Vera lowered her voice. "There was a man outside the fence at her school." Her voice dropped to a whisper. "He *exposed* himself."

Joe was flooded with disgust and relief. He wanted to lay bare hands around the guy's neck and strangle him and do something not much less violent to Vera for the emotional roller coaster ride he had experienced during the past few minutes while under the impression that his four-year-old angel had been seriously hurt. But perhaps there was more; sure, there must be more to the incident.

"Did he touch her?"

"Certainly *not*! Keri and the little girl she was playing with screamed and ran to the playground supervisor. She called the police but the man disappeared before any adult got a good look at him."

Joe picked up his beer and took a swallow. "So you said this was an emergency. What exactly do you want?"

"What I want," Vera said tersely, "is to take Keri to a sexual abuse specialist. That is not covered by the children's health care policy."

"For what? So she can tell the shrink what she told the playground attendant and her teacher and the police and you? How many times do you want her to have to repeat it, for God's sake?" Joe exploded.

Vera's voice came across the line with icy calm. "Until someone who knows children and *cares* about their feelings can determine that she hasn't been scarred by the incident."

"Is she afraid to go back to school? Having nightmares or anything like that?"

"No, she has been too distracted by the kitten. Which was *my* idea, while I was waiting for you to get back to consult with you as to what should be done."

Joe, who was taking another sip of beer, almost choked on that one. Vera had never consulted him on a damned thing concerning the girls, other than when, exactly, he was going to write the next cheque. Which was what this was about; him writing a cheque to some high-priced specialist to deal with a non-existent emotional trauma.

"I appreciate that," he said after he had cleared his throat and wiped the sputter of beer off the mouthpiece. "Tell you what, Vera. I'll come over and take her for a ride and have a talk with her. If it seems like there's a problem—"

"I *want* her seen by a specialist," Vera snapped.

And what Vera wants, Vera gets, Joe finished silently. Well, not this time, baby. Aloud he said, "I don't think it's that big a deal, Vera. Getting her a kitten was probably the best thing you could've done."

"Joe—"

Vera's tone was ominous, but he didn't let her finish. "Since she hasn't *been* sexually abused, I don't think it's necessary to send her to a sex abuse specialist. But if that's what you want to do, I won't object. As long as you pay the bill." Up to that point, he managed to keep his voice neutral, but his last words came out dripping with sarcasm. "Which I'm sure you'll be willing to do if it's as important as you seem to think it is."

Two weeks in Cuba had dulled his reflexes, which is why he didn't get the receiver away from his ear in time to avoid a third shattering screech. "You cheap bastard! Your own daughter—"

Joe eased the receiver back onto the hook. He had been in this mental space before, this insane mixture of helplessness, vindictiveness, uncertainty, disgust, and anger. Been there many times and knew exactly how to get himself out of it.

He dropped a Gloria Estefan CD into the machine, cranked up the volume, and went into the bathroom. He turned on the water and let the tub fill to a depth that would just cover his testicles, then stripped and lowered himself into it. The warmth of the water and rhythm of the music was precisely what he needed to get his own rhythm going. He closed his eyes and let images of Celia, Gloria Estefan, and the big-breasted woman who had kept rubbing her thigh against his on the plane kaleidoscope through his head.

Afterwards he showered, slipped into a cool silk dressing gown, and with the smell of dinner wafting from the microwave, sprawled in his leather-covered recliner with profound pleasure at being back in his own space. Again he took in the cluttered apartment, most of it visible from where he sat. Funny, he could visualize Celia astride him in any bed, but no way could he imagine her in this room. Not that he would bring her here. He'd want something more appropriate for the two of them, and—he winced at the thought—probably space for Liliana at least part of the time.

His brow wrinkled as it occurred to him that Celia would not find the kind of upscale neighbourhood Vera had demanded to her liking at all. Where then? Miami had neighbourhoods with houses built back in the 1950s that weren't all that different from ones you'd see in Santa Fe, Cojímar, or parts of Vedado. They were comfortably middle-class there, lower middle-class here. However, Celia had moved out of Vedado in order to live on the ocean. Where could he offer her that?

Given what he'd sunk into Vera's dream house and what he was paying out monthly for the girls, he could hardly pop for a beachfront condo, which would be the nearest thing Miami had to offer to the place Celia lived now. Not that there was any comparison between that dilapidated four-storey public housing unit and a modern Miami high-rise. If he could ever get her here, once she got used to it, how could she not like it?

The microwave dinged and Joe went to take out the chicken whatever-it-was. He found an open bottle of white wine toward the back of the refrigerator and emptied the last of it into a glass. "Fit for a king," he muttered as he peeled the wrapper off the TV dinner, sipped his wine, and breathed the aroma of hot, instant food.

Just about everything he'd ever dreamed of owning was in this apartment, in his office, or parked downstairs in the garage. But there was no denying that it would be nice to have Celia sitting across from him, challenging him to find his way through her prickly words into the yielding softness he knew was underneath. Celia, once he got her here, would be the ultimate antidote to that goddamned poisonous Vera, an ever-present reminder of what a stupid jerk he'd been to let her get her hooks into him in the first place.

FORTY-FIVE

CELIA drove out of Trinidad feeling better. Almost intolerable thoughts of Liliana prostituting herself to middle-aged or elderly sex tourists had been replaced with the possibility Magdalena had suggested: that she might have hooked up with foreign young people who, like her, only wanted to explore Cuba and have a bit of fun. If they treated her badly and she dared not return home for fear that the authorities would cart her off to a re-education camp, she might well have hitchhiked on to Santiago. The notion that Liliana would at any moment land in Franci's lap was a comforting scenario—one Celia needed as much as she needed Franci's wise counsel.

The drive was slowed by frequent stops to pick up hitchhikers: students, teachers, medical personnel, farm workers, women carrying children to the nearest clinic for a checkup, and many more. Celia handed out flyers to her passengers as they got out of the car and asked them to post the notice in a public place in their town. Everyone promised to do it, and as she pulled away, she saw them reading the information she had not felt like sharing in person.

Darkness descended around Holguín and she saw that she wasn't going to make it to Santiago. Trinidad, she now understood, had been barely a third of the way to Santiago, not halfway as she had imagined. But in another hour she would be in Bayamo. She could overnight with Joaquín and his wife, Sylvia.

She had last seen Joaquín when he came to Habana for a fencing event six years ago and was billeted near the Pan American stadium with his team. Celia took Liliana to see the match and invited Joaquín to dinner. At Liliana's request, he brought a rapier and showed her some moves. She watched with intense interest, but informed him, with ten-year-old seriousness, that he should tell the team members to be careful and never mess around without their masks because you could put out somebody's eye with that thing.

Celia's own eyes blurred as she thought of that sweet, clingy child who had so inexplicably disappeared into an adolescent whom, it seemed, she did not know at all. Angelica had assured her that the running-wild adolescent would come back, and Celia believed that. But the child she had cared for since infancy, had lived with for nine years, who felt like an extension of herself—how did one bring back that person?

Celia parked in front of Joaquín's stucco house, flat-roofed and square as a box, its stark facade broken only by curving wrought-iron steps leading to the terrace. If she had been less tired she would not have stopped. Having gone through the whole sorry story of Liliana's disappearance only that morning with Angelica, she dreaded recounting it again for Joaquín almost as much as she dreaded the conversation they certainly would have about Luis Posada Carriles. Yes, she had read *The New York Times* article in which Posada had claimed credit for bombing seven Habana hotels. Yes, she knew Posada was now in jail in Panama for an attempted assassination of Castro; she had read a statement by the Panamanian security forces stating that if the bomb planted by Posada and his collaborators had detonated it would have killed not only Fidel but also the two thousand-plus medical school students and staff assembled to hear him speak. Yes, but—could she just say to Joaquín that she had enough pain on her plate at the moment without dredging up past losses and injustices? Especially now that Posada was behind bars.

It was not Joaquín or Sylvia who answered the door. An auburn-haired woman, speaking not the Spanish of Cuba but that of Spain, said the couple was out for the evening. Celia explained that her family and Joaquín's were old friends, she was en route from Habana to Santiago and had decided to drop by on the spur of the moment. With that she would have been on her way, but when the woman understood that she intended to continue on to Santiago, she would not hear of it. "What would they say if I told them you had come all the way from Habana and I allowed you to leave? I'm Sylvia's sister Lydia, by the way. You must stay, you must!"

"Well . . ." Celia murmured indecisively. She had reached that point of tiredness when the take-charge attitude of a woman like Lydia was hard to resist.

Lydia stepped out onto the terrace and called down to a couple of boys playing baseball in the street, "Pietro, Juan! Open the garage door for my friend."

Again Celia protested, "Please, no! I cannot take their garage space."

"Oh my dear!" Lydia laughed. "They don't have a car. Nor does anyone else on this street. When Joaquín's family traded their house in Habana for this one, it just happened to have a garage. A taxi driver one street over normally parks his vehicle there but it is at the mechanic's now so it's quite empty. And here"—she walked back inside and motioned to a door that opened off the living room—"you can sleep. The bathroom is there. Rest a bit, shower if you like, and we shall have dinner."

"Oh no! Really! I do not need—"

"Ah, but *I* need the company. Would you have me eat alone?" Lydia gestured dramatically toward a long table at the far end of the big room. "Go!" she commanded. "Put the car away. And when you come back—oh, I almost forgot! Don't turn on the air conditioner while you're running the shower. The water heater and air-conditioning unit together trip a circuit or blow fuses or something like that. We shall end up in the dark."

"Thanks for warning me." Celia laughed.

When she returned from putting the car in the garage, Lydia was nowhere to be seen. Glancing about the living room, a pair of crossed rapiers on the wall above the sofa caught her attention. When she and Joaquín were children, those rapiers had hung exactly so, above the sofa in his family's Vedado home. They had belonged to Joaquín's father.

On the other side of the room was a cabinet that held trophies. The ones on the top shelf she had seen before; they, too, had belonged to Joaquín's father. The next shelf held ones Joaquín had earned while still in his teens, and on the bottom shelf, those from his years on the Cuban Olympic team.

She heard kitchen sounds and thought of offering to help Lydia prepare their meal. But tiredness compelled her to opt for the shower. When she came out twenty minutes later she found the table set for two and nothing resembling Cuban food in sight. Instead, there were two delicate green salads, hot garlic bread, and a heaping dish of paella redolent with unfamiliar spices. Lydia was already seated, sipping a glass of wine. Celia sat down, feeling blessed to be in the company of a hospitable stranger with whom she could converse on impersonal subjects.

"How wonderful of you to take me in like this," Celia said. "This truly is beyond the call of hospitality."

"Not *Cuban* hospitality," Lydia disputed. "I cannot count the times Cubans I barely knew opened their homes to me. I hope a little of that openness has rubbed off."

Lydia was not exaggerating about Cuban hospitality. Had a stranger appeared at Celia's door claiming to be Joaquín's friend, she would have shown the same hospitality, albeit not the same ability to throw together a gourmet meal on the spur of the moment.

"Do you come to Cuba often then, to visit your sister?"

"To visit my sister, no. We are too far apart in age and interests to be friends." Lydia smiled brightly. "However, our relationship is not so strained that we can't use each other. When Joaquín's work takes him to Spain they stay with me, and from time to time I come to here to pursue my love affair with Cuba."

The turn of phrase piqued Celia's interest. She knew Joaquín's wife was from a cultured Spanish family, yet neither sister showed the condescension toward Cubans that Celia had often encountered among Europeans.

"I grew up with Joaquín," Celia explained. "Our families lived across the street from one another. But I don't know your sister very well, nothing about her interests."

Lydia leaned forward confidentially. "Sylvia's interest, singular, has always been sexy athletes, plural. Fortunately Joaquín is intense enough to hold her attention, which, let me tell you, has been a great relief to the family. If Joaquín hadn't come along and touched her, God knows where she would have ended up."

Celia barely concealed her surprise, both at Lydia's characterization of her sister and the notion of Joaquín being sexy. Intense, yes, but sexy? Well, maybe he was in a bone-thin way, especially when all that dancer's grace was on display in the sport at which he excelled. "And you?" Celia asked, diplomatically turning the conversation away from the private life of the absent sister who was technically her host. "What is it you like so much about Cuba?"

"The art." Lydia promptly launched into a discussion of Cuban painters that left Celia feeling as if she had been subjected to a seminar on the subject.

"But here in Bayamo?" Celia asked, when Lydia finally paused for breath. "I would have thought that the best Cuban artists are based in Habana."

"Not necessarily," Lydia contradicted. "I don't think there's a finer sculptor in Cuba, or in Europe for that matter, than Lecuey, who lives right here in Bayamo. I find the Afro-Caribbean influence at this end of the island very appealing. And many of them as yet undiscovered. For example, there is a tiny community on the coast, not far from Santiago, called Los Mamoncillos. The government set it up especially for artists with free housing and a gallery to display their work. But it's so isolated—"

The sentence was cut short by shouts from the street. One was female, high-pitched, and defiant. The other was male and angry. Celia glanced with alarm toward the open window, but Lydia waved airily as if shooing away a mosquito that had buzzed in on the warm night air. "They're home," she announced.

"Puta! You showed him everything!"

"Hijo de puta! It's mine to show to whomever I please. At least he *noticed*."

Celia had no desire to witness a domestic quarrel or to spend an evening in the company of a quarrelling couple pretending for her sake that everything was fine. Leaping up from the table, she said hurriedly, "Please excuse me. I—"

Lydia laid a restraining hand on her arm. "There is no need to hide. It will be over in a moment." She leaned forward and whispered, "Joaquín is insanely jealous. When they go out socially, my sister taunts him. They quarrel all the way home, then fall into bed and make up, passionately." Celia must have looked shocked because Lydia laughed. "Don't you see? It is a game. Like fencing."

"But it sounds so—"

"Intense? Of course. It is the thing that attracts them to each other."

As if to dramatize her statement, the front door flew open so hard that it banged back against the wall. Joaquín stalked in, looking like a cinema outlaw in tight black jeans, black boots, and a black V-neck T-shirt that revealed every ripple on his slim torso. He half turned to snarl at Sylvia. She was right behind him, wearing a leather miniskirt that hugged her hips even tighter than Joaquín's jeans hugged his. As Sylvia stepped through the doorway she lifted a foot to take off one high-heeled shoe. For a second Celia thought she was going to hit Joaquín with it. He must have thought so too because he raised a hand as if to fend off a blow. At that instant it apparently registered with Sylvia that at the opposite end of the room, her sister was not alone at the table. The shoe remained suspended in mid-air.

"Madre de Dios!" Sylvia gasped. "Celia Cantú! Where did you come from?"

That brought Joaquín's head snapping around, and both of them rushed toward her. Joaquín reached her first because Sylvia, with one shoe in hand, paused to remove the other. Joaquín swept Celia into his arms and hugged her so tight that she could feel his heartbeat. She was fairly certain that its pounding had nothing to do with the surprise of seeing her but was from adrenalin generated by the interrupted quarrel.

Both proclaimed joy at seeing her, fussed over her, and chided her for not calling so that they could have been there when she arrived. Lydia shooed them toward the sofa and went to fetch coffee. Celia sank down in one of the overstuffed armchairs—not a common luxury in a Cuban household, as island-made wooden rockers were more durable and less expensive. Joaquín moved a footstool into place for her comfort and took a seat across from her on the sofa. Sylvia slid down beside him in a reclining position and thrust her shoeless feet into his lap. Joaquín wrapped his long thin fingers around one foot and began to gently stroke the underside of the arch—an intimate gesture he seemed unaware of as he quizzed Celia about their Habana friends.

Lydia soon returned with the coffee. She smiled sardonically at Sylvia's provocative pose. Sylvia gave her a defiant look and perhaps to provoke her older sister, squirmed so that the short skirt rode up even higher on her thighs.

"Enough about people I don't know!" Sylvia interrupted Joaquín. "Tell us, Celia, what brings you to this end of the island? A conference?"

"No, this trip is personal. I—well, here. Let me show you." Celia rose and went into the bedroom to get something from her bag.

She heard Lydia say, "Have you no shame, Sylvia? You're behaving like a child."

And Sylvia's petulant response, "I'm tired. And Celia is family, yes, Joaquín?"

"Claro, Celia es familia," Joaquín was saying as Celia re-entered the room. He gazed indulgently at his supine wife. Neither seemed to remember the insults they had hurled at each other not thirty minutes earlier.

On another occasion Celia would have found an excuse to retire, leaving them to pursue their passion. But her mission took precedence. From a manila envelope she removed copies of the flyer and passed them around. Just as the mood had changed in a heartbeat from heated quarrel to warm welcome, so it changed with dramatic suddenness in response to the information on the flyer.

"Dios mío!" Lydia gasped.

"Que terrible!" Sylvia cried, sitting bolt upright.

Celia realized that these women, being Europeans, assumed the most frightening possibilities, such as a kidnapping or Liliana being spirited out of the country against her will. She was about to explain how those things did not happen here when Joaquín offered a similar thought. "What do you mean, 'missing,' Celia? This is not Argentina."

Briefly Celia told them what had happened. She did not mention that she had broken off her engagement with Luis, only that he had made the flyers and was helping distribute them. She asked if she might leave a few for them to circulate in Bayamo or anywhere else on the island where they happened to go.

"Claro, claro!" they assured her.

"Joaquín is about to take his team for demonstration matches in all the provincial capitals," Sylvia said. She tapped the notice in her hand. "I'll make more copies and he can circulate them everywhere he goes."

"Tomorrow I will be going to that artists' community I told you about," Lydia said. "There are four resorts along the coast east of Santiago. I will ask at each of them."

Joaquín was still staring at the picture, frowning. "Cuban girls don't go missing," he insisted. "They just don't."

"I know," Celia said. "But she did."

"In Cuba," he said stubbornly, "children are safe."

"Yes," Celia said, although as a doctor she knew it was a qualified kind of safety. She had never heard of the kind of abductions and child murders in Cuba that so often made the news in North America, but social workers had brought her young girls who had strayed into prostitution. She had first-hand knowledge of the damage some had sustained. She also knew that time was of the essence; that the longer it took to get them into care, the greater the chance of irreparable damage. She wasn't sure she was doing all she should be doing, but was certain that the collective approach was the best, the Cuban, way. The more people who joined the search, the better.

They sat for a moment, saying nothing. Then Sylvia stood up. "This is such a sad thing, Celia. I will pray for your little girl tonight." She kissed the air next to Celia's face and, with a meaningful look at Joaquín, left the room.

Lydia clasped Celia's hands in hers. "I am glad you told us. We will spread the word. If your lovely niece is in this area, someone surely will be able to tell us."

Lydia left the room and Celia started for her own. Joaquín put out a hand to keep her. "This is terrible news. And on top of the other—you must be devastated."

Celia's heart leapt into her throat. "What other?" Too late she realized that it would not be some new terrible thing, merely some new version of the old. Joaquín was already answering the question she wished she had not asked.

"Luis Posada Carriles is on the loose again."

His words struck her mind like the slap of an open palm against her cheek. "No!" she burst out. "Impossible!"

"It was the president of Panama, that bitch! On her last day in office she pardoned him. Of course the release was brokered by the United States—or so we can surmise, since Posada and his little terrorist entourage left Panama on a US government plane."

"You mean he is back in the United States?"

"The plane put down in Teguchigalpa for a press conference. When it was time to reboard, Posada had disappeared. Who can say where he is now? You know he brags about all the passports he owns, how he can travel anywhere, anytime." Joaquín made a sudden slashing motion with his arm and jabbed the air with an imaginary rapier. "That's what it will take to stop him. Just that! Through the heart, to the spine!"

Although the news shook her to the core, Celia pulled back. "Let it go," she said in a low voice. "I have said this before, Joaquín. We have to let it go."

Joaquín wrapped his arms around her. She could feel him shaking with the intensity of his hatred. "You say that," he choked, "but you can't, no more than I."

"We must," she insisted. "Posada will get what he deserves. If not in Panama, if not in Venezuela, if not in the United States, then somewhere."

"Do you really think so?"

"I am sure," she replied, although she was not at all sure. She pointed in the direction Sylvia had gone. "Go, old friend. Your wife is waiting."

Joaquín stared hard into Celia's eyes. She knew he was looking for what he had always looked for in her—a reflection of the pain and frustration he himself felt. What he sought was not there with the intensity it once would have been, but he must have seen enough to validate his own emotions. He kissed her cheeks and bade her goodnight.

The old anguish was there, of course; a knot in Celia's stomach told her as much. But where Joaquín had had no new emotional upheavals to take its place, apart from those he and his wife created for their own amusement, she had one so fresh and raw that news that her father's killer had again gone free did not generate the same turmoil it once would have. It was a reality, but it was not hers—not now.

FORTY-SIX

CELIA arrived at Franci and Philip's place in mid-morning. The door was locked, and when she walked around back to see if the mothers were about, she found that they, too, were out—no surprise, as most Santiagans tried to get their errands done before the city's sweltering heat reached its zenith. As she passed the bedroom window she peered in and saw that it was exactly as she had left it a little over a week ago. Even the teddy bear, a gift from Philip to Franci once when they mistakenly thought she was pregnant, remained propped against the pillow where Celia had placed it. The hope that Liliana might be here died within her.

She got into the car intending to drive to Franci's office but decided instead to get gas and go into downtown Santiago for—what? Clues? Luck?

In central Santiago she found a line of tour buses disgorging tourists into Parque Céspedes. She went into Hotel Casa Granda to phone Alma, Emily, and the hospital and to leave a flyer at the reception desk. Then she climbed the wide marble stairs up to the terrace. She took a seat at one of the small tables that flanked the balustrade, where she had a clear view of the park, and ordered a plate of pasta.

There were numerous jineteros in the park and almost an equal number of police. While visitors wandered about collecting impressions of the historic square, police and jineteros eyed each other suspiciously. The police were authorized to arrest any Cuban who approached a foreigner with the intent of hustling, but where did simple sociability end and harassment begin? If they moved to intercept hustlers too soon, foreigners were likely to perceive it as police interference in a harmless exchange. Yet if the police held back, foreigners were quick to complain that the police had looked on and done nothing while they were being harassed.

Perhaps the police were being particularly vigilant in Parque Céspedes that day because the only contact between Cubans and foreigners that Celia observed occurred in alcoves along side streets where the odd visitor wandered alone. Even at a distance it was easy to tell when a foreigner was being approached because almost all the tourists were white and most of the jineteros were black. This would not have been true in Habana or Trinidad, but Santiago, having the island's largest Afro-Cuban population, naturally had a higher percentage of black jineteros. If Liliana had got hold of an outfit more appropriate than the shorts and halter top she was wearing when she disappeared, she might be mistaken for a tourist, but she would have stood out among so many dark-skinned jineteras.

Celia finished her pasta and went down into the park. She approached several of the policemen and showed them Liliana's picture. They shrugged, neither interested nor helpful. Their job was to keep hustlers away from tourists, not to look for missing kids. If the compañera wanted to file a report with the youth authorities . . .

The compañera did not. She walked up Aguilera Street to the Plaza de Dolores. In sidewalk cafés around the plaza there were many people, some exactly the kind of young foreign "backpackers" Celia had begun to imagine Liliana might have hooked up with. She stood in the shade of a tamarind tree and scanned the area.

Three gay men sat on a bench exchanging witticisms probably meant to be overheard by a lesbian couple on a nearby bench. The women caressed each other, pretending to ignore the men. However, given the relatively small number of Cuban homosexuals who were out of the closet, Celia guessed that they would all end up at the same party that evening. One of the men rose and, flinging a forelock of black curls out of his eyes, came toward her. She recognized him from the café in Playas del Este. He was the one who, when she passed around the notice with Liliana's pictures, had made a facetious remark about her not being "his type."

"Hello," he said. "I don't suppose you remember me, but—"

"I do remember you," Celia said. "We met at Mi Cayito."

He looked embarrassed. "That's right. I just wanted to tell you that I have been on the lookout for your daughter. I've got the numbers, see?" He took a thin wallet from his pocket and from it extracted a slip of paper, which did indeed have the three telephone numbers listed on the notice.

The thoughtfulness, coming from such an unexpected source, brought tears to Celia's eyes. "Gracias, compañero," she murmured.

"Don't thank me," he protested. "I haven't done anything."

"Yes you have. You have made me feel less alone in my search."

"Oh." He looked down at his shoes. "Then I guess—I mean, you shouldn't feel alone, okay? Not in Cuba."

No, Celia thought as she walked back along Calle Herida. Everywhere she had been so far, she had come away knowing she had the support of friends and strangers. Whatever the problem, in Cuba one need not shoulder it alone.

She walked until she heard the voices of a classical choir floating on the hot midday air, then changed directions to return to Parque Céspedes. As if to emphasize Santiago's collage of musical traditions, she was barely out of earshot of the choir when she paused to listen to a street band of guitarists, flautists, and drummers. When the charanga ended, Celia approached the plump female vocalist, showed her Liliana's pictures, and asked the tired question.

Everyone in the band glanced at the pictures, but briefly, anxious to get back to their music. "Don't know as we'd notice her out here on the street," the woman said apologetically. "Try the clubs."

As Celia cut across Parque Céspedes toward where her car was parked, she noticed an elderly black man seated on a bench watching the human circus. Judging him to be a park regular, Celia sat down next to him. After exchanging pleasantries, she showed him Liliana's pictures and asked if he had seen her around.

He studied the photos, then called to an ebony-skinned young man with Rastafarian hair. "Julio! Come tell me if you seen this little girl around." To Celia he said, "Julio play son over at the Casa de la Trova. You got time to catch the show this afternoon, he way better than most."

The younger man strolled over and took a seat next to Celia, his dreadlocks brushing softly against her bare arm as he leaned to look at the flyer she held. "This one I not seen. Not too many white jineteras around here."

Celia flinched at the word and started to slide the poster back into her purse, as if to shield her niece from that interpretation. But the old man reached out with arthritic fingers and took it from her to study the pictures. Finally he shook his head.

"The boy speak true. This child most likely gone to Habana."

Celia rose and nodded her thanks. "If you see her, would you tell her—" She hesitated. "Tell her that her tía is looking for her."

"For sure," the young musician promised.

The old man patted Celia's hand. "And you know, no pretty girl like that gonna come in this park without Julio seeing her."

"Ha!" Julio tossed the long Rastafarian locks in a way that Celia suspected drove women wild. "This old man got more girls sitting down by him in a day than I got in a week. And taking his picture. He make more money looking colourful than I make playing music."

"That's true and that's justice." The old man winked a cloudy eye at Celia. "Learning to be a music man don't take no time at all. Learning to be old, now that take pretty near a man's whole life."

FORTY-SEVEN

CELIA parked the convertible at the curb, relieved to see that the Fiat was now in the driveway. "Hello?" she called through the screen door. "Anybody here?"

"Celia?" Franci called from the hallway even before she saw her. She emerged pulling a purple tank top down over white shorts. "Hey, girl! What brings you here again so soon? Why didn't you call so I could meet the train?" Not waiting for answers because the answers didn't matter, Franci wrapped Celia in a hug. "Come *in*. I can't tell you how glad I am to see you! How did you get here? Don't you have a bag?"

As Celia opened her mouth to speak, the telephone rang. Franci snatched it up. "Oh, Philip, guess—"

Franci's eyes widened in alarm. "I'll be right there!" She hung up the receiver, grabbed her car keys, and turned to Celia. "That was Philip. Come. Something has happened at work."

"Is he—?"

"It's not him. At least, that's what he said. But some kind of emergency. He needs me there as quickly as possible."

As Franci backed out of the driveway into the street, she saw the convertible. The top was up and road grime dulled the glossy yellow paint but it was still an eye-catching car. She frowned and turned her gaze on Celia. "That can't be how you got here."

"It is," Celia admitted.

"And it belongs to?" Franci stomped on the gas, causing the Fiat to leap forward. "Don't lie! That is a José Lago car if I ever saw one."

"It is José's car, but it's not what you think, Franci."

"What I think is that it better *not* be what I think!"

"Franci," Celia said, reaching for the seat belt. "You have other things on your mind. So drop it. For now, okay?"

"Okay," Franci agreed. Every part of her body, even her blown-out Afro hair, seemed electric with tension. "He should have told me *something*. He must have known I'd worry every second till I get there."

"Maybe there was somebody there he didn't want to talk in front of."

"Oh! That could be. In fact, that's how he sounded."

Celia grabbed the armrest as Franci swerved around a horse-drawn cart, cutting it so close with oncoming traffic that she flinched. Fortunately it was not far to Philip's office. Celia drew a breath of relief as they approached the nondescript government building at the mouth of the harbour—then went rigid with fear when Franci drove right past the sentry without so much as a nod. He looked startled, and Celia could have sworn he lifted his rifle in both hands before he realized who it was and waved.

By then Franci had braked to a stop in front of the harbour master's office. She was halfway up the steps before Celia caught up. They entered Philip's office together, expecting anything, perhaps, other than what the room was about to reveal.

Philip, looking much as he always looked when he was in uniform, sat at his desk. He rose and held out his hands to Franci. Before she could ask anything, he said, "Just stay calm and act natural."

As far as Celia could tell, the only *un*natural thing was Philip's terse warning to act natural. Her eyes swept the room. In a dim corner, half-concealed behind a coat rack, she saw—at first she didn't know what she was seeing, only that it was dark and moving.

Philip took Franci by the elbow and led her toward the dark thing. Speaking in a soft voice, he said, "C'est ma femme, Franci. Franci, voici mon amie, Josephine."

Franci held out her hand. The child, for it was a child Celia now saw, drew back. Philip pulled Franci away and jerked his chin toward the door. Outside, still speaking in a low voice, he explained, "She's a stowaway. From Haití. Her father got caught, I guess it was six months or so ago. They turned him over to me and when I discovered he had the little girl—they hadn't found her yet and that was actually how they caught him, trying to get her off the ship—well, I should have reported them but I didn't."

Franci wrapped her arms around him. "Oh, Philip!"

He gently disentangled himself from her embrace. "Let me finish, Franci. After that, the guy dropped around occasionally, looking for work. I tried to give him spare change, but he didn't like handouts and would hang around until I found something for him to do."

"Where is he now?"

Philip ran fingers through his wavy blond hair, already mussed by what Celia recognized as a repetitive worry gesture. "Good question. She showed up here about an hour ago asking for a shovel. Maybe he's sick, maybe she wants to make a garden, I don't know. All I know is I don't have a damned shovel and I've got a ship coming in. If she hangs around they'll pick her up for sure because she doesn't speak a word of Spanish. I was hoping you—" He seemed to notice Celia for the first time. "And Celia, yes. Maybe the two of you could find a shovel for her and take her home?"

"Claro!" Franci exclaimed. "Where's home?"

"When I last saw the man, maybe three weeks ago, I asked where they were living. He just waved." Philip waved his own hand to the mountains rising along the southeastern side of the bay. "Somewhere up there. Probably in some thrown-together shelter. Having entered the country illegally, it's not as if they could apply for housing."

"What would happen if they were turned over to the authorities?" Celia asked.

"They'd be put on the next boat back to Haití." Philip gave Celia a look that begged her to understand why he had not done the legally appropriate thing. "But they had a reason for leaving. Wrong political party or something. The guy's been whipped to within an inch of his life; his back is a mass of scars. He said his wife and another kid were killed."

Celia and Franci looked at each other, overcome by a mixture of horror and gratitude at the unearned good fortune of having grown up in a country where, in their lifetime, there had been no such violence.

"Let me talk to her," Franci said softly.

Philip smiled. "With your French? Good luck!" But there was relief in his voice.

They found the girl where she had been, in the dimmest corner of the room. In French, Philip told the child that he must go now to bring in a ship, and she must go with these ladies, that they would find her a shovel and take her home.

Franci put out her hand. The girl, as ragged a child as Celia had ever seen, stared at it a long moment, then placed her own dark hand in it. "Je suis Josephine," she said.

Franci, although she had already been introduced, touched herself on the chest and repeated her own name. Then motioned to Celia. "Ma amie, Celia."

The girl barely glanced at Celia and—Celia felt certain it was because of her colour—edged closer to Franci.

When they reached the car, Franci tossed her keys to Celia. "You drive."

Celia obediently slid behind the wheel. Franci got into the passenger seat and held out her arms to the child, inviting her into her lap. The girl obliged but did not lean back the way a normal child would. She held herself bolt upright so that her starvation-thin body made minimal contact with Franci's.

"Where to?" Celia asked.

"Home," Franci said. "Mamá is doing a garden. That's probably what Josephine wants the spade for. It's that time of year. They must be trying to live off the land."

Observing Josephine from the corner of her eye, Celia guessed that although she looked to be about eight, she might be older and small for her age due to malnutrition. The girl had fine features and almond-shaped eyes looking out of an oval face as dark as Franci's. The depth of her colour was less apparent on the rest of her body due to scaly dryness and a coating of dust. Josephine's tension increased as they left the harbour and entered what Celia supposed were to the child unfamiliar parts of the city. When they stopped at the house, Josephine pawed at the door latch. Franci opened the door but clung to the girl's hand as if fearing she might bolt. Celia trailed them to the back of the house.

"Mamá!" Franci shouted.

Franci's massive mother appeared in the doorway of the cottage. "Franci!" she exclaimed. "Where you get that scrawny child? You bring her inside this minute, I give her something to eat."

"Mange?" Franci pantomimed eating.

Josephine shook her head. She was scanning the yard, and when she saw the spaded area, headed straight to it. She returned clutching the shovel.

"She seems pretty focused," Celia commented. "Maybe we can take some food out to them later, when we see what their situation is."

"Good idea," Franci said, and to her mother, apologetically, "She just wants to borrow your shovel. Is that okay?"

"She gonna bring it back?" the old lady demanded. "How come she take it just like that, don't say nothing?"

"She doesn't speak Spanish. Only French," Celia explained.

"Mon Dieu!" came the piercing voice of Madame Morceau from the window of her garage apartment. "You have a child who speaks français?"

"We'll bring the shovel back," Franci promised, hurrying after Josephine, who was already at the car. Waving up to Philip's mother, she called, "I'll explain later."

Again Franci pulled the little girl into her lap. Celia pried her fingers off the shovel and placed it in the back seat where it would not interfere with the gear shift and headed for the harbour. She hoped Josephine would be able to direct her from there.

The girl remained upright and attentive to landmarks. She relaxed visibly when the harbour sparkled in the distance. Suddenly she pointed to the left and said, "Ici."

As soon as Celia turned on to the highway that ran along the southeast side of the harbour, the girl's demeanour changed. She allowed her body to relax against Franci's and, unsmiling, began to chatter.

Celia and Franci glanced at each other. "Did you get any of that?" Franci asked

"Les chiens? The dogs?" Celia suggested hesitantly. "And something about rocks."

"I thought she was talking about her father." Franci frowned. "I think she's saying he's sick. But where?" To Josephine, she said, "Où est ta maison?"

Josephine's small grimy hand gestured in the direction they were driving, a highway rather grandly called the Carretera Turística, although it ran for at least two kilometres through an industrial wasteland before emerging into open countryside.

"Mais où?" Celia persisted, as the highway twisted and climbed toward the great fort that guarded the mouth of the harbour. To Franci she said, "We have come a good five kilometres. I find it hard to believe she walked this far alone."

Again Josephine rattled off a long explanation in her quaint Haitian French, which left Celia and Franci more perplexed than before.

"Le grand homme? The big man? Oh, why did I let my college French lapse?" Franci muttered in frustration.

"I think she said *under* the big man. Could she mean the Frank País monument?"

"Under the statue?" Franci looked bewildered. "Oh, like somewhere on that hill, lower down?"

As if in answer to both of them, Josephine suddenly bounced on Franci's lap, pointed to the parking lot for the País memorial, and squealed, "Ici, ici!"

Celia braked sharply and turned into the parking lot. Josephine had obviously observed how the car door worked because this time she had it open before Franci got to it. Celia took the shovel from the back seat, intending to carry it, but Josephine took it from her and clutched it to her chest as if it were a beloved toy. They locked the car and followed the child up the steps, at least two hundred of them, to the top of the hill. There in a grassy park as big as two soccer fields stood an enormous bronze likeness of Frank País, the young schoolteacher who in 1956 had led an attack on the Santiago police headquarters to divert attention from the landing of the boat bringing Fidel and his fellow revolutionaries from México. Two months after the *Granma* landing, the police spotted Frank País walking down the street and shot him in the back. The young teacher's funeral turned into a massive rally led by the mothers of Santiago, followed by nationwide protests against the dictator's brutality.

Josephine crossed herself as she passed under the shadow of the huge statue. Celia wondered whether she considered the statue a deity, a demon, or simply a giant whose goodwill she wished to keep. Josephine waited on the far side of the park until they caught up to her, then moved rapidly down the slope through a tangle of undergrowth. Celia had noticed a network of scratches on the child's bare arms, and as she collected a few on her own, realized that this was how she had got them.

"Like following a goat," Franci muttered. Celia glanced back and saw that Franci, in shorts and tank top, was having a rough go of it. Her grumbles turned to ouches as they trailed Josephine through a thicket of thorn bushes that, had they been hiking on their own, they certainly would have avoided. Suddenly the head-high bushes opened onto a small clearing. One side was walled by a rock face down which trickled a pencil-thin stream of water. Near it was a hut, barely bigger than a dog kennel, built of cardboard and torn plastic. Josephine did not enter the hut but went immediately to an area where the soil had been turned up.

"Look," Franci brightened. "She *is* making a garden." Franci bent to pick up something. Holding it up for Celia, she exclaimed, "Can you believe this? A broken spoon! She was trying to dig a garden using a tablespoon!"

Celia looked at the soil, already turned up to a depth of about fifteen centimetres. It was longer than it was wide. She was struck by an awful suspicion. "Ou est ton papa?"

Without looking up from her digging, Josephine pointed to the hut. Celia moved to the burlap-covered doorway and called, "Monsieur?"

There was no response. She pulled aside the burlap. It was dark inside; she could see nothing. Celia went down on her knees, which was the only way for a grown person to enter the hovel, and crept forward.

Franci called from behind her. "Tell him he needn't be afraid of us."

Slowly Celia's eyes adjusted to the dim interior. Near the entrance was a rusty pail and beyond it a pile of rags. Then she saw that it was not a rag pile; it was a rag-covered man. She thought his face moved, as if he were trying to speak or smile. She leaned closer. The movement was not his. It was that of flies and ants, claiming what they could from the corpse. She automatically reached for his wrist to check for a pulse, although the smell had already told her that there would be none. Celia backed out.

"What?" Franci demanded.

"He is dead," Celia said, although Franci must have understood the simple words the child flung over her shoulder as she shovelled dirt: "Il est mort."

Franci's lips parted but she said nothing. She simply walked over and took the shovel from Josephine.

"What are we going to do?" Celia asked.

"Help her dig the grave."

"Franci, this is illegal! You can't bury a body just anyplace. The authorities—"

Franci picked up the pace of her digging. "If you want to leave, go." She glanced up at Celia with a grim smile. "But if you notify the authorities, I'll kill you."

Celia had no trouble following Franci's thought processes, both the ones that led to her sudden decision and the ones that flowed from it. She sighed and started scooping soil with her hands. "Another shovel would make this go a lot quicker," she muttered.

Josephine looked from one woman to the other, then dove into the hut. She came out with the pail of water. She dumped it and handed the bucket to Celia.

"Merci," Celia said and began using the pail to remove dirt from the hole. Josephine busied herself sorting stones from dirt, heaping the rocks to one side.

The sun blazed down and the smell of putrefaction coming from the hut intensified. An hour later, when Franci reached down to wiggle loose a rock, Celia saw that her hands were blistered. The blisters had broken and were bleeding. She rose and took the shovel from her. "You work the bucket for a while," she said.

Franci looked at her hands ruefully. "I noticed Josephine's hands had big broken blisters on the palms. Now I know how they got that way."

Celia's hands fared no better, but by the time she felt she could stand the pain no longer, at least they had a hole. It was not deep but it would have to do. The clearing had been in shadow for an hour; the sun would be setting soon.

"C'est bien?" she asked Josephine.

The child stared at the hole. Celia could tell that she was not satisfied but she too must have realized that they were running out of time. She shrugged and, in a tiny voice, said, "Oui."

"How are we going to get him out here?" Franci asked.

"Very carefully," Celia responded. "He is lying on a piece of canvas. If we each grab a corner, I think we can drag him to the grave."

As Franci started for the hut, Celia warned, "Don't touch the body. And once you have touched *anything*, keep your hands away from your face. He could well have died of something contagious. I have already touched him, so I will drag him to the door. Then you grab a corner of the canvas and pull."

The old man—or perhaps he wasn't that old, merely ravaged by life and death— was surprisingly light. Just before dragging him out into the light, Celia brushed the insects off his face. No need for his daughter to see that.

Josephine had not come to help them bring out the body. When they reached the grave she was in it on her knees, smoothing it with her bare palms. Franci held a hand down to her. The girl hesitated, then took it and climbed out. Holding opposite sides of the canvas, the three of them lowered the body into the ground.

Celia went back into the hovel and came out with an armful of rags that she spread over the body, not for the man's sake but for the child's, to give her the illusion that her father had gone to rest in the nearest thing to comfort they could provide.

When Josephine saw what Celia was doing, she took one of the rags, a small scrap of brown velvet, and laid it over his face, soft side down. Franci pulled the child to her and held her while Celia shovelled in the dirt. When the body was covered, although by barely half a metre of soil, they started to leave. But Josephine, who had neither wept nor spoken during the process, squatted and began piling the rocks she had set aside on top of the grave.

Celia and Franci knelt down to help, at last understanding what Josephine had said back in the car. Her father had to be buried, and the grave must be covered with rocks to prevent the dogs from getting at it.

FORTY-EIGHT

CELIA, Franci, and Josephine reached the top of the hill as the last ray of sunshine lit the bronze head of Frank País. They passed by the statue, Josephine again crossing herself, and descended the long stairway down to the parking lot.

"Do you think," Franci asked as they were driving back, "that she might have caught whatever it was he died from?"

"She might have," Celia admitted. "If she develops fever or diarrhea, you will get her to a doctor, won't you? One you can trust with her real history, insofar as you know it. She may need to be tested for diseases not common here in Cuba."

Celia was aware that she was speaking as if the child would remain with Franci. She probably had known the second Josephine lay her hand in Franci's back in Philip's office that this was how it would turn out. Perhaps they all had known.

Josephine was quiet on the ride back. She had taken nothing from the hut, nor had she asked where they were going. She lay limp against Franci, as if where they went or what they did now could not possibly matter.

"What do you propose doing with her?" Celia asked.

"Feed her, of course. My mother's right, you know. She is half-starved."

"Clean her up first," Celia said as they pulled into the drive. "Wash her hands and yours with soap and water, plus alcohol if you have any, before touching anything."

Josephine showed no reluctance going into the house but clung so tightly to Franci's hand that Celia wondered if the two could be pried apart long enough to be washed. Celia went into the kitchen for water, and when they came out of the bathroom, she handed a glass to each of them. It had been a blistering hot day and all three of them were dehydrated. Then Celia placed a mandarin on the table in front of Josephine.

"That's not enough!" Franci exclaimed, heading for the refrigerator.

Celia laid a hand on her arm. "Wait, Franci. I have never seen a case of malnutrition this serious but I have read about it. We have to be careful not to overload the system. The mandarin will pick up her blood sugar level. Then—let me think. Philip's seafood bouillabaisse would be perfect, or a light vegetable broth."

"Surely she needs more—"

"Much more," Celia agreed quickly. "But pay attention, Franci, to what I'm telling you. Go *slow*. No fried foods or anything heavy."

Josephine consumed the mandarin and licked the pink undersides of her small brown fingers. Noticing the short fingernails, some of which were cracked vertically, Celia said, "She has a calcium deficiency too. Do you have any yogourt?"

"No, but I can fix—"

"You bathe her. I am going to the pharmacy to see if I can find some vitamins and"—Celia opened the refrigerator and scanned its contents—"fresh vegetables. I'll make a soup."

As Franci held out her hand to Josephine, Celia said, "You are going to have to watch the mothers like a hawk. Yours will want to stuff her and Philip's is a sugar addict. Josephine should have no sweets for a while. Everything she puts in her mouth should be nutritious. And no big meals. Just small amounts through the day. Can you manage that?"

"Claro," Franci called over her shoulder as they headed for the bathroom. "I'll just tell them not to feed her and they'll sneak it to her bite by tiny bite behind my back."

Celia drove to the nearest pharmacy for what she needed there, then stopped at a farmers' market and got carrots, a tomato, a few green beans, boniato, and garlic.

When she got back to the house she found Franci on her knees beside a tub so full of bubbles that Josephine's small head was barely visible above them. Celia set a package on the bathroom sink. "Have you shampooed her hair yet?"

"Nope," Franci replied. "We've done fingers, and now we're doing toes."

"Use what I got at the pharmacy."

"Why? I have some lovely coconut—"

"This is for lice," Celia interrupted.

"What?" Franci spun around on her heels. "Who said she had lice?"

"A precaution," Celia said firmly. "You saw the conditions they were living in."

"I don't even know what a louse looks like!" Franci wailed.

"Look in her hair for nits—the eggs. If there are any there you will see them."

"Ugh!" Franci grimaced with distaste. "What have I got myself into?"

They looked at Josephine, or rather at her close-cropped black curls. Sensing something negative in their expressions, she paused in the act of blowing a handful of bubbles, holding the breath she had just sucked in.

"Oh, just a child." Celia grinned.

"Very funny, Doc!" Franci swatted at Celia's ankles with the washcloth. Josephine let her breath out in a whoosh, sending iridescent bubbles floating into the air around them.

Celia put a pot of water on to boil, threw in spices, and minced the vegetables. While the soup simmered she wrote out a list titled Instruciones de la Doctora. It detailed the kinds of foods Josephine should and should not have and how much of which vitamins. She also advised Franci to get the girl tested for internal parasites as soon as possible.

The telephone rang. "Get that, will you?" Franci called. "It'll be Philip."

"I just got in," Philip told Celia when she picked up the receiver. "How did it go?"

Briefly, Celia told him what they had found and what they had done.

"How terrible! I suspected he was sick, and Franci—and you—I was relieved to see you, Celia, because if he was sick you'd know what to do."

"We did," Celia assured him. "Or I should say, Josephine knew what she had to do and Franci knew what she wanted to do. I was just along for the ride."

"How is Franci?"

"Well . . ." Celia teased him with a long hesitation. "Right now, Philip, your

Franci is wearing the happiest smile and the dirtiest shorts I have ever seen on a grown woman."

When Celia returned to the bathroom, Franci had Josephine out of the tub and was towelling her dry. A lump filled Celia's throat as she recalled drying Liliana in exactly that way when she was small.

"It was Philip," she said when she could speak. "He will be here shortly."

Celia returned to the kitchen. On the back of the instructions she had listed for Josephine's care, she wrote, *I'm sorry, I should have told you sooner, but I can't stay. I have to be*—she hesitated, trying to think where she might reasonably say she had to be, then wrote—*somewhere by morning. I will call when I get back to Habana.*

FORTY-NINE

CELIA wondered, as she drove out of the brightly lit city and into the dark foothills of the Sierra Maestra, what exactly she would have told Franci if circumstances had allowed her to tell her anything. Details of Liliana's flight and the conflict with Luis that preceded it, of course. Plus her own fear that if she brought in the youth authorities they would accept Luis's recommendation that, once Liliana was located, she be sent to a re-education camp. Or perhaps they would come to that decision on their own, depending on what they discovered when they investigated Liliana's recent history.

But Franci, she knew, would dig deeper. She would want to know what Celia herself wanted to know: Why had Liliana not trusted her? Why had she run away rather than coming to Celia—or even to Franci—when she felt threatened?

She could almost hear Franci saying, "That is a significant change, Celia. When did it come about?" And her whispered answer, "I do not know."

Franci would look down, then, to keep her from reading anything judgmental in her gaze. But not before Celia would have seen astonishment in her dark eyes, a look that said, clearer than words, "You don't *know*?"

Franci, well-trained professional that she was, would sit quietly as Celia explained the double shifts she had been working and how tired she was when she got home, how Liliana had become so much more social this year, away at school three weeks out of the month and much of her week at home spent at the beach. How she had encouraged that because it seemed to her that it was a good thing that Liliana had lost the clinginess that had characterized most of her childhood and was choosing to be among friends her own age. Good kids they were, and a well-run campismo it was where they spent most of their time—the very same one where she and Franci and their friends had partied, played loud music, danced, and swam when they were in their teens. It had all seemed . . . so right.

All of which would explain why Celia had not noticed, but would not explain why the change had taken place. So Franci would back up and come at the mystery from a different direction, asking another question Celia had already asked herself repeatedly: *when* did the change come about? At that point in their conversation, had there been such a conversation, Celia would have broken down and wept, "I do not *know*. My child went away and I did not see her go! Did not even miss her until her body disappeared too."

Had Franci been in the car instead of back at the house falling in love with an orphan girl, she would have tried to console Celia. That would have been a waste of time, Celia knew. Some things you try to do must be done right the first time because there are no second chances. Some things, when you lose them, you will never get back. All one can do at such a time is move on. If only she knew where to go from here.

Suddenly the physical exertion and emotional drain of the day caught up to her.

Celia felt as if she could not keep her eyes open one moment longer. She pulled off the highway onto an unpaved side road and cut the engine. As she sat waiting for the vibrations of the car to leave her body, she saw the smokestack of a sugar mill like a black cutout against the star-whitened sky. At this midnight hour the old central was silent. There was no odour of crushed cane, nor did the smell of burned fields and dust from tractors bringing fresh-cut cane hang in the air. Maybe it was too early in the season. Or maybe this mill was a relic from a bygone era and had been decommissioned. She got out of the car and walked to the fence. The cavernous building, sheathed in rusty metal, seemed a familiar place. She saw it not from the outside, but from the inside, and not in starlight, but by candlelight . . .

Fidel and his commanders hunched over a map spread on the desk, Fidel pointing to Santa Clara, captured by Che yesterday. His finger moved along the Carretera Central to Habana. Mañana, he told them, New Year's Day, Che and Camilio will be in Habana, and we will be in Santiago. He glanced up at her, read her mind, and backtracked.

He could not actually read her mind, but she did believe that until much later, when, laughing, he told her how facial expressions give her away. A steady gaze said, You are right; we are of one mind. A slight frown: I have a doubt; let us discuss this. A deep frown: No, that will not work; we must find another way. Now Celia was looking across the map with a deep frown, wondering if he did not remember what she had said earlier about how they should not enter Santiago on New Year's Day, but should wait one day more, until the garrisons at Camp Columbia and La Cabaña had surrendered, and Che and Camilio had taken control in Habana. He did remember. He lifted his finger from the map and said, No, not mañana. Mañana we rest. Then we take Santiago, and the war is won; Cuba will be in our hands.

They were all weary, drained, and pained from the battles they had fought and the compañeros lost in the ten weeks since leaving La Comandancia. When Fidel finished describing what was likely to happen in Habana mañana, and in Santiago the following day, his commanders went out into the main part of the mill and curled up against burlap bags of sugar, to dream or sleep dreamless in the sweet truth that a just war has been won.

Only Celia remained in the office, taking off her boots as Fidel took off his, loosening the laces and placing them just so, so the boots could be pulled on in half a second should an alarm be sounded. They spread bedrolls on the rough wooden floor and lay down, although she could tell by the brightness of his eyes in the instant before she extinguished the candle that he was far from sleep. He was probably formulating what he would say on Radio Rebelde in the morning; the ultimatum he would give the Santiago garrison, to surrender or be attacked. This time there would be no slaughter of idealistic students, this time no defeat. This time, Moncada would fall.

Celia, for all her bone weariness, was not swift to sleep either. She was aching for the compañeros who died in the final days of battle, and the ones before that, whom they buried in the sierra. She was aching for the sierra.

She did not miss the bed. She learned long ago to sleep on the ground, the floor, in the back of a truck, anywhere. Here in this black, windowless room, foul with the smell of fermenting cane juice and rat droppings, what she missed was the openness of their small room at the Comandancia, its wooden flaps lifted to let in cool air at night and bird songs at dawn. She missed the silence.

She missed those things in the same way she missed the compañeros who had fallen, the way one misses someone or something that will never be again. As she missed Fidel, although he lay next to her at that very moment.

As if in response to her profound loneliness, he turned on his side, folded one long leg across her hips, and wrapped an arm just below her breasts. As close as they were, it was not so close as before. Now they slept with the fabric of his and her uniforms between them, sleeping in their clothes as soldiers must, not as lovers, each wrapped tight in the skin of the other. Again, someday, perhaps they would. Or perhaps, never again.

"The war is over," he whispered into her hair. "Now La Revolución can begin."

"Sí," she whispered, holding back the rest. It was only to her heart that she said, Our time in the sierra is over. That place where I alone was all you needed—lover, sister, mother, nurse, cook, critic, confidant, challenger, commander, and more—is no more. Tomorrow begins La Revolución. I will hold on to as much of you, for you, as I can, and perhaps, a little for me. But in the end, Cuba will have us both. It is the only way to make a revolution.

Celia Cantú stood at the gate of the old sugar mill, fingering a padlock. She could not go inside to see if burlaps bags of sugar really were piled about, or whether there was a windowless room at the back with a scarred wooden desk stained by candle wax. Those things might or might not be real. The greater reality, it seemed, was this feeling of, just moments ago, lying on a hard wooden floor next to a body warmer than her own.

In the distance a dog let out a single yap. A bat swooped past, soundless. She walked back to the car, wondering how far from the main highway she had driven. She wondered if she would reach the Sierra Maestra before dawn.

FIFTY

IT was a little before four in the morning when the Chevy chugged up the final steep section of concrete highway leading to the Comandancia trail head. Celia parked and got out. This time she had no flashlight, but the trail felt familiar to her feet. She moved slowly and did not stumble. The moon, just a night off full, was very bright.

She had not looked for landmarks on her previous trip and feared she might miss the narrow path leading to Miguel's cabin—which in fact she did. She realized that she had walked too far only when she turned around for a view of the sky, which had gone from black to pearl grey with just the faintest tinge of pink. That was when she saw a thin curl of smoke coming from a cottage lower on the mountain.

She retraced her steps along the main trail until she found the path. Winding narrowly through the forest, it was crisscrossed with dew-covered spiderwebs. There were so many that she wondered if they could have been built in one night, or if Miguel had a special appreciation for webs that caused him to walk around the more elaborate ones rather than brush them aside.

There was no clearing around the cabin. Celia was almost upon it before it came into full view. It looked to be a single room with a thatched roof that extended out over a porch about two metres deep. The windows had wooden shutters that lifted like those in the Comandancia cottage. The shutters and the front door were wide open.

Miguel stood with his back to her, cooking. He was wearing jeans, unbelted, low on his hips. The lack of shirt and shoes and the way hair tousled about the nape of his neck suggested that he was not long out of bed. A coffee pot simmered on one burner. He lifted the skillet, flipped something into the air, and caught it coming down.

He turned toward the table and saw her standing there. As when he had first seen her at the Comandancia, he stopped mid-motion, suddenly so still that he seemed not to be breathing. It must be a skill he had taught himself for his work, Celia thought; to freeze like that when he sighted a wild animal so as to not startle it.

"I'm sorry," she stammered. "I have interrupted your breakfast."

"Not to mention my life," he said with a smile, setting the skillet down on a table.

Only when he walked toward her with his hands held out in welcome did Celia realize how wrong this could go. "I did not come for what you think," she said quickly.

The welcoming smile became mocking. "What I *think*?"

"I am not—that is, things are different now."

"You mean you're not Celia Sánchez? I'm not Fidel Castro? We're just ordinary Cubans?" He turned back to the stove and picked up the coffee pot. "In that case, may I offer you an ordinary cup of coffee?"

Celia stepped inside the cabin, arms wrapped around herself, feeling foolish. What in God's name had possessed her to come? Why had she not foreseen how awkward it would be? She might explain how she was searching for Liliana, how she had left notices at beach resorts and given them to people to distribute in every city between Habana and Santiago. But how could she explain why, when she reached Bayamo, she had not continued west, back to Habana, but had veered south for a two-hour detour to the trail leading—exactly here?

He shoved a stack of books and papers to the back of the table, poured two cups of coffee, and sat down without looking at her. Celia hesitated, but sitting seemed the only civil thing to do, so she sat.

Miguel began spooning a dark thick liquid into his coffee. "I haven't got any sugar. This is honey. From wild bees. Want some?"

"Por favor," Celia said in a voice that sounded prim even to her.

He passed the spoon to her. While she transferred honey from the jar into her coffee, he cut the pancake thing he had been cooking in half and offered part of it to her.

"The honey's good on skillet bread too. It's got royal jelly in it and probably bee larvae. I don't bother to strain it."

"I don't mind a few baby bees. They are protein, right?" Celia was determined not to sound prissy again. All the same, she was glad there were no larvae to be seen in what she spooned into her coffee.

"Looks like you could use some," he said, without looking at her.

"Some what?"

"Protein. You must've lost two kilos in the past ten days."

Celia stared at him. Not only had he kept track of how many days it had been since he saw her, but with barely a glance he had been able to guess almost exactly how much weight she had lost since Liliana's disappearance.

"So you gave up eating for Lent, or what?"

"For your information," Celia informed him crisply, "I had perfectly nutritious rice and beans all last week." She held up a hand in his face, fingers spread, and began ticking off what she could remember of recent meals, not bothering to note how little of each she had actually eaten. "Saturday, I visited a friend in Trinidad who fed me picadillo and sautéed yucca, and on Sunday I dined with a Spanish lady in Bayamo who served pallea with green salad and white wine. Yesterday in Santiago—" Celia paused, trying to remember whether she had eaten either before or after getting together with Franci.

Miguel caught her hand and held it, frowning. "What happened to your palm?"

Embarrassed, she pulled her hand back. "It's from digging. A grave."

"Is that what brought you back to this end of the island? A funeral?"

"Not a funeral. A burial."

He rose, and from a shelf took a brown bottle and a square green can. "Hydrogen peroxide," he said, unscrewing the cap on the bottle. He held out his hand for hers.

Meekly, she gave it to him. Miguel poured the hydrogen peroxide onto the blisters of each hand. Together they watched the fizz. Then he opened the green can and smeared a Vaseline-like substance into the damaged flesh.

"What is that?" Celia asked.

"Bag Balm. A Canadian colleague sent it to me. It's used for cuts and scratches on the udders of milk cows."

"*Cow udders?*" Celia sputtered. "You're putting cow medicine on my hands?"

"That's right, Doctor. Apparently when dairymen rubbed Bag Balm on the cows' teats to heal minor cuts, they discovered that it helped heal their hands too. According to my friend, it's now used by all sorts of people who have never been near a cow. I use it myself when I get scratched in the bush."

As he spoke, Miguel rubbed the salve into her palms and fingers, then slowly up her sunburned forearms. As if sensing her readiness to pull away, he stopped at the elbow and put the lid back on the green can. "This person you buried—was it a close friend?"

"No."

They sat in silence for several minutes before Celia conceded that since she was the one who had arrived unexpectedly, she would have to do the explaining. As the dead man was the most recent thing that had happened, that seemed the place to start. So she told him who Franci and Philip were, how Philip had let the Haitian stowaway slip into the country because he had a little girl, and how that girl was now in Philip and Franci's care—the black, part-French child they had not been able to have.

As Celia talked, Miguel stared out the cabin door, watching the morning light come up. When she finished he said, softly, "Que milagro! Little orphan girl stories don't often have such happy endings in real life."

Celia blinked fast to keep her eyes from overflowing. "Are there happy endings?" she asked in a strangled voice. "In real life?"

He got up and walked out onto the porch. A large juita came from the forest and stood at the bottom of the porch steps looking up at him. He came back inside and picked up the piece of skillet bread, which she had only nibbled. "Are you going to eat this?"

Celia shook her head.

He tossed it to the tree rat and said, "Come. Let's sit on the porch."

She followed him outside and sat down in a rocker. The fact that in this remote place, at a cabin where a man lived alone, there was an extra chair on the porch as if inviting a visitor to sit and chat, was so Cuban and friendly that it made her feel better.

"It must have been a chore to carry these rockers up the mountain," she said.

"They weren't carried up. I made them here."

Celia took a second look at the chairs and saw that they were well built, with intricate designs carved into the back and arms. "Is that your hobby, woodworking?"

"One of them. What are yours?"

"I don't think I have any. Just my work."

"But after work," he persisted. "What do you do with yourself?"

In an almost inaudible voice, she said, "There was my child."

He laid a hand on her cheek and turned her face toward him. "Was?"

In a clipped, reporterly way she told him why instead of being at work she was roaming Cuba from one end to the other. When she finished she got up and walked to the end of the porch. The sun, higher now, was hot. The forest had grown quiet.

"You blame yourself," he said.

"Of course! Myself and—everybody! All the lies, the deception! They say our children are contented! And when they aren't, some claim it's because we're too permissive. Others say it is because there is not enough freedom! That more choices or," she spoke bitterly, "at least more *dollars* will solve everything."

He shook his head. "Nothing solves everything. Simple answers provide comfort, not solutions."

The rising temperature of the air seemed to ignite her own anger—anger toward Luis for his interference, anger toward José, who might have put ideas into Liliana's head, anger toward Liliana that until this instant she had not allowed herself to feel. "They are no comfort to me!" Throwing up her hands, she whirled to face him.

"I ask you, Miguel, is this what our parents fought for? So their children could become bureaucrats and their grandchildren could trade it all for consumer trash?"

"Do you think that's what's happening?"

"I don't *know* what is happening! I just want to know what happened to the Cuba they promised us! Where is the Cuba we thought we were building? *Where is my child?*"

Of course he could not answer those questions, nor did he try. He became very still, the way she would learn that he always did when tension thickened the air. The jutia crept onto the porch and squatted near his foot.

As quick as her anger had flared, it turned to ash. In a more controlled voice she explained to him, and to herself, why she had come. "I was trying to find her, but I kept losing my bearings. I needed to be with someone who knows who I am. Someone I have not kept secrets from."

"You mean the Celia Sánchez thing?"

She shrugged and did not answer.

"That's still an issue for you?"

"It is not an 'issue,'" Celia snapped. "It is *me*."

He looked beyond her, into the trees. She also stared into the trees, and at last began to take some solace from their quiet way of being alive. She said, "Celia Sánchez didn't want to leave here, you know."

"Then why did she?"

"She had . . . responsibilities. Things no one else could do."

He did not respond. After a few minutes, she asked, "What are you thinking?"

He reached down and absently scratched the juita's back. "With most animal behaviour there are patterns. I was wondering if there are any patterns to these Sánchez 'visitations' or whatever you call them?"

Celia had asked herself the same question, and knew the answer, more or less.

"They seem to happen when I come to a place I don't know but feel I do, sort of a deja vu thing. It is often a place where Sánchez spent time. Sometimes I knew that, like when I came to the Comandancia. But there are times when I did not know. It might be only my imagination that she spent time there." She gave a self-deprecating laugh. "After all, where on this island *didn't* she go?"

"Anything else?"

Celia wiped sweat from her neck. "I seem most likely to feel that I have become her—or vice versa—when I'm weak, drained. Or totally exhausted." She gave him a wry smile. "Like now. Only right now I am not in her space, or her in mine. I am just here and tired as sin."

"Aye!" He jumped up from the rocker so suddenly that he startled the tree rat, which skittered off the porch. "I didn't think! You must have driven all night!" He went down on his knees and began tugging at the laces of her running shoes.

"Miguel! What are you doing?"

"Putting you to bed. There." He pointed to the cot in the cabin. "It's all yours."

When she opened her mouth to object, he held up her runners, laces dangling, and grinned. "Strings attached, but only to your shoes. See?"

As Celia drifted to sleep it occurred to her that long ago she had become the one who dealt with others' aches and pains, removed shoes, and insisted on naps. She could not recall the last time somebody had done those things for her. How strange that the one who would was a near-stranger whose closest companion might well be a big tree rat.

FIFTY-ONE

THE guerrillas wound their way down the mountain; Fidel leading one column, Che another, Cienfuegos another, Tete another. Tanks rumbled along the highway. Fighter planes roared into the air. "Fidel! From the south!" Celia shouted into the microphone. "They're coming!" She pressed the headset tight against her ears but could not hear his voice. What she heard was gunfire, shrieking metal, and a shout, "Take cover!" She saw the battle as if she was there although she was not. A girl from Tete Puebla's female brigade leapt onto a tank. A soldier emerged from inside the tank. They struggled, hand to hand. He flung her over the side. As she fell her body twisted and Celia saw the face: Liliana.

Celia's feet hit the floor before she was fully awake, the image from the dream searing her mind. "Miguel!" she shouted.

Her T-shirt was glued to her body with sweat. She wanted water. She wanted her shoes. She saw them on a chair. There was a note stuffed into one. She spread the note on the table and read it as she pulled on the shoes.

> Had to check some track traps and wildlife cameras. Back before dark.
> Make yourself at home. Don't mind the juita. He's used to having the run
> of the place. —Miguel

She picked up a stubby pencil and on the bottom of his note scribbled, *So sorry, I must go.* She wanted to explain but it would take too much time. She did not have time.

She ran back along the path to the main trail and started swiftly down. The way she had found easy in the dark seemed treacherous in broad daylight. She stumbled repeatedly and fell twice. Only after the second fall, when she banged her knee on a rock, did she force herself to slow down and exercise caution appropriate to the rough terrain.

The late afternoon sun was blazing. She was drenched in sweat and recognized her lightheadedness as dehydration. How foolish not to have drunk water before she left the cabin! Just as she felt she would faint from thirst, she came around a bend and saw a small stream. It tumbled down a rocky incline and crossed the trail in a wash so narrow that it could be crossed in a single step. She had scarcely noticed it before.

Beyond the stream a mule stood tied to a tree by a short rope. The animal's foam-covered lips fluttered helplessly toward the water he could not quite reach. Sharp as her own thirst was, it struck Celia as outrageously cruel to have tied the animal in such way, in sight of water but unable to get to it. She stepped across the stream and untied the mule. He promptly plunged his muzzle into the water. Celia moved upstream a metre to where it cascaded down the rocks into a basin-sized pool and drank. She ducked her head into the cool water and, eyes shut in ecstasy, poured handfuls over her shoulders, soaking herself front and back.

She opened her eyes to see a stocky man emerge from the trees. Without a word he grabbed the mule's lead rope and jerked its head up.

"He was thirsty," Celia said, her voice reflecting the indignation she felt that the man had not allowed the animal to finish drinking. "He wants water."

"Dumb beast doesn't know what it wants." The man's eyes, flat and stupid, fastened on the front of Celia's wet T-shirt.

As Celia scrambled to her feet a second man emerged from the forest. When he saw her he stopped short and grinned. Celia felt goosebumps rise on her wet skin, not from the coolness of the water that still dripped from her hair down her back and between her breasts but from what she felt as clear and present danger.

Traitors! You would sell your neighbours to Batista for a sack of rice, or for a bottle of rum, your own son. But not me. I go where I please in these mountains and you will not be the ones to stop me.

Instinct told her it was useless to turn and run back up the steep trail. They would be on her like dogs. She could dash into the forest but they must know the terrain better than she. Forward, down the trail, would be fastest. But how to get past them?

The man holding the mule continued to stare at what the wet T-shirt revealed of her breasts. The second man stood just beyond the mule, on the lower side of the trail. He held a burlap bag from which protruded orchids. Celia registered the orchids and guessed that since this was a national park, they were probably poaching them for sale in town. The man dropped the bag on the ground and started toward her.

The mule, still prevented from drinking by the man who held its lead rope, had swung its rump around so that it blocked the trail. It stood with one hind leg slightly forward, cocked. Its ears lay flat against his head. Celia had never had any dealings with mules, but she understood that body language. The mule rolled its eyes to watch the man approaching behind him.

Another step put him within range of the mule's kick. Its leg shot out, caught the man square on the thigh, and sent him flying sideways off the trail. Simultaneously the animal jerked free and plunged up the mountainside.

"Corre!" Celia shouted, and she ran.

Adrenalin flooded her veins and sent her racing down a last steep incline. Then she was on the broad flat part of the trail that led to the parking lot, running as she had not run since some long-forgotten track meet back in secondary school.

It was dark by the time Celia reached Bayamo. She did not stop there or anywhere else until she needed gas. She made a final gas stop just before getting on the autopista. By then it was into the wee hours of the morning and she was feeling drowsy. She put down the convertible top and drove the rest of the way with the wind whipping her hair and smoke from burning sugarcane fields on either side of the highway stinging her nostrils. In her mind images from the dream, of Liliana being thrown from the turret of a tank, replayed again and again. The red flames and smell of burning cane fields were real. The wind in her hair was real. The ones who died in battle were real. What she did not know was whether the night wind and cane field fires and loved ones who had died were real then or now—or both.

In the grey dawn, the Pan-American stadium loomed off to her right. The next exit was for Habana del Este and home.

Celia parked at the curb in front of the apartment building and glanced at her watch. It was five-thirty in the morning—exactly twelve hours since she had left the parking lot at the Comandancia trail head.

FIFTY-TWO

CELIA woke to the shuffle of feet outside her door, soft voices, hesitant knocks. At first she did not know where she was. In her apartment, yes, but why on the sofa and not in her own bed? Then she remembered. She had only meant to catnap until eight, then call around to find out whether anyone had heard anything. Late morning sun blazing through the apartment's east windows told her that she had slept much longer.

A man's urgent voice was shouting, "Dr. Cantú? Dr. Cantú!"

"Who is it?"

"The Gómez family. We have your child."

Celia sprinted to the door.

At first she did not see the faces of the man and woman, nor did she notice the three children behind them. All she saw, hanging between them like a limp doll, was Liliana. She was wearing the same white shorts and red-and-white-striped top she had had on when Celia last saw her. Exposed skin was scratched and scraped, with blood still oozing from some of the wounds. Liliana let go of the couple supporting her, stepped forward into Celia's arms, and fainted.

Together they lifted her to the sofa. Celia knelt beside her, taking vital signs, running hands over her scalp, feeling for broken bones. The visible damage told her something of the nature of the accident, although not its severity. She had treated children with similar injuries who had been tossed off fast-moving bicycles, and once a boy who had been thrown by a horse over the edge of a steep bank. A *thorn-covered* bank, she corrected herself, noting the thorns imbedded in Liliana's flesh. Again her hands went to Liliana's head, feeling for bumps that might signal a concussion.

The Gómez family hovered behind her. "We probably should have taken her to the hospital," Mr. Gómez began in a tentative voice.

"But she said you were a doctor?" his wife said in a dubious voice.

Only much later would Celia understand why they sounded so doubtful; what they had seen when she opened the door: a bleary-eyed woman wearing a filthy T-shirt and even filthier jeans, knees darkly stained with dirt from the grave site. But she was unaware of the impression she made on them. In fact, she was scarcely aware of them at all until the children began to chatter and the adults chimed in with information she needed.

"She fell out of a car!" the taller boy exclaimed.

"No! He pushed her!" piped the younger one.

"Be quiet!" their mother scolded.

"This car," explained Mr. Gómez. "It was some distance ahead of us. The passenger door flew open and it swerved off—"

"Right off the road!" the taller boy finished.

"I said, 'Look at that pig, throwing garbage,'" Mrs. Gómez began.

"I thought he was dumping a dog," Mr. Gómez cut in.

The youngest child, excited by the drama of it all, chimed in with her version. "I said, 'Stop, Papí! It's a girl!' He said I had an overactive imagination. But he stopped."

"We couldn't believe it was a person. Not when the car kept going!" Mrs. Gómez perched nervously on the edge of a chair, hands fluttering in the manner of a person who wants to be helpful but has no idea what to do.

Celia glanced at her. "Bring me some water, please. Take a pot from the kitchen."

"It was a new car, like tourists drive," Mr. Gómez offered.

"And it didn't even stop," the younger boy repeated.

The little girl leaned closer to Liliana, awed by the blood and the damage. When the child's face came into Celia's frame of vision, she said, "Bring me a washcloth and a towel from the bathroom, please. That's a good girl."

"The skid marks showed where the car went off and came back onto the road. I thought it was going to roll," Mr. Gómez continued. "The bank was so steep. I wouldn't have stopped except Gladys—that's our daughter here—was so sure it was a person."

Mrs. Gómez returned with the water and set it at Celia's elbow. The girl Gladys put a washcloth in Celia's hand. "My brothers climbed down first, but they couldn't get her up, so Papí and Mamí went to help them. They all got scratched all over."

"It took forever to get her up the bank," Mr. Gómez explained. "She was conscious when we found her. She gave us her address, yours, and said you were a doctor, otherwise we would have taken her straight to the hospital."

"You did the right thing, bringing her here," Celia assured him, still unaware that they were having difficulty perceiving her as a doctor. "There are no lumps on her head and I am not finding any broken bones."

"But her face! It's so messed up!" Gladys gazed in fascinated horror at the blood caked on nose, lips, brow, and cheeks. "Is she going to have scars?"

Celia ran the washcloth over Liliana's face. The skin was more scraped than gashed, and her cheekbones felt intact. For the most part it was surface damage. Speaking in her calm, doctorly voice, she said, "She is badly bruised. And some thorns have penetrated quite deeply. When she has rested a bit I will take her to the hospital for a checkup." She stood, for the first time acknowledging the family who stood in a semicircle around her. Eyes brimming with tears, she said, "I don't know how to thank you."

"Not at all. I mean, it's what anybody would have done!" Mr. Gómez assured her.

"*Anybody* might have left it for others to cope with. You abandoned your own plans to help her. You brought her home. You probably saved her life."

"I do hope she's okay." Mrs. Gómez herded her brood toward the door. "Please give us a call and let us know. Ignacio Gómez. We're in the Santa Fe phone book."

"I will, Mrs. Gómez. I promise."

It was difficult for Celia to walk away from Liliana, even the few steps it took to show the family to the door. But she forced herself to do it, to shake hands with father, mother, and sons, offering (and glad when they declined) to treat their thorn scratches. She hugged little Gladys and whispered, "Gracias, niña. Gracias, gracias, gracias! Estás mi heroína." She smiled with more gratitude than she had ever felt toward anyone, until they understood her need to attend to Liliana and urged one another out the door.

Then she rushed into the bathroom for more hot water, fresh towels, scissors for cutting off what was left of Liliana's clothes, and antiseptic for a more thorough cleaning of the wounds. She was not sure why Liliana had fainted, whether it was from shock, pain, or relief, but she hesitated to move her more than was necessary until she was awake and could answer questions about where she hurt. The two steps Liliana had taken on her own made it unlikely that she had a spinal injury or a broken leg, although ribs or internal injuries were another matter.

Once she got the clothes off, Celia focused on parts of the body she could see and did not try to turn her. It was Liliana herself who moaned and rolled over, face against the back of the sofa. Celia began cleaning the wounds on her back, trying to visualize the trauma that had caused them.

She could imagine the car swerving, the door flying open, and Liliana spilling out as it jerked back onto the pavement. She had landed on her right side, shoulder first, perhaps in soft sand; this Celia deduced from the sand she found under the strap and in one bra cup of the halter top when she cut it off. Momentum had carried Liliana down the slope, where she stopped in, or was stopped by, thorn bushes. She had not been knocked unconscious because minutes later, when the Goméz family arrived, she had been able to tell them where she lived.

As Celia attended the visible injuries, none of which appeared life-threatening, she looked for clues that might reveal more serious damage. Liliana's breathing was shallow but regular. Her colour had improved and her pulse was strong. She did not seem to be in severe pain. However, two things puzzled Celia.

One was skin tone. Liliana was wearing the same shorts and halter top she had been wearing when she disappeared, so there should have been a clear differentiation between parts of her body always covered and skin regularly exposed to the sun. But the tan line was indistinct. Previously tanned skin was pale, closer to the colour of skin never exposed to the sun. Had she been indoors the whole time?

The other thing that caught Celia's attention was a wound different from the others. It had not been made that morning; in fact, it was practically healed. What struck Celia about it was its *neatness*. It crossed the throat in a thin semicircle from ear to ear. It had not been deep but what could have caused it?

By the time she finished cleaning all the wounds, she was certain that none were life-threatening. Her greater concern was the girl's silence. Apart from gasping when Celia pulled a thorn or cleaned a raw wound, Liliana communicated nothing.

Celia knew that physical traumas were often matched by emotional traumas, and she also knew that the emotional responses of adults and children were not the same. Adults in need of medical attention tended to blame whoever they perceived as the cause: the husband who drove too fast, beer drinkers who had left a broken bottle on the beach, or the cook whose food had caused gastric distress. Children blamed themselves. Maybe it was because they'd been told, "Change into dry clothes or you'll catch cold." Or "Don't run out into the street without looking." Indeed, many parents, in an attempt to shed their own guilt, lashed out at the child with "I warned you!" Because children blamed themselves, their anger was turned inward. Yet it was not so simple as that. At some deeper level they seemed to know that they were not entirely to blame, that they had a right to be angry at the driver of the car that hit them or the parent who made them go to school when they said they were not feeling well. But it was a helpless, hopeless kind of anger that, in Celia's opinion, often hurt the child more than the physical injury.

Celia gazed at Liliana lying nude on the sofa, at the full womanly breasts and the slim girl's hips and legs, and did not know whether the battered body was that of a woman or a child.

FIFTY-THREE

CELIA dozed in the rocker. Sounds from other apartments, neighbours shouting off balconies to friends below, and children playing in hall did not disturbed her. Yet her head snapped up each time Liliana moaned or shifted position. Seeing that Liliana was still asleep, Celia again fell into a doze. Not until the apartment was flooded with the hot sun of late afternoon did Celia open her eyes to find Liliana awake.

"That's the dirtiest shirt I ever saw," Liliana said. "You look like you've been working in a cane field."

Celia smiled. "You look like you were in a fight and lost. How do you feel?"

"I need to go to the bathroom."

Celia's instinct was to help, but she waited to see how Liliana managed on her own and what movements seemed to cause her pain. Liliana coughed, stood up, and hobbled toward the bathroom. She had not shown pain when she coughed, so there were probably no cracked or broken ribs. Afraid she might faint again, Celia followed closely. "Are you hurting any place in particular?"

"All over."

Celia trailed her into the bathroom. Turning her back while Liliana tinkled, she tossed the dirty towels into the laundry and reached for clean ones. Liliana rose to wash her hands and screamed.

"My face is *ruined*. Oh, the bastard!"

Celia, trembling from the shock wave sent through her system by Liliana's scream at such close quarters, put her arm around her shoulders and said in a controlled voice, "Once your mother was standing close to where a grenade exploded and her face looked a lot worse than yours. A year later you would never have known. There was just this one little moon-shaped scar that your dad liked to kiss." Celia touched a crescent-shaped cut on Liliana's brow. "Like that one. Of course, you could let your hair curl down over it. But Carolina never did."

Liliana leaned forward to examine the cut more closely, then groaned, put her hands to the small of her back, and hobbled back to the sofa.

"Since you are able to walk, we should run over to the hospital for some X-rays and a couple of tests," Celia said casually.

Liliana gave her a suspicious look. "What kind of tests?"

Celia simply looked at her.

"What *kind* of tests?" There was an edge of hysteria to Liliana's voice.

"To see what else the bastard did to you," Celia said tightly.

Liliana folded her arms tight across her naked breasts, squinched her eyes shut, and shook her head violently. "No! They'll ask a bunch of questions."

Celia sat back down in the rocker and studied her niece. Her own theory about sexual abuse, rape, and the like ran counter to the popular belief that it was best to talk about it. She felt, especially in the case of children, that letting it fade like any ordinary memory might be less damaging than having to repeat the details over and over to a string of doctors and therapists until there was no possibility of erasing the incident from one's mind. On the other hand, there was no dealing with any trauma without knowing some of the gory details.

"If you want to tell just me," she said finally, "I will see that nobody else questions you. But you must be tested."

"You're talking about tests for STDs, aren't you?" Liliana accused her.

"Sexually transmitted diseases, yes. And pregnancy."

"I can't be pregnant!" Liliana screamed and broke into hysterical sobs.

Celia pulled the naked girl into her lap, draped a towel around her shoulders, and rocked her as she might a five-year-old. It was a good twenty minutes before Liliana ceased to sob, but she continued to cling to Celia, alternately sobbing and hiccupping. Celia rocked on. Finally tears and hiccups faded. But the child remained.

Liliana lay back down on the sofa. A thin skim of sweat beaded her upper lip but Celia knew from having held her that she was not feverish. Her eyes said that the pain was coming from inside. Briefly, Liliana had allowed herself to feel anger toward whoever hurt her. Now she was turning the blame back on herself.

For several minutes Celia felt as helpless as she had ever felt in her medical career. Then the fragments of information she had been collecting all afternoon coalesced into a diagnosis, and with it, a course of action.

"You need not go for tests this afternoon," she decided.

Liliana looked at her dully. "No?"

"Tomorrow will be soon enough. Today you must talk to the police."

Liliana's swollen lips parted in disbelief. "Are you going to—?"

"*I* am not going to anything. *You* are going to give them a description of the man who did this to you. Not just for your sake, but so they might be able to catch him before he does the same thing to other girls."

"I can't talk about it!"

"You do not have to talk about 'it.' You must tell them what you know about *him*. They can take it from there."

Liliana shook her head. "It's no use. He's a foreigner. He's gone by now."

"Maybe," Celia conceded. "Or maybe not. Finding him is the responsibility of the police. Your responsibility is to give them something to go on."

She wondered if she was heaping too much responsibility on the girl in her frail condition. Then thought, No. No burden is heavier than guilt. I will not have my child carry the guilt for this, not now or ever. Her mother was a fighter. She will be a fighter.

"If he has left the country there is nothing to be done. But if he is still here—well, I ask you: do you want him roaming around Cuba doing the same thing to other girls?"

It seemed a long time before Liliana answered. "No."

Celia reached for the telephone.

FIFTY-FOUR

LUIS sat at his desk reading the alternative energy report. One of his skills was the ability to plow through the most boring reports, identify key points, and remember them in sufficient detail to discuss them intelligently later. Since the relationship with Celia had blown up in his face he seemed to have lost that ability. Exasperated, he flipped back to the beginning of the report and began skimming it for relevant points he had not absorbed the first time through. He tried to memorize statistics on recent increases in solar-generated energy and made a mental note to find out what components Cuba was manufacturing and which ones must be imported. How many scientists did Cuba have working in the field of solar technology and doing what exactly?

The report also noted an increase in wind-generated energy, but the overall percentage of power being supplied by that method was infinitesimal. Not much hydro power either, but what could you expect? The island hardly had an abundance of big rivers rushing down mountainsides and through narrow canyons where dams could be easily built as, for example, had been done in México's Sumidero Canyon. Too bad North Korea's economy collapsed before its government got around to providing the aid promised to realize the Río Toa hydroelectric project. Luis stopped reading and sat tapping his pencil. What about small hydro-power units that could be installed on any creek with a year-round flow? What about methane gas? Did it have to come from animal manure? If so, it would not be practical because animal manure was needed for fertilizer. Could methane be produced from vegetable matter? Damn! He hated reports that raised more questions than they answered.

The phone rang. Grateful for the interruption, he picked it up and identified himself. When Celia's cool, familiar voice came over the line, his heart, he was sure, skipped a beat.

"Luis? Liliana is back."

"Bueno, bueno! Is she okay?"

"Not entirely. She was assaulted. It was very serious and must be reported."

Luis barely repressed a sigh. Surely Celia did not have in mind reporting that Liliana had been raped—even though that was probably what Liliana had told her.

"You rejected the idea of bringing in social services before," he reminded her. "Why report it now?"

"Not to social services. Or the police. This is outside the scope of their resources. The Ministry of the Interior. It involves a foreigner."

"MININT?" Luis could not believe he had heard right. "Celia, they deal with matters of state security. Not crimes against individuals."

"I expect that rather depends on the crime," she said crisply.

"Well, yes, I suppose, but certainly not rape or—you said assault, right?"

"Attempted murder."

Luis had a sinking feeling in the pit of his stomach. He knew she was asking him to make the necessary contact in MININT because he could move laterally, to someone in the ministry at his own level, whereas she would have to work her way up the bureaucratic ladder, which would take forever. He did not want to do it because he did not believe a word of what she had just said. When the truth came out, whatever the truth was, he would look the fool for having asked for the investigation of an incident in which the only "criminal" behaviour would turn out to be that of a manipulative teenager skipping school and fucking a foreigner for her own financial gain. Luis felt like putting his head down on his desk and crying because as surely as he knew that participation in this charade would hold his reputation up to ridicule, he knew that he could not say no to Celia Cantú.

Leandro Quevedo had changed little in the decade since Luis had last seen him, other than that his hairline had receded to midway on his head. The loss of hair made his face seem more round, and in it his hooded eyes were humourless. He was a serious, unflappable sort of person. Under the circumstances, Luis found that reassuring.

Quevedo's companion, Gloria Muñoz, was one of those women who, while not really plump, seemed so because there was little difference between bust, waist, and hip size. An attempt to give herself a figure by pulling the belt of her uniform extra tight caused hips and breasts to push more firmly against the khaki fabric. She had a dimple in her chin that Luis would have found appealing if he had been less nervous about the errand they were on. They did not speak on the drive to Celia's apartment. It was his glum conclusion that the less said the less the officers would remember later, when there would be every reason to want the incident forgotten.

Celia must have heard them coming because she was in the hallway outside the apartment when they reached the top of the stairs. Luis was surprised to see her in crisp hospital whites. He knew she had not been to work that day because he had called the hospital earlier. Besides, she usually shed her work clothes the minute she entered the apartment. He guessed that she had dressed as a doctor deliberately, in order to be taken more seriously. He introduced her with the formality her attire invited. "Dr. Cantú, this is Capitán Leandro Quevedo and Lieutenant Gloria Muñoz, from MININT."

Quevedo cleared his throat. "We won't take much of your time, Dr. Cantú. I presume the girl is inside. Did you wish to give us some background before we go in?"

"Thank you for coming, compañeros. I would not have imposed on you for purely personal reasons. But this incident has broader implications. My niece disappeared nine days ago. She said she was taken prisoner by a foreigner. He held her until this morning, then tried to kill her. She will give you the details—about him and his attempt on her life. Not about what he did to her during the time she was with him. She does not want to talk about that."

"Dr. Cantú!" Gloria Muñoz said sharply. "You must see how inappropriate it would be for us to agree to limit our interrogation."

Celia's eyes glittered in a way that gave Luis a chill. *Oh God*, he thought. *This is going to be worse than I thought.*

"Excuse me, Lieutenant, if there has been a misunderstanding. This is *not* an interrogation. My niece has been assaulted and wants to provide information about the man who did it. Not for her own sake but because he may still be in Cuba and may engage in similar acts of terrorism against other young girls." Celia paused and gazed into the eyes of the ranking officer. "Perhaps you have a daughter yourself, Capitán? If so, you will understand why, when the child is already traumatized, I as her doctor could not allow her to be questioned in a way that might worsen her condition."

Luis could scarcely believe how adeptly Celia had used phrases like "the child," "acts of terrorism," and "a daughter yourself." In fact, Quevedo had four daughters, although Celia would not have known that.

At Quevedo's nod of acquiescence, Celia walked ahead of them into the apartment. Liliana sat on the sofa wearing clean white shorts and a new blue T-shirt that Luis recognized as the one José had bought her in Varadero. She was cut, scratched, scraped, and bruised from head to foot. One eye had a particularly nasty cut above the eyebrow. Celia made introductions and motioned the two MININT officers to the rocking chairs. She sat down on the sofa next to Liliana. Luis brought a chair from the dining table and placed it to the side and back a little, where he could exercise his best skill: that of making himself invisible while observing everything that passed between the others.

Celia said, "Compañeros, Liliana wants to tell you about this man, so that if he is still in Cuba, you might be able to find him."

Liliana said nothing.

Quevedo took a notepad from the pocket of his khaki uniform. "Your aunt said you thought he was a foreigner. From what country?"

Liliana took a deep breath. "He spoke Castellón with a lisp, the way people from Spain do, so I asked if he was from Spain. He said no, he was from Argentina. He said he was a colonel in the Argentine army. Or used to be. I'm not sure if he still is. He wore a uniform but it didn't have anything like that on it." She pointed to Quevedo's insignia.

"How old was he?" Quevedo asked.

Liliana seemed perplexed. Then, looking carefully at Quevedo, she said, "Older than you. Quite a bit older. About your build, but more—" With her hands she described a large paunch. "Not fat exactly, but big. He was a big man."

"How did you meet him?" Muñoz asked, cutting her eyes at Celia as if to say, *I know my business, and don't you go interfering.*

Liliana looked at Muñoz, found her gaze unsympathetic, and shifted her eyes to Quevedo. "I was hitchhiking," she said. "Going to visit some friends at Playa Jibacoa. He said that was where he was going too. And it was. To SuperClub Saturno."

Luis glanced at Quevedo and knew exactly what the man was thinking. *This was not an abduction.*

"You went there with him?" Quevedo asked.

Liliana's expression became sullen but she answered the question. "He said they had Jet Skis, and if I wanted to walk down to the beach with him, he would show me how to ride one. He said he had to stop at his cabaña first to change into his swimsuit."

"So you went to his cabaña with him," Muñoz concluded, pursing her pretty little mouth in a way that deepened the dimple in her chin.

"I walked over there, yes. It was on the beach. The farthest one at the end. I said I would wait outside. I was just about to sit down on the porch when he grabbed me and pulled me inside." As Liliana spoke, her voice rose. "And don't ask me what happened because I already told Tía Celia I'm not going to talk about it!" She finished in a shriek of barely controlled hysteria that did not seem to Luis to be feigned.

There was a silence, except for the sound of Quevedo's pencil moving on his note pad. Luis could see the pad. Quevedo was not writing, but doodling. Luis wondered if his friend was visualizing one of his own daughters in that situation, testing it in his imagination for veracity.

"Surely you had—" Muñoz began in an accusatory tone, but Quevedo cut her off.

"So we won't talk about what happened there. Just tell us how you got away."

"I didn't get away—not exactly." Liliana cast a fierce look at Muñoz. "How could I? There are guards all around the perimeter fence of that place. He was handing out money to everybody to keep them away. Maids, gardeners, everybody. That's why the security guy at the gate let me in in the first place. He gave him money. The kitchen people, when they brought our meals, stopped way back at the other cottage, and he walked out to meet them. He told them to do that, so nobody came close to where I was."

Luis recalled the way the security guard at SuperClub Saturno had treated him when he went there to drop off a flyer. Unconsciously, he became less skeptical of Liliana's story.

"So how did you get away?" Quevedo asked again.

"I was still asleep. Well, pretending to be asleep. He went out for a few minutes, and all of a sudden he was back. He jerked me out of bed and threw my clothes at me and—"

"You were naked?" Muñoz asked, pen poised as if on the verge of writing down a significant detail.

"Yes, I was naked!" Liliana screamed. "Stark naked for nine damned days! On the very first day when I smashed a bathroom window trying to get out he took my clothes and cut my throat and that's the last I saw of them till he threw them in my face at whatever time it was this morning!"

At the phrase *cut my throat*, four adults gasped simultaneously.

"See?" Liliana threw back her head. "It was cut, wasn't it, Tía Celia?"

Celia laid trembling fingertips against the red line of a nearly healed cut across the girl's throat. Her face had turned deathly pale. "Yes," she said in a low voice. "Not a deep cut, but the skin was scored. Was it a knife?"

Liliana slumped back against the sofa and shook her head. "A piece of the broken glass. He said if I tried to get away again he'd do it for real and lock me in a closet where I'd bleed to death before anybody found me." She glared at Muñoz. "I guess *you'd* have been brave enough to try again. But I wasn't."

Muñoz seemed unable to take her eyes off Liliana's throat. Nor could Luis. The story was incredible; he would have said such things never happened in Cuba. But Liliana's emotional outburst and that raw red line demolished his complacency.

"After he gave you your clothes," Quevedo prompted. "What happened?"

"He threw his stuff in his bag and we left. Not through the lobby but the back way to the parking lot. He had his arm around me and told me to keep smiling. He said if I made one sound he'd kill me. Which he tried to do anyway."

Luis was watching Celia. She seemed as stunned as the rest of them. He guessed that at least some of what Liliana was telling them Celia had not heard before.

"How?" Muñoz whispered the question.

"He was driving along the Vía Blanca really fast. All of a sudden he reached across and opened the door on my side and gave me a push. I almost fell out. I just barely grabbed hold of the frame of the door, so I was sort of half in, half out. He pushed me again and when he did, the car swerved off the road. Then he put his foot up and kicked me. And I went out."

"What happened next?" Quevedo asked.

Liliana looked at Celia. Celia laid a hand lightly on her knee, which Luis noted was swollen to twice its normal size. "There were witnesses," Celia said. "A family in a vehicle some distance back. All five of them saw the car go off the road and saw Liliana fall out. When the driver didn't stop, they did. She was conscious long enough to tell them that I was a doctor and asked to be brought home rather than to a hospital."

The room suddenly seemed quieter. Conversation continued, but the emotional crackle of skepticism had disappeared.

Celia handed Quevedo a scrap of paper with a name written on it. "This is the family who witnessed it. They live in Santa Fe. The wife said they are listed in the telephone directory."

Quevedo was staring into space. "Nine days. If he was here on a two-week package he might have a few more days. I wonder what caused him to bolt?"

Luis cleared his throat. The way the others turned to look at him showed that they had forgotten he was in the room. "I can speculate about that."

"Please do." Quevedo's serious eyes were perplexed.

"I had some notices made from family photographs." Luis swallowed hard and looked at Celia. "Do you have one to show them?"

Celia reached for her briefcase at the end of the sofa, took out two flyers, and handed one to each MININT official.

"Saturday I circulated them in Varadero. I also left one at SuperClub Saturno." Luis could not bring himself to meet his friend's eyes. The very fact that he had done this revealed what he thought Liliana was up to, and how close he was to the family.

Quevedo frowned at the flyer. "That was four days ago. If she was at the resort then, why do you suppose the management failed to act on the information?"

"There was something . . . obstructionist . . . in the manager's attitude. So rather than ask him to share the information with his staff, I told him to post the notice. His said he would, but I got the distinct impression that he had no intention of doing so. Yesterday I had business at the thermonuclear generating plant in Santa Clara del Norte. It's not much farther to SuperClub Saturno, so I decided to drive out and see if he had posted it. As I suspected, he had not." Luis paused. "So I myself put up the notice and made it clear that there would be repercussions if it was taken down. This was yesterday evening. Around six."

Muñoz was studying the flyer. Liliana reached for it. Muñoz passed it to her, giving Liliana's hand a squeeze. "You're a very pretty girl," she said in a low voice.

"Not anymore," Liliana mouthed back.

"So the abductor might not have seen it last night," Quevedo mused. "But may have seen it in the lobby this morning. That would have alarmed him."

"Possibly," Luis agreed.

Quevedo glanced down at the name, Ignacio Gómez, on the slip of paper Celia had given him. "Do you know these people?" he asked Celia.

"No. I had no idea who they were when they brought Liliana in this morning."

"What time would this have been?"

"I did not look at the clock. Late morning, I'd say."

"Why didn't you call the police immediately?"

Celia turned to stare at Liliana, causing all of them to do the same. Her face was badly swollen. The eye with the cut over it was on the verge of closing.

"Capitán, if someone brought your daughter home in this condition, would your priority be medical attention or talking to the police?"

"I take your point. So you attended her and—" Quevedo paused delicately. "Is there anything about her condition that we should know?"

Celia gave Quevedo what Luis recognized as her let's-just-drop-this-for-now look. "She is scheduled for tests tomorrow. I will forward you a copy of the results."

Quevedo cocked his head at Liliana with an expression that was almost, although not quite, a smile. "Young lady, can you draw?"

Liliana gave him a puzzled look and shook her head. "Not really."

He handed her his pad and pencil. "Would you give it a try? See if you can give us the shape of the man's face, or something?"

Liliana poised pencil above paper. Hesitantly, she drew a squarish face with a squiggle of lines meant to represent a short haircut that was flat on top. She added eyes, without eyebrows. She glanced at Quevedo. "He had eyebrows but they were so light you'd hardly notice them."

The pencil dropped to the page again, and she drew in a small mouth, almost a woman's mouth, Luis thought, which seemed ridiculous in the large square face. "I'm sorry, I can't do noses," Liliana said apologetically. "But that's how his mouth was. Little. It seemed kind of silly at first, but later I saw how it really was."

"How it really was?"

"Mean." Liliana looked back at the sketch lying in her lap. "I don't know how to make it like that. But that's the shape."

"Is that the shape of his face too?" Muñoz asked.

"Sort of. But he had jowls." She held the pad out to Muñoz. "Can you do jowls?"

Muñoz glanced at Quevedo. He nodded. She took the pencil and sketched jowls. "Like that?"

"Yeah, but bigger," Liliana affirmed. "It was weird because he had hardly any wrinkles on the front of his face, but these big floppy jowls on both sides." She pointed to the picture. "Will you do the nose too? It was a big nose. Fat at the bottom."

Muñoz sketched in a slightly bulbous nose. "How's that?"

"Not exactly. But yeah, sort of like that."

"I don't suppose he gave you a name?"

"He said his troops back in Argentina called him 'Colonel Boots.' I thought about that—that's the last thing I remember thinking—when his big old black boot came up and kicked me out of the car."

As Quevedo was writing *Boots* on his pad, Liliana leaned forward. "But I might know his real name. Mario Baaker, spelled with two A's. I don't know if that *is* his real name, but I did see it this morning when he was packing. It was on his bag."

"Excellent," Quevedo said and added the name to his notes. He looked up at Liliana. "You have been very helpful, young lady. Can you think of anything else we should know?"

Liliana shook her head and looked at Celia. "I have a terrible headache. And my knee hurts. I can't remember much of anything right now."

Celia rose. Quevedo, Muñoz, and Luis did likewise. Quevedo wrote his name along with two numbers, tore off the page, and handed it to Celia. "The first is my office, the second my home. Feel free to call either place if anything else comes to mind."

"And the medical report? Where shall I send it?"

"Tell the lab to call me with the results. If we need a copy, we can get it later."

He turned to Liliana who was still seated on the sofa. "There is no assurance that we can find him. But we will try."

Liliana struggled to her feet and held out her hand to Quevedo. "Gracias, Capitán." Then she smiled shyly at Muñoz. "Gracias, Teniente."

Luis had not seen civil behaviour from Liliana in so long that he had forgotten she was capable of it. He was just thinking, Of course, she couldn't be bothered to extend it to me, even though it was me who saved her ass, when, with a flicker of her eyes in his direction, she said, "Thanks for putting up that notice. Is it okay if I keep this one?"

It was thin acknowledgment but that hardly mattered. When Luis felt Celia's warm hand on his arm, heard the tremulousness in her voice as she thanked him, and looked into eyes brimming with gratitude, he needed nothing more.

The seriousness with which the MININT officials seemed to be taking the case further reassured him. "Hard to know what goes through the mind of a person like that," Quevedo mused on the drive back. "If this guy is what he claimed to be, well, you know what they got away with in Argentina. Some of them just moved on to other countries and ran amok there. They are an arrogant lot." Quevedo gave Luis an apologetic look. "You know chances of catching him are slim. If he thought she was likely to report the incident he probably caught the next available flight."

"Especially if he realized that others witnessed the incident," Muñoz added. "Shall I contact the Habana and Varadero airports?"

"Yes, do that. Right away."

No more was said until Luis rounded the Plaza de la Revolución and stopped in front of MININT headquarters. Luis thanked both officers and they shook hands all around. Waiting until Muñoz started into the building, Quevedo leaned toward Luis and spoke in a confidential tone. "Be assured, compañero, we will nail the bastard if we can."

That evening Luis sat on the sofa listening to his mother humming in the kitchen. The room was semi-dark, illuminated only by a flickering candle Alma had lit before the statue of the Virgin in thanks for her prayers being answered. For the first time in weeks, Luis was happy. He thought of how Celia had looked in her hospital whites, how much he liked that image of the dedicated professional, which was what he knew her to be. What he would not give to see her day after day, coming home dressed like that, to him.

FIFTY-FIVE

CELIA had to urge Liliana forward as they approached the door of the hospital. "They won't ask what happened," Celia assured her. "When I made the appointment I told them I already had your case history. This will only be a physical examination. All they will ask is where it hurts."

"What will they do to me?" Liliana's voice was thin with anxiety.

It was not the question of an adult, who would have wanted to know only if the procedures to be faced would fix whatever was wrong. This was a child asking, "Are they going to hurt me more than I am already hurting?"

"There will be an internal exam first and a blood test. Uncomfortable but not painful. Then they will X-ray your knee and that shoulder."

Celia knew she was dealing with a mixture of embarrassment, repressed anger, and physical pain. The bruises were every colour from black and blue to grey and yellow. The swollen knee was causing a pronounced limp and both eyes were swollen to slits.

"What about my face?" Liliana whimpered.

"The doctor may think the cut over your eye needs stitches." Experience had taught Celia that it was not only adults who needed some sense of control over their own bodies. Children were equally resistant to being "done to" without having any say in the matter, so she added, "But it's up to you. You can decide whether it gets stitches or not."

Knowing that Liliana would be most nervous about the internal exam, Celia had scheduled it first and requested that it be performed immediately upon their arrival with a particular nurse in attendance. The nurse, a wiry black woman called Orquídea, came striding into the examining room, clipboard in hand. "Ah ha! So you're that niece Dr. Cantú is always going on about. Girl, aren't you a mess this morning! Well, let's get this show on the road. Get yourself naked, child, and up on that table. I'll be right back."

Celia helped her undress and waited in the room until she heard Orquídea coming back down the hall, singing a pop tune in a voice good enough to have given her a chance at a musical career had she chosen to pursue it.

"Doc's on his way," Orquídea announced cheerfully. And to Celia, "El Jefe wants you upstairs, Dr. Cantú, and, sorry to say, we got no use for you around here."

Although Celia and Orquídea had entirely different "bedside manners," their respect was strong and mutual. Orquídea often tried to get Celia involved with very young girls who had developed health problems due to high-risk sexual activity because she felt Celia was more sensitive than some of the hospital's male doctors. And Celia called on Orquídea whenever possible to deal with difficult teens. Orquídea's breezy irreverence never failed to captivate adolescents, just as it now held Liliana's attention, distracting her from the dreaded internal exam.

Orquídea glanced over her shoulder. "You still here, Doc? The boss is gonna chew your—oops, sorry. Forgot we had a minor in earshot."

Liliana laughed. Celia waved. "I'm going. I'm gone. See you later, mi corazón."

The door to Dr. Leyva's office was open. The secretary nodded Celia in. He was on the telephone. His hunched posture gave her a view of the top of his head. Celia was again surprised at how white his hair had become, considering that he was not yet fifty. He glanced up and motioned her to a chair. Dropping the receiver back into the cradle, he said cheerfully, "So you found your niece and you're back. As of today, or tomorrow?"

"Actually, there are complications. You see, she was injured."

"Oh?" He fastened his grey eyes on her in the way she remembered from their previous interview, which said he wanted the whole story, quickly, and it would have to be good to convince him to give her more time off. "I understood that she was coming in for some fairly routine tests."

"It's not the visible damage. It's . . . she was abducted, you see. Held prisoner. Then the man tried to kill her by throwing her out of a speeding car."

Leyva's gaze remained level, but his eyes conveyed the same skepticism initially conveyed by Luis, Quevedo, and Muñoz. "I presume you contacted the authorities?"

"MININT is looking into it. Because the man was a foreigner. They interviewed Liliana yesterday. Today they will be talking to witnesses."

"There were witnesses?"

"To the vehicle incident, yes."

There was a silence during which Leyva processed this information. Celia supposed that he was trying to decide whether, in the absence of a serious injury, Celia's staying home was really necessary. She had to give him a convincing reason.

"Besides the physical injuries, she has been traumatized. She cannot return to school immediately and I cannot leave her alone in the apartment. There are only the two of us. My parents, her parents, the grandparents, are dead. Most of my friends are at work and hers of course are in school. There is no one I could ask to stay with her."

Of course there were neighbours, dozens of them, whom she might have asked to look in on Liliana. Leyva would know that and would guess that this was not her real reason—or at best, was only part of it. He was silent. Celia used the technique often enough herself. If you don't get the whole story, keep quiet until the other person spills it out. The director was waiting, not with the greatest patience, for the real reason. She sighed, bowed her head, and told him.

"Something went wrong, Dr. Leyva. She seemed so happy, many friends, good grades, no health problems. But she took a wrong turn. I do not know exactly when, or why. It was months ago. She started skipping school, hanging out at resorts. Her focus shifted to clothes, cosmetics, jewellery—all the superficial, appearance-related things they sell in dollar stores. I never noticed. That was the problem. I never noticed."

Celia looked up, her eyes anguished. "I missed it because I was working too much. If I go back to full time, I will go on missing . . . whatever it is I need to understand. I must not make the same mistake again."

Leyva's changeable grey eyes changed yet again, to an expression she could not read. He was no longer looking at her, but at the picture of his two daughters. Celia sensed a connection but had no idea what it might be.

"Your daughters," she ventured. "They must be grown now."

Leyva turned the picture around so she could see it: two girls close to the same age, dark curls and sparkling brown eyes, waving to whoever was taking the picture.

"The one on the left is twenty-two now. She is an intern at Children's Hospital in Manzanillo. She'll soon be a doc like her papá." There was a very long silence, in which Celia felt he was deciding whether to say more. At last he said, "The one on the left, the younger one, is dead."

Celia was stunned. Hospital gossip being what it was, she could not believe she had never heard of the director having lost a daughter. His wife, yes, everyone knew she died of colon cancer two years ago. And it was common knowledge that he had a daughter who was following his footsteps into medicine. If anyone on the hospital staff had known there was younger daughter, they would have assumed she was still in school.

"She was a good student," Leyva said. "Probably the brightest person in our family. And full of self-confidence. But restless. Easily bored. During her last year of pre-university she became involved with a boy. He seemed fairly ordinary. But he got it into his head to build a raft to go to Florida and convinced her to go with him."

He paused and shook his head. "Or maybe that was not what happened. Some of their friends say that she was the one who pushed the idea and the boy only carried it out to prove that his daring matched hers. We will never know. The raft was found, with their things. But the bodies were not recovered."

Leyva lifted the picture to study the girl's face. "Who would have guessed that she would become a balsera? Why did she make that choice? Where did we go wrong?"

In the outer office, Celia could hear the secretary telling someone that the director was busy, and in the hallway, the usual sounds of a busy hospital. She could even hear traffic noises from the street below; the bicycle bus pulling in to pick up cyclists to carry them through the tunnel and into Centro Habana. But in Leyva's office silence lay as heavy as sand. Celia stared at him, beyond him, and back into her own mind. Those were the very questions she had asked ever since Luis raided Liliana's room and dumped that armful of awful dollar-bought trash under her nose. The answer, which had eluded her from one end of Cuba to another, was now forming in her mind.

"Have you ever considered . . . ?" she began tentatively.

Leyva gave her a weary look that said, My dear, there is nothing I *haven't* considered. But with the trained courtesy of a good doctor, he waited for whatever she was about to say.

"We do everything we can to ensure our children's physical health. Proper rest, good diet, enough exercise. We take that approach because it is impossible to prevent them from being exposed to pathogens. The best defence is a strong immune system.

We know that. At the same time, we know that no matter how healthy they are, some pathogens can breach the immune system. HIV, for example. Hepatitis. Swine flu. Besides the really nasty viruses, we know that some pathogens are deadly because there has been no previous exposure, no opportunity to build up defences."

Leyva was watching her with a small frown. He was not making the connection, which to Celia suddenly seemed crystal clear—not merely obvious but undeniable. She leaned toward him. "I think there is a social parallel. We have raised our children in an environment rich in healthy values like service, social justice, and sharing. But when new elements are introduced—for example, the hedonism of recreational tourism with all that false freedom and illusion of endless pleasure—I think our children may be as susceptible to that as Cuba's indigenous population was to small pox."

It was a long time before Leyva responded, but Celia did not need his assurance that she was right. She knew this was what had happened to Liliana and possibly to Dr. Leyva's daughter and to countless other young Cubans. They were of a vulnerable age. The pathogen was there. They had no immunity.

He did not respond at once, but when he did she knew he had grasped her point. "It's not just tourism," he said sadly. "It's what's over there." He waved his hand toward the window from which could be seen, a kilometre away, the Strait of Florida. "They can imagine the wealth of America from here, but not its violence and inequality."

Celia nodded. "All that glittering materialism. Descriptions from relatives who have emigrated, plus what they see on television. But tourism is what brings the *reality* of materialism here, to Cuba."

"The government never wanted recreational tourism," Leyva mused. "Everyone was aware of how it warped the fabric of Cuban society back in the '40s and '50s. In the '60s, when I was a boy, tourism meant trips around the countryside to show off the successes of the Revolution. And in the '70s, there was medical tourism. Which to this day remains the best showcase for our health professionals, pharmaceutical advances, and the humanitarian values of our Revolution."

Celia nodded as she picked up and pursued her analogy. "Good medicine, yes, but it was not strong enough to save us when we lost Soviet support. The government was forced to encourage recreational tourism. Strong medicine for an economy that was close to death. And it worked. It saved our economy and our way of life."

Leyva nodded. "That it did. And still is doing."

Celia continued. "But the stronger the medicine the worse the side effects. Like chemotherapy—look at the damage it does in the process of affecting a cure!"

Celia suddenly stopped speaking. She had no more to say. She, like Leyva, was hearing her words for the first time. She needed time alone, quiet time, to consider their ramifications and test them for veracity against her own experiences.

The secretary, who unbeknownst to Celia had been hovering in the doorway behind her, took their mutual silence as an intermission in which to interject, "Dr. Leyva, your eleven-thirty appointment—did you wish to cancel?"

He rose immediately. "No, no. Show him in." To Celia he said, "I have long been aware of your skill as a pediatrician. And as an administrator, since you became jefa de la sala." He smiled. "But only now am I discovering what an analytical mind you have."

"Gracias." Celia moved slowly toward the door, hoping he had not forgotten her original question. Apparently he had, so she asked, "About time off . . . ?"

Leyva looked at is watch. "Let's discuss that over lunch. Meet you in the cafeteria at twelve. You and your niece."

FIFTY-SIX

CELIA found Orquídea where she had left her, but Liliana was not there. "She's in radiology," the nurse informed her. "But hold on. The doc who did the internal wants a word with you."

The gynecologist entered the room and began scrubbing for his next exam. It struck Celia as a little unprofessional that he had turned his back to her. Perhaps he was still young enough that it embarrassed him to speak with someone of the opposite sex about sexual matters? Or was it what he had to tell her that caused him to turn away? She drew a breath and prepared for the worst.

He must have heard the intake of breath because he turned from the sink to look at her, eyes saying that he did indeed find it difficult. "The violation was primarily anal. Quite rough. Your instructions were to not ask questions, so I didn't. But I did say to her, when I saw the anal lacerations, 'This must have been a painful experience.'"

"How did she respond?"

"She said, 'That's all he wanted. To hurt me.'"

Celia flinched. She did not need to be told that while the rapist's focus on anal penetration reduced the chance of pregnancy, it heightened the risk of HIV and hepatitis.

The young doctor must have seen the blood drain from her face, but he didn't spare her. "The lesions are severe. We drew blood for serological testing so we'll have a baseline in case anything nasty develops. And swabbed the area."

Clean hands in the air, he looked at Orquídea. She opened the door to the exam room for him and answered Celia's unasked question. "Already sent to the lab, along with the pregnancy test. I told them to expedite and to call you directly, Dr. Cantú."

"Thanks," Celia mumbled, too shaken by the graphic information to say more.

"Oh, by the way, there's that knee too," the doctor said as he started out. "They'll be able to tell you more about it in radiology."

Liliana sat in a plastic chair, head leaned back against the wall, eyes closed. At a light table, the radiologist was studying an X-ray. "Want to see your bones?" he was asking Liliana as Celia stepped into the room.

"No."

"I do," Celia said.

"It's the collar bone." He put his finger on a faint line across the collar bone. "Hairline fracture." He winked at Celia. "She'll look cute in a neck-to-waist cast."

Liliana looked away and said nothing.

"What about the knee?" Celia asked.

He laid another X-ray on the light screen. "No broken bones. Soft tissue damage. But that wouldn't show up here."

"We will keep it elevated and ice-packed awhile and see how it goes," Celia decided. "Thanks for the quick feedback."

"Can we go home now?" Liliana whined. "I'm hungry."

"We'll have lunch here, in the cafeteria. I haven't been shopping in almost two weeks and there's not a scrap of food in the apartment."

Grocery shopping would take well over an hour and require her to leave Liliana alone, whereas lunch here would be immediate and take no more than thirty minutes. Also, Celia wanted Dr. Leyva to see Liliana and judge her condition for himself.

Liliana put her hands over her face. "I can't go in there. Everybody will stare at me. They'll throw up!"

"Liliana, we will be in the staff dining room. Everyone in there will have seen patients who look just as bad as you, and some a whole lot worse."

"For sure." The radiologist spoke over his shoulder. "There was a bicycle accident victim in here less than an hour ago. Somebody opened a car door in front of his bike. The boy went sailing right over top and I don't know how far along the pavement on his face. One cheek was sanded right down to the bone."

Liliana shuddered. "Let's get out of this place. Please?"

"We are having lunch *in* this place," Celia informed her. "Dr. Leyva is my boss and it was not an invitation. It was an order."

Dr. Leyva was waiting when they entered the dining hall. He waved for them to join him in the cafeteria line.

"This is my niece, Liliana," Celia said, falling in behind him.

"Encantado," he said with barely a glance in her direction as they picked up lookalike plates of pork-flavoured congrí and grated cabbage salad.

As they were placing their plates on the table Leyva had selected, he leaned forward and peered at the cut over Liliana's eye. "That's a nasty one. No stitches?"

"I decided not," Liliana informed him.

"No? Why?"

"My mother was a soldier. She had a scar like that over her eye."

"I see."

Dr. Leyva tucked into his meal and said nothing more. Celia did likewise, and Liliana, after pushing the food around on her plate for a few minutes, began to eat. Not until they had cleaned their plates, and Dr. Leyva had gone and come back with demitasses of hot sweet coffee, did he address Liliana again.

"Are you aware that your radical aunt has got this hospital into hot water?"

Liliana turned to stare at her aunt. "Tía Celia? A radical?"

"Who, me?" Celia laughed, wondering what the joke was. Then, with a sinking feeling in her stomach, she remembered. It was no joke.

"She presented a paper in Santiago wherein she blamed the government for the high incidence of asthma in Cuban children."

"Oh that." Liliana was clearly disappointed. "She's always on about smoking."

"It's one thing to be 'on' to family and friends. It is quite another to stand up in public and accuse a government that considers itself to have one of the best health systems in the world of being negligent in the area of a preventable illness like asthma."

"Is it preventable?" Liliana looked from one to another. "I thought it was like, you know, just something some kids had."

"Not according to Dr. Cantú."

"But Dr. Leyva!" Celia protested. "You saw my data and the outline of my presentation. If you thought—"

"I thought they were fine. And I expected rebuttals. But I had no idea it was going to create such a furor. Discussion groups are being organized all over Cuba. Not only in the field of medicine and, I might add, not generally in support of your position."

"It's not a 'position.' What I presented were the results of two years' research. And there is nothing *radical* about the conclusions. It has been thirty years since the US surgeon general warned against the harmful effects of second-hand smoke!"

"Ah yes." Leyva smiled with one side of his mouth. "But his warning was based on US research. Where is the *Cuban* research?"

"Besides mine, you mean?" Celia waved her coffee spoon in the air. "How do I know? Maybe others sat on their studies to avoid controversy. Or maybe the data were excluded from scientific publications for fear of government disapproval."

Liliana, who had shown a spark of interest at the beginning of the conversation, appeared to have tuned out.

Leyva sipped his coffee, the grey eyes noncommittal. "Well, Doctor?"

"Well what?" Celia tried to address his concerns, but she was distracted by Liliana's withdrawn manner. "What do you want me to do about it?"

"Defend our good name, naturally."

"You mean retract—"

"Of course not. I mean more studies. Develop protocols in your unit, with focuses on specific age groups, onset of exposure, whatever. If we are going to be attacked from all sides, the least you can do is help me man the barricades." He reached for the sugar and added another teaspoonful to the already-sweetened coffee. "Oh, and put together a couple of generic protocols too. Something I can pass out to other hospital directors who challenge me, to give them something to work with if they want to run their own studies."

Celia could scarcely believe that in response to her request for time off, he was piling all this additional work on her. She was on the verge of protesting when he looked at Liliana and asked, "Can you type?"

"I've never used a typewriter. But keyboard skills I've got. Doesn't everybody?"

"Your aunt has requested some time off." He looked again at Celia. "If you could come in for a few hours a day, to keep the pediatrics unit from slipping into total chaos, you could spend the rest of the time at home, working on the protocols. Maybe Liliana can help input some of the data."

Liliana slumped lower in her seat and did not respond.

Celia frowned. The casual way Leyva had handed her the home leave she had requested and at the same time burdened her with a huge assignment was enough to give her vertigo. "I could not do it without a computer, not in any reasonable length of time."

"The hospital has just been offered some used ones from Pastors for Peace. You can have one of them."

Celia nodded, but her eyes were on Liliana. All she wanted to do was get her home. Enough was enough.

FIFTY-SEVEN

CELIA felt sure, when they got home and Liliana tumbled into bed, that the girl would sleep for a couple of hours, so she hurried to the bodega, the bakery, and the agromercado to replenish the apartment's bare cupboards and refrigerator. When she returned Liliana was still sleeping. Celia went to the kitchen and prepared a vitamin-rich vegetable soup, certain that the aroma would wake her.

It did not. As night fell, it became apparent that she would sleep on. Good, Celia thought. There was no better pain reliever than natural sleep. Liliana would wake up in the morning fully rested, one day further removed from her traumatic experiences and one day closer to recovery.

Celia was so grateful to Dr. Leyva for having given her the time off that she did not even wait until the computer arrived but began at once to jot down ideas for short-term studies of a year or two that she and the other doctors in her unit could carry out.

She went to bed early and woke refreshed on Sunday morning. Liliana, though, remained asleep. After breakfast Celia tried to work but as Liliana slept on she became increasingly distracted. She found herself looking in on her niece every half hour, then every fifteen minutes. Sleep was a normal response to physical and psychological trauma, but twenty hours at a stretch? Just before noon, Celia reheated the soup, woke Liliana, and insisted that she get up and eat. Liliana complied groggily, then headed for her room.

"Don't go back to bed," Celia said. "The computer person is coming soon. I want you to learn to operate it too, in case you want to use it."

"I have a headache," Liliana said.

"Then lie on the sofa. At least you can listen and help me if I get into trouble later. You know I am not as computer-literate as you are."

Celia could not have said what she thought a Pastor for Peace would look like, although she probably had in mind someone similar to the excessively scrubbed, excessively serious, excessively perspiring Mormon missionaries who sometimes showed up in tandem at her door. That hardly fit the description of the ponytailed beanpole who stood there holding a computer. He wore denim cut-offs, a Pastors for Peace T-shirt, and sandals from which protruded toes that had not been well scrubbed, if at all.

"Hi. Dr. Cantú?" At Celia's nod, he said, "I brought you a pet dinosaur. It's too old to learn new tricks, but it is housebroken. Where do you want him to live?"

Celia looked around. There was little choice; it was either the coffee table or the dining table. "The dining table," she said, deciding that it would be easier to eat on the coffee table than to work there.

He placed the computer on the table and walked over to Liliana, who was lying on the sofa with her injured knee elevated. "Hi," he said, sticking out his hand. "I'm Jimmy. Who're you?"

"Liliana," she murmured, offering him a limp hand.

"Bet I know what happened to you. You took a spill on your bike, right? I had one on mine about five years ago and got scraped up the same way. 'Course, I looked worse than you to start with, so I naturally looked worse after."

"Are you a pastor?" Liliana asked suspiciously.

"Naw. Pastors for Peace are just a bunch of blockade runners I like to hang with. They started that program of rounding up American kids from the ghetto who want to be doctors and getting them into medical school here in Cuba. But their main thing is running the blockade to bring down stuff y'all have a hard time getting. I like it 'cause it's a way of helping out and saying 'up yours' to our government at the same time."

He turned to Celia. "Ma'am, there's still the monitor and printer." He glanced down at her well-muscled legs. "Maybe you want to help me lug 'em up? The quicker it's all in here, the quicker I can get you started."

"Of course!"

By the time she had slipped on her thongs he was out the door and clattering down the stairs, blond ponytail flying. She caught up to him at the van and accepted the small monitor he placed in her arms. He followed with the printer, surge protector, a tangle of cords, and ten reams of paper.

"Looks like they expect you to do a lot of homework," he said in a slightly breathless voice that told Celia that she was indeed in better condition than he was.

"I don't mind. It's a favour, allowing me to stay home with Liliana until she feels better. I like my work."

"That's the thing about you Cubans. So many of you really like what you're doing. I bet you never once told your daughter she ought to go into some particular field because that's where the money is."

"She is my niece, but no, I would never tell her that. I want her to do what makes her happy—and hope that whatever she chooses, it will *not* be for the money." As Celia said those words, an unexpected image of the music box stuffed with bills brought tears to her eyes. She was glad Jimmy was behind her on the stairs and unable to see them.

They piled the rest of the computer equipment on the table. Jimmy looked around admiringly. "I really like the way you folks fix up your places."

"I'll bet," Liliana muttered with heavy sarcasm.

Celia scanned the room, trying to see it through his eyes. The only "fix-up" in the sparsely furnished room was two framed photos, one of her parents and one of Liliana's parents, and a blue vase that sometimes held flowers but now did not. Celia laughed, embarrassed both by Liliana's tone and by the compliment, which she did not understand. "What do you mean?"

"You go in for space instead of stuff. An apartment this size back home"—he waved his lanky arms around—"would be jammed with stuff. Even if the family was on welfare. They'd be collecting crap from garage sales or flea markets or what people gave them till they couldn't turn around. Then they'd hate the place because it would feel too little. Most everybody I know thinks where they live is too little. That's because they've not left themselves room to breathe. Me, I gotta have elbow room." He flapped his elbows and grinned at Liliana. "Don't you?"

"Yeah," she said and closed her eyes.

Jimmy suddenly dropped to his knees and crawled forward. "Ah, there it is. I was looking for an outlet. Now that's something I don't much admire about Cuban houses. Not enough electrical outlets. 'Course, old houses in the States are like that too. My grandma's house has one outlet per room. You can guess how many fuses she's blown."

Throughout the afternoon, as Jimmy installed what he called "the old 386" and showed Celia how to operate it, Liliana remained withdrawn. She opened her eyes only when Celia asked her to pay particular attention to something Jimmy was saying.

Jimmy did not directly address Liliana again until he was getting ready to leave. He squatted next to the sofa and said conversationally, "Sorry I couldn't bring you any games, but the old 386 is text only. Can't handle graphics."

Liliana opened her eyes. "I thought all computers had graphics capabilities."

"Now they do. Probably did even when your aunt was in school. But not back in the olden days."

"Actually," Celia said, "When I was in medical school in the early '90s, because of the blockade and it being the Special Period, we had very few computers."

"Oh yeah," Jimmy stood up. "I see the shortage even now. That stupid blockade!" He looked back at Liliana. "But at least *you've* got them, right? In school?"

"Yeah." She closed her eyes and frowned as if in pain.

Perhaps she was in pain, Celia thought as she thanked Jimmy and said goodbye. Perhaps there was more pain than she could imagine or Liliana would ever reveal. Not that it mattered. What mattered was that Liliana find a way to cope with it, and heal.

Celia placed her hand on Liliana's forehead. She was sweating but it was from the heat of the afternoon, not fever. Celia picked up a pillow from the floor to exchange it for the sweat-dampened one under Liliana's head. That was when she noticed the telephone. She had taken it off the hook and covered it with a pillow from her bed so its ringing would not disturb Liliana. Reluctantly she put the telephone back on the hook.

"Is it okay if I go back to my room now?" Liliana asked.

"Yes, if you feel more comfortable there. Do you mind if I stick my head in occasionally?" Celia smiled. "I need to reassure myself that you are really here."

"If you want."

It occurred to Celia that she could prevent getting calls by placing them herself—which she ought to do anyway. She dialed Alma first.

"Celia, mi hija! We have been trying to reach you. How is Liliana?"

"Better. We were at the hospital yesterday and today she slept until noon. I took the phone off the hook so it wouldn't wake her and forgot to put it back on. I am sorry."

Celia gave Alma a quick rundown on Liliana's condition, omitting only what the doctor had gleaned from the internal exam. "I want her to sleep as much as she can for the rest of the day, but I have to go back to work tomorrow. Would it be possible for you to drop by in the afternoon? It is not that she needs anything done for her. Just company."

"Claro," Alma exclaimed. "I'll bring lunch too, and some games."

"Buena idea," Celia encouraged. "I will leave the door unlocked, so just walk in. If she is asleep, please wake her." She lowered her voice. "She is not herself yet. A little ashamed, I expect. Not quite able to face up to what happened."

"Well, naturally! Poor child! I drove an ambulance for twenty-five years, and I can tell you, I never heard of anything like this."

Celia rung off, relieved that Alma had not insisted on coming over immediately. She saw all too clearly how such a visit would have unfolded. Being Sunday, Luis was not at work so he would have driven her. While Alma focused on Liliana he would try to get Celia alone, to let her know how desperately he wanted to revive their relationship. As if, when she was saying goodbye to him and the MININT officials, his face had not been plea enough. The happiness in his eyes when she thanked him showed that he was incapable of understanding that what she felt was gratitude, not love. But then, how good was she at distinguishing the two? Was it not that very confusion that had led her to become engaged to him in the first place? The whole situation shamed and depressed her.

Celia called Joaquín, Angelica, and Emily to let them know Liliana was back and asked Emily to tell Magdalena and Danilo. When she finished the calls she peeked in on Liliana, who was again sleeping. A good time to become familiar with "the dinosaur," Celia decided. The computer was to be used only for word processing so she would start with personal letters. She was, after all, still on "personal time."

She began with a thank-you letter to the Gómez family, followed by one to Franci. She told Franci everything—except about the Sánchez hallucinations and her encounters with Miguel Ortega Ramos.

There was one more letter she wanted to write, but not on the computer. She shut it down and moved to the sofa, pad and pen in hand.

Dear Miguel,
I am sorry about the way I left. I dreamed that Liliana was hurt, and since I didn't know where she was, I had to go home and hope she would come. Strangers brought her home the next day. She has been hurt, although it was nothing like the dream, so it wasn't a premonition or anything like that. Just luck that I got here before she did. I would like to visit again, if I am still welcome. But I don't know when.
Celia Cantú

Seeing that she had signed her last name, she smiled. As if he knew a lot of Celias. Well, two at least. He might be curious as to which one of them had written the note. She had no idea what Miguel's address was, so she posted it to the park headquarters in Santo Domingo. Guides went up and down to the Comandancia every day. Someone would take it to him.

It was past midnight when Celia finished her correspondence. She heated a bowl of soup and took it out onto the balcony to eat. She wanted to take advantage of this quiet time to process the events of the past week, but hardly knew how to go about it.

Given what she had been through—Liliana's disappearance, helping Franci bury Josephine's father; returning to Miguel with the desperate desire to ground herself in the multilevel intimacy they had had or she had imagined they had on their first encounter, only to deny that was what she came for and to flee without saying goodbye; the danger posed by those men on the trail and her and the mule's adrenalin-fuelled dashes to escape; the surreal all-night drive back to Habana, slipping from one Celia persona to the next until she did not know, moment to moment, who she was; then Liliana's return, her shocking story, their day at the hospital—how did one go about processing all that?

She thought of an old sugar mill her class had once visited. Muscular young men, showing off for the gaggle of secondary school girls, had dumped one wagon load of cane after another onto the conveyor belt that carried it into the maw of the crusher. Some spilled off along the way, but the silly boys so overloaded it that the belt overflowed the crusher, causing the decrepit old mill to choke, sputter, and shut down.

Celia wondered if her own system was doing that—spilling bits of her experiences off to the side, to be scooped up later, or never. Would she be able to assimilate what remained without breaking down? Perhaps, if she didn't rush it. She gazed at the stars and decided that on this warm clear night the only thing she would "process" was the fact that Liliana was now safely asleep in her own bed.

But beneath that thought her body was processing something quite different: the knowledge that at the other end of Cuba there was a man whose bed she had shared, and might share again, who knew she was two Celias in one skin and did not seem to mind.

FIFTY-EIGHT

LUIS knew the meaning of Celia's phone being off the hook. The request she made of Alma could not have been clearer if she had shouted it in his face. All night he alternated between depression, hopelessness, and anger. Not until Monday morning, when he reached his office and sat at the familiar desk, did his mind began to work in a clear and methodical way. He was not without resources. Using the resources at hand, had he not come up with a way of flushing out Liliana that was more effective than José's flashy convertible? Using those same resources—concentration, planning, and patience—had he not won Celia before, after José lost her? And so he would again. Even as he reassured himself of this, Luis wondered if he believed it only because José had left Cuba. Would his hope dry up like a splash of water on hot pavement as soon as his brother returned?

Luis's gaze fastened on the portrait of Che Guevara, as it often did when he was trying to get himself in the right frame of mind for serious work. José had never set foot in this office and if he ever did, Luis knew he would make some sarcastic remark about the clichéd image, repeated ad infinitum all over the island. But it meant something to Luis, which was why it was the single picture that adorned his office wall.

Che never compromised his ideals. After the war in the sierra many combatants tried to repay themselves for the hardships they had endured by behaving so decadently that their lifestyle had come to be known as *la dolce vita*. Not Che. He lived a spartan existence in Cuba and faced even greater hardships in the Congo when he sought to contribute what he could to the Africans' struggle for independence. But he had found the behaviour of the Congolese rebels too barbaric, and so had returned to South America to help the Bolivians liberate themselves from a brutal dictatorship. Che had opted for a life of honour and service to humanity over a life of bourgeois ease, as had he. Luis Lago had not fought in the Revolution but he would defend it to his dying breath.

Luis left his desk to gaze out the window at waves splashing against the seawall along the Malecón. An oil tanker was visible on the horizon. For a moment he tried to imagine what it would be like to see ships there and know them to be those of an invasion force, and that he and all Cubans must swiftly take up arms to defend themselves.

He made a scoffing noise at himself for the silliness of imagining that it could happen like that now and replaced the invasion image with a real image from his own past: walking on the Malecón with Celia, Liliana atop the seawall, he holding the child's hand, she squealing with delight as the salt spray drenched her.

That would have been before Celia moved to Habana del Este, when she still lived just down the street. In an effort to give Liliana a semblance of family to replace the one recently lost, Celia had begun spending almost as much time at the Lago house as at her own. Alma encouraged it, having identified Celia early on as the ideal wife for one of her sons. Luis knew Celia could scarcely tolerate Alma's religiosity, different as it was from her own mother's irreverent ways, but she appreciated the surrogate mothering, if not for herself, certainly for Liliana. Just as Luis gained the trust of his co-workers by helping them achieve their ends, he gained Celia's trust by helping her achieve hers.

For instance, there was the conflict that arose every Easter, with Alma begging Celia to allow her to take Liliana to mass. For two years he watched Celia agonize over what to do, wanting to repay Alma for her daily kindness yet reluctant to have Liliana subjected to religious dogma. Then Luis had unobtrusively taken charge of the situation. He arranged for all of them to spend Semana Santa at the beach, in a location where Easter Mass was not an option. Later, after he achieved a high enough rank that a state car was made available to him, he had diversified their activities. Thus he had begun to court Celia without her even being aware of it. Could he not do the same thing again?

Luis regularly arrived at work an hour ahead of everyone else, but that hour had somehow slipped away. He heard other state employees coming along the corridor, some calling out to him as they passed his open doorway. He greeted them in his usual respectful fashion, then, like a tardy schoolboy, hastened to his desk and went to work. The work, blessedly uninterrupted by calls or consultations, quickly absorbed him. It was two-thirty in the afternoon before he looked up again. He had not gone to lunch, having decided to leave early in order to drive Alma to Habana del Este.

Luis stopped on the way to the apartment to pick up a bouquet of flowers from the big outdoor market. Silly to pretend they were not for Celia, but he understood that they must not be. It was by doing things for Liliana that he gained Celia's trust before, and through his ineptness in handling Liliana that he had lost her. Now it was Liliana with whom he must court favour if he was ever to get close to Celia again.

When they arrived at Celia's place, Luis was chagrined by the sight of the yellow convertible parked at the curb. José's way of marking territory, he thought irritably, like a dog's yellow piss against the curb. Oh well. At least the car meant she was at home.

However, stepping inside the foyer, he saw that her bicycle was gone. Celia's obvious rejection of a luxury José had tried to provide strengthened Luis's resolve. As he climbed the stairs behind his mother, he did not feel entirely confident but neither did he feel hopeless.

Alma knocked then walked in, calling Liliana's name as she headed for the kitchen. Luis hesitated in the doorway. He was standing there when Liliana came from her bedroom wearing a short nightgown. Her face was sleep-swollen and patchy with ugly bruises. She looked even worse than she had three days earlier. Alma stopped short, set the things she was carrying on the table, and took Liliana in her arms.

"Aye, Preciosa! Gracias a Dios for bringing you home!" she exclaimed.

Liliana returned the hug, but over Alma's shoulder she fixed Luis with a cold eye. When Alma released her and went to put the food in the kitchen, Luis thrust out the flowers. Liliana folded her arms across her chest, refusing to accept them.

"You just wasted your money. She's not going to take you back."

"They are for you," he lied.

"It's no use," she repeated. "It's over."

Luis tried and failed to keep the fury from his voice. "What makes you so sure?"

He thought he saw a flicker of uncertainty in Liliana's eyes before she ducked her head and mumbled, "You don't know her."

"And you do?" he questioned sarcastically.

Liliana brought her swollen eyes up to meet his. "Not really."

Alma returned from the kitchen. "Here," she said, taking the flowers from him. "Let me put them in water." To Liliana she said, "Won't they look nice in that blue vase you gave Celia for her birthday!"

"Claro, Tía," Liliana said sweetly, but continued to glare at Luis.

It infuriated him that the apology she owed him—owed all of them—would not be forthcoming. On the contrary, to even get past that malevolent stare he would have to be the one to apologize. He opened his mouth to do it but that was not what came out.

"Listen, Liliana," he said in a low voice, so that Alma, in the kitchen filling the vase with water, would not overhear. "There is no way we can avoid each other. We should not make it hard on the people we love by fighting."

"So don't come here," she hissed.

"That is Celia's decision. She and you have always been welcome in our home, and I find it hard to believe she will make us unwelcome in hers, no matter what misunderstandings there have been."

Liliana turned away in what might have been embarrassment. If she had been inclined to more overt hostility, Alma's return to the living room caused her to stifle it.

"I brought the boys' chess set," Alma said brightly, not letting on that Liliana's appearance was anything other than normal—a talent she had probably perfected during three decades as an ambulance driver. "And dominoes too. Would you like a game? Or shall I fix you something to eat first?"

"Dominoes, please," Liliana said in a small tired voice.

"Oh, good," Alma enthused, clicking the domino tiles onto the coffee table. "We can all three play. Come, Luis, pull up the other rocker."

Luis was staring at the computer. "Where did that come from?"

"A man gave it to Tía Celia," Liliana said with a hint of satisfaction. "A friend of hers. Not somebody you know."

Alma glanced up sharply. Luis smiled at his mother, the smile genuine, because his first thought was that José had bought the computer. Liliana's answer, calculated to make him jealous, did not. He knew every friend Celia had, male and female. Clearly the hospital had lent it to her so she could work at home.

He pulled up the rocker and took his dominoes, recalling as he did so the hours he had spent teaching Liliana to play the game. He remembered, too, how often he had let her win. No más, muchacha. Nunca más.

240

FIFTY-NINE

CELIA had intended to get home much earlier, but with one doctor absent and so much work having piled up in her absence it was after eight when she entered the apartment that evening. She climbed the stairs swiftly, still buzzing from the rush of her day.

"How are you, mi vida?" She motioned toward half a sandwich lying on a plate on the coffee table. "I see you fixed yourself something to eat."

"Tía Alma brought it."

"Let me make myself something and I'll join you. I am so hungry I could faint."

"You can have that."

Celia hesitated. "Are you sure you don't want it?"

"I didn't even want the first half. I only ate it to keep from hurting her feelings."

Celia sat down on the tile floor with her back against the couch and kicked off her shoes. She picked up the half-sandwich and although she could have downed it in three bites, forced herself to eat slowly.

"I see she brought flowers too. That was sweet."

"Luis brought them," Liliana replied, cutting her eyes at Celia, no doubt checking for a reaction to the dropping of tío from his name.

"Oh. Nice they both came to see you."

"It was *you* he came to see."

"They both knew I was working," Celia said patiently. "If they chose to visit when I wasn't here, it would have been to see you."

"Tío Luis hates me," Liliana sulked, this time giving the *tío* a sarcastic intonation.

"Oh? Why?"

"He blames me for you dumping him."

"If he does, he would be wrong."

"Then why did you?"

"It's . . . complicated. I would rather not discuss it now."

For a moment Liliana was silent, but the fretful, almost asthmatic sound of her breathing told Celia that the mood had not passed. Celia swallowed the last bit of sandwich. It went down dryly. She rose to go to the kitchen for a glass of water.

"Tía Celia?" Liliana waited until Celia stopped and turned around before asking, "Why do people keep secrets?"

"All sorts of reasons, I suppose. Afraid of punishment? That would be why you didn't want me to know you were skipping school. Or fearing disapproval. I expect that was Luis's reason for not telling me he was calling in the youth authorities."

"You knew!" Liliana cried, sitting up on the sofa so suddenly that she winced with pain. "You planned it together! You just don't want me to blame *you*!"

Celia was so surprised that her mouth fell open. "Surely he did not tell you that!"

"You think I'm totally stupid? You were the only person who knew what time I was getting home. 'Noon,' I said. And that was when he showed up with those youth cops. Right at noon! If you didn't tell him, *who did*?"

Gazing at her agitated niece, Celia saw again that the injuries to her body were merely the easiest to identify. How many days, weeks, months would it take to locate the others? How should she treat them, and how long would they take to heal?

She took a deep breath. "I did tell him you would be home by noon. He said he wanted to talk to you. I knew nothing about the youth authorities. Alma did, but even she had no idea that he had arranged for them to take you. That came out later."

Liliana lay back on the couch, not entirely mollified. Celia went into the kitchen for the water she craved. She drained the glass and, feeling almost as drained herself, leaned against the counter. Not an hour ago, while cycling home from work, she had vowed to shorten her hours at the hospital, spend more time with Liliana, and have more meaningful conversations with her. Yet here was Liliana, creating an opening for all sorts of shared confidences, and all she wanted to do was escape. She forced herself to return to the living room. Liliana watched her walk toward the sofa with dark soulful eyes so like those of her dead mother that Celia's heart wrenched.

"That's not the only secret in this family," Liliana muttered.

Celia took the comment for what it was: an acceptance of her explanation, combined with an accusation of—what? What specific thing did Liliana have in mind?

"Probably not," Celia agreed, mentally shying away from her own secrets, only to be bludgeoned by an image of dollars stuffed into the bottom of a music box. "Do you have one you want to share?"

"Do you?" Liliana shot back.

"I might, but not tonight. Some other time, when you feel better and I am less tired." She picked up Liliana's limp, sweaty hand, kissed the palm, and headed for the bathroom. It was not avoidance, she told herself. It was only that she would feel more rested after a shower. Then maybe—well, would she?

No. As she closed the bathroom door behind her, Celia knew there was not a chance under the sun that she would tell Liliana anything about her two most closely guarded secrets. She could not see either lasting forever, but as long as they did last they would form a wall that shut others out, and shut herself—or part of herself—in. However much she wanted to be as open with Liliana as she wanted Liliana to be with her, there was no way to explain to somebody else things she could not explain to herself.

She came out of the shower refreshed, determined to sit down and let Liliana talk about whatever was on her mind. That, she knew, was as important from a therapeutic point of view as antiseptic was for the skin abrasions. But Liliana had gone to bed.

Celia went out onto the balcony, sat down in one of the plastic chairs, and stared out to sea. Lights twinkled on the surface of the black water, the lanterns of night fishermen in small dories or fat tubes converted into rubber rafts. Each one alone, each with his own secrets, out there in the dark.

The breeze had died down. The air was warm and uncommonly soft. Soft, too, were the sounds from other apartments. She had been on the balcony perhaps ten minutes when Liliana appeared in the doorway. "Tía Celia?"

"What is it, mi corazón? I thought you were asleep."

"There's one thing I have to know. One of your secrets."

Celia's heart lurched. She had only two, neither of which she could bear to reveal.

"Only one?" she said with feigned humour. "Come. Sit down."

Liliana did not come, nor did she sit. She remained in the doorway; her face, white in the moonlight, framed by dark bedraggled curls. "Are you going back to Luis?"

"I very much doubt it."

"Are you going to get re-engaged to Joe?"

"That is not going to happen either."

"Didn't he give you that car?"

"It was not a gift. He only loaned it, so I could look for you."

"You looked for me?" The surprise in Liliana's voice reminded Celia that she had not even mentioned to Liliana the lengths to which she had gone to find her.

"Of course I did. From here to Santiago. And distributed notices. Except in Varadero and SuperClub Saturno. Luis circulated those." She smiled up at Liliana. "I expect you're famous all over the island by now."

Liliana did not smile back. She stared out at the lights winking on the surface of the water, thinking her own thoughts. Celia waited. When at last Liliana spoke, the words pierced Celia in a part of her psyche so delicate that she had shielded it even from herself.

"You will."

"What?"

"Go back to one of them."

"Why do you say that?" Celia asked, her voice sharper than she had intended.

Liliana took a step back, but faced Celia long enough to say what was on her mind. "You're just not strong enough," she said sadly.

Celia knew her entire family had always believed that. Her older sister, her courageous mother, even her gentle father, had seen her as the baby, the weak one. The one in perpetual need of protection. It was the last thing in the world she wanted to hear from the child she was sworn to protect.

SIXTY

JOE looked out the window of the plane as the western tip of Cuba drew nearer. Had anyone told him, when he watched the island's coastline recede ten years ago, that he would someday feel a sense of freedom upon entering Cuban airspace, he would have laughed so hard he'd have been in danger of falling overboard.

On that summer morning he saw Cuba only as a place of limited opportunities, with a government that practised what many viewed as the greatest crime of all: that of preventing its citizens from becoming rich. He was just a kid when then-President Ronald Reagan said, "I want America to be, above all, a place where people can still get rich." Cuban leaders ridiculed Reagan for the greed that remark encouraged, but from the time Joe heard it he harboured a desire to go to the country where he along with everybody else would have the freedom to "get rich."

Not once during the decade he was clawing his way up the economic ladder had Joe felt nostalgia for Cuba, only pride at having escaped. That was why, as the turquoise sea below was replaced by the verdant green of Península Guanahacabibes, he took notice of the lightness that loosened his muscles and caused him to take a deep breath of relief. The emotion was so unexpected that he let *The Wall Street Journal* fall to his lap. Once he had analyzed the feeling, he was less surprised. It had to do with the divorce or, more specifically, its aftermath.

He had not silenced Vera as easily as he had imagined with that one phone call. Within two weeks she had hauled him into court in an attempt to squeeze a large sum of money out of him for a shrink for Keri. How with Miami's overloaded court system she had been able to do it so fast he had no idea, but the episode was resolved even faster. A fuzzy-headed black judge with a very unfuzzy mind had listened to the story dramatized by Vera's lawyer, then opted to discuss the matter privately with Keri in chambers. Joe couldn't know what Keri told her, but the judge promptly dismissed the case, with a sharp reminder to Vera that as part of the divorce settlement she had agreed never to bring her ex-husband to court for additional financial assistance of any kind.

Striding out of the courtroom Joe felt his non-entanglement policy reinforced; again he was a free man. Again he was wrong. Keri broke away from her mother, ran after him, and his determination to not see the girls anymore went to hell. With Keri wrapped around his legs begging to know when he was coming to take them out, he did the only thing he could do. Right there in front of Vera's lawyer, his lawyer, and a gaggle of strangers, he asked Vera, "How about I pick the girls up after school tomorrow?"

Kneeling down to disentangle Keri from his legs, Vera had replied sweetly, "Of course, Joe. As long as you have them home in time for dinner, which as you know is at six. We all feel better when we get to bed at a reasonable hour, don't we, Keri?"

His daughters were home in plenty of time for dinner because the outing never took place. Vera conveniently failed to notify the school that he was to pick them up, and the school, under strict instructions to not allow the girls to leave with anyone other than their mother, the maid, or their maternal grandparents, would not allow Joe to take them. The superintendent had tried to reach Vera by phone but only got the maid, who would not confirm anything, other than that she would be right over to get the girls if Miss Vera wasn't there. Vera of course was unreachable.

Leaving Amy in tears and Keri in the midst of a full-fledged tantrum, Joe had stormed downtown to his lawyer's office. Three hours later, a letter was hand-delivered to Vera. It was sufficiently threatening that when Joe drove up in front of the house the following morning the girls were ready and waiting. He didn't even have to ring the bell.

By then he had a new game plan. The trouble with the previous one was that he had only aimed at solving the problem of the moment. He thought he could prevent Vera from manipulating him by not asking anything from her, not even access to his own children. Now he saw that he'd have to factor in the girls' desires.

One of their desires was to spend time with animals. Joe himself had no time for a pet, and until the advent of Fluffy the kitten, Vera had objected to pets on the grounds that they harboured diseases. Probably as a result, their petless children were fascinated with all visible life forms, from sea slugs to elephants. For that reason (and to annoy Vera), most of Joe's post-divorce time with them involved animals. When they had a day together he took them to the zoo or Sea World. If their time together was brief, it might entail pony rides or a trip to a park where they could feed the ducks. On that particular Saturday, because it was what Joe figured would be his last visit with them for a long time, he had something special in mind. When the girls quizzed him about where they were headed, he said, "To a really scary part of the Everglades, to see *alligators*."

Amy, who was just beginning to develop her mother's habit of implying that nothing was quite enough or good enough, turned down the corners of her pretty mouth and said, "We saw alligators at the zoo. They just lie there. Boring."

"Yeah, but these are wild alligators. We'll be lucky if they don't bite the paddle in half and leave us stranded out there in the swamp all night."

In fact, Everglades alligators were so accustomed to sightseers that they did lie among the reeds like logs. But the airboat driver thrilled the girls by coming in close enough that, had he had a paddle in hand, an alligator could have chomped it.

Later they visited an alligator farm where a Seminole Indian "wrestled" an alligator. Joe, who didn't care for the stupidity of the so-called sport, stood back, preferring to admire his beautiful children as they clung to the wire fence, their blond hair wildly tangled from having been blown about during the airboat ride.

Watching them brought to mind a trip he had made with Celia to the Laguna de Tesoros back in their college days. She had been fascinated by crocodiles in a fenced pond behind the restaurant. This was a similar scene—pretty girl pressed against a wire fence, beyond which lay a body of water infested with ugly reptiles. His feelings, though, were in no way similar: paternal pride now and something altogether different then.

He had stood behind Celia, admiring her well-shaped legs and imagining their upper reaches, concealed by shorts snug against her firm ass as she leaned over the fence to get a better look. He wanted to bed her right then and there in one of the romantic cottages scattered about on small islands in the lagoon. But that was impossible; far beyond his means at the time. Instead, they had returned to Jagüay Grande on the bus and stayed with a friend who obligingly lent them one of the family's two bedrooms.

The alligator-wrestling show was appropriately concluded by a helper who, in throwing fish to the big reptiles, revealed a hook in place of a hand. The girls came screaming to Joe in delicious horror, and he assured them that, yes indeed, the hand had been bitten off by a gator. Which he supposed it could have been, given the nature of the "entertainment" on offer.

They lunched in a diner at the alligator farm. As soon as they had settled into one of the red vinyl booths, Joe told the waitress, with a wink, "Three gator-burgers, two orders of fries, two orange juices, and a draft beer."

When the girls had exhausted their repertoire of gagging sounds—not allowed in front of their mother—Joe brought up the reason for the day's rendezvous.

"I'm not going to be able to visit you much anymore," he confided.

"Why?" Keri demanded.

Joe mentally flipped through the answers he had prepared, trying to decide which would best serve his plan. Amy beat him to the punch with the truth.

"Because it makes Mommy mad," she said, without looking up from the drawing she was creating on the back of her paper placemat—an alligator with a large, four-fingered hand dangling from its mouth.

Keri frowned at her sister's drawing, then smiled brightly at Joe. "We could sneak down to the corner and meet you. She wouldn't know."

Joe's heart went out to his youngest daughter. Like Amy, she was a preschool version of their doll-pretty mother, all fair skin, blond curls, and deep blue eyes. But Keri's soul was pure Joe Lago. Where Amy was quick to learn the rules and follow them for adult approval, Keri was just as quick to look for a way around them to achieve her own objectives. Even as Joe recognized this quality of himself in his not-yet-five-year-old daughter and loved her for it, he felt compelled to say, "No, Keri, I don't think that would be a good idea."

"Why?"

Again Amy answered before Joe could. "Because we might get grabbed. By a pervert."

"A pervert wagged his weenie at me," Keri informed Joe solemnly and collapsed against her sister in a spasm of giggles.

"Wagged his weenie!" Amy echoed. Amidst chortles, they chanted, "Wagged his weenie, wagged his weenie!"

Joe couldn't help laughing even as he shook his head with incredulity. Was that what Keri had told the fuzzy-haired old judge? If so, had Her Honour also wondered where a preschooler might have learned such slang, let alone its meaning?

Seeing the waitress heading their way, he shushed the girls. For the next two minutes they behaved like well-designed robots programmed with perfect table manners. However, the second the waitress turned her back, Amy drowned her fries in half a bottle of ketchup, while Keri opened her bun and with delicate, none-too-clean fingers lifted the patty off the burger and placed it on Joe's plate.

"It's not really alligator," Joe protested. "I was just kidding."

"It was a live something," Keri stated. "I don't like eating live things."

"Why not?" Amy smirked and pushed aside her plate so she could admire her drawing. "Some of them want to eat you."

"I don't care." Keri again examined her sister's drawing of the alligator and the hand. "Where's the other finger?"

"I told you," Amy said, although she hadn't. "He ate it."

Keri leaned back in the booth and began picking at the bun of her now-vegetarian burger, scattering broken bits on and around her plate. Something, or perhaps everything in their lunchtime conversation, had clearly upset her.

"Like I said," Joe tried again. "I'm not going to be visiting you very often from now on. But I've got a surprise for you." From the pockets of his khaki cargo pants he produced two small, beautifully wrapped packages.

The girls ripped off the wrapping and squealed with such ear-piercing delight that the waitress on the other side of the room turned to stare, then smiled. It was a cellphone for each girl in what he knew to be her favourite colours: red and gold for Amy, turquoise and silver for Keri. They were familiar with cellphones; Vera had one and occasionally allowed them to use it; for example, when they were out together, to call the maid to let her know what time they could be expected home for dinner.

"The house is programmed on number 1," Joe explained. "Just like on Mommy's. Mommy's cellphone is number 2. Why don't you try it, Amy?"

Amy punched number 1. Vera promptly picked up. "Mommy," Amy said breathlessly. "Guess what? Daddy gave me a cellphone!"

"Me too!" Keri shouted into the mouthpiece of her sister's phone.

Joe could hear Vera asking where they were. He held out his hand for the phone. Amy passed it over. "Hello, Vera. I thought it would be a good idea for the girls to have these in case of, well, something like before. I programmed the house number in on 1 and your cell on 2. Is there another number you'd like me to program in on 3?"

"Not yours?" Vera asked in a tone that implied he hadn't included his own number because he didn't want to be bothered.

Joe smiled at how accurately he had predicted her response. "Well, sure, I could. But since these are mainly for use in case of emergency, and I'm out of the country so much now, maybe somebody more accessible, like, I don't know. Your parents, maybe?"

There was a long silence, during which his smile grew broader. He knew Vera was trying to figure out his game and knew she could not. At last she said, "My parents, yes. That would be fine."

"Give me the number, then, and I'll program it in right now." To the girls he said, for Vera's sake, "Finish your lunch, girls. I'm putting Grandmother's number in on 3."

He repeated Vera's parents' phone number after her, programming it as he went. When he finished, he said, "Okay, great. See you in a couple hours." He hung up before she could ask anything else and turned his attention back to his daughters.

"There's something special about these cellphones. A secret."

"What?" Two pairs of blue eyes fastened on his face, expectant.

Joe pointed to Numbers 8 and 9. "These are my numbers. If you call this one you'll get the apartment. If you call this one, you get the office. Go ahead, try them. You, Keri, call the apartment. And you call the office, Amy."

Each girl punched a number. Being Saturday afternoon, the secretary had left the office so Amy got the answering machine, as Joe had known she would. "This is Mr. Lago's daughter," Amy said with stiff pride. "His daughter calling for him to call me."

Meanwhile Keri had reached the answering machine at the apartment. "Daddy, it's me, Keri," she giggled, then hung up.

Amy touched each button in turn, reciting what it was for. Then she lifted her eyes to Joe. "Why, Daddy?"

"Why what?"

"Why are your numbers secret?"

"They're not really secret," he said. "Your mother has them. But it's a secret that they're on your phone. If you tell her, I expect she will make them go away."

Both girls fell silent. Joe's heart ached. Why the fuck did it have to be like this, children so young already learning to distrust not just strangers but their own parents?

Keri got up on her knees in the booth and leaned across to Joe. "I will *never* tell. Cross my heart." She drew an X on her chest, leaving streaks of ketchup across the happy face on the front of her yellow T-shirt.

"Me either," Amy said, although to Joe's knowledge there was not a word he had ever said to her that she hadn't repeated to her mother under cross-examination. She was, after all, the child who most wanted to please.

"You can tell her if you like," Joe emphasized. "Because it's your secret, not mine. But if you do, you know what will happen. As long as they're there, though, you can call me anytime, day or night. If you get the machine and I don't call right back, it's because I'm out of the country. But if you leave a message, I promise to call back the minute I get home."

He repeated that last to them, with variations, until he was fairly certain that they had grasped the fact that they couldn't expect him to be immediately accessible, but they could expect a call from him as soon as he returned. On the way home they practised calling until he was sure the programmed numbers were fixed in their memory. Just as surely, he knew Vera would gain access to those memories. In a matter of weeks, if not days, she would de-program his numbers to prevent unmonitored conversations.

Cellphone memories she could erase. What was in the girls' memories she could not. They would remember this day. They would remember the alligators, remember he had given them the wonderfully adult gift of their own personal cellphone, remember that by programming in his numbers he had made himself accessible.

They would likewise remember when their mother took the numbers, and possibly the cellphones, away from them, thereby cutting off that access. Amy would cry and Keri would tantrum and Vera would do it anyway, trusting them to get over it, which they would. But ten years from now, at an age where mother-daughter relationships were at their most poisonous, it would be one more thing for them to hold against her; the fact that Daddy had tried to stay in touch but Witch Mommy had driven him away, even to blocking their phone calls. Joe wasn't concerned about missing out on childish babble, which he wasn't much interested in to start with. He was looking ahead to the future; say, ten years from now, when the girls would be a lot more interesting to spend time with and he'd be the favourite parent.

Joe tucked the newspaper into the seat pocket in front of him and straightened his seat back as the plane descended toward Habana's José Martí airport. If he had remained in Cuba and married Celia, would he be divorced now? Probably, given that at least half of Cuban marriages did end in divorce. Besides, he had never limited himself to one woman and Celia wouldn't have put up with philandering. But a divorce in Cuba wouldn't have been the same.

The plane came in low over squared-off fields and slid to a stop on a runway rippling with heat waves. As Joe's foot touched the asphalt he again felt the strange sensation—not of coming home, but of coming to a place where, even in the heavy heat, it was easier to breathe.

In the immigration line, his thoughts went back to the difference between divorce in the States and in Cuba. It wasn't that complications didn't arise in Cuban divorces; after all, what was the Elián case if not a complication? Not to mention the hassle Fidel had had in getting Fidelito back to Cuba after his ex-wife moved abroad. But those were exceptions. Most Cubans viewed kids as indivisible community assets, and community went well beyond parents to include the extended family if not the entire nation.

Of course, Celia, in her fury at Luis had called Liliana, "*my* child." But Joe would bet the contents of his moneybelt that once Liliana came back—and he was sure she was back by now—differences had been resolved in a way that prevented Liliana from being torn apart the way his own girls would be torn apart if he tried to hang on to his fair share of them.

The immigration official took his passport and spent an interminable amount of time doing whatever it is they do with passports out of sight behind the counter.

Waiting for her to ask his reason for the trip, Joe wondered what she would say if he replied, "I have come to father a few kids in a country where I don't have to eat shit every time I want to visit them. Are you by any chance free tonight?"

The uniformed woman looked up and, perhaps picking up vibes from his copulation fantasy, quickly averted her eyes. Without asking the purpose of his visit, she slid his passport back and called, "Next."

A sudden tropical downpour made visibility next to nil. Joe slouched in the back seat of the taxi and for the first time wondered if the States was the best place for his children to grow up. Each of his daughters had in her room such things as a Cuban child could not imagine. But what good was that if the whole of their childhood was to be spent in a barbed wire no man's land between two warring parents?

As quickly as the storm had broken it blew over. Joe rolled down the window and took a deep breath of fresh air, slightly spiced with salt as they approached the coast. Anybody's definition of freedom had to reference what they were running from: poverty, violence, ignorance, or in his case laws that forced him to pay a ridiculous sum of money for the privilege of spending designated hours on designated days with his own children.

"Screw you!" he wanted to shout to Miami, Dade County, Florida, USA—his own personally chosen place in the universe. "Your ball-busting 'family law' can't touch me here!"

SIXTY-ONE

CELIA sat alone in the small conference room at a large round table. The elegant but scarred piece of furniture had not been easy to acquire, nor could she have got it without Luis's help. When she insisted that in order to handle her then-new job as jefa de sala for the pediatrics unit, she needed to be able to meet with her staff in the round rather than with herself at the head of a rectangular conference table, he had quietly gone about getting the addresses of homes confiscated by the government from families who had departed Cuba permanently and had taken whatever steps were necessary to gain access to the houses. They prowled the abandoned properties until they located a round table, and Luis had obtained permission for it to be moved to the hospital for Celia's use. It was one of the many favours for which she had repaid him out of her own body—or as she now saw it, out of her own weakness.

Neither the table nor Luis was on her mind as she counted the protocols her secretary had Xeroxed that lay on her left, and copies of the presentation she had given in Santiago that lay on her right, and waited for the doctors in her unit to arrive.

They entered the room in a clump, continuing animated conversations already begun, raising their voices to compete with the scraping of chair legs on the bare floor. Celia never felt that she was actually in charge. Like many in her generation, she had been promoted young and perhaps too rapidly. In the 1990s, the brain drain of doctors leaving the island for better-paying positions abroad had brought swift advancement for herself, Franci, and other classmates who chose to remain in Cuba. Only lately had Celia realized that unless the government took preventive measures, an in-country brain drain caused by doctors leaving medicine to take jobs in tourism would create the same problems for the post-2000 generation—albeit the same opportunities for advancement.

Only one doctor in the group was older than Celia. Ana Menendez had been passed over as jefe de sala because her husband, also a physician, had gone to Spain on a government-funded trip and had not returned. The supervisory position required attendance at conferences abroad, and as Ana's husband had defected, she was considered unreliable. In Celia's view the administration was wrong about that. Ana was far too attached to parents, siblings, children, and grandchildren to ever leave the island, even to be reunited with her husband. She was a fine doctor, yet so anxious to prove her loyalty that she would never have taken the kind of risk Celia had just taken in speaking out against government policy. For that same reason, she could not be counted on to participate wholeheartedly in what Celia was about to ask of her doctors.

Next to Ana Menendez sat the two youngest doctors in the group, Carlos Urrutia and Beto Alfonsín, small wiry men, one of African descent, one of European ancestry. Both were graduates of the same medical school Celia herself had attended, although eight years behind her. They shared a keen sense of humour, took the social benefits of the Revolution for granted, and displayed irreverence toward Cuba's leadership typical of their generation. If there was a raised eyebrow, a sideways smile, or a joke to be told about Cuban officialdom, it was sure to come from them. Their favourite line was that between them their initials spelled CUBA, and to know their hand-to-mouth financial status was to know everything one needed to know about the nation's economy.

Opposite them at the table were two Oriental-looking doctors who might have passed for brother and sister, but their background could hardly have been more different. Ancestors of Lia Fong had been brought to Cuba in the mid-1800s to replace recently freed black slaves in the cane fields. But the Fongs, like many free blacks, had migrated to town. Lia had grown up in Habana's Chinatown, where her family ran what was said to be the best Chinese restaurant in the city.

The similar-featured young doctor next to her, Kunio Saki, had grown up on the Isla de la Juventud. His Japanese-immigrant grandparents had been snatched off their vegetable farm on the main island in 1942, taken to Cuba's largest offshore island, and there, together with five thousand other "enemy aliens" had been crowded into a US Navy prison called El Presidio. After the war the Saki family, having lost their mainland farm, remained on Isla de la Juventud and eked out a living as door-to-door vegetable vendors. They were staunch supporters of the Revolution, it being the education policies of the Revolution that made it possible for Number One Grandson to become a physician. Dr. Saki was fond of reminding people that just a decade after his grandparents were prisoners in El Presidio, Fidel Castro was locked up there by the Batista regime and "surely ate some of the vegetables my grandparents delivered to the prison."

Doctors Saki and Fong, like Doctors Urrutia and Alfonsín, were bright and energetic. If they went along with Celia's new approach it would not be because they felt compelled to submit to her authority but because they saw it as a more effective way to do their job.

The strongest opposition to the directives Celia planned to give her doctors was likely to come from Esther Cohen, sitting directly across the table from her, chain-smoking. Esther's family history was one of good fortune and tragedy, which, it seemed to Celia, had shaped the woman's conflictive personality. In 1939, Hitler had allowed a shipload of Jews to leave Germany, in a calculated move to show that Jews were no more welcome in other countries than in his own. He was very nearly proven right. Neither the United States nor Canada allowed the ship to land. It was permitted to dock in Cuba but only two children were allowed ashore. The ship returned to Europe, where other countries finally accepted the passengers. Most perished in concentration camps when the Nazis overran Europe.

One of the two children allowed to enter Cuba was Esther Cohen's grandmother. Parents and grandparents had bequeathed to Esther a deep loyalty to Cuba for having saved a tiny portion of their family, entangled with equally deep bitterness toward Cuba for having forced others to return to Europe and to their deaths.

Celia valued Esther for her analytical abilities but found her tendency to take a contrary stance on just about any subject tiresome. Sometimes it seemed to Celia that Esther did so because she considered herself to be the better doctor. At other times Celia suspected Esther of taking the opposite point of view as a form of mental exercise, merely to show off her considerable debating skills.

Whatever her motivation, Esther Cohen could be a formidable opponent, Celia thought, as she unobtrusively studied her from across the table. She noticed that Esther's smooth white skin was already beginning to show signs of aging from the effects of smoking. Celia smiled at the younger woman. Esther flashed a quick but challenging smile back. Celia knew then, if she had not known before, that unless she said exactly the right thing there would be polarization, some doctors siding with Esther, some with her. Even if the majority voted with Celia to pursue the studies she was proposing, those on the losing side would do so with less commitment than she wanted.

"I have copies here of the presentation I gave in Santiago," Celia opened the discussion. "I want you to see exactly what I said at the conference because as you know," she paused and looked around the table, "we are under fire."

Someone, Celia wasn't sure who, murmured, "We?"

Celia gave a wry smile. "That is Dr. Leyva's view. He says that various groups may try to bring the hospital in general and this pediatrics unit in particular into disrepute because of the link our data show between second-hand smoke and children's respiratory ailments. He has asked for our help in 'manning the barricades.' According to him, the way we do this is with more studies."

"And if they fail to support previous conclusions?" Esther asked sharply.

"If that should be the case, would it not be better for our reputation if the refutation comes from us than someone else?"

There was silence, Esther choosing to respond with an enigmatic smile.

Celia looked around the table. "Comments, anyone?"

"Is that all? Just more studies?" Lia Fong asked.

Celia gave the young doctor her attention. "Not quite, Dr. Fong. Based on the evidence we already have, I think it is time we made an all-out effort to ensure that parents understand how important it is for their children to have a smoke-free environment."

Next to her, Dr. Menendez shifted uneasily. "There are community workers who discuss the health effects of smoking. That would be their responsibility."

Naturally Ana would not want to do anything that might be construed as anti-government, Celia thought. If the Ministry of Agriculture suddenly decided to market cocaine, Ana Menendez would probably find a way to avoid criticizing it.

Celia turned to her. "True, Dr. Menendez. But as pediatricians, our word carries more weight. I do not want any of you to let a parent leave this hospital without a clear understanding of the damage second-hand smoke can do to their children—or has already done. No matter how many times you have told them before, or in how many different ways, tell them again. Is that clear?"

From the corner of her eye, Celia saw Esther Cohen's lips curl upward in a tight smile as she blew a stream of smoke toward the middle of the table. "Given what all Cubans have been asked to give up, I don't see how we can ask them to give up smoking too."

"I agree. Smoking is very much a personal choice." Celia paused just long enough to let it sink in that she was not asking Esther to forego her personal choice to damage her lungs and dry her facial skin to the consistency of a well-smoked ham.

Esther could not very well take exception to what, on the face of it, was agreement. When she said nothing, the other five doctors looked to Celia. Her next remark was phrased as a question, but there could be no doubt that it was a directive. "However, as specialists in children's health, we should, don't you agree, encourage them to not smoke around their children, particularly indoors, or with infants in arms?"

She was rewarded with nods of approval from Carlos and Beto. Celia had expected that from the two young doctors. Both were new fathers and, contrary to Cuban custom, forbade smoking in their homes. Ana Menendez, always quick to express agreement with whatever she perceived as the prevailing mood—unless it ran counter to the official position—bobbed her head in what might have been a nod of agreement.

Kunio Saki leaned toward Lia Fong and whispered something. She nodded. Then he asked, "This is to be primary research, using protocols developed here?"

"That is the idea." Celia tapped the second pile of papers. "I have outlined ten possible areas of research. You can review these—" She glanced at Esther. "Or submit ideas of your own. Then we will take a vote as to which ones the department will pursue. Dr. Leyva's only stipulation is that they be in areas where a substantial amount of data can be compiled in a relatively short period of time, say, one to two years."

"I hardly see how anything we do can be original," Esther sniffed. "The effects of second-hand smoke have already been studied ad infinitum in the United States and Canada."

"Exactly the point I made with Dr. Leyva," Celia nodded, again leaving the woman without a sparring partner. "But he insists we need *Cuban* research." Celia flashed an ironic smile around the table. "Maybe he is hoping Cuban tobacco will prove less harmful than what is grown in the United States."

That brought a laugh from the younger doctors. Beto's dark face split into a wide grin. "How about a study designed to show the health *benefits* of smoking?"

"Yeah!" Carlos crowed. "Like, if kids learn young, from their parents, they might be less likely to set themselves on fire by smoking in secret."

"Whatever, as long as we be on the same side as the powers that be," Beto said with a comic roll of his eyes that put a lie to his concern about pleasing "the powers."

Lia Fong leaned forward and injected a point that Celia had intended to make. "The bureaucrats in the Ministry of Agriculture may not be ready for this yet, but I listened to the speech Fidel gave in Buenos Aires. He cautioned young people against smoking. If that isn't a change in the way the wind—or should I say, the smoke—blows, I don't know what is. I think the government may begin a serious anti-smoking campaign within a year. We could be ahead of the curve on this one."

Celia understood Lia Fong's remark for what it was: a reminder to Ana Menendez and any others in the group who might be hesitant about doing studies that were likely to provide data that would undermine Cuba's tobacco industry, that the nation's highest power, not to mention its best mind, would approve of such research.

"Very perceptive, Dr. Fong. Dr. Leyva seems to feel the same way." Thus Celia reinforced the fact that some people in positions of authority shared her thinking on this particular subject. She handed off the papers on either side of her to be passed around. Next to Lia Fong, Kunio was nodding, smiling. Next to Celia, Ana Menendez was not smiling, but she had taken a paper and was studying it intently.

Beto grabbed one of the protocol outlines. "Man, this is radical!" he exclaimed, without even reading it. Carlito snatched it from him. "Then it's mine. You can study the effects of second-hand smoke on babies' breath."

Esther snubbed out her cigarette, took the remaining protocol outlines, and began flipping through them. Celia saw her lips part and thought, She's hooked. It is going to be a unanimous vote.

Celia rose to signal the end of the meeting. "Sorry I have to run, but there is not much to discuss until you have all had time to digest these materials. We will meet again next week and take a vote. Parent counselling should of course begin immediately."

Celia was not in as much of a hurry as she pretended; she merely wanted to adjourn the meeting before Esther Cohen could challenge her again. Cohen would do that anyway, but in private Celia did not mind. She already knew that Esther would play the contrarian to the end, then very likely turn in more comprehensive and better-analyzed research data than anyone else. That was why she considered Esther a valuable colleague. It was only in group situations where Celia was aiming for a consensus and Esther was trying to create competition that the woman became a thorn in her side.

As the doctors skimmed papers or stuffed them into briefcases to be read later, Celia headed for the door. She did not stop at her office but went out of the building to where her bike was parked. She flung her leg over the seat as if mounting a steed and raced off. She might lack the strength of her mother and sister, but on her own turf she had held her ground, perhaps even gained some.

The one thing she might have wished was that Liliana could have been there to see her take charge like that. While basking in the glow of success, another thought brushed Celia's mind: that without Liliana's blunt characterization of her as "not strong enough," she probably would not have gone into the meeting so determined, remained so completely in control, or come out of it with exactly what she wanted.

SIXTY-TWO

CELIA opened the door and saw Liliana as she had found her every afternoon that week, sprawled on the sofa in underpants and a stained T-shirt. On other days Liliana had been staring dull-eyed into space, but now she held the black receiver to her ear.

"She's just come in," Liliana said. "You can talk to her. Chau, Capitán."

Celia took the receiver from Liliana.

"Capitán? Thank you for calling."

"Buenos tardes, Doctora. I knew Liliana was upset, or—" He corrected himself. "I knew any of my daughters put through such an ordeal would be suffering, so I considered it important to let her know what we learned."

"Thank you," Celia murmured and waited.

"We found his reservation, confirmed, for a flight out of Habana, so we waited, expecting him to show up. We also posted surveillance at the airport rental car agency, where we assumed he would return the car."

There was a long pause, so long that Celia did not have to be told that this had failed. Finally Quevedo said, "The long and short of it is that the guy outsmarted us. He turned the car in on Cayo Coco, so its return wasn't immediately registered in Habana. He rented another one, then drove to Holguín and left Cuba from there."

"To Argentina?" Celia asked.

"To Costa Rica. We checked with the Argentine military and learned that he was one of those forced out after the dirty war. He is now running a police training program in Honduras. The Argentines couldn't be more specific than that, and of course we got no co-operation from the Hondurans. So that's more or less the end of the trail. Even if we managed to locate him, Honduras being under the US thumb as it is, would never extradite to Cuba."

"Will he ever be able to return?" Celia asked. She glanced at Liliana, who was staring into space with the dull-eyed gaze Celia found so disconcerting.

"No," Quevedo assured her. "We contacted the Honduran authorities and although they denied ever having heard of him, I am sure they will communicate to him the fact that he is a wanted man in Cuba. That should give him second thoughts about returning. Also, as I explained to Liliana, his data is now in our computer systems. Even if he returns under an assumed name and with a different passport, there is a good chance he will be apprehended."

"You have been more than kind, Capitán. Liliana and I are grateful to you."

"It was only my duty," he replied stiffly.

"Your duty to investigate and to follow up so thoroughly. But a kindness to treat the incident seriously in the first place and to let us know the outcome."

"All part of defending our Revolution," he said brusquely. "Good luck to you and your niece." He hung up before Celia could proffer more thanks.

She kicked off her crepe-soled hospital shoes and started unbuttoning her smock, anxious as always to strip, shower, and rid herself of hospital smells. "So," she said to Liliana. "I guess he already told you everything."

"Yeah. How old Boots got out of the country." Celia was halfway to the bathroom when Liliana added, "*After* he beat up another girl."

Celia stopped in her tracks and turned around. "*What?*"

"He didn't tell you?" When Celia shook her head, Liliana continued. "A girl from Las Tunas. He picked her up on his way to the airport, messed her up, and threw her out of the car just like he did me. Well, not quite like me. He dumped her while the car was stopped. But she was already messed up. At least, that's what Captain Quevedo said the girl told them at the hospital." Liliana paused. "She remembered the boots too."

Celia returned to the sofa, knelt by Liliana, and kissed her. "You were so brave!"

Liliana shook her head. "No I wasn't."

Later, standing under a tepid shower, Celia understood the remark for what it was: evidence of yet another wound in Liliana's psyche. Perhaps she would not have noticed nor felt it so keenly had she not been struggling with the same question: exactly how brave was she? Was it that she—or Liliana, for that matter—actually lacked courage? Or was it that they had not demonstrated it in a convincing way; in particular, not when they felt they ought to have taken a stand?

Yet if Liliana had been bolder she might not even be alive now. As for herself—well, there was really no comparison between the kind of courage required of Liliana to deal with physical abuse and death threats and the kind a woman needs to hold on to herself when a man is trying to manipulate her. The only similarity was that, in both cases, to not capitulate required some sort of inner strength. Failing that, the challenge was to reclaim self-respect. How in the world did one go about doing that?

Refreshed by the shower, Celia went into the bedroom, slipped on shorts and a top, and brushed damp hair. "Did Alma come by today?" she called through the open door.

"No, but she phoned. So did Magdalena. She might come over later."

"What do you want for dinner?"

"I'm not hungry."

Celia grimaced at the response, which was identical to what it had been all week.

There was a single knock, the sound of the living room door opening, and José's voice: "Not even if we go out to dinner and you can order anything you like?"

"Not even," Liliana responded as Celia came from the bedroom.

José walked to the sofa and looked down at the girl. "So. She found you."

"I *wasn't* lost," Liliana muttered.

"Hello, José," Celia greeted him. "I didn't know you were back."

"Just got here. The taxi's waiting downstairs."

"Oh. You can let him go." Celia reached into her purse. "Here are your car keys. And what's left of your money."

"What money?" Liliana asked, but Celia ignored her.

"Maybe you should keep the car a while longer," José said, trying to push the envelope with the remainder of the cash back at her.

"Thank you, but we have no need of it now," Celia said firmly, stuffing both the keys and the money into his jacket pocket.

"We do!" Liliana objected, although not once since her return had she shown the slightest interest in leaving the apartment.

José stood there for a moment, looking from Celia to Liliana and back, assessing the situation. Then he said, "I don't have anything on till Monday morning. How about we take this beat-up chica to the baños in Viñales tomorrow?"

Celia hesitated, but when she saw what she thought was a flicker of interest in Liliana's eyes, she replied, "All right. If we leave early. I'd like to get back before dark."

"Easier on everybody if we stay the night," José said casually.

Too casually, Celia thought, narrowing her eyes at him. "You should not keep the taxi waiting. Come. I will walk down with you."

José followed her out and down the stairs. After he had paid the taxi driver and shifted his bags to the convertible, he turned to Celia and asked, "Well, what's the story? Was she—"

"Yes," Celia said shortly. "But she is not pregnant and there is no sign of a sexually transmitted disease."

He rested his backside against the fender of the convertible. "So what's wrong with her? Other than she got the shit beat out of her."

"Thrown out of a car. Luis can give you the details. But there is more to it."

"Like what?"

Celia rubbed fingertips across her forehead, smoothing out wrinkles that seemed always there. "Something isn't right. I obviously was not aware of what was going on with her before she ran away but at least she seemed happy. Now there is this sense of hopelessness or something." Celia closed her eyes, feeling the shame that engulfed her when she thought about how much she had not seen coming and how little she understood of what it would take to make Liliana "right" again.

Her eyes opened with a start as a warm hand pressed the small of her back and a familiar voice said, "Hi, Dr. C."

She turned and saw Magdalena. She was wearing black lycra shorts and a black halter top. Her spiked hair had changed from metallic orange to jet black.

"Hello, Magdalena," Celia greeted her, but Magdalena's eyes were on José.

"You wouldn't be Fiancé Number One, would you?"

"I'm not used to being called that," José replied with a wary grin.

"How about Dumpee Number One?" Magdalena smirked. "Although I don't know why—not if this is your máquina." She pushed a black fingernail with a gold lightning bolt design along the fender of the car, stopping just short of where José's backside rested. "Or Uncle Joe? Can I call you tío too?"

"His name is José," Celia cut in on Magdalena's attempted cuteness. "José, this is

Liliana's friend Magdalena." Putting an arm across Magdalena's shoulders, she said, "I am glad you came. Liliana has been waiting for you."

To her surprise, Magdalena shot her a grateful smile. It occurred to Celia that given the way the girl dressed, she was probably unwelcome in many homes. Celia smiled reassuringly. "I would like to visit with you too. You can tell me how you managed that." She pointed to the designs on her black nails. "Liliana will be dazzled."

"You think so?" Magdalena beamed, then frowned. "Is she okay?"

"Well . . ." Celia hesitated. "Not really. I think she is depressed. Go on up. Maybe you can make her feel better."

"Claro!" Magdalena turned and almost ran up the walk to the apartment building. Just as she reached the door she remembered her manners, manners that, Celia noted, she did have after all, although not regularly on display. She turned and waved. "Chau, José. Nice to meet you."

"You too, Magdalena," José called back.

As soon as the door closed behind the girl, he cocked a questioning eyebrow in Celia's direction. "*That's* one of Liliana's friends?"

"One of her roommates from school."

"That might explain a few things."

Celia frowned. "Not really. Maybe they fed each other's fantasies, but I am almost certain that it was not a case of Magdalena talking Liliana into something."

"How about Viñales then? The thermal baths might be just the ticket. She could have a soak when we get there and again Sunday morning before we drive back."

"It couldn't hurt," Celia conceded.

José grinned. "You look like you could use a little relaxation therapy yourself, Doctora. Of the hydrotherapy variety," he added quickly.

Too quickly, Celia thought, reading a sexual suggestion into what she was sure was exactly that. "I would appreciate it," she said tightly, "if you would accept the fact that I'm not going to sleep with you, and I did not have to fend you off the whole time."

He lifted his hands into the air. "Word of honour."

They settled on ten the following morning. José left and Celia went upstairs. She paused outside the apartment door, hoping to hear the murmur of girlish chatter mingled with giggles. What she heard was a low humming sound. Entering the apartment, she saw Liliana lying with eyes closed, her head in Magdalena's lap. Magdalena was crooning a lullaby. The absurd Goth makeup was streaked, and one wet tear clung to the underside of her chin.

When Magdalena finished the song, Celia sat down in a rocking chair across from the girls and said, "I thought you would be talking."

Magdalena shook her head. "She can't. It hurts too much. The sex thing, I think." She cut her eyes at Celia to see how she would take a reference to "the sex thing."

"Liliana did not have sex," Celia said, watching not for Magdalena's reaction but for Liliana's. It was instantaneous. Liliana's eyes flew open. Celia looked directly into them. "What happened to you was not sex," she stated. "It was violence."

"I don't get it," Magdalena said. Liliana's eyes conveyed the same confusion. Celia took a breath and did her doctorly best to see that both girls "got it."

"Sex is something you do with somebody else. Sometimes it is great and sometimes it's not. But it is always both people's choice. Violence is one person's decision, meant to hurt somebody else. They might use a sexual part of the body, but that does not make it sex."

She then risked an awful example, but one she knew they would get. "Remember those stories in the news about torture victims in that prison in Iraq, men being forced to masturbate and do things with other men?"

Magdalena nodded. Liliana turned so pale that Celia almost lost the nerve to make her point. But she was too far in to back out. "Torturers used sexual parts of the body but it was not sex. It was violence. So is rape. The only one at fault is the one who inflicts it."

There, done. She had said what she knew to be the truth, but whether it was the right thing at the right time, or if it would make any difference, how could she tell? Celia felt the panic of a professional who has strayed beyond her area of expertise and may have done more harm than good. She wanted to scream, We are not prepared for this kind of danger! Not doctors, not parents, not children! How can we know the right thing to do?

Magdalena began to hum the lullaby again. Liliana closed her eyes. When the song ended, Liliana sat up. "I think I'll to go to bed now, if that's okay." She glanced apologetically at Magdalena. "Thanks for coming by."

"Wait," Celia said quickly. "We are going to Viñales with José tomorrow. Would you like to come with us, Magdalena?"

"Fabuloso!" The skinny girl popped up from the couch like a puppet jerked on a string and clapped her hands. Then, as if strings had been dropped all over, her arms flopped to her side and the corners of her mouth turned down. "Ay, no! It's my grandfather's seventy-fifth birthday. I'm in charge of just about everything for the party. Family's coming from all over the island." She smiled hopefully. "But next time? I would *love* to ride in that máquina." Hugging Liliana, she said, "Do get better soon, Lili. School's awful without you."

Liliana accepted the hug with a wan smile. "Sure, 'Lena."

They listened to Magdalena clatter down the hallway. "Too bad she couldn't come," Celia offered. "Viñales will be a nice change, don't you think?"

"If you want to be with Joe, that's fine with me."

"I want to be with *you*," Celia corrected, touching the girl's pale cheek.

Liliana turned away and headed for her bedroom. "Nobody's with me," she said in a low voice. "And I don't want to be with anybody."

SIXTY-THREE

JOE sighed, happier than he had been in days. It didn't occur to him that he was making this trip as a compensation for a previous trip to Pinar with Liliana that had foreshadowed a lot of bad things to befall her afterwards. Or that Celia's readiness to let him do a fatherly thing for Liliana was something of an antidote to the poison Vera darted him with every time he tried to play dad to his own girls. Joe's motive for the trip, as far as he knew, was much simpler. But at the moment he was not thinking of it either.

As he cruised along the Habana-Mariel autopista, a big navy base on his right, with a duty-to-serve-the-people quote from Fidel painted on the side of a cement block building like "Jesus Saves" on the side of a barn in the southern United States, reminded him of his military service. In retrospect it didn't seem so bad. Two years, required of all Cuban males, hadn't been a great loss at that point in his life, since he did not yet have a sense of direction. He did know, within weeks of induction, that he did not want to be a military professional in Cuba's armed forces or any other.

One thing he had got from his stint in the navy was confidence on the water. As the various small craft to which he was assigned piddled around offshore, a recurring thought was that, weather permitting and the right compass setting, one could make landfall in Florida in a matter of hours. That awareness metamorphosed into a determination to make the journey.

The day he mustered out of the military he applied for permission to emigrate. A year later he had it. Not that permission from the Cuban government meant much without a corresponding entry visa from the country one wished to emigrate to—in José's case, the United States. The United States issued few visas. The Cuban government distributed those few by lottery. With little hope of being one of the lucky ones, Joe enrolled in medical school. It was a casual choice, made because several women he was hot for at the time were there. But he was only killing time.

It was 1994, and Joe was halfway through med school and nowhere near the top of his class when the rules suddenly changed. Castro, fed up with the way the United States was encouraging dangerous illegal sea passages by granting undocumented Cubans instant status as "political refugees" while accepting only a few of those who had exit visas in hand, suddenly announced that anyone wishing to leave was free to do so. A wave of Cubans, fleeing the hard economic times brought on by the recent loss of Soviet support, headed for Florida. A panicked Clinton administration promptly started negotiations, demanding that Cuba go back to restricting the number allowed to leave.

Joe had not waited for the outcome of negotiations. Three days after hearing that those who wished to leave were free to do so, he was on a boat bound for Florida. His leave-taking was from the port of Mariel. A grey dawn it had been, and no one to hug him goodbye. Or as he saw it then, no one to hold him back. Prior to his departure, nothing had sparked his interest except sex. But that day his whole body was stoked. His heart felt like it was pumping more adrenalin than blood. Flying as he now did would never match the thrill of that first crossing, he thought, as he left the Habana–Mariel autopista, cut across to the Habana–Pinar del Río autopista, and continued west.

Celia's silence lasted for the better part of the three-hour drive. Only when they crested the last mountain and the Valle de Viñales spread out below them did she gasp, "Oh, lovely!" She turned and said, "Liliana, wake up, mi corazón. Look at the mogotes."

"Are we there yet?" Liliana asked in a small-child voice.

Joe glanced in the rear-view mirror. Liliana sat up, swaying slightly. She was as pale as any Cuban he had ever seen. "I'm carsick," she moaned.

Joe immediately pulled to the side of the highway. "Get out and walk around," he advised and got out himself to admire the strangely shaped limestone formations that rose like gigantic camel humps out of green tobacco fields in the valley far below. Celia got out with him, but paid less attention to the spectacular view than to Liliana, who shook her head at the suggestion that she walk around.

When it became apparent that Liliana was going to remain in the car, Joe motioned Celia back into the convertible. "We'll be there in five minutes," he promised. To Liliana he added, "And five minutes after that, you can be cooling your nalgas in the pool or warming them in a thermal bath."

Joe had booked two cottages on the forested grounds of the villa, but the fantasy of shoving Liliana into one and sharing the other with Celia was dashed within minutes of check-in. Liliana brought it out in the open as she took one of the keys from him and said to Celia, sullenly, "You might as well sleep with him and get it over with."

"We didn't come here for a romantic holiday," Celia snapped, snatching the key from Liliana's hand and marching off in the direction of the cottage. Liliana shrugged and followed. Joe watched them go, feeling a little discouraged.

In his own cottage, changing into his swim trunks, it dawned on him that he had been thinking about Celia in the wrong way. All this time he had been treating her like a woman he had already courted and slept with. But hadn't she put him on notice that she wasn't the woman she was back then? If she was a different woman (not that he saw it that way, but if she did), then he was in effect starting from scratch. For Celia, this outing might have the emotional content of a first date—or given Liliana's presence, maybe not even that. Maybe it was merely a pre-date, the sort where you made the lady receptive by being kind to her parents/children/ younger siblings— whoever she brought along to keep you at arm's length, and whom you treated with special kindness in order to put her in a receptive frame of mind.

Joe tried to see himself as Celia might, but only succeeded in seeing himself the way he always did—as a man on the move, determined to lay hands on what he wanted. Surely Celia was not unattainable. Standing on the outer edge of youth, she was bound to be ripe for something more than his stick-in-the-mud brother. While pumping himself with possibilities, Joe was realistic enough to admit that this wouldn't be an easy conquest. It had to do with what he had inadvertently confided to Liliana that night in Pinar del Río: the fact that he did not seem to have anything Celia Cantú wanted.

"Bullshit," he said aloud, annoyed by the notion that he had nothing to offer. Yet something was bothering him. He sat down on the bed and stared at the wall, trying to figure out what it was. Then he got it. He was changing. Fucking—changing.

From the minute he laid eyes on Celia on the day of his return he'd wanted to bed her, to relive the wild abandon of those heady days when he had been her first and only lover. He had not thought beyond that or wanted more than that. Seriously, he had not.

Yet when he returned to Miami, hadn't he fantasized Celia there? Wondered where he could buy a house she'd find acceptable? And the day with Amy and Keri, hadn't he imagined Celia standing between them at the railing of that slimy alligator-wrestling pond, the breeze tossing her brown hair as it was tossing their blond curls, all of them "his girls"?

Somehow it had snuck up on him, the desire to have Celia as his—what was the term they used nowadays?—"significant other." He had not recognized it sooner because he had never wanted a woman like that, not even Vera, whom he had married only because he was out-of-control hot for her and that was the price she charged to quench the fire. He had been drawn into that relationship by lust, and lust was still the driving force in his life. But there was definitely more going on where Celia Cantú was concerned. It made him profoundly uneasy.

Joe lay back on the bed and examined the possibilities as he might a business deal—a Cuban business deal, which, as he had already learned, was complicated by the fact that few Cubans in positions of power admitted to being interested in business. Yet didn't they give foreign businessmen the red carpet treatment? Each upscale hotel with a "business centre" geared to corporate tastes—what was that if not an enticement to the business class? Even as *Granma* damned capitalism, every issue seemed to announce a new joint venture.

It was probably the same with Celia. She wanted what a capitalist lifestyle could offer as much as Cuba did, but it wasn't politically correct to admit it. So—okay. Just as he'd come back to Cuba to get something he wanted by showing its heavies that he had something they wanted, he'd do the same with her. Not by grabbing—that would only get his hands slapped. He would take the cerebral approach. Lots of women liked to think of themselves as intellectuals, brains over hormones and all that. He doubted such women existed, but didn't mind pretending he viewed them that way if that was what it took.

Feeling much more sure of himself, Joe wandered into the bathroom to pee, then stepped out onto the porch of his cottage and looked toward the pool. Celia sat in a white plastic chair, wearing a black swimsuit. She had to want something. Didn't everybody?

She said she wanted a chaste weekend. So fine, that was what they would have. She'd talk, he'd listen, and by the end of the outing he would have a clearer idea as to what she *really* wanted. Meanwhile, he would be Mr. Cool. Nothing like indifference to stir up a little insecurity. And that—a woman's uncertainty about her own attractiveness—was something that always worked in Joe Lago's favour.

He meandered across the lawn, dove into the pool, and swam a couple of laps. Then, dripping, he pulled himself out near her feet.

"Where's the kid? Soaking?"

"Sleeping."

"Sleeping? She slept all the way here."

Celia sighed, not the romantic sigh Joe would have liked to hear, but one that bespoke worry. "It has been like this ever since she got back. She sleeps more hours than I would have thought possible. I have no idea what it will take to snap her out of it."

Joe saw his opening and moved into it with the alacrity of a soccer player driving a ball toward the net. "There is one thing." At Celia's questioning look, he said, "Something you asked about before, but I guess you forgot."

He paused, and with sympathy in his voice to give the impression that this was something he hated to remind her, said, "She wants to leave Cuba."

SIXTY-FOUR

CELIA knew that. Or had been told that. She chose to think of it as untrue, and since Liliana's return had given it no thought at all. When José reminded her—and it angered her that he had—she reacted the way she often did when something threatened to send her emotions into turmoil: she slammed shut some inner door on her feelings and called upon the analytical part of her brain.

"Are you suggesting a connection?" she asked coldly.

José shrugged. "I suppose Cuban doctors have heard of depression."

"Spare me the condescension!"

"Sorry. But I've been there. I know what she's going through."

At Celia's incredulous look, he said quickly, "Remember in college when I developed claustrophobia? All I could think of was leaving." He paused and added, "If I had stayed, I might've got over it. Or committed suicide."

"Suicide is *not* one of our health problems," she snapped, not entirely accurately.

"Unless you count the ones who head out to sea in floating caskets."

"Liliana is not a potential balsera! This has nothing to do with a schoolgirl's fantasy about going on a shopping spree in the States. It has to do with being held prisoner, the rape, and someone trying to murder her—all that barely two weeks ago! She will get over it!"

José shrugged. "You're the doctor. But in case she doesn't, just bear in mind that I can get her, or both of you, out of here."

Celia was on the verge of another retort when the penny dropped. She shook her head. "José Lago, you are incorrigible. Is there any situation you *wouldn't* take advantage of to get a woman into bed with you?"

He put on an aggrieved, misunderstood-boy look. "I'm not asking you to jump in bed with me, Celia. Not that I'd object, if that was what you wanted. But I wouldn't make it a condition. You could have your own apartment in Miami."

Celia leaned across the table and looked straight into his confident brown eyes. "Do you have any idea what it would cost me to leave Cuba?" she asked with soft fury.

"Nothing as far as I can see. Liliana's your only real family."

"And my work, is that not 'real'?"

"So you could practise in the States. Or you could switch fields."

"Become, say, a pharmaceutical salesperson?" she asked caustically.

"What's wrong with that? Fidel's sister Juanita has certainly done well in Miami; made a damned good living with her pharmacy on Calle Ocho."

"Now there's a parallel," Celia sniffed. "Juanita chose making money. Fidel chose trying to improve life here in the island for the average Cuban."

José grinned. "So who do you figure has been most successful?"

"History will decide *that*." She paused, thoughtful. "Or 'success' might be measured by how happy each is with what they chose. Fidel, Juanita, you, me—would any of us have been happy if we had made the opposite decision?"

José, grin still in place, tilted his chair back on two legs. "Are you saying you're completely happy with your position at the hospital? That's all you want out of life?"

Celia shook her head. "You really do not get it, do you, José? My 'position' means nothing to me. What counts is my contribution."

He laughed. "To what? La Revolución?"

"You think that is funny?"

He sobered. "The funny thing is, I thought we were alike."

"Us? Alike? Now that *is* funny."

"How so?"

"You were always so *determined*. To get out, make a better life for yourself, all that American dream stuff. Whereas I am—*dedicated*. Or trying to be."

"Maybe you're trying too hard," he said quietly.

Touché. He had aimed the small sharp words at her chest and with the tiniest twist could have made her bleed. What had she been doing if not trying too hard to be a good and dedicated doctor while Liliana slipped away, went astray?

"You . . . do not understand," she said, fearing that he did.

"And you're not answering my question."

"What question?"

"What's keeping you here?"

Celia picked up the bottle of repellent and began applying it to her bare legs, noticing, as she did so, that she had already been bitten a couple of times. José got up and walked to the edge of the pool, then turned around, she supposed, to watch her. He had always admired her legs. His gaze said he still found them attractive. She recapped the bottle and looked up at him. "Sit down, José."

He sat.

"I want to see Cuba become a better place, a happier place, than it is now. I know what I am doing can make a difference."

He shrugged. "That's noble, Celia. But why you?"

"Because my parents and Camilio and Che and Celia Sánchez—they're all dead!" she cried. "Don't you see? It is up to our generation, ours and Liliana's, to carry on!"

"Why?" No sarcasm now, just the one uncomprehending word.

"Because if we don't, *who will?*"

José cocked his head in mock thoughtfulness, "Duh? Luis?"

She shook her head. "Luis is a good man. Dedicated and intelligent. But he only cares about keeping things the way they are, not the way they could be."

Celia immediately regretted her disloyal words, a betrayal of good boy Abel to his malicious brother Cain. However, José's next remark told her he had deduced something altogether different from them.

"You're not in love with Luis," he pronounced in a cocksure way.

"So what?" she shouted. Then, lowering her voice, hissed, "That does not mean I am ready to pick up and go to Miami with *you*."

To Celia's surprise, José suddenly pulled back, emotionally and physically.

Shoving his chair away from the table, he stood up, stretched, and said, "Okay. How about we just pick up and go to dinner?"

It took Celia a moment to drop the defensive posture he had manoeuvred her into and to gather her wits. "What about a pizza and we eat out here?"

"So you can keep an eye on the cabin in case Liliana comes out?"

Celia glanced toward the cabin, which showed no sign of life. "Do you mind?" she asked, her earlier anxiety returning in a rush.

"No. But you tell her, in the morning she gets her little butt into those thermal baths or I'm going to drag her out and dunk her myself."

Celia laughed. "I will tell her that. I will even help you."

José walked past her, close enough that the black hairs of his thighs brushed her arm. One hand passed over her hair, casually, oh so casually. He headed for the restaurant to order the pizza. Wearing only swim trunks, his skin copper in the late afternoon sun, he had the confident bearing of a man conscious of the attractiveness of his own body.

Watching him stride across the lawn in that fluid, muscular way, all predator and prowl even when there was no prey in sight, caused Celia to remember something and smile. It was Franci, who had gone out with José only one time, back in high school, who said, "That José Lago is compliant as a cat. He doesn't ask a thing of you as long as you let him lie in your lap and knead you with his paws."

Celia's gaze turned inward, trying to see herself in his world. How bad would it be, she wondered, to wake up in a Miami apartment with José Lago rubbing his ever-ready penis against her? And after that? What would fill her days? She could not imagine.

Then she thought of Liliana. Liliana and José had driven to Pinar and back, had been together the whole of that night and half of the next day. Liliana had told him things she had never told Celia. What if he was right? What if a schoolgirl fantasy of taking a boat ride had been transformed, first by José's return and then by the psychic wounds she had sustained, into a desire to leave Cuba? What if nothing else would revive her spirits?

The late afternoon sun was hot but Celia's arms prickled with chill. It was a price she might be willing to pay. But could she?

SIXTY-FIVE

CELIA and José did have to drag Liliana from bed next morning, but in the end she soaked in the thermal baths—all of them did—for as long as the therapist deemed healthful. It might or might not have done Liliana good, but Celia felt better afterwards. She had not slept well; had awakened exhausted from what seemed to have been a night of running from an indefinable terror, or hiding and waiting for it to spring upon her. They had a late breakfast in an open-air restaurant and started back.

José drove north, through La Palma, rather than the shorter route via Pinar del Río. Celia did not ask why, assuming that he either did not want to be reminded of the night he had taken Liliana there or was in no hurry to get back to Habana.

They had been driving about an hour when she asked, for reasons of her own, "Would you mind if we stopped at the Cueva de los Portales? Just for a few minutes?"

She wanted to visit the cave, another of those historic spots where groups of schoolchildren were often taken on field trips, because it had figured in her dream. When she woke she could not remember the details; only that the dream had taken place there.

"Good idea," he said with an alacrity that confirmed her suspicion that he was not anxious to return to the city.

"Did you go home Friday?" she asked. "Do Alma and Luis know you are here?"

José chuckled. "And leave the very next morning to take Luis's ex-girlfriend off for what he'd be dead certain was a weekend of sex, drugs, and rock 'n' roll? Now, what do you think?"

From the back seat, Liliana snickered. It was the first sign they had had from her since leaving that she was not asleep. Celia turned in her seat and spoke to the girl. "You can be my witness, Liliana, if your sneaky tío gets caught. There was none of that."

"I was sleeping," Liliana murmured, her eyes squinched shut. "How do I know what you two did?"

"A fine chaperone you are," Celia teased, her heart soaring at this tiny indication that Liliana's sauciness was returning. "Sit up and enjoy the scenery, mi corazón. It is very wild."

Liliana sat up. "Where are we going?"

"Cueva de los Portales," José replied. "Have you been there?"

"No," Liliana replied shortly. "I don't like caves."

When did this come about? Celia wondered uneasily, recalling José's remark about wanting to leave Cuba so badly that he had developed claustrophobia—and not recalling that Liliana had ever expressed a dislike of caves or other closed-in spaces.

"It is not much of a cave," she assured the girl. "Small, with a river flowing through. Che made it the headquarters of the Western Army during the October Crisis."

Liliana frowned. "Did we really think the United States was going to nuke us?"

"Well, I think so," Celia began tentatively. "All of Habana was evacuated."

"Damned right," José cast a glance over his shoulder. "We weren't born yet but our parents evacuated Habana along with everyone else in the city; it was that close."

"José! Watch out!" Celia cried as they hit a pothole. The fifteen-kilometre road through Parque La Güira was paved, but there were small washouts at the bottom of some of the gullies that caused them to bounce in their seats. As they soared up short steep hills and plunged down the other side, the ride took on the quality of a roller coaster—or so Celia imagined, although she had never ridden one, only seen them on television. Liliana shrieked, showing enjoyment for the first time on the trip.

They parked in front of a campismo consisting of unimaginative cement block huts. José paid the attendant a small fee and told him, "We don't need a guide; we've been here before. We know the way and all the stories."

Liliana hung back, whining excuses for why she should be allowed to remain in the car. But José cajoled her and then walked with her along the path leading to the cave, telling her stories he had heard as a boy of what it was like when Cuba was on alert, everyone in Habana believing that it might be America's next Hiroshima.

He led Liliana up a ladder toward one entrance of the cave. Celia took another route, following the river that flowed into the cave and through the cavern's largest room. The room, which had been used for planning, was empty except for a long rough table.

Opening off that room was a tiny stonewalled cell where Che had slept. She entered and stood next to the narrow cot, listening . . .

Out in the main room, Che was insisting, Take my room. Just for tonight. Go on, you haven't seen her for weeks. Fidel arguing that he is the commander-in-chief and does not take orders from Che. At last—would it be the last?—laughter.

Then Fidel was there, holding a blanket, holding her, through the longest night of their lives, the longest night ever in the history of the world. He spoke of strategy, how they would organize themselves after the attack, how they would survive. She thought, during all his can-do, must-do, will-do talk, that he had somehow overlooked the fact that if Cuba were hit with nuclear bombs it would be a thousand times worse than Hiroshima because the bombs were no longer atomic but hydrogen; that there would be no survivors. But of course he knew and later they spoke of that too. If I don't die, she whispered, don't let me live. Promise you will not let me live sickened by radiation, dying day by day in that awful way. I do not want to be weak. He shook his head. What you are asking would take more courage than I have. Only you can promise yourself that. Then I will, she said, and held him closer than breath. The night went on and on and on, and they make love worthy of the night that might have been the last night of their world. Then dawn came and no bombs fell. We are alive, she breathed. Our children are alive. Cuba lives.

Celia touched the metal frame of the cot lightly and walked to the door. For an instant she wondered why the war room was not swarming with soldiers. Then she saw Liliana's pretty sandalled feet on the ladder leading down into the cave and remembered.

"It's not too scary," Liliana said. At Celia's bewildered look, she added, "This cave, I mean. Like you said, there's not much to it. And the river running through, that's nice. I wonder if bats live in here."

"Yes," Celia said. "There are bats."

She did not add, And ghosts.

SIXTY-SIX

CELIA had hoped the weekend excursion would be a turning point, but when she begged Liliana to go to school the following week, she flatly refused.

"At least have breakfast and go sit on the balcony," Celia urged. But Liliana remained in bed, staring moodily at the ceiling of her room.

Celia worked at the computer until noon, distractedly, then dressed for work and tried again to engage Liliana. She sat down on the edge of the bed and looked into the girl's expressionless face. "What are you thinking about?"

"Prison."

"What prison?"

"Any prison. What're they like?"

"You must have read in school some of the things Fidel wrote about when he and his compañeros were locked up at the Presidio for their attack on the Moncada Barracks. Most of the time he was in solitary—"

"That was fifty years ago. I mean now."

"I have no idea. Look, mi corazón, you really should get up."

"Why?"

"Because the longer you stay in here the worse you are going to feel."

"How do you know how I feel?"

"All right," Celia sighed. "The longer you stay in here the worse *I* feel."

"*I* feel like I'm in prison," Liliana muttered.

"Why? Who or what do you feel is keeping you there?"

Liliana got up and shuffled into the bathroom. As she closed the door, Celia heard her say, "Everybody. Everything."

Celia was blessedly busy at the hospital, although less with patients than with paperwork. Besides normal managerial responsibilities, it seemed that all of her doctors required consultation on something. There was a note on her desk that Dr. Leyva wanted to see her. Celia had not seen Dr. Leyva since he assigned the task of writing protocols and her team had voted on the ones it would pursue. He probably wanted a status report.

When she entered his office he was at the window, gazing into the distance. "You wanted to see me?" she asked.

He turned. "Yes. How is your niece?"

"Physically, she is virtually healed. Emotionally she is—" Celia hesitated, not knowing quite how to characterize Liliana's strange behaviour. At last she said, "Not very accessible."

"What does that mean?" he asked with a puzzled frown.

"Liliana was always very open with her feelings. Joy, anger, rebellion, insecurity, a desire to please—whatever it was, she radiated it. Now whatever is going on inside her seems bottled up. Whether by choice or something beyond her control, I do not know."

"Do you think she needs psychiatric help?"

"I do. But she has refused."

"And you allow her to make that decision?" His steady grey eyes held hers.

Celia did not look away, although she wanted to. "Yes. I let her decide."

"That may be a mistake."

"I know."

Leyva sat down but did not ask her to sit, so she remained standing. She sensed that he wanted to say more, though, and so did she. Whatever he had intended to discuss with her, apparently he had decided against it. There was dismissal in his eyes when he looked up, until he saw the uncertainty in hers. "You had a question?"

"I—yes. But it may not be answerable."

He arched his finely shaped eyebrows, which, like his hair, had changed in the years she had worked under him, from bushy black to bushy white. "Well?"

"Why would a girl who has everything—friends, family, freedom—feel trapped?"

"Your niece? That's what she says?"

"Yes." It was a question Celia felt compelled to ask Leyva because she knew it was one he must have asked himself a thousand times after his own daughter took to the sea on a homemade raft. Perhaps he had found an answer.

He swivelled his worn desk chair around to look out the window. His view was of the hospital parking lot, the Vía Monumental, the apartment complex where Celia lived, and beyond it, the ocean where his child had perished. With his back to her, he said, "It probably has something to do with types."

"Types?"

He turned back to face her. "Let's say you have two adolescents, both bright and full of energy. One has a focus—a career she's looking forward to, a hobby, even a boy she wants to marry. She puts her energy and imagination into that. The other one has the same amount of energy and imagination but no focus. She bounces from one enthusiasm to another. Such a young person, the one who wants to go, see, do it all, feels restrained."

"Our children are not restrained!" Celia cried. "They have opportunities to travel around the island, can participate in sports, spend weekends at the beach. Associate with others of any race, play their music as loud as they like, choose a career—"

Leyva cut in on her defensive response. "It's not parental; it's geographical. Cuba is an island, not a continent. Possibilities are limited. For some, what we have to offer is enough. For others, apparently not."

The chair went round again, putting his back to her. Celia felt that the decent thing to do would be to steal from the room and leave him alone with the despair that she, in attempting to deal with her own, had revived in him. But one does not disappear from where one has been summoned by one's superior.

"Was there anything else?" she asked tentatively.

The rickety swivel chair came back to face the desk. Leyva picked up a notice and gave it to her. "A conference at Children's Hospital in Manzanillo. Can you get away?"

She was surprised. "They have invited me to make a presentation?"

He grinned wryly. "They haven't invited you at all—merely asked that I send 'an appropriate delegate.' Since one of the unlisted activities will surely be refuting your Santiago presentation, I thought you might want to be there to defend yourself."

"Not really," Celia protested. "And Liliana is not—"

"I understand that," he interrupted. "But give it some thought."

SIXTY-SEVEN

LUIS was about to enter Celia's apartment building when a woman carrying an armload of books approached. When Luis held open the door for her, she gave him a startled, grateful smile. Her dark intelligent eyes seemed, like his mother's, almost too big for her face. The books, clutched to her chest like a schoolgirl, pushed her breasts upward. They were fuller than one would have expected on a woman so slender.

"Thank you!" she exclaimed, as if he had performed an exceptional service.

"Let me help you carry those." He reached for the books.

"Oh, but I'm going all the way up to the fourth floor," she protested.

"So am I." He scooped the books out of her arms and saw as he did so that they were pre-college textbooks. "Are these by any chance for Liliana?"

"Why, yes. How did you know?"

"I am a friend of the family. Luis Lago." He cradled the books in one arm and held out his hand. She shook it warmly.

"Compañero Lago! We spoke on the telephone when Liliana went missing. I am Emily Solana, the secretary at her school."

"Of course, Compañera Solana. At your service."

"You are." The woman gave a tiny laugh, indicating the books he had taken from her. "Are you here to visit Liliana too?"

"Just checking on her. In case Celia is at work and there is something she needs."

"How thoughtful!" Emily paused on the next landing and waited for him to step up beside her. "It must have been such an ordeal for poor Liliana," she said in a low, breathless voice. "What a shame they didn't catch the brute who abducted her."

This clued Luis in to the fact that Captain Quevedo had telephoned the school, as he had requested. He knew that a call from a MININT official would be taken more seriously than a call from Celia or himself. Once Quevedo explained what happened, whether he provided many details or none, no questions would be asked regarding Liliana's past or future absences.

"Young people recover quickly. I expect Liliana will be back in school soon."

"I don't know." Emily sounded doubtful. "When Dr. Cantú called this morning she said Liliana was likely to be out the rest of this week."

Emily turned and headed up the next flight of stairs. He thought her legs, bare and pale, were pretty. Not as muscular as Celia's, but then, he didn't often see Celia's legs, since she generally wore slacks.

"You aren't working today?" he asked.

"Oh, I am. I was sent into the city to run some school-related errands." They had reached the fourth floor. Emily went ahead of him down the hall and knocked. There was no answer.

"She has been sleeping a lot," Luis said and reached around her to try the door. It was not locked so he pushed it open and called, "Liliana?"

274

There was no reply, but he glimpsed a movement on the balcony. Liliana entered the living room hesitantly, carrying a partially eaten plate of food. She wore a shapeless white T-shirt spattered with old and recent food stains.

"Oh, hi, Compañera Emily." She seemed genuinely glad to see the secretary. She cast a nervous glance at Luis and said, "Tía Celia is at work."

"She was not there this morning," Luis remarked, hoping to get some feedback as to what Celia's new schedule was.

"I guess she slept in," Liliana said nonchalantly. But Luis caught the malicious glint in her eye and a telltale glance at the computer.

"Or working at home," he said. He put the stack of books down next to the computer and flicked off the monitor that Celia had inadvertently left on.

Emily touched the geometry book on the top of the pile and said, "Your aunt asked me to bring these over. Each one has a note in it from the teacher, to let you know what was covered during your absence and what each class is working on this week."

"Thanks," Liliana mumbled.

"Oh, Liliana!" The words rushed out of the woman, charged with emotion. "We all miss you. Do come back as soon as you can!"

"Okay." Liliana looked dully at the floor and offered no excuse for why she was well enough to sunbathe on the balcony, well enough to eat, well enough to stand here and talk to them, but not well enough to go to school.

"I wanted to visit awhile," Emily said earnestly. "But there is only the one bus this afternoon, and if I miss it—" She gave a tiny wave and backed toward the door.

"I'll be going too," Luis said and felt a flash of resentment at the relief in Liliana's face. At the door he said to Emily, who was already out in the hallway, "Don't worry about the bus. I'll drive you back." Then, without premeditation, he said in a voice meant to carry back into the apartment, "Maybe you'd like to join me for lunch first?"

He would have given a lot to see Liliana's face but did not look back. He was amazed at his own audacity. It was what his brother might have done in a situation where a woman was jerking him around, but for him it was completely out of character. Just imagining Celia's feelings when Liliana told her gave him satisfaction. He closed the door behind him before Emily responded, in case her answer should be a rejection.

Emily turned around to look at him. "Compañero Lago! How kind of you!"

He chose Las Terrazas because it was in Cojímar, just three kilometres up the coast. Foreigners who dined in what had been a favourite Hemingway haunt paid in dollars, but there was a peso menu for Cubans. "Would you like a drink?" Luis asked as he held open the door leading into the cool dark interior of the street-level bar.

"Heavens no!" Emily laughed in her high-pitched yet melodious way. "If I went back to the office with alcohol on my breath that would be the end of me!"

He caught Emily's small-boned elbow and steered her upstairs to the dining room. A group of tourists was just departing, leaving the place in something of a mess but pleasantly empty. Luis picked a table near the window overlooking the bay.

Emily gazed around, eyes luminous. "I've never been here. What an adventure!"

How many times had he brought Celia here, and how many times had she thanked him with unfailing courtesy? Yet never had she indicated that it mattered, that she wouldn't have been just as satisfied to pick up a pizza on the street or, for that matter, to eat alone at home. Luis felt Emily's gratitude as a man in a parched desert might feel the miracle of rain: something to be absorbed through the very pores of his skin.

"Are you a Hemingway aficionada?" he asked.

"Well . . ." Emily looked out across the Bahía de Cojímar, ruffled with small whitecaps by the afternoon breeze. "I do like *The Old Man and the Sea*, it seems so true to life as it was for the poor before the Revolution. It really deserves to be the classic it is. But in general, no. Furthermore," she added with sudden passion, "I don't see why we make so much of him! Many Cuban writers are as good or better. And scores of first-rate Latin American writers have lived and worked in Cuba."

"It is done for economic reasons," Luis explained.

"Economic reasons?" She leaned toward him, lips slightly parted.

"Few foreigners have heard of our writers, but most have heard of Hemingway. There are these 'literary groupies'—tourists who want to visit Sartre's grave, or take a boat down the river Mark Twain wrote about, or sit at the bar where Hemingway sat."

Emily's eyes sparkled with humour. "Do you think our elbows are on a table where Hemingway put his? Should that be inspirational in some way?"

"I will let you know," he said. "After I have finished writing my next dry-as-a-bone report on Cuba's energy options."

As they studied the menu, Luis revelled in his own wit, which he had never thought of as quick. Emily brought it out in him, he decided. He could not remember ever feeling so easy with a woman he had just met. Emily ordered little, with an eye to prices. She cleaned her plate thoroughly, letting nothing go to waste, which he also liked.

After lunch he drove her back to the school. The trip would have taken two hours by bus but by car took barely thirty minutes. When they arrived he did something he had not done for a woman in years. He walked around the car and opened the door for her.

Emily exited gracefully. "It was a wonderful afternoon, Compañero Lago," she said, her eyes still sparkling with the unexpectedness of it all. "I am so glad we met."

"So am I," Luis said and knew, in the few seconds he held her fine-boned hand in his, that if they had had the privacy of darkness she would have accepted a kiss as well as, or in preference to, a handshake.

Driving back to the city, it occurred to Luis for the first time that he might be more in love with his dream of loving Celia than with the woman herself. She was no more attractive or intelligent than a lot of other women he knew. Not all of them were available to him, but some would certainly appreciate the attentions of a man who held so high a position in the government. Who was to say that some weren't better company than Celia Cantú? Why was he so addicted to her? What did she offer that he couldn't find in other women? He could easily have a woman like Emily Solana, younger than Celia by five years or more, who would be thrilled with him—and maybe, under the right circumstances, thrilling.

But old habits die hard. As the hospital where Celia worked appeared off to his left, the Fiat, as if of its own volition, exited the Vía Monumental, rounded the traffic circle, and steered itself to a spot in the hospital parking lot that would allow Luis to see Celia when she exited the building.

SIXTY-EIGHT

CELIA was removing her bike from the rack when she saw Luis walking toward her. He was too close to pretend she had not seen him. She forced a smile. "Hello, Luis."

"Hello, my—Celia." he answered, cutting short the endearment. "I tried to reach you on the weekend, to ask how Liliana is doing. I guess you weren't around."

"The bruises still show, but I think the soreness has gone out of them. The cut over her eye hasn't healed and the knee is weak but she is not limping as badly." Celia pushed her bike along the sidewalk avoiding his eyes. "How are things with you?"

"Not bad. José is back. Of course you knew that, since he came for the car."

"Yes."

As they reached a spot of shade cast by a jacaranda tree, Luis caught hold of the bike handlebar, forcing her to stop. Celia stiffened. She did not want to discuss their relationship, which she was sure was what he had come for. Quickly, by way of distraction, she threw out a question. "Luis, have you ever visited a prison?"

He gave her a baffled look. "Several. Last week, in fact. I was with a team evaluating three for possible installation of solar panels. Why do you ask?"

"Liliana was asking what conditions were like. I had no idea what to tell her."

Luis sighed. Celia supposed he understood that the question was tangentially related to his threat of sending the girl to a re-education camp. "The ones I saw in Camagüay Province were basic, as you would expect. Forty or fifty men in dorm-type barracks. Line-ups for the bathroom. The food is your standard rice and beans, with meat not more than once a week. After all, that's how we lived during military basic. In fact, that's how our medical school students are housed right now, including the foreign ones here on scholarship. It would hardly be acceptable for convicted criminals to live better."

"Do they work?"

"Of course. Each prison grows its own food, so there is agriculture, a garage for equipment maintenance, and so on. They also have exercise and education programs. As I said, incarceration is not all that different from what José and I had to put up with when we did our compulsory military service."

"You never saw anything that suggested . . . abuse?"

Luis shrugged irritably. "Of course not!"

"Well, you know there was—"

"Twenty-five years ago! There were those run by compañeros who distinguished themselves during the war but being illiterate could not be brought into the government. It was obviously one of the mistakes of the Revolution that they were put in charge of prisons. Their attitudes toward homosexuals, and some of the religious groups—well, what could you expect? As soon as the abuse was brought to the attention of responsible people in Habana, it was corrected," he huffed. "I hope José isn't bringing Liliana Miami newspapers. Which as you well know, are crammed with lies about Cuba."

"He did not leave any reading materials," Celia said coolly. "Or anything else."

"Celia, Celia!" Luis dropped his head and said in an almost-broken way. "Please! I know it was my fault. But it's over. Liliana is back where she belongs. Can't things go back to where they were?"

"No. We are not—I am not who I was."

"I am! I have made mistakes, I know! But I am the same person! Why do you treat me like a stranger? Worse than a stranger! Like an enemy!"

Celia stared at his hand, squeezing the handlebar of her bike so tightly that the big knuckles were white. She felt as if the hand was latched on to her own flesh. "I'm sorry, Luis. I do not want you to feel badly. But it is over between us. Finito."

"Oh, I know that!" He laughed bitterly. "I knew that the minute José showed up."

Before Celia could react—and she was not sure how she would have reacted, not sure how much José's return had to do with anything—Luis turned on her a gaze so pleading that it almost broke her will. "I know I have lost my fiancée, Celia. Have I also lost the nearest thing I ever had to a sister?"

She could not bear to look into his eyes, to see all that pain reflected just inches from her face, and not want to do something, however inappropriate, to alleviate it. She looked away. "We are family, Luis. We always have been. I simply need some distance."

"Why, Celia? What are you afraid of?"

Myself, she wanted to say. I am afraid of my own inability to say no. Instead, she struggled to articulate another version of the truth. "You want something. If it is not to renew our relationship, then I do not know what it is."

His answer was pathetic, but there was no doubt in Celia's mind that it was sincere. "What I have always wanted. To understand you."

She sighed and shook her head. "We haven't got time for a seminar in *that*."

The response angered him, which had not been her intention. "Not for *me*!" he shouted. "But José got a seminar, didn't he? *He* understands you."

Celia's resentment at being pushed to explain herself flared just as swiftly. "As a matter of fact, he did not," she snapped, snatching the bike out of his grasp. "Like you, he just makes a lot of pigheaded assumptions!"

She swung onto the bike and pedalled off, anger fuelling her exit from a situation that, had she had the courage to be honest at the outset, would never have happened.

SIXTY-NINE

CELIA woke up tangled in bedclothes. It had been a nightmare of running, hiding from torturers, searching for compañeros who had disappeared but whom she was sure were not dead. She lay there for a moment, considering the difference between the nightmares, of which she had had several lately, and the daytime hallucinations where she imagined herself to be Celia Sánchez. In the "Sánchez moments" she was often in danger but coolly coping; mind and body working in unison so that what she hallucinated doing was either the right thing or all that was possible, with nothing more to be done. Celia Sánchez was not afraid of dying.

By contrast, she was herself in the nightmares, although often in Sánchez's world, with bombs falling, armies clashing, torturers trying to lay hands on her. The dreams were terrifying because in them she did not know if she was making the right choice or about to open a door into some ultimate terror leading to a long unquiet death.

She got out of bed. It was a bright moonlit night so she did not turn on a lamp. She tiptoed into the kitchen to make a hot drink in hopes of calming her nerves. She opened the refrigerator and saw a cup of cocoa made for Liliana at bedtime that the girl had not drunk. Leaving the refrigerator door ajar for light, she poured the brown liquid into a saucepan, heated it, and poured it back into the cup. Then she quietly closed the fridge door and moved back into the living room.

Three doors stood wide open—the one to her bedroom, the one to Liliana's room, and the one to the bathroom. From the time they had moved into this apartment, those doors were left open at night, as it made the small apartment seem more spacious. Celia tiptoed toward Liliana's doorway and looked in to see if she was asleep, or if she was awake, to ask if she would like to share a wee-hours cup of cocoa.

Moonlight spilled through the jalousied window, casting silver bands of light across the sheets. What the moonlight revealed caused Celia to gasp. Liliana was not there! She was not in the bed, not in the open closet, not in the room. Celia spun around, eyes searching the living room through which she had walked. Rocking chairs, sofa, chairs at the dining table, the floor itself—empty. She could see into the bathroom as well: the white gleam of sink and toilet, beyond them the shower stall. Empty.

The door leading out into the hallway was closed. Could Liliana have opened it, walked out, and shut it behind her without Celia hearing?

A cool breeze brushed her cheek. Celia turned. The balcony door, which she normally closed at night in case the wind should rise, was open. And there was Liliana. Her dark curls merged with the darkness around her but the white night-gown was clearly delineated against the black sky. She was not in a chair or standing by the railing. She sat *on* the railing, facing outward, feet dangling four storeys above hard ground.

Celia was not aware of setting down the cup of cocoa but she must have because when she reached the balcony door her hands were empty.

Liliana, holding to the railing on each side of her body, let go with one hand. For a breath the hand hung in the air, pale as a moth. Then Celia's fingers closed around her wrist with a steel grip. She braced herself for a jerk, the sudden drop of weight that could have dragged her over the railing with the girl. But it did not come. Celia's other arm encircled Liliana's waist. She drew her tightly against her own body, and in a voice as smooth as silk, murmured, "Come, Liliana. I have made you some cocoa."

Liliana neither spoke nor resisted. Celia again braced herself as Liliana swung one leg and then the other back to the balcony side of the railing. Celia wrapped arms around her and they walked, staggered, really, into the living room. Celia let go with one hand and reached behind herself to flip the lock on the balcony door that she had never locked before.

Celia sat Liliana on the sofa and retrieved the cocoa. She handed Liliana the cup and knelt in front of her. Liliana's expression was trancelike, eyes dark and unfocused. She remained so for perhaps two minutes. Then she began to sip, holding the cup in both hands like a toddler.

"Were you thinking of jumping?" Celia asked softly, not sure Liliana was even aware of what had transpired.

There was a long silence. Then Liliana replied in a distant voice, "I was thinking of flying. It seemed like if I could just lift my arms, I'd be able to fly. But I couldn't let go." Tears slid silently down her cheeks. "I was afraid."

When the cocoa had been drunk, Liliana went to bed. She did not protest when Celia got in beside her. They slept spoon-fashion as they had when she was a little girl, in the first years after Carolina's death.

When the bedside clock showed 6:00 AM. Celia got up. She went into the living room and dialed Franci's number.

"Franci," she said quietly, "We need help."

SEVENTY

JOE and Luis both looked up when the phone rang, but as usual, waited for Alma to answer it. As soon as she heard the voice on the other end of the line, her face brightened. "Oh, Celia, I'm so happy you called!"

Joe had been recording notes for meetings with potential joint-venture partners in his daytimer. He began doodling in the margin so as to follow the conversation without appearing to do so.

"Aye María, Madre de Dios!" Alma gasped. Blood drained from her face as Celia, on the other end of the line, did all the talking.

"What's up?" Joe demanded.

"Que pasa?" Luis echoed.

Alma dropped the receiver back in its cradle, dark eyes like saucers in her stricken face. "Liliana tried to commit suicide last night. Although maybe she was sleepwalking. Celia is not sure. She caught her on the balcony railing just as she was about to jump."

There was a stunned silence. Then Luis flew into a rage. "Nobody can raise a child alone! Celia's going about it all the wrong way, refusing help—"

Alma held up a hand. "Silencio, hijo. She *is* getting help. She is taking Liliana to Santiago. To see Franci."

"Franci?" Joe was momentarily confused. "Why Franci?"

"She is a psychiatrist," Alma explained.

"Franci, a shrink?" Joe was surprised, then remembered. "I guess that always was her thing, wasn't it? Trying to figure out people's motives."

"As if we don't have hundreds of psychiatrists right here in Habana!" Luis ranted. "Right in her own hospital, for that matter. Doctors who could see Liliana regularly, over a period of time, which is obviously what she needs." He paced the length of the narrow room, unable to contain his agitation. "I will go see if I can talk some sense into her."

Alma picked up her rosary and began drawing beads through her fingers in a distracted rather than a prayerful way. "Celia said she would rather we didn't come over right away. She said wait till they get back from Santiago."

"Why?" Luis demanded.

"She wants a professional opinion as to the best way to handle it. Otherwise she's afraid talking about it might do more harm than good."

"Makes sense," Joe said. By way of dropping an oblique reminder to his brother of his less-than-cordial relationship with both Liliana and Celia, he added, "At least Liliana won't have a reason to rebel against Franci's advice."

Joe saw Luis deflate and knew the point had been taken. He picked up his daytimer, sighed in a way meant to suggest that he didn't know what *he* could do about it, and said, "Well, you two sort it out. I've got back-to-back meetings all day."

Ignoring Alma's bead-fingering, which now seemed to signal serious prayers, he kissed the top of her head. "See you at suppertime, Mamá. Try not to worry too much."

As he went out, Joe heard Luis ask, "Did Celia say when they plan to leave?" Joe paused in the hallway long enough to hear Alma's reply.

"She said she had to tie up a few loose ends at the hospital but planned to take the afternoon train."

Joe had two meetings scheduled that day, one before lunch, one after. He stopped at Hotel Habana Libre and phoned to reschedule both of them. Then he called Celia.

He spoke firmly, without preliminaries. "Mother said you needed to tie up some loose ends at the hospital before leaving for Santiago. I know you won't want to leave Liliana alone. I'll come over and stay with her till you get back."

"José!" Celia's voice was shrill with stress. "I specifically told Alma—"

"That you'd handle it. Sure you can. But here's one thing you might want to consider." He paused until he heard a ragged intake of breath on the other end of the line.

"What?"

"Liliana took me into her confidence that night we were in Pinar. Things I don't think she has told anyone else. If I had an hour or two alone with her, she might—look, Celia. I won't keep anything from you. We all want to see the kid get back on track."

Joe looked through the phone booth glass at hotel guests passing in the hallway, waiting for her answer and already knowing what it would be. After a long silence Celia's voice came over the line, small and uncertain. "How soon can you get here?"

"Right away. I'm at the Habana Libre. I'm going to pop into the boutique and pick up a CD for her. Or a cassette. Which?"

"She has a portable CD player," Celia said tiredly. "A friend gave it to her."

Yeah, right, Joe thought. A "friend" she met in Varadero who thought he could buy sex with a Cuban teenybopper for the price of a cheap CD player.

"I'll be there in thirty minutes and stay till you get back. And, Celia, don't worry. I won't push her to talk about what happened last night. Just, you know, peripheral stuff that you might want to know or pass on to Franci."

"Thank you, José. That is very . . . sensitive of you."

Joe stepped out of the phone booth smiling. Celia had sounded relieved, and if he wasn't mistaken, a little surprised at his "sensitivity." He was definitely making headway.

He knocked and at Celia's "Pase" walked in. Celia was at the computer, Liliana on the couch. Both had dark circles under their eyes and looked emotionally drained. Celia promptly shut down the computer and stood up. "Hello, José. I'm due at the hospital ten minutes ago. Liliana can entertain you. If you want lunch, I expect you can find something in the kitchen."

"Wanna go out to lunch?" Joe asked Liliana.

"No," she said, not even glancing his way.

"Then I'll raid the fridge," Joe said cheerfully. He puttered noisily in the kitchen before settling for a reheated cup of coffee and a piece of stale white bread. He still hadn't readjusted to the paltry selection of edibles in the average Cuban kitchen, or at least in his mother's and Celia's kitchens, which he took to be average.

"Chau," Celia called, and was gone.

He meandered back into the living room and sat down in a rocker across from the couch. "Want a bite of bread?" he asked, thrusting the white roll toward Liliana.

She made a face and turned her head the way Amy, the pickiest eater of his two daughters, had done when she was a toddler.

He laid the roll down on the coffee table and reached into his jacket pocket. "Want to see the CD I brought you?"

"What's the point?"

He dropped the CD back in his pocket and munched on the roll, more to show disinterest than because he wanted it, which he didn't. Bread from Cuba's government-run bakeries made America's white bread seem downright tasty. He looked Liliana over. What he saw, from unbrushed hair to bits of pink polish clinging to dirty toenails, was not attractive. "How's the knee?" he asked.

"Who cares?"

"Looks like you're going to have a scar over your eye."

"Who cares?"

"Probably nobody, if you kill yourself."

She flashed him a quick look, her expression guarded.

"Isn't that what you tried to do last night?" he asked, stuffing the last of the bread into his mouth, as if it didn't matter to him one way or another.

"What if I did?" She began gnawing at her fingernails, nails that he had noticed on the weekend were ragged but not bitten down to the quick as they now were. "I might as well be dead if I can't get what I want."

He took a sip of coffee and held out the cup to her. She made a face, so he sipped it himself. "What *do* you want?"

The passivity suddenly gave way to agitation. "Come on, Joe! You know what it's like!" She glowered accusingly. "You just don't give a damn. None of them do."

Joe sat there rocking in a way that might have seemed relaxed, but a lot of things were running through his mind while way too many other things churned around in his gut. He knew now, as he had not known when he left Cuba at age twenty-four, that one reason for his obsession to get off the island had been the sense that his life was going nowhere; at least, nowhere fast enough to hold his interest. His peers were getting on their career horses and galloping off in all directions—Carolina into the military, Celia and Franci into medicine, Luis into the bureaucracy, Joaquín to international-level sports. He was as smart as they were and had a good deal more on the ball than his brother, but there was not one thing on the Cuban horizon that excited him. Except maybe owning a car like the one he had recently purchased. His lips twitched at the thought that had somebody offered him a car or the means of earning the money to buy one he might never have left. The same could probably be said for thousands of other Cubans.

On the other hand, there were several million, including just about all the kids he grew up with, who tolerated the lack of luxury—if *luxury* was the right word for an ordinary car. To him, luxury was the BMW parked in the secure underground garage of his super-secure Miami apartment building. But that was now. In those hard times after the USSR pulled the plug on foreign aid, he would have considered a bicycle a luxury. But not even Cuban kids thought that way now. Television, tourism, and Miami relatives had given them a mental catalogue filled with all kinds of goodies.

To escape Liliana's glower and to give himself time to run down other threads he was trying to prevent getting tangled up in his head, he went to the bathroom for a piss, then back into the kitchen for a second cup of coffee.

Convincing Celia to let Liliana go to Miami was clearly the key to getting Celia there. Once there, he would persuade her to let Liliana attend a South Florida boarding school, or better yet, one out of state. Expensive, but at least they wouldn't have the little sulker underfoot seven days a week. However, it was a given that Liliana's appetite for "neat stuff" would be, like that of all US-born and immigrant kids, insatiable.

The smart thing would be to take the advice he had given his brother: just forget about Celia until Liliana was off to college. Then he could coax her to Miami without the baggage of a moody adolescent. The only problem with that approach was that Joe Lago was not the kind of guy who waited around—for anything.

He set the second cup of coffee down with a thump that made Liliana jump. "Okay, kid. What if I get you to Miami? What then?"

Liliana gazed at him, a little wearily, he thought, then dropped her eyes. "You know how far I was willing to go in Pinar. If that's not what you want, just tell me. I'll do whatever. Go to school, scrub toilets, work three jobs—same as you did."

Joe was about to make a sarcastic rejoinder to the effect that Cuban kids lived such easy lives, never expected to do a damn thing except go to school and hang out at the beach or play sports and she didn't have a fucking clue what it was like out in the real world of south Florida sweatshops and stoop labour where no small number of immigrant teenagers were employed right now. But Liliana spoke first.

"If I have to kill myself to get off this island, then I'll kill myself."

Joe stared at his coffee, growing cold. I don't need this, he thought. I should have left fucking well enough alone.

Minutes passed. At last he took a deep breath and said, "I'll talk to Celia."

"What's the point?"

"The point is, I'm willing to help you. But not behind her back."

Liliana said nothing. He walked into her bedroom, where he found the portable CD player on the night stand. He wound the head set cords around it, carried it back into the living room, and dropped it on her flat little belly. From his pocket he took the CD and tossed it onto the coffee table. She reached for it. Her lips parted with pleasure as she recognized Los Van Van, a band popular on both sides of the Straits. "Gracias, Tío."

He was surprised to see that there were tears in her eyes. They were startlingly like Carolina's eyes as he remembered them the night at Joaquín's house after they'd watched that TV program on CIA terrorism, that being a time when he still lusted after Carolina and was only toying with her less flamboyant younger sister. Liliana's eyes had that same dark intensity and naked emotionalism. They forewarned him that he would do well to paddle away from this particular female before he was in over his head.

Joe went out and sat on the balcony. He wished he had asked Celia how long she would be gone. He did not fancy eyeballing the ocean for the rest of the day.

An hour later he saw her bike turn the corner at the far end of the street. He went back into the living room where Liliana lay on the sofa, headphones in place, her expression calmer than it had been earlier. He waved a hand in front of her face. She lifted the headphones off her ears. "What?"

"Adios. I'm leaving."

"Tía Celia's not back yet."

"So?"

She gave him a little smile that was half feigned hurt, half challenge. "What if I get depressed and fling myself off the balcony?"

He leaned down so that his face was just inches from hers. "Your T-shirt will fly up and you'll land with a terrible, messy splat. People will come running from all over and everybody will get a good gander at your bloody naked ass."

She gasped, and he added as he headed for the door, "So if that's what you decide to do, better put on some bloomas."

"You're crude!" she shouted after him.

"Yep," he said cheerfully and closed the door behind him with a click.

He met Celia in the foyer. "How is Liliana?" she asked anxiously.

"Listening to music. Let's take a walk."

"I haven't got time—"

"Oh, sorry. I thought you wanted to know what's going on with her." He reached for the door to let himself out.

"Well, of course! I mean, did she talk to you?"

"Probably nothing she hasn't already told you . . . about why she did it."

He stepped outside. Celia was right behind him. "José! Wait!"

It had begun to rain, a soft drizzle. He made a dash to put up the top on the convertible. When he turned around, Celia was standing under a nearby bus shelter. He waved for her to get into the car, but she motioned for him to come there. He went.

It was early afternoon. They were alone in the shelter except for a man on the far side making a repair to a shabby bicycle. "What did she tell you?" Celia demanded.

"That she's going to leave Cuba or else."

"Or else what?" Celia asked, but before he could answer, her expression turned to horror. "Or—? No! She could not have said that!"

"I'm afraid she did."

"She does not know what she is talking about! She has never been anywhere! She would hate the States! I know she would!"

"Yeah, well, that's the problem, isn't it? Cuban kids have never been anywhere. They don't get a chance to compare island life with life anyplace else."

"Can I help that?" Celia hugged herself. She was damp from the drizzle and there were chill bumps on her bare arms. "Oh, José! What should I *do*?"

The man repairing his bike cast a discreet glance in their direction and even though it was still raining, wheeled off, probably to give them privacy.

"Let her figure out what she wants. She is at that age, you know."

"Let the person I love most disappear from my life? No!"

"It doesn't have to be forever," he tried to reassure her.

"Oh? Maybe just a decade?" she said sarcastically.

"Dammit, Celia! I wish you'd believe me when I tell you I wanted to come back. But it was all so 'us and them.' I felt like I had to choose. You *forced* me to choose, all of you!" Joe swung his arm in a wide arch, to take in everything from Cojímar to Habana.

She glared at him. "And so you did."

"Yeah," he said bitterly, looking down at the cement and grinding his heel on an already ground-out cigarette butt. "I chose. But only because it took me ten fucking years to figure out that the us-and-them thing is just a mindset. Lots of Cubans go back and forth all the time. From now on that's what I intend to do."

"You are an adult! Liliana is a child. You have money. We do not!"

"Ah, Celia." Joe softened his tone and tried a different tack. "I know you want what's best for her. Which, you're probably right, is here in Cuba." He paused to let it sink in that he was in agreement with her. Then added with deliberate harshness, intended as the verbal equivalent of slapping a hysterical woman, "But it's not going to do her any good if she kills herself."

It had the intended effect. Celia collapsed on the bus stop bench and sat shivering as if she had contracted some instant form of malaria. "Do you really think she might?"

"A kid that age *might* do anything."

"What should I do?" she asked again, this time in a smaller voice.

Joe squatted down beside her and took her cold hands in his. "Cut a deal with her. Offer her a trip to Miami if she promises to come back and finish school."

She looked into his eyes, her own all but hopeless. "How can I? Permission to travel abroad, I mean, it is possible. I do it every year. But it is complicated."

"Luis could arrange it."

"He would never do it."

Joe grinned. "Us Yanks have an expression: 'never say never.' Just give the word, Celia, and I'll talk to him. Maybe I can sell him on the idea."

She rose and walked to the edge of the shelter, seemingly unaware that she stood under the drip from the edge of the roof and was getting wetter than if she had been out in the rain. She gazed across the choppy grey water in the direction of Florida, which, Joe was sure, must seem incalculably distant to her.

He put an arm around her shoulder and drew her back under the shelter. "My place is right over there," he said, pointing across the water. "As close as Viñales."

For a moment she allowed his arm to remain, then moved away. "This is not something I can decide this minute. I have to go, now, or we will miss the train."

"Go pack," Joe said. "I'm going to make a run into Cojímar. Back in fifteen minutes. Be ready and I'll drive you to the station."

Celia smiled wanly. "I have Liliana to pack too. Give us half an hour."

"When are you coming back?" he asked when they reached the station.

"Sunday, on the overnight train. We should get in early Monday morning. I would stay longer, but that was all the time off I could get."

"Wait here," Joe instructed and went inside to get the tickets.

The three o'clock train to Santiago was gone, and tickets on the six o'clock express were sold out. He made a phone call, then went back to the car.

"No seats," he told Celia. "The best I could do were these for return on the Tren Francés." He tossed the tickets into her lap. "How about the Viazul bus?"

"The Viazul? But—"

He knew what she was going to say. Viazul buses were primarily to accommodate tourists, who couldn't be expected to ride overcrowded local buses. Naturally the Viazul fare would be in dollars, which Celia naturally did not have.

"Doesn't matter," he interrupted. "The bus to Santiago is leaving right away. Not sure we can make it, but I'll give it a try."

SEVENTY-ONE

CELIA felt that she should have protested José buying their tickets, but she did not. Maybe she was tired of protesting, or maybe she had forgotten why she should. She watched him fork over one hundred dollars for their tickets as easily as she might have paid the ten centavos for a bus into Centro Habana, and wondered what difference it made anyway.

They hurried to the bus, which was already boarding. José seemed surprised at how little luggage they had; Liliana only a book bag and Celia an oversized shoulder bag in which were two changes of underwear, one shirt, a notebook, and a few toiletries.

"Wait!" José said to Liliana as she was about to board. He ran to the car and returned with two large paper bags.

"What is that?" Celia asked, as he handed them up to Liliana.

"Road food. There's a dinner stop, but it's going to be a long night."

"This is not food," said Liliana, nosing into one of the bags.

The chofer urged them up the steps before José could reply. They found their seats and Liliana, who had taken the one nearest the window, promptly slid open the window and called to José, "A *sweatshirt*? What for?"

He came to the window. "A jinetera I met in a bar told me they keep Viazul buses air-conditioned really cold. She had just come from Santiago and said she almost froze to death." He grinned. "Of course, she wasn't wearing as much as you are."

Without looking at him, Celia could imagine the self-satisfied smirk that was making Liliana smile as the bus pulled away. Celia tried to hide her uneasiness as Liliana dug through the bags. The smaller one contained two bottles of water, four cartons of Tropicana juice, and a dozen packets of crackers and cookies. Celia imagined José striding into the little market across from Hotel Panamericano and without checking the price on anything, grabbing some of every kind of junk food within reach. Then, as was apparent from the contents of the other bag, he had gone across the street and bought two jogging suits.

"They're huge," Liliana exclaimed. "For fat people!"

"We are going to need fat people clothes if we eat all that," Celia remarked dryly, although she saw that the big sizes would be perfect for pulling on over their jeans and T-shirts if they got cold. The air conditioning was set to such a low temperature that it was already beginning to bother her.

What was really bothering her, though, was Liliana's animated response to the gifts and a feeling that they were both being "bought." It wasn't only the gifts that seemed to be co-opting her feelings. It was that they showed thoughtfulness as well as generosity. Would it be so wrong to let him look after them like that on a regular basis?

Perhaps Liliana was thinking similar thoughts because later, as they were rolling swiftly along the autopista, she asked, "Was Tío Joe always like this?"

"I suppose. Although before he went to the States he did not have the kind of money he does now. He and Luis have always been good to us," she added loyally, not wanting to leave the impression that José had ever been more generous than his brother.

Liliana was silent, sucking on a lollipop. Then asked, "What's wrong with him?"

Celia looked over at her. "What do you mean, 'What's wrong with him?'"

"Why didn't you marry him? Or why don't you now?"

"For one thing, he never asked me. Not then and not recently. I was his novia as in going steady, not as in engaged to be married. Our families just assumed marriage would follow." She did not add, And so did I.

"Oh." Liliana looked reflective—or as reflective as was possible with a lollipop sticking out of her mouth. "He's after you now, though."

"He is looking for an available woman. Not necessarily me."

"Yes, you," Liliana insisted. "He really cares about you." She cut her eyes at Celia. "He told me so. In Pinar. Only he figures he hasn't got anything you want."

Celia looked past Liliana to the cane fields swishing past. "He is probably right about that." She said "probably" because she was not altogether certain he had nothing she wanted. She wanted Liliana to be happy, happier, at any rate, than she had been in recent months. She doubted that such happiness could be found in a Celia/ José/Liliana trio, but maybe she was wrong. It certainly would not be the first time she had been wrong where Liliana was concerned—or herself, for that matter.

"So?" Liliana persisted. "What else?"

Celia stirred around in the food bag until she found a packet of bread sticks, the only non-sweet thing in the bag. "I was 'José's girl' for two years and I admit I was loca for him. It was only later that I noticed a few things about him, things that hurt me at the time but that I didn't register then as being part of a pattern."

She nibbled on the bread stick, recalling painful episodes and trying to put them into words that did not sound bitter. "Some men want one woman who is theirs alone. Some like to play the field. José wanted it both ways, all the time. There would be his Number One woman, who for a time was me, and there would be the others."

Liliana shrugged. "So? As long as you're Number One."

"Only in a situation like that you aren't," Celia tried to explain. "Because the passion, with José, anyway, would be focused on whoever he was chasing, not the one he had already caught. He has never said why his wife divorced him but I will bet you this bag of junk"—she nudged the bag of snack foods with her foot—"that he was playing around on her."

"You think that if you married him he'd play around on you?"

"Almost certainly."

"Even if you lived with him in the States, so you could be together all the time?"

"Even if."

Liliana made no further attempt at conversation, but fell into a state of apathy, sprawled in the seat much as she had sprawled on the sofa in recent weeks. The only difference was that instead of refusing to eat, which had resulted in a thinness that was almost anorexic, she was munching steadily, and apparently miserably, on junk food.

It bothered Celia that Liliana seemed not to have factored in cultural differences between Cuba and Miami. Cuban television regularly showed slum dwellers in the States, people doing drugs in public places, unemployment lines, schoolchildren being frisked for weapons, race riots, and police swinging clubs into people's heads. Those images seemed not to have registered. Nor were they the things that Miami relatives chose to talk about when they returned. Cuban Americans, as well as other sources, supplied different images.

Celia suspected that the sudden mood shift was the result of her having pulled the plug on Liliana's fantasy in which the three of them lived in a pretty house with a parklike lawn or in a high-rise condominium with an ocean view like the ones pictured in glossy magazines. That fantasy would entail beautiful young people flirting on the beach or skimming the waves in expensive boats, plus trendy clothes, elegant dining, nightlife, parties, and dancing. Perpetual fun and perpetual happiness.

As Celia fretted about the unrealistic notion of life in Miami that Liliana had pieced together from movies and magazines, she was unconscious of the attraction those same images held for her—images of a life they might live if she let José lure her to Florida. Not that such a superficial, entertainment-focused existence attracted her; in its own way it seemed as revolting as the more violent side of life portrayed in CNN news clips rebroadcast on Cuban television. For Celia, the hook was one small detail: those happy teenagers cavorting with their friends. Once she had had such a child—or imagined she had. Now what she had was this depressed lump of a girl next to her.

Hoping to jolly Liliana out of her moodiness, she said teasingly, "Of course, *you* could marry José. He wasn't bad in bed."

Celia expected a wry smile and wrinkled nose, or banter of the sort they used to have when discussing "girl stuff." Instead, Liliana turned scarlet, not merely her face but her ears and all the way down her throat. "That's disgusting!" she hissed. "He's old enough to be my father!"

"I'm sorry," Celia said, and she was. Oh, how she missed the saucy, lighthearted girl who less than a month ago could prance in and gloat about having gone dancing with her tía's "two fiancés!" Celia wanted to put her head down and cry.

Liliana pulled the jogging suits out of the bag and examined them. She pushed the blue one at Celia and kept the red one for herself.

Celia kicked off her sandals in order to get the sweats on over her feet. "My feet are so cold they hurt. Yours probably are too."

"There are socks in here," Liliana said, retrieving them from the bottom of the bag and handing one pair to Celia. "Tío Joe thought of everything."

Maybe it was Celia's imagination, but she thought the comment carried a hint of rebuke for what Liliana seemed to feel was a lack of appreciation on Celia's part. Celia said nothing, just pulled the socks on and drew Liliana's head against her shoulder.

"You are in for a surprise when we get to Santiago."

"What?" Liliana murmured.

"Franci and Philip have a little girl."

"What!" Liliana jerked up so suddenly that the top of her head collided with Celia's chin. "They had a *baby*?"

"Not a baby. A little girl. We are not sure how old she is. Ten, maybe. Possibly even twelve or thirteen, but quite small. She is Haitian and speaks only French."

"Where did they get her?"

"It's a long, sad story. But with a happy ending, I think." She pulled Liliana back against her and told her all of it.

When she finished, Liliana was silent for some minutes. Then she asked, "What about Josephine's mother? Where is she?"

"Philip thinks she was killed back in Haití, before they escaped to Cuba."

"Then she knows too," Liliana said in a voice so low Celia wasn't even sure that was what she said.

"Knows what?"

"Sooner or later everybody disappears on you."

Celia's arm tightened around the girl's shoulders and she whispered into her hair, "Not everybody."

SEVENTY-TWO

CELIA had asked José to call Franci to let her know that they would be arriving by bus rather than on the train. He apparently had done so because Franci was waiting at the Viazul station. Philip was not with her but Josephine was. The child watched intently as passengers descended. The minute Celia's foot touched the steps leading down from the bus, Josephine tugged at Franci's hands and cried, "C'est Tía Celia!"

"And Liliana," Franci added, nudging Josephine forward. "Are you going to say hello to them?"

"Bonjour, Tía." Josephine turned her cheek shyly up to Celia for a kiss and whispered, even more shyly, "Buenos dias, Liliana."

Celia knelt to greet the little girl, first in French, then in Spanish.

Franci hugged Liliana. "It is so good to see you, you big, beautiful thing, you!"

"I'm not all that big," Liliana protested.

"Compared to my Josephine," Franci insisted and introduced the girls.

Crossing the street to the parking lot, Josephine held tightly to Franci's hand, walking so close to her hip that a couple of times she almost caused Franci to stumble. But when Liliana slid into the back seat of the Fiat, Josephine slipped in beside her.

Franci smiled over the top of the car at Celia. "Guess you'll have to ride up front, hermana. The back seat appears to be occupied."

Philip was waiting with breakfast. It was largely wasted on the girls, Liliana having no appetite and Josephine apparently too filled with repressed excitement to do more than dutifully nibble at what was put on her plate. Celia satisfied her own appetite with healthy servings of soft-scrambled eggs, fruit salad, and coffee.

"I'm surprised you could get away again so soon," Philip remarked. "Did your boss give you a hard time?"

Celia shook her head. "Not really. He made it conditional though."

"How long can you stay?" Franci asked. "And what are the conditions?"

"I have to be back at work on Monday. And I must attend a three-day conference in Manzanillo. I didn't want to go but that Leyva is a negotiator. When I asked for time off to come here, he said he could justify it only if I attended the conference while I was at this end of the island."

Celia spoke casually, but her eyes asked Franci, *Will that be enough time?*

Franci's faint shrug said, *I don't know.*

Immediately after breakfast Philip rolled his Flying Pigeon out and cycled off to work. Josephine came around the table to hang at Liliana's shoulder. Liliana smiled at her and Josephine motioned for her to come. Celia held her breath, fearing that Liliana might show the same lack of interest in the child that she showed toward everything nowadays. However, Liliana rose and followed Josephine out into the backyard.

"Josephine's going to show her off to Las Madres," Franci explained. "She does that with every new thing. First my mother, who feeds her, then Philip's mother, who gives her sweets." She waved at the child's barely touched breakfast. "That's why I don't worry too much about what she eats here."

"How is the mothering going? With Las Madres, I mean," Celia asked.

Franci shook her head in wonderment. "Unbelievable. Mamá loves her because she's black and the redhead loves her because she speaks French. On top of that, the kid's a natural diplomat. Whenever one or the other gets into a jealous snit—and they do at least twice a week—she finds a way to pacify them. They spend so much time doting on her that Philip and I have almost got our lives back."

"How wonderful! I can hardly believe that little mahogany beauty is the same waif you almost drowned in bubble bath less than a month ago. Health problems?"

"None," Franci said. "Except for parasites, which we got rid of right away."

"Is she sleeping well?"

"Not at first. I'd check on her through the night, and if I found her awake I'd lie down with her. Sometimes Philip would wake up and find me gone, and he'd join us." Franci laughed. "That's why she's got a big double bed—one that can hold all of us. I hope you don't mind that I put Liliana in there with her?"

"Of course not. That is a wonderful idea," Celia said, although she worried about the effect it might have on the younger girl if Liliana lapsed into one of her hours-long uncommunicative moods. "What do you think about me going off to Manzanillo for three days and leaving Liliana here? If you think it might be a problem, I simply will not—"

"Go," Franci interrupted, pouring coffee into the cup Celia held out. "It will give me more one-on-one time with her. Josephine is with a tutor in the morning."

"Oh!" Celia set her cup down with a jolt. "Then Liliana will be here alone?"

Franci reached out and patted her hand. "Not to worry, Mamacita. I have been off work since Josephine came and will be till the end of the month. I'll overindulge and overanalyze yours same as I do mine."

Celia took the train to Bayamo only to discover, when she arrived, that the one on to Manzanillo was out of service. She had no idea when the next bus ran, or how she would get to the bus station with the rain coming down in sheets. As she stepped out of the train station, a collective cab pulled to the curb. A young woman, also waiting for transportation, called out, "Where to?"

"Bartolomé Maso," the driver called back.

Bartolomé Maso was not precisely on the route to Manzanillo, but it was fifty kilometres or so in the right direction. From there, Celia reasoned, it would be no more than an hour on to Manzanillo. It might be easier to catch a bus or truck from there than trying to cross town in this deluge and waiting for the next overcrowded Astro bus.

She slipped into the back seat of the taxi between two passengers as rain-dampened as herself, one the woman who had called out, the other a silent campesino who rode with a machete between his knees. Celia wondered what he might have been doing with a machete in the city, until she noticed that it was new. He opened his legs a couple of times to look down at it like a boy with a new toy and carefully wiped away raindrops with a kerchief.

He got out at a rural cottage and was greeted by joyous shouts from three small children who showed nothing of their father's taciturn nature as they bounded toward him like puppies. The young woman remaining in the back seat smiled and waved at the children and they waved back, although she said later that she did not know them.

Celia learned that she was a teacher in a school with only five students, ages six to ten. Celia had heard of such small schools but knew no children who attended them. "Is it difficult," she asked, "teaching children who need instruction at different levels?"

The woman ran her fingers through hair that dampness had caused to curl into tight ringlets and replied, "No more difficult than to mother five children, I expect. Maybe easier. We do have a video hook-up with educational programs from Santiago and Habana. The parents are very co-operative too. I feel so appreciated." She glanced at Celia with open curiosity. "You're not from around here, are you?"

"No. From Habana. I am going to Manzanillo for a medical conference."

"Oh!" the young woman exclaimed. "You should have taken a colectivo to Yara."

"I know, but I didn't see one. Is it not possible to get there this way?"

"Oh sure. Easy."

"Then I am not entirely lost," Celia smiled. "Where is your school?"

"Las Humanitas," she replied. "Beyond Santo Domingo. Beyond the end of the road even. The last part I have to go on foot. I won't make it back tonight. But I can overnight in Santo Domingo." She smiled. "My boyfriend manages the villa there."

Celia only vaguely recalled the talkative young man who, on the night she stayed at Villa Santo Domingo, had deflected the unwanted attentions of an agriculture inspector by walking her to her cabin.

"He's a pilot," the young teacher said proudly.

"Really!" Celia wondered why a pilot would be working as a villa manager in an area far from any airfield. In the next breath the woman answered the unasked question.

"When he was in the air force, that is. But he didn't like the military."

"No? Why not?" Celia asked, more for conversation's sake than because she was interested in the man's background. It did occur to her, though, that if he had remained in the service long enough to become a pilot, that would have been voluntary. It was difficult to get into flight school. Carolina's very bright husband had tried and failed.

The woman was silent for a moment, then said, "Raúl is a hard man."

Few questioned Raúl Castro's competence as a military commander, but there were many stories about his intolerance of anything that deviated from what he deemed politically and professionally correct. Celia had heard from Carolina, among others, that Fidel's younger brother was more dogmatic and less forgiving of infractions than Fidel.

"Also, I wasn't there; I was here," the woman added. "I didn't want to leave this area. So he came back. For me." As she spoke she ran a fingertip lightly over her full lips. Celia wondered if she was thinking of the love she and the pilot-turned-villa-manager would make when she arrived in Santo Domingo. Rather than intrude on the woman's private musings, Celia turned and stared out the rain-streaked window.

In her mind's eye she saw the small wooden sign in the parking lot at the end of the road, wooden arrows that pointed in different directions, indicating trails to Pico Turquino, Las Humanitas, and La Comandancia. Images of someone she had assured herself she would not see on this trip, or perhaps any other, formed in shadowy parts of her mind. They were not all that clear, but the longing was.

I could go with her, she thought. Catch the same ride she does to Santo Domingo, and from there walk. But such spontaneous acts were for younger, freer people than she. Dr. Cantú was far too responsible to do any such thing. Instead, she reached for the bag under her feet, took out a notepad and pen, and scribbled a short note.

> I will be at a conference in Manzanillo on Thursday and Friday.
> Afterwards, that is, after three on Friday, I shall visit the Sánchez
> Memorial on Calle de Caridad. I must return to Santiago on
> Saturday. Celia.

She folded the note and wrote "Miguel Ortega Ramos" on the outside. She had no envelope or any way to seal it to make it private. Did that matter? She hesitated, then turned to the young teacher and asked, "If I gave you a note, could you drop it off at the park office in Santo Domingo?"

"Sure. I'll be walking right by there." She glanced at the name with no sign of recognition and stuffed the note into her purse.

Celia arrived in Manzanillo just before dark and just after the rain had stopped. The trip from Santiago, with its unpredictable transportation, had taken all day. She had not needed a bus from Bartolomé Maso after all, but had stayed with the colectivo that circled through Yara on its return to Bayamo. In Yara she had waited by the side of the road for a bus, but a truck stopped first and she accepted the driver's offer of a ride. Within the hour he let her off on the outskirts of the Manzanillo, directly across from the Celia Sánchez children's hospital. She bought a pork sandwich from a vendor on the corner and ate it before crossing the busy intersection to the hospital.

She showed her credentials and was directed to the dorm accommodations provided for conference attendees. By that time neither professional challenges nor romantic possibilities were on her mind. All she wanted was to shower and sleep, which she did, with more pleasure in those simple acts than she would have imagined possible.

SEVENTY-THREE

LUIS'S heart physically ached. Celia's telephone call to Alma to convey the message that she intended to handle Liliana's crisis without his help was bad enough, but that was not the worst of it. The next day he accidentally ran into Captain Quevedo. The MININT official, who lived in the suburb of Nuevo Vedado, mentioned that on his way home he had he had seen Celia and Liliana boarding a Viazul bus.

"How is the girl?" Quevedo asked.

Luis told his friend about the possible suicide attempt, and that Celia was taking her to Santiago to spend time with a close family friend who was a psychiatrist.

Quevedo could not have known that the expression on Luis's face came from learning, in so casual a way, that while he had respected Celia's request to leave them alone, his brother had charged ahead, grandly purchasing tickets for them to travel on the Viazul line.

Probably supposing that Luis's pained expression was related to Liliana's problems, the captain laid a comforting hand on Luis's shoulder. "May the bastardo rot in the mud of Honduras."

"Bastardo!" Luis echoed fervently, fully aware that the foreign bastard Quevedo referred to was not the homegrown bastard he was thinking of.

When Luis came dragging into the apartment that evening Alma met him with news that, while not so crushing, was more unclear as to its meaning. "José is not coming home this evening. He is in Varadero. He wants you to meet him there in the morning."

She smiled hopefully at Luis, like a nurse, he thought, making a recommendation that she hopes might help a patient but is not altogether sure.

"What for?" Luis asked, thinking he might do that, might drive all the way to Varadero just to kick his brother in the balls.

"He has chartered a boat to take some socios fishing. He said some are men you wouldn't know but others are government officials you probably do."

She watched Luis face anxiously. "Go," she urged. "It will do you good." And added, "I have been praying for you, mi hijo."

Luis was too depressed to offer a dismissive rejoinder along the lines of, if she was going to waste her time praying for favours, how about asking the Almighty to stop sending hurricanes ripping across Cuba every year instead of begging Him to intercede in the private life of a single individual. Luis merely nodded, excused himself from a good meal he had not done justice, and went to his room to brood.

He could see no good coming out of a trip to Varadero. On the other hand, he had no clear idea of what his brother had been doing in Cuba. This trip might shed some light on his moves, past and intended. Maybe he would find out something about the bastard's activities that could get him booted out of the country for good.

Luis pulled into the Marina Gaviota parking lot at 7:00 AM. He saw José standing at the stern of a fishing boat. As soon as José saw him, he waved and called, "Luis! Over here!"

Luis strolled up the gangplank, not realizing until it was pulled up behind him that the boat was so close to casting off. A nice entrance, he thought. Dignified.

José clapped him on the back. "Glad you made it, hermano. I thought you were going to blow me off."

Luis acknowledged his brother with a nod and turned to shake hands with the several officials he knew: Dr. Armando Portillo, head of Habana's largest hospital, Dr. Juan Torres from the Ministry of Health, and Dr. Xaviar Lazaro, one of Cuba's best-known scientists in the field of cancer research. José introduced him to the others.

"Clifford Jones from the American Interest Section, Frank Sturgis with Sherritt International, and Guillermo Garcia with the Gaviota chain. My brother, Luis Lago."

Luis wondered briefly why a representative from the Canadian nickel mining company and another from Cuba's most upscale hotel chain would be among those with whom José was trying to curry favour. Then he recalled that Sherritt had its fingers in a lot of pies in Cuba besides mining; maybe it was funding some new bio-tech research. Gaviota might be seen as a possible market for José's medical equipment, massage tables and the like, since most resorts had doctors and professional masseuses on staff. Given the range of interests represented in the small gathering, it appeared to Luis that his brother was leaving no stone unturned. All this time and expense, and as of yet, it wasn't even possible for Yanquis to do business in Cuba!

Before the boat reached open water a muscular young man in a tightly stretched T-shirt began passing around a tray of drinks. The subdued conversation soon became more animated, but in Luis's view no more interesting. The interesting thing was the ease with which his brother moved among these important men, none of whom he could have known very well. Luis overheard nothing that could be construed as either business-related or sucking up. Rather, José seemed to leave each man with the impression that he had invited him along purely for the pleasure of his company. Which left Luis wondering why *he* had been invited.

"How many of you are fishing?" called a member of the crew.

All of the guests surged forward to choose and test the gear on offer, except for Luis. When José noticed, he came back to him. "Wanna fish?" he offered.

"No thanks. You?"

José shook his head. "Bores me out of my gourd. The only good part is being on a boat. Remember Papá letting us take the dingy out to paddle around Cojímar Bay?"

Luis smiled at the memory. "And we would pretend we were pirates attacking the fort?" He avoided looking at his brother as he said, "I guess the real invaders do it differently. Nowadays, at least."

José pretended not to take his meaning and wandered off to see that his other guests got their lines in the water. Then he drifted back to Luis.

"I kind of remembered that you didn't care for fishing," he admitted. "But I wanted you to see this." He pointed to the prow of a sunken ship sticking out of the water. "Know what it is?"

"Sure," Luis replied. "A decommissioned Russian patrol boat. The Ministry of Tourism sank it there. Divers love posing for pictures astride the rocket launchers."

"Know what that proves?" José asked.

"What?"

"The Cold War is over."

"Hmp!" Luis grunted. "Tell that to the US Congress."

"They may be the last to figure it out, but the penny's going to drop. Soon. The question is, will Cuba be ready?"

"What are you driving at?" Luis demanded, impatient with his brother's build-up to whatever sales pitch he was about to make.

"People from other countries, the States included, come here a lot. They're learning Cuban culture but Cubans aren't getting a handle on theirs."

"Plenty of Cubans travel. I do. Celia does. Our scientists, doctors, teachers—"

"I was thinking of the younger generation. Liliana's age."

So that was it, Luis thought bitterly. José was going to come up with some pop psychology theory about Liliana being out on the balcony dreaming of new horizons. His brother was still talking, and Luis was not pleased with what he was saying.

"I know," José said in a low voice. "The government has almost stopped giving scholarships to study abroad because so many are defecting. There's a reason for that."

"Yeah," Luis grunted. "They're gusanos."

"No," José said evenly. "They're *kids*. Being shut up on this island, they romanticize other places. If they had a chance to visit, to see the limitations of other cultures, well, sure, some of them would stay. But a lot of them would come home."

"A lot of them *do* come home," Luis corrected.

"So what's the problem with letting them go?"

It took longer than Luis thought it should have taken for his antennas to pick up the message José was sending. When he did get it, he felt more tired than angry.

"So you want to take her to Miami with you, is that it? You think Celia will follow. Then you will convince her that Liliana ought to go to school in some other city. Leaving just the two of you in a love nest that you'll have ready and waiting."

José gave a harsh laugh. "That's the fantasy, all right. But it's pretty hard to romance a woman who turns a verbal blowtorch on you every time you get within shouting distance. Celia would burn in hell before she'd move to the States."

Luis was glad his brother was still staring out to sea and did not notice how astonished he was by the admission. He asked, "So why the pitch for Liliana to travel?"

José turned back to him, frowning. "Because we have no idea whether the kid is jerking our chain or actually contemplating suicide. You can't rule that out—not when some do. And others risk their life in anything that floats for the sole purpose of leaving."

Luis stonewalled. "Maybe you have a solution but I don't. Not when Celia has made up her mind to handle the situation without any input from us. From me anyway."

José laid a hand on his shoulder. When he spoke his voice again had an intimate quality, as if the two of them were alone on the boat, not with half a dozen other guys loudly mouthing off about inconsequential things a few metres away. "What we do know is this, Luis. If Liliana suicides, we'll feel guilty forever. Mamá would cry every day for the rest of her life. And it would flat-out kill Celia."

A swell tilted the boat sharply. José grabbed the rail. Luis took advantage of it to move beyond his brother's reach. "I do not work in Immigration," he said, knowing even as he spoke that the distance he had placed between them was not great enough.

José looked at him in a way Luis remembered from childhood, when he was asking something that Luis considered absolutely impossible. It was a look that said the thing being asked *was* possible, and all statements to the contrary were irrelevant.

"But you could get her a passport, couldn't you?"

In fact, Luis could not get her a passport. He probably could get a visa for a one-time trip, but did he want to?

When José had gone back to schmoozing with his prospective socios, Luis considered the pros and cons. To let Liliana go would be an admission, of sorts, that Cuba could not meet the needs of its own young people and they must go abroad to find a decent life. However, Luis had always believed that Cuba was better off without gusanos and for that reason alone, those who wanted to leave should be allowed to go—and *not* allowed to return. As he saw it, Cuba had little to lose by letting a materialistic little mutt like Liliana leave. And in his view, better *before* the government invested a small fortune in providing her with a university education. Then there were the reasons José had given, which, Luis had to admit, were not frivolous. The thought of Celia defecting with Liliana was terrible—but the suicide scenario was infinitely worse.

Luis thought he was beginning to get queasy as a result of the swells that kept the deck rolling under his feet. He hadn't zeroed in on the fact that what was actually churning his gut was the knowledge that if Liliana left and Celia did *not* follow her, that could generate a whole other agony. Up to now he had been able to explain away Celia's failure to respond to him with any degree of passion, then her refusal to set a wedding date, and now her apparent determination to cut him completely out of her life, as having to do with Liliana. What if Liliana was not around to explain Celia's holding back?

Although Luis had worked none of this out in his head, he felt it. It was not dissimilar to the despair he felt the day Celia broke off their engagement. Then he had held out hope that it would all blow over and things would go back to being as they were. This time it was worse. Whatever his head told him about the possibility of a future relationship with Celia Cantú, his sloshing gut told him that she had made up her mind that he was not the man with whom she intended to spend her life.

Maybe that man would be his brother. Or her boss at the hospital, a widower who apparently gave her permission to do whatever she wanted, even if it meant bending the rules. Or maybe she would end up like her mother, welcoming compañeros to drop in for food, music, conversation, and when she felt a sexual urge, that too.

SEVENTY-FOUR

CELIA stood at the bottom of Calle de Caridad, looking up. The steep street, lined with small stuck-together stucco houses, wasn't exactly a street anymore. It was now two blocks of broad steps paved with terra cotta tiles to create a memorial to Celia Sánchez. Ascending the steps, Celia paused to admire beautiful ceramic tile murals that the artist Lecur had placed on walls, displayed above windows, and tucked beneath stairs: here a sunflower, there a stylized tree, farther up, a heron in flight over the moon.

Celia loved the art but for her the genius of the memorial was that it incorporated the homes on either side. Most were accessed by half a dozen steps built close to the side of the house and railed in wrought iron. Children dashed up and down those steps and played tag on the larger terracotta steps of the memorial as if it were their playground. Elders placed their chairs in the shade of buildings on whichever side of the street was providing shade. Women washed their own stoops and came down onto the steps of the memorial and cleaned those too. They were pleased that the street where Sánchez and her doctor-father once lived had been made into a memorial. But as an old man had told Celia on a previous visit, they did not need the memorial to remember Celia Sánchez.

Celia started climbing the steps a little nervously, concerned that with all this Sánchez history surrounding her she might be swept into a hallucination. That was the last thing she wanted right now! She scanned the memorial street, thinking that if Miguel was coming he would be here already, but his not being here told her nothing. Maybe he had not received her message. Or had received it and had chosen to ignore it.

She decided she would spend an hour at the memorial, and if he was not here by that time she would walk on to the train station. She could not get back to Santiago tonight, but she could travel as far as Bayamo and stay at Joaquín's place. That would be easier than remaining here in Manzanillo, feeling rejected.

She climbed the steps slowly, taking her time at the small pieces of art along the way, each of which she found simple, imaginative, and exquisitely rendered. At last she reached the memorial's focal point. A large ceramic tile mural about four metres square, it stood alone at the top, backed by blue sky. The panel was covered in a wild array of green leaves, yellow sunflowers, and white doves. Topping it was the face of Celia Sánchez in profile, her neck extending into the mural's profusion of flowers, leaves, and vines as if those were an integral part of herself, her body.

Having studied many photographs of Sánchez taken at all ages, Celia could see that the artist had given the profile sharper features than Sánchez actually had. The way the sharp-featured face was thrust forward captured the strength of Sánchez that a softer, more feminine likeness would not have. Lecur had rendered the head of a woman who might have graced the prow of a ship, as she had graced the prow of the Revolution throughout the war and for twenty years to follow. Sánchez's softer side was reflected by a single small flower woven into her hair. It was not the most compelling feature. That detail belonged to eyes that gazed fearlessly into the future. At the bottom of the mural was a quote from Amando Hart, calling her la flor más autóctona de la Revolución. For the hundreds of poems written to Sánchez and about her, during her life and afterwards, those few words were enough. She was not a woman who would have wanted more.

The name Celia Sánchez rarely appeared in public unless it was the official name of something like the children's hospital where the conference had been held. In any part of Cuba, but particularly on this end of the island where Sánchez had spent the first thirty-nine years of her life, one often saw roadside paintings of flowers or birds, unsigned and unexplained. If there were any words, it would be a phrase like, "We have not forgotten you." But never her name. She had shunned publicity in life and that preference had been generally respected after her death. Thus it was not surprising that in this two-block-long memorial, there was only one place her name appeared. It was on a small mural on the side of a building, a blue field with a single white bird, and one word, *Celia*.

She would look at the mural with the name, then one more, a large one tucked into an alcove. Then she would leave. She turned right to walk around the large mural and saw him standing in the alcove. He wore khaki pants and a sleeveless, multi-pocketed vest of the same tan fabric. His dark hair, longer than she remembered it, lay in untidy curls along the neck of a white T-shirt. She had almost reached the entrance of the alcove before he turned and saw her.

"Hello, Miguel. Have you been waiting long?"

"No, not long."

For a moment they stood in awkward silence like the bare acquaintances they were, studying the mural's flowing design and soft yet sensuous colours. Then Celia noticed that he had no bag. "Where are you staying?" she asked.

"Nowhere yet. What about you?"

"Nowhere."

"That's all you have?" He indicated the worn leather bag slung over her shoulder. She smiled. "You don't seem to have this much."

"Ah, but I have pockets." Grinning, he reached into one and held up a toothbrush.

So he *had* come planning to stay the night, she thought, feeling less uncertain. "I was hoping you could suggest a place."

"They did put you up at the hospital, for the conference?"

"Yes, of course."

"You could have stayed there."

"Not with you."

It was then that he kissed her. It was not their first kiss—or was it? She could not remember. She only knew one thing: it would always be like this. He would wait for her, not move until she moved, for fear she might fly away. She would always be the one to choose. It was a reversal of roles, although not entirely. He had come to where he thought she would be. He had been there as if to wait for, but not pursue, some wild thing.

Celia took his hand as they walked along the sidewalk, moving slowly in the heat of the afternoon and dissuaded from conversation by noisy traffic. Not until they reached the relative quiet of Manzanillo's shady central square did Miguel say, "I know a casa particular, if that would be okay with you?"

She said it would and let him lead her to a doorway with a red triangle sticker to show that it was licensed to rent rooms. It was a narrow townhouse of colonial vintage, three storeys squished between equally shabby houses on either side. The owner, a pear-shaped woman with a light quick step, answered Miguel's knock. She took them in at a glance, and before he had the question fully out of his mouth, opened the door widely and motioned them inside. "Claro, we have a room." As she led them into the parlour, she bellowed, "Don Renán! Bring the guest book!"

A man of perhaps seventy, with the look of a decrepit Spanish grandee, entered the room carrying a registration book in one hand and a beautiful old guitar in the other. He inclined his wispy white beard in their direction, handed his wife the guest book, and retreated from whence he had come.

The woman watched as Miguel and then Celia wrote their names and ID card numbers in the guest book. "Biologio. Doctora," she murmured with approval, reading their professions upside down. "Bueno."

She led them up two flights of stairs, each steeper and narrower than the one before. Celia was beginning to wonder if the next one would be a ladder when they emerged onto a sunlit rooftop surrounded by a metre-high wall. Along one side ran a line of flapping laundry, beyond which was a stunning view of the sea. On the other side was a boxlike room that Celia supposed must once have housed a servant. Oven-hot it would be, as it received no shade from any direction. But the late afternoon sun would soon be below the wall and in an hour or two would drop below the horizon. Even now there was a stiff sea breeze that caught the thin white curtains of the room's large window, causing them to billow inward. Maybe it would not be as hot as she imagined.

The landlady handed Miguel a key that she explained was to the front door, in case they decided to go out later. They did not need a room key, she said, since no one would come up to the roof to disturb them. Would they want dinner later?

Celia and Miguel exchanged a glance, each waiting for the other to reply. Celia realized that neither had the faintest idea of what would please the other.

"No," said Celia, when it was clear that Miguel was not going to answer for them. "Thank you, but we will be going out for dinner." She knew that food prepared by the housewife would be superior to anything they could buy in town, but how did she know what would transpire in the next few hours, and when or whether they would want to eat?

The woman gave Celia a knowing smile, snatched an armload of breeze-whipped clothes from the line, and disappeared back down the stairs.

Then they were alone, this time two real people in real time.

SEVENTY-FIVE

IN the whole of her life, Celia had taken the lead only at work, and even there she did so in subtle rather than overt ways. The habit dated back to childhood when as the younger sister she had been expected to follow and felt comfortable doing so. However, as she stood in the doorway of a room that was about to become a love nest, with a man she barely knew, she understood as she had at the memorial that she must take the lead. It was that, more than the impending intimacy, that almost caused her to lose her nerve. Then she looked into Miguel's eyes, saw the stillness, his waiting for her to move either toward him or away, and let the voice of her self tell her what she wanted to do.

The white-walled room, so unlike the rain-darkened cottage at the Comandancia where they had made love before, was ablaze with light from the slanting afternoon sun. It was empty save for a double bed and a straight-backed chair—just that and breeze-filled white curtains.

Beyond the bed was a doorway into a tiny bathroom.

Celia was wondering what the protocol for such a situation might be when Miguel said, "I'm so hot and sweaty . . . I didn't take time to . . . I'd like to take a quick shower."

"Claro!" Celia said, relieved that at least one of them had a notion of what to do next. "What time did you leave this morning?"

"At ten. As soon as I got your note."

"You only got it this morning?" she exclaimed.

"That's right. I went out as usual before sun-up. It was there when I got back."

She looked at him wonderingly. "And you came? Just like that?"

"Well, sure. Did you think I wouldn't?"

She did not answer. Had she thought he wouldn't? Or that he would? She did not know what she had expected, only what she had hoped.

"I usually go for a swim after work," he explained. "But if I had taken time to do that I couldn't have made it to Manzanillo by three. So"—he was edging toward the bathroom as he spoke—"if there's running water in here . . ."

She kicked off her sandals and fell face down on the bed. Soon there was the sound of running water. When it stopped, she rolled over and saw him step out of the shower. She had seen him nude before, of course, but only in near-darkness. Now he stood dripping wet in bright light, unselfconsciously giving his hair and beard a cursory wipe with the towel, then his almost-hairless chest and furry pubic area.

His visible readiness ignited her own. She felt her breasts harden and a hot hollowness between her legs that wanted filling. Her mind seemed to shut down altogether as emotion overwhelmed her and fastened on the man who, without yet touching her, had roused a level of sensuality that caused her breath to go ragged and her eyelids to flutter shut.

When she opened her eyes he stood over her, nude and ready. She was just as ready, but most awkwardly, fully clothed. She wished she had undressed while he was in the shower. She unzipped her jeans, wondering how they had come off so easily before, so easily that she could not, in fact, even remember taking them off that other time. He knelt at the side of the bed and pulled them over her feet; then she remembered.

She caught the tail of her T-shirt and lifted it over her head. When it was half-way up, she felt his mouth on her breasts and gasped. She pulled the shirt off and saw him reach into the pocket of his vest, which he had hung on the back of the chair next to the bed. From it he took a condom, opened the packet, and began rolling it on.

"I'm sorry," he said as he moved over her, "for putting you at risk before."

"We put each other at risk," she corrected him, remembering all too well who had initiated their previous intimacy.

"Not much," he grinned. "Weren't we Celia and Fidel? Their lovemaking was all pre-AIDS."

"But not pre-pregnancy," Celia quipped.

His eyes widened in alarm and she saw that he had misunderstood. "Oh no! Not to worry! Last time was safe." She touched his sheathed penis. "But we do need this now."

She put her arms around him, feeling the wetness of his back that he had not dried. A pulsing motion that felt as powerful as an ocean wave bore down on her and lifted her past the pain of the first thrust. Again her mind went blank. There was neither fear nor fantasy, only a physical need that sucked everything else into its vortex. As before, he climaxed before her but kept the rhythm until she came. Then she rolled on top of him and as before, they slept. The difference was that this time she woke unafraid, knowing who he was, who she was, and exactly where they were.

From downstairs came the notes of a Spanish love song, played, she was sure, by the old gentleman they had met when they arrived. Earlier he had been playing flamenco with a driving rhythm appropriate to the intensity of their lovemaking. Celia wondered if he played the music in that order deliberately, knowing that it was likely to coincide with the activities of guests who disappeared into his rented room in mid-afternoon. Perhaps he used the music to fuel his own fantasies. Or to give life to memories of when he himself might have been the young man making love in the afternoon.

When the music ended, she rolled off Miguel and went to shower. She returned with a towel. Seeing he was awake, she tossed it to him. He wiped himself and glanced out the window. It was growing dark.

"Would you like to go out to dinner?" he asked.

"If we can go somewhere close by."

They stood on the street holding hands as they waited for the vendor to bake two pizzas in a split oil drum recycled into an oven. She paid, because the vendor was unable to change Miguel's one-hundred-peso note. Then they walked until they saw a blender in an open doorway and from its owner ordered fruity milkshakes. Again Celia paid for lack of change on the part of Miguel or the vendor.

"Generous woman!" Miguel grinned. "I could get used to being a kept man."

"Oh really? I was just beginning to consider the benefits of being a kept woman," Celia joked, choosing not to remember that only three days earlier she had considered exactly that—with Miguel not the keeper she had had in mind.

They sat in the park and ate slowly, admiring the Andalusian Moorish architecture around the square. An organ grinder cranked out a tune that probably dated back to the late nineteenth century, when many such instruments were imported to Manzanillo from France. Although quaint, the music was not as romantic or well played as that from the guitar that had serenaded them earlier.

"How was the conference?" Miguel asked.

"Not too devastating."

"You were expecting devastation?"

"It was a definite possibility." Between sips of milkshake, she told him about her Santiago presentation on the role of second-hand smoke in children's asthma and the furor caused by her laying blame at the feet of the government.

"Fortunately," she concluded, "in the month since I gave my presentation nobody has had time to collect data to refute it, if it can be refuted, which it cannot. I expect that was why it was ignored by presenters at this conference. Even so, when we broke into working groups, no matter what group I was in, it seemed that there was a 'designated hitter' who attacked me and forced me to defend my methodology, my conclusions, my credentials, my politics, my—" She looked at him from under her lashes. "I guess if the conference had lasted any longer, they could have attacked my morals too."

"You could have told them your morals are squeaky clean. I'd vouch for you."

They kissed like adolescents, kisses the flavour of fresh mangoes. Then they wrapped arms around each other's waist and walked back to the casa. The stairway leading to the top of the house was dimly lit, but when they emerged onto roof, the moon glistened gorgeously on the ocean. Celia turned away from the view, it causing some uneasiness in her for which she could not account.

Miguel switched on the light. Celia immediately began removing her clothing. With smiling eyes, he did the same. He hung his vest on the back of the chair and reached for something in the pocket, what she took to be another condom. As she sat against the headboard waiting for him to prepare himself, he pulled one of her feet into his naked lap and from a tiny square of paper, unwrapped what he had taken from the vest pocket.

She could not believe . . . *a glint of gold, long sensitive fingers, trembling just slightly as he fumbles with the clasp on the thin chain now looped around her ankle.* Celia gasped and jerked her foot back as if the gold were burning hot. Miguel's mouth opened in surprise, his expression confused, and hurt.

"I'm sorry," he mumbled, balling the gold chain into his fist. "I just thought . . . that is, I know ankle bracelets aren't politically correct. But when I was in Santiago a couple of weeks ago, an old woman on the street was selling them and I thought—"

"Surely you know," Celia interrupted tersely, "that Celia Sánchez wore an anklet." What was he trying to do, force her into a hallucination she had managed to avoid until this very moment? Why would he deliberately jerk her back in time like that?

"Well, no, I didn't." Hurt mingled with perplexity at her tone of accusation. "Pictures I've seen of Sánchez, she is usually wearing army fatigues or slacks. I wouldn't have thought she went in for jewellery."

He tried to rise, to reach for his vest to discard the rejected gift. But Celia pressed her foot into his lap, holding him there. "Wait," she said, taking a deep breath. "Just . . . wait a minute. It's not what you think."

Of course she had no idea what he thought. He lapsed into stillness, waiting for her to calm and collect herself. She struggled to regain composure that the coincidence had startled out of her, to erase the sensation of that split second when the hands had been not Miguel's but those of someone else, someone with longer, more tapering fingers that trembled while trying to fasten the clasp of a fine gold chain, just as his had.

"Celia Sánchez did wear an anklet. I saw it when my mother and I visited her. I liked it. I liked it on her and—" She took a deep breath. "I think I would like it on me."

He said nothing, nor did he look at her. Clearly he was not convinced.

She leaned forward and touched his arm. "But you must find it strange, Miguel."

When he did look up, she saw that the flecks of gold in his eyes were almost as bright as the glitter of the delicate gold chain, but the brownness of those eyes, which was most of their colour, was very steady. "Strange that I think you have beautiful ankles? That Fidel noticed hers? Not really."

Celia believed what he said, believed that for some inexplicable reason she was trying to turn mere coincidence into a mystical moment. She wanted to believe that, so she did. And would go on believing . . . until the next hallucination. She wiggled her foot, which still lay in his lap, provocatively close to his penis. "Put it on, please."

He unclenched his fist and looked at the anklet. "It's not like a ring that might get in the way of a woman carrying a rifle—or a stethoscope."

"It's perfect," she said softly. "Trust me."

What she meant was, Trust yourself. Not me. I am as unreliable as they come.

Later, after they had made love again and were lying on their backs a little apart, Celia held her leg aloft to admire the slim gold chain around her tan ankle.

"Are you sure you like it?" Miguel asked.

"Very much. Which is odd, because normally I don't care for jewellery." She paused, considering that that too was a similarity between herself and Sánchez. She said nothing to indicate that she was thinking of the other Celia, but from the way Miguel was watching her she knew he guessed where her thoughts had taken her.

What point was there in trying to conceal them? So she asked, "Why do you suppose Fidel loved her?"

He folded his arms behind his head and stared up at the white plaster ceiling. "That's easy. Because she was totally devoted to a cause they shared. And to him."

"A lot of women in his circle were that."

"Yeah. But from what I've heard, Celia Sánchez was different."

"In what way?" She had been immersed in the Sánchez persona, or the Sánchez myth, so long that she had lost track of what normal people thought about the woman.

"She was also totally independent."

"Totally devoted yet totally independent? Isn't that a paradox?"

"Maybe. But any halfway intelligent man, when he meets a woman like that, can't help but love her."

Celia rolled onto her side. She could not tell if there was something personal in the assertion or not, so she asked, "Do you think I am like her?"

Miguel cut his eyes toward her and smiled. "Hard do say when I've only met one of you." He turned full toward her and pulled the sheet up to cover her breasts, as if to keep from being distracted by them. "When your personality gets mixed up with hers do you feel like a different person?"

Celia had asked herself the same question more than once. "Not a different person. A stronger one. Like I could, if I had to, pick up a rifle or survive prison or face torture. I could stand my ground against Fidel himself if I thought he was in the wrong. Neither his political power nor his physical size would intimidate me."

"Sounds like an infusion of the Sánchez spirit would be a gift for anybody."

It had not occurred to Celia that her mental aberrations might have value. She turned the idea over in her mind a while before replying. "I think it has helped me in my career." Then she added, shyly, "And without it I would never have had the audacity to walk into your arms the moment I saw you."

He stripped off the sheet he had just pulled up and pressed himself against her. "Celia," he said in a voice between a groan and a whisper. "Celia, Celia!"

It might have been three in the morning when she got out of bed. Miguel gave a moan of contentment but didn't waken. She wrapped herself in a towel and tiptoed out onto the rooftop.

Because what she called "Sánchez moments" generally came when she was in a place known to have been frequented by Sánchez, she had considered the possibility that such places remained the woman's haunts after death—not that she *believed* that, but the notion had occurred to her. It surprised her that here in Manzanillo, where Sánchez had lived and worked first with her doctor-father and then for the revolutionary cause, that she had not experienced the sensation of her persona merging with that of Sánchez. Even at the memorial, on the very street where Sánchez once lived, Celia had been cognizant of the fact that she was one person and Celia Sánchez had been a very different person. The only slippage, and it was a mere fraction of a second, was when Miguel's fingers had suddenly seemed those of another man, her ankle that of another woman.

That had been enough, though, to tell her that she had not exorcised Sánchez from her psyche. Moreover, the fact that she was now creeping out onto the moonlight rooftop proved that she did not want to, that on the contrary, she was courting a hallucination. Seeking from it—what? The strength she had revealed to Miguel that she felt in such moments? Was that what she was after? And why now? In this safe place, wrapped in the presence of a man who wanted her with an intensity she had not experienced with anyone else, why was she trying to evoke an aura of strength that the other Celia had embodied, and which she almost certainly did not?

There was no waiting. As she approached the wall of the roof the moon slid behind a cloud. Her eyes strained to see through the darkness.

There was no moonlight to reveal what she sought: the boat bringing Fidel and his men from México. Why had they not reached the point of rendezvous hours ago? How could Fidel have let this happen? If only there was a god to whom she could pray, plead that this not be another Moncada, with men and women, boys and girls, tortured and destroyed because they confused idealism with reality and could not distinguish between leadership and charisma. Dear non-existent God, she half-prayed, give me the Granma *and its courageous fools to go with the fighters I have recruited from the sierra; put them in my hands and there will be no more Moncadas. Ah, but you don't exist; better I pray to the waves. Bring that boat ashore, Black Tide, and let me find it before Batista does. Just that, Ocean. Give me men and I will be all that Fidel is not, and this time, we will win.*

Celia's eyes ached from trying to see into the darkness, for how long she did not know. She heard a whisper of footsteps crossing the roof toward her. For an instant she floated between two times, unwilling to choose between them. Then she turned and saw Miguel come toward her.

Wrapping his arms around her, he murmured, "You're cold. Don't you want to come back to bed?"

"Yes," she whispered. "I want to come back."

SEVENTY-SIX

CELIA stirred and came fully awake. Miguel slept soundly beside her, but she remained awake and troubled. It was not that the lovemaking had gone wrong, not at all. It had been almost equal to the first perfect time at the Comandancia. But not quite.

That first time, when she had not known who he was or who she was, she had imagined that they had not only a physical and emotional connection but an intellectual marriage—a shared purpose that would survive as long as either of them lived. She was absolutely certain that with Celia Sánchez being the kind of woman she was and Fidel Castro the kind of man he was, the intellectual had come first. It was their strongest bond, the one that would hold them together if one of the other strands weakened or broke.

It had not been like that with Celia Cantú and Miguel Ortega Ramos. In the hours just past she had loved him with her body, fevered with extreme emotions. She had not thought about whether it was wise or fair or permanent or passing. There had been no intellect in it, none at all. Once during the night she had fled his embrace to conjure a hallucination, but that was not thought. That was probably . . . fear. She had likely been trying to infuse herself with some of the "Sánchez spirit" to gain the courage to continue this reckless uncharted course with a man she barely knew. In the throes of such mindless behaviour, how could there have been an intellectual connection?

Celia Sánchez would have fallen in love with the man's mind and only then given her heart and body. Celia Cantú had led with her body and followed with her emotions. Where was her mind in all this? Where was his? Those were the questions that gave rise to her unease as she lay beside him that morning, and which caused her to pick at her food when they went downstairs to take breakfast with the landlady and her husband.

The old gentleman, Celia decided, resembled a good many representations she had seen of Don Quixote. She thanked him for his guitar music of the evening before, and Miguel thanked his wife for breakfast. Then, in morning sun already blazing hot, they walked to the train station. If it ran on time Celia would be in Santiago by mid-afternoon. Miguel would ride as far as Yara, then find other transportation up into the mountains.

The train did leave on schedule. They sat next to each other in the tan vinyl seats, his hand resting on her thigh, fingers interwoven with hers. Celia wondered how many such morning-afters Miguel had experienced and whether he was always so tender, yet withdrawn. The enormity of what she did not know about him weighed heavily. She wanted to lighten her burden of ignorance but did not know how.

She had told him about Liliana's abduction and its aftermath, and how Franci was trying to get at some of the girl's feelings. There was, in fact, very little about herself that she had not told him, with the exception of her relationships with Luis and José, which she was determined to think of in the past tense. Miguel, though, had told her nothing of himself, and now she desperately wanted information about anything in his past relevant to the man he was, the man with whom she had repeatedly made love yet barely knew.

She searched for a question that would not seem as obvious as, Who are you, stranger, and what are your intentions concerning me? She waited awhile, hoping he would initiate conversation, but he did not. Finally she asked where he was from.

"Baracoa," he told her. "My family has lived there for generations. Some relatives even claim Taíno blood, but I doubt there's any truth to that."

"I would find it easy to believe that you carry a few of Chief Hatuey's genes."

He smiled. "Oh, I don't think so. There is a bust of him in the park in Baracoa. If it looks anything like the actual man, he was much fiercer than I am. A warrior."

"Maybe he was only that out of necessity. For all we know, he might have been a naturalist until the Spaniards came and he felt compelled to lead his people against them. Although the way he died—" She shuddered.

"That's another difference between me and that ancient non-ancestor. When they were about to burn him at the stake and the priest offered him a chance to enter heaven if he would become a Catholic, he told them that if there were going to be Spaniards in heaven he'd rather go to hell."

"You would not have made that choice?" Celia asked.

"I wouldn't have bothered to choose because I don't believe in either place." Miguel looked past her, across rolling green pastures to the purple silhouettes of mountains against a faded blue sky. "My paradise is here."

Although their fingers were still entwined, Celia felt that he was slipping away, that he had just entered those distant mountains without her.

"Have you ever been married?" she asked suddenly.

"No."

"Engaged?"

"Three times."

"You have had *three novias*?" she exclaimed in astonishment, then laughed as she realized that was only one more than she had had.

"That's right," he mumbled.

"What happened?"

He did not laugh or smile. He continued to gaze past her, toward the mountains. "That," he said, waving his hand toward the window.

She looked out the window but saw only grazing cattle. "What?"

"La sierra." Still looking past her to dark mountains sharply defined against pale sky, he said, "Everything I want is there. Not necessarily in the Sierra Maestra, but in the Rosarios or the Escambrays or the Cuchillas de Toa. I have spent time in all Cuba's mountain ranges, but those around Toa, where I grew up, are my favourites." He smiled in memory of the place. "The last ivory-billed woodpecker seen in Cuba, that's where it was. There may still be some there, although none have been sighted in decades."

Celia was listening but not hearing what she needed to hear, which was how a love of mountains connected to the termination of his three previous love affairs, and how, she sensed, it might have the same effect on theirs. He must have known what was in her mind and wanted to avoid the subject. But they were entering Yara. He may have thought, as she did, that this was not the time to leave something crucial unsaid.

"My novias were women of substance, all of them. In Cuba's most rugged mountains I find everything I need. But there are no universities there. No possibilities for political power. No place for an architect to realize her urban renewal ideas." He squeezed Celia's hand but did not look at her as he added, "No hospitals."

The air was sliced by shrieks of metal against metal as the train braked to a stop.

Celia said, "But there are children who need doctors, no?"

He kissed her lightly, hardly more than a brush of his lips against hers. "Yes," he said. "There are children."

Then he was gone.

SEVENTY-SEVEN

CELIA had called Franci when she changed trains in Bayamo to let her know when she would be arriving. Franci was waiting for her at the station, alone.

"Where are the girls?" Celia asked at once.

"Philip took them to the Centro Cultura de Africa. It was that or let Las Madres drag them to the Basilica de Nuestra Señora del Cobre." Franci grimaced as she unlocked the car doors. "Josephine has already been twice, once with each of them,"

"Just what you were afraid of."

"So it was," Franci said, but smiled. "That Josephine! You wouldn't believe how she's got those old ladies wrapped around her little brown finger. She chatters away in French about the Virgin to Philip's mother, then in pidgin Spanish tells my mamá how Ochún is the same goddess her mother prayed to in Haití. Both mothers are absolutely convinced that she sees things through their own religious lens."

"Does Josephine actually believe in either the Virgin or Ochún?"

Franci shrugged. "Yes and no. She told me one can't have too many gods, but also said she asked all the ones she'd ever heard of to save her mother and father and baby brother and none of them responded, so she is doubtful they exist."

"A thoughtful conclusion," Celia mused. "Agnosticism is unusual in a child."

"Josephine is an unusual child. Our personal miracle."

"You and Philip deserved a personal miracle," Celia readily conceded. Trying to keep the anxiety from her voice, she asked, "What about me? Do I get one now?"

Franci's face clouded. "I hope so. But don't count on it happening this week. You've got a pretty complicated situation on your hands, hermana."

"Where are we going?" Celia asked, noticing that Franci had turned the opposite direction from her house and was taking the road along the harbour that they had followed to find and bury Josephine's father. "Not to visit a grave, I hope!"

"No, no!" Franci looked horrified. "I'd never go back there unless Josephine asked to. So far she hasn't mentioned it. It's just that with Philip and the girls out all afternoon, I thought we could get off by ourselves. Sin Mamá, sans Maman."

Franci pulled in at the Castillo El Morro and led Celia to a restaurant on the opposite side of the parking area. Entering the restaurant, Celia saw that the view of the coast far below was breathtaking. "Thanks, Franci. This is a real treat."

They sat at a table recently vacated by a group of tourists and placed orders. Then Franci leaned back and made eye contact in a way Celia recognized as her "conference" mode. "Okay, here's what I've found out. Liliana wants to leave Cuba. Preferably go to the States." At Celia's silence, Franci said, "I take it this is not news to you?"

Celia swallowed. "No."

"I haven't seen Liliana in a while, but when I last talked to her, less than a year ago, I'm almost certain nothing like this was in her mind. She was full of questions about medical school here in Santiago—what kind of grades she needed, what approvals she would need to attend here rather than in Habana, whether she could stay with us if she didn't like living in the dorm. Remember those conversations?"

"Yes," Celia nodded. "And she did follow up with the authorities to find out what the procedure would be."

"So when did this change come about?"

"I can't say for sure. She started cutting classes about three months before she ran away. That would have been in January."

"What was going on in her life then?"

The waiter set drinks and a plate of banana chips between them. Celia heard Franci crunching into the chatinos without really hearing and looked down at the spectacular coastline without really seeing. She could hardly remember a time before the emotional earthquakes of the past month, a time when their life had been steady to the point of humdrum. Finally she fastened on Christmas as a date she could recall in detail. Neither her family nor the Lagos had ever done much more during the holidays than get together for a big meal. Alma of course went to Mass. Sometimes Liliana went with her, sometimes she did not. Last Christmas Eve, she had.

Franci interrupted her thoughts. "Try to remember what you were doing."

What Celia had been doing Christmas Eve, while Alma and Liliana were at Midnight Mass, was giving Luis his "Christmas presents"—first sex, then a promise that she would set a wedding date within the next few months.

"Around Christmas Luis was pressuring me to get married but I didn't tell Liliana. Oh, and her best friend moved away. Her parents joined a literacy team to Venezuela and she went to stay with her grandparents in Las Tunas. But Liliana has so many friends . . ."

Celia stopped speaking. Franci pointed to the chatinos, "Eat. Some pieces are starting to fit together, but I want to get them—well, you know how it is with a jigsaw puzzle. It helps to get all the pieces right side up before you try putting them together."

Celia munched on banana chips and managed to stay silent for perhaps two minutes. Then said, "Enough already, Franci! Think out loud!"

Franci was running a finger around the rim of her daiquiri glass, periodically stopping to lick the salt off it. "Children don't have to be told when something's going on with the adults in their life. Liliana would always have a pretty good idea of where your relationship with Luis stood. Don't you think she knew marriage was in the wind?"

"Probably." Celia took a deep breath. "I *was* on the verge of giving in. I really did not want to marry him, but I was also tired of living in limbo."

"You could have broken it off."

"I wanted to but I guess I was not strong enough. Not strong enough to say no when he asked me to marry him, not strong enough to break it off after I had said yes. I kept drifting. Making excuses instead of decisions."

"Then José came back and that changed everything."

"No. Then Liliana ran away and *that* changed everything."

"Are you saying José being back *hasn't* changed anything?"

Celia hesitated. The hesitation was enough to give her away to someone who knew her as well as Franci. "Maybe it did. Maybe it has. But that was later."

"Like now?"

Celia did not answer.

"Answer me, Celia. Are you thinking of taking up with José Lago again?"

"I don't *want* José," Celia said in a voice that was almost a whine. "But he keeps pushing me, and if it is what Liliana wants—"

"Wait a minute. Who said that's what Liliana wants?"

"What *does* Liliana want?" Celia cried. "Come on, Franci, *help me!*"

A crowd of Italians who had just finished touring El Morro burst into the restaurant, loudly disputing whether Giovanni Bautista Antonelli, the sixteenth century Italian engineer who had designed the fort, was merely a talented man or a true genius.

"It's too noisy to think in here," Franci decided and signalled for the check.

As they drove back into the city, Franci said, "There's one more piece that fits in somewhere." She glanced across at Celia. "This is a tough one."

Celia felt a headache coming on, caused, she supposed, by the fact that they were driving directly into the bright afternoon sun and she had had only a daiquiri and banana chips for lunch. "Go ahead," she said, closing her eyes.

"Liliana told Josephine that her parents abandoned her."

Celia's eyes flew open. "*Abandoned* her? Why on earth would she have said—?"

"Exactly the question I asked her. I didn't get a straight answer, but I think it has to do with what you told her, or maybe what you didn't tell her, about how they died."

"You think I should have given her all the gory details?" Celia cried. "Young as she was?" Was Franci accusing her of overprotecting Liliana, as Luis so often did? Implying that if Liliana had known the truth she would not be going off the rails now? "Look, Franci, just because Josephine handled the harsh reality of her parents' death doesn't mean Liliana—"

Franci interrupted sharply. "Let's not be making comparisons like that, Celia. We have no idea how Josephine is going to handle it, especially once she reaches her teens. I am only pointing out that Liliana is not a young child anymore, so some of the things that haven't been explained to her—"

"Like what?" Celia cried, still feeling as if she was being accused.

"Like why both her parents were in Angola in the first place. Her impression, and this is more what I got from Josephine than from what she said to me, was that they just dumped her with her grandmother—your mother—and went off to have a romantic war because they wanted to be heroes."

"That is not true!"

"I know," Franci said as they pulled into the driveway. "So maybe you want to tell her how it really was."

Philip had not yet returned with the girls, which was fortunate because by then Celia's head was pounding and she could not have explained anything to anybody. She claimed exhaustion—true in view of how little sleep she had gotten the previous night—and went to lie down. She immediately fell asleep and was only vaguely disturbed by the sounds of the girls returning and Franci shushing them because Tía Celia was resting.

SEVENTY-EIGHT

CELIA woke to darkness. Her headache was gone. Dishes were being washed in the kitchen, indicating that she might have missed dinner. There were thumping sounds and occasional single-person applause coming from the living room.

She meandered out to see what was going on. Josephine, whose short hair had been blown out into a smaller version of Franci's Afro, was twirling around the living room in a white dress made of a lacy fabric very like that of a curtain panel now missing from the window of the guest room. Liliana was pirouetting in an ankle-length red skirt that Franci must have loaned her. Her dark curls had been transformed into a cascade of tiny beaded braids that would have taken hours to do. That, Celia guessed, was how Franci had kept her sitting still long enough for an intimate conversation.

Philip stood in the doorway of the kitchen in his white dress uniform, the wavy blond hair and blue eyes giving him the appearance of a storybook prince. He applauded as the girls leapt and curtsied in front of him.

"What," Celia exclaimed, "is going on?"

"Tía Celia!" Liliana squealed. She twirled her way across the room and flung herself into Celia's arms. "We thought you were going to sleep forever."

"Je suis une ballerine," Josephine announced, pointing her toes. "Liliana est ma professeur."

Celia chuckled. Years ago, as a student, she had attended a lecture by Alicia Alonso. The great ballerina had achieved worldwide acclaim for her use of ballet as therapy for disturbed children, her theory being that children whose emotions were out of control were calmed and reassured by being able to control their body to the degree demanded by ballet. Although initially skeptical, Celia observed some of Alonso's dance therapy sessions and was impressed with what she saw. Not long afterwards Liliana lost her parents, then her last grandparent. Celia arranged for her to take ballet lessons, not because Liliana seemed more upset than any normal child would have been, but as a precaution. However, the teacher was no Alicia Alonso and Liliana did not have the makings of a dancer. By age ten she had grown bored so the ballet lessons ended. As far as Celia knew, this was the first time she had pointed a toe since.

Franci came to the kitchen door and slipped an arm around Philip's waist. Seeing Celia, she said, "This gorgeous man is taking our glamorous girls out on the town."

"Oh really?" Celia sprang forward to catch a lamp toppled by the outflung arm of one not-quite-in-control dancer. "Are they mature enough for an evening out, Philip?"

"We're going to a National Ballet performance," Philip explained. "If they don't try to steal the show, I think they can handle it."

"We can handle it, ma chère tante." Liliana waved her hand airily. "I can handle anything."

"You can go with them if you like," Franci offered.

"Thanks, but I think I'll stay home and eat leftovers—if there are any."

"Leftovers and more." Franci headed back into the kitchen while Philip shooed the girls out to the car.

At the door, Liliana suddenly dashed back and gave Celia a hug that was so tight it felt almost desperate. "I'm so glad you're back!" she whispered, then rushed out to join Philip and Josephine.

Celia stood there a minute, still feeling the warmth of the girl's arms. Then she went into the kitchen where Franci was reheating croquetas. "Do those look good!" Celia exclaimed. "Just what the doctor would have ordered for the doctor."

"Naturally you haven't eaten since breakfast," Franci scolded.

"Daiquiris and chatinos don't count?"

"Not really. I don't know what you did at the conference, or more to the point, *after* the conference, that you came back more in need of sleep than food."

"I met a man," Celia said.

Franci, who had been standing at the stove adding a helping of rice to the plate with the croquetas, dropped the serving spoon with a clatter. "You *what*? Never mind, I heard you the first time. Who? Where did you meet him? Will you see him again?"

Celia shook her head. "I can't talk about it—him—right now."

Franci placed the plate of food in front of her and sat down. "And why not?"

"Because I need this time to talk to you about other things. About Liliana."

"Okay," Franci said. "Eat. Then we'll go for a walk and talk as long as you like."

Although the Morceau home was only a few blocks off Avenida de las Américas, there was little traffic on the quiet suburban streets along which they strolled. Franci did not chatter nor initiate conversation, giving Celia time to organize her thoughts.

"When I went to sleep it made no sense to me," Celia confessed. "But when I woke up it was all there. So neat I'm suspicious of it. What I need is a reality check."

"Which is exactly what we have always been for each other," Franci reminded.

"Okay, here goes." Celia held up a hand and began ticking off on her fingers. "One, child's parents disappear, leaving her with her grandmother. Two, grandmother dies, leaving child with aunt. Three—flash forward nine years—aunt is about to marry a man whom child believes doesn't want her around. At the same time, best friend moves away and a new friendship develops. She and the new friend egg each other into taking certain risks until she is over the line—and she knows it. All of a sudden, stepfather-to-be is standing there *in her home*, threatening to have her put in a re-education camp."

Franci nodded. "Thus the runaway."

"Which was not really a runaway. Liliana said she only intended to stay with some friends until she had a chance to call me and make sure that—well, that I would take her side against Luis, I guess, although she did not say that."

Franci took up the thread. "Meanwhile, José blows in with a flashy lifestyle that feeds her fantasies. If he can walk out on family and come back at will, why can't she? Especially since, in her mind, what's left of her family is about to dump her anyway."

Celia swallowed hard. "Do you think she might have thought that?"

"Very likely. But the suicide attempt, if that's what it was—how does that fit in?"

Celia didn't answer. She thought she knew the answer but wasn't quite ready to talk about it. She pointed to a grassy knoll, atop which was an arrangement of large granite blocks, forming a monument of some type. "What is that?" she asked.

"El Bosque de los Heroes."

"Funny name," Celia mused. "Why would they call it 'forest of the heroes' when there is not a tree in sight? Maybe from the olden days, when there was a forest here?"

"I don't know about the forest, but the heroes aren't from all that long ago. It's for Che and those who died with him in Bolivia."

They climbed the steps to the top of the knoll. Circling the monument, Celia saw that the names of those who died in Bolivia were listed, except for Che's. He was recalled in just one place: a granite block with an inscription of his most famous quote, "Hasta la victoria, siempre."

"Until the victory, always," Celia murmured, feeling sad, as she always did, when she thought of how things had turned out for Che and his courageous band. Not to mention poor Bolivians, who, partly because of that failed revolution, remained to this day among the most destitute in the hemisphere.

"You know," she said to Franci, "Che was as incorruptible as they come. He walked away from leadership positions in the revolutionary government and never showed the slightest interest in creature comforts or personal popularity. In fact, I have always believed that the reason he left Cuba was because he was sickened by the excesses of some of the compañeros once they were in power and had access to resources of the state." She paused. "Naturally I am glad Che was with us, but why should *he* be the symbol of Cuba's Revolution when he only spent seven years here? Celia Sánchez was every bit as incorruptible and she worked flat out for more than twenty years to keep our leaders focused on their original humanitarian vision. Why should the whole world know about Che while hardly anybody has heard of her?"

Franci shrugged. "You can't blame him. He shunned publicity as much as she did. And revolutions have always been seen as a macho activity, with women relegated to the background."

Celia stopped in front of the list of combatants who had died with Che in Bolivia. "Like Tanya. Although she was no Celia Sánchez, not by a long shot."

Franci looked at her oddly. "What makes you say that?"

"Oh, I know Tanya was as dedicated to Che and the cause of Bolivian liberation. But there was more to Sánchez. She was organizing and fighting in the sierra long before she met Fidel. The campesinos, men and women, joined the struggle because of her. In Bolivia, Tanya was an outsider like Che. She could not support him the way Celia supported Fidel."

Celia thought of other ways Sánchez had supported Castro that were not noted in any historic account, and which, if she mentioned, Franci might think she had invented. She concluded lamely, "It seems to me that when a woman takes up with a revolutionary she should bring more to the struggle than sex and guns."

"I expect they do, but their male partners choose not to remember it." Franci paused and asked, "Are we finished with the Liliana discussion?"

Celia's mind had drifted from Liliana's problems, and, in fact, had drifted from Cuba's revolutionary heroes and the women who stood beside them, to a different man of the sierra and what kind of woman it would take to share his life. But the instant Franci mentioned Liliana, Celia's thoughts veered back.

"No," Celia said, heading down the steps of the monument. "There is the question you asked before, about how the suicide attempt fits in. Do you have a theory?"

"Not really," Franci admitted as they crossed the grass back to the sidewalk. "Has she talked to you at all about it?"

"Only a few words the night it happened. She spoke of wanting to fly—not kill herself. She didn't say another word about it. At least, not to me. But she told José that if she couldn't get off the island, she would kill herself."

Franci frowned. "Was she saying that was why she was up on the balcony railing? Or was she just using the incident to manipulate him into—well, whatever?"

Celia looked down at shifting patterns caused by the light from street lamps filtering through trees lining the sidewalk. "You are the mind doctor. You tell me."

"About that I can't say. I can tell you that she only had one period of withdrawal while you were away. It was after I took her to the medical school. I introduced her to some teachers and we visited one of the dorms. Afterwards she retreated to the bedroom for several hours. Finally Josephine cajoled her into coming out and little by little she lightened up. Today—well, you saw her. Do you think she seemed suicidal?"

"No," Celia admitted. "But is it possible? When we get home and there is only the two of us, do you think she might be . . . at risk?"

They had arrived back at the house. Franci picked a red hibiscus from a bush growing next to the driveway. She twirled it in her slim brown fingers, studying it as if the petals were tea leaves and she could read the future in them. But her reply said not.

"You know better than to ask me a question like that, Celia. Psychiatrists are no better than anybody else at predicting human behaviour. Even though some think they can, available evidence shows that we can't."

"I know." Celia could not keep the disappointment from her voice. "But if you were in my situation, what would you do?"

"I'd take some precautions. Just in case."

Celia did not want to reveal to Franci what precaution she was thinking of taking. She walked on up the driveway without speaking. But as Franci unlocked the front door and Celia followed her inside, she realized that there was no point in holding back.

"José has offered to take her to Florida. To take us."

"Aye, yi yi!" Franci's hands flew to the top of her head as if to hold it in place. "Offered Liliana or offered you?"

"Me. I don't know if he mentioned it to her or not."

"If he did, that could change everything!"

"How?"

"Liliana might see that as the answer to this imagined problem—this notion that she's on the verge of being abandoned. She'd get to leave before everyone leaves her. Better yet, you'd come along so she wouldn't lose a thing."

"I am the one who would lose," Celia whispered, unable to stop the tears.

Franci embraced her the way they always embraced each other when faced with a challenge that seemed insurmountable. Countless times one or the other had said the words that went with that particular hug. Franci wasn't saying them now, nor, with Franci's arms around her, did Celia need to hear them. The hug said, I'm here for you, sister, but even if I wasn't you'd cope, because you're Cuban and Cubans don't give up.

That had been easier to believe when they were twenty years old. Now it helped but was not enough. Celia dropped onto the sofa and pulled Franci down beside her. "Surely you have some advice, Franci."

Franci stretched out long, jeans-clad legs and stared at her sandalled feet. Celia knew she hated giving advice because for a psychiatrist it wasn't the correct thing to do. But for a friend, when asked, it was. It would just take Franci a minute to give in to the demands of their friendship.

Finally Franci asked, "When is your next trip abroad?"

"México, in about two months."

"What if you took Liliana with you? She'll be out of school for the summer—"

"If I can even get her to go back," Celia muttered.

"Offer her a trip to México on the condition that she goes back and makes up the work she has missed."

"And that will fix everything?" Celia asked skeptically.

"It might not fix anything. But I get the feeling that she's tired of being depressed. Her natural energy is asserting itself. Didn't you notice that?"

Celia thought of lively way that Liliana had swirled about this very room in Franci's red skirt. "I did, yes."

"At the same time, there's this heaviness inside her." Franci balled her fist against her stomach, to suggest an undigested lump. "She doesn't feel good and doesn't want to go back to her old life feeling that way. It may take something new to inspire her."

"A trip abroad," Celia said in a flat voice.

"You don't like the idea?"

"I do not," Celia concurred. "And you know why."

"Because you don't like to travel."

"True. But what I like even less is that I cannot do it on my own. I would have to ask Luis for help getting travel documents and ask José for the money."

"I thought you said José already offered."

"He did. In fact, he suggested the same thing."

Franci looked surprised. "What?"

"That I 'cut a deal' with Liliana. Of course, he was talking about a trip to Miami, not México. And I am fairly certain he had me figured into his plan."

"I get the picture," Franci grimaced. "But you see what you're up against, don't you? José has already put the possibility into her head."

Celia sighed. "I think the possibility was already in her head. What he may have done is tell her that he could make it happen."

Franci got up and circled the small living room twice. Then stopped in front of Celia and said, "Okay. That's *his* game plan. But there's nothing to stop you from making a different one in which you take her to México and bring her home. So José buys the ticket, so what? If he can samba in and buy that convertible you were driving last time, I'd say he can afford it. If he offers you some cash for expenses in México, take that too. If he doesn't, well, there's plenty to do there that's practically free. She'll love it."

"I am sure she will," Celia said morosely, thinking that what Liliana would really love would be shopping in the Zona Rosa, which neither of them could afford.

Franci must have guessed her thoughts because she said, "Naturally she'll be dazzled by all the shops. But Liliana is a sensitive girl. Seeing rich people side by side with child beggars, that's going to make an impression on her too."

"I have to think about it," Celia said. "I do not know if José would buy her a ticket only to México, and I doubt Luis will go for it at all. I just do not know."

"Incredible!" Franci shook her head wonderingly. "We've known those Lago boys all our lives and don't have a clue what they'll do. It just goes to show how much there can be that you don't know about people you've known forever."

SEVENTY-NINE

JOE woke early, as he always did. Luis lay in the twin bed opposite, barely an arm's length away. Both brothers slept nude, had since their teens. So Luis was now, belly down, sheet tangled around his waist. The deep sleep wasn't surprising, considering that he hadn't come in until four in the morning.

Joe had asked him, at the end of the fishing trip, if he would like to join some of them for dinner. Luis had not given him an answer right off, but had gone into the marina restaurant to place a phone call. Then he begged off, claiming a previous engagement. Joe figured it was just an excuse, since Luis seemed to have no social life other than a Sunday morning chess club. He did frequently go out at night for job-related meetings, but not on weekends. Joe concluded that Luis refused the invitation because he didn't want to leave the impression that he was into a modern version of La Dolce Vita, as some Cuban bureaucrats were nowadays, frequenting top restaurants and resorts at the expense of capitalists seeking to set up joint ventures.

Joe got up quietly and moved sideways between the beds so as not to bump Luis's arm, which dangled over the side. Luis's clothes were piled on the floor, except for the white shirt he had been wearing, which hung on the bedpost. Joe noticed the shirt and bent for a closer look. Lipstick? But Celia was in Santiago. Anyway, she didn't wear lipstick. He suppressed a chuckle, and thought, Why, you old dog! You grabbed a piece of ass last night. I oughta throw your shorts against the wall to see if they stick.

Still grinning, Joe picked up his own clothes and tiptoed to the bathroom. If Luis had another woman, that put a different light on things. It might explain why he couldn't get a clear reading as to how Luis felt about helping arrange a trip for Liliana.

Coffee was waiting in the new electric percolator, but Alma must have gone to early Mass because she was not around. Joe poured a cup and went out onto the porch. From a wooden rocker that had been there as long as he could remember, he watched the street coming alive, slowly because it was Sunday morning. The sun just touched spires and turrets of the shabby mansions. Their faded colours were pleasant to the eye and the sounds that escaped from inside were soft and unhurried.

Joe rocked, sipped coffee, and reviewed the previous day, measuring what he thought had been accomplished against what he had set out to do. The hospital director had been evasive; Joe judged him to be more interested in donations from capitalists than in doing business with them. The minister of health seemed less interested in Joe's product line than in his willingness to provide stuff on credit. The bio-tech researcher he considered a potential friend. At dinner they had discussed the man's rather fascinating area of cancer research, which had been on the verge of becoming a joint effort with a US university until President Bush nixed it. The others, from Gaviota, Sherritt, and the US Interest Section, were not potential customers, just guys good to know on a first-name basis and to touch base with occasionally. He doubted that he would ever call upon any of them for more than an introduction to somebody else.

Then there was Luis. Joe would have bet the farm that he was brooding over Celia and bearing a grudge a mile deep for what he took to be Joe moving in on "his" woman. But the truth—or one version of the truth—had worked like a charm. Joe's lips twitched with amusement when he recalled the expression on Luis's face when he said he couldn't get within shouting distance of Celia without her frying him with a verbal blowtorch. He figured that only by convincing Luis that he, Joe, had no chance with her, would he get Luis's co-operation.

Joe considered himself a salesman, not a manipulator. He had never looked at the overlap between the two and if he had it wouldn't have bothered him. Since he only sold people things they needed or wanted anyway, what was wrong with nudging them along?

At the outset, when he was one more underpaid slang-speaking Latino immigrant in a sea of same, the only thing he'd had to sell was himself—a product he had finessed until he could promote it with pride. Next it was medical supplies for the asshole son of a Cuban banker who'd arrived in Miami with money back in the old days. By the time Joe came to work for the company, said heir was in the process of losing the family fortune with bad business decisions and futile Castro-bashing politics. When Joe knew the medical supply business well enough and had built up a good client list, he left, taking the list with him and starting his own company. Later he added a line of pharmaceuticals. And very soon, he would launch both right here in his native land.

That was the ten-year plan. But if he wanted a hand in raising his daughters he couldn't wait ten years. That was where Celia came in. The only blatant lie he had told Luis was that Celia would go to hell before she'd move to Miami. She'd move to Florida because she couldn't bear to let go of the last blood relative she had on earth—a girl who looked more like the sister she'd lost with every passing day. Once Celia got there, he'd make damn sure Miami worked out better for her than hell.

It came to him clear as a bell on that soft Sunday morning that the way to do it was to promise that it was only temporary. Maybe it would be. Next year or five years from now a US president would strap on some balls and terminate the travel ban. Then it wouldn't matter where they lived. They could set up housekeeping either place or both places and commute back and forth. His daughters would learn Spanish after all and could drive their mother fucking crazy talking to him and each other in a language *she* couldn't understand.

Joe left before Alma returned. He might have stayed for breakfast, then parked himself on the sofa and opened his laptop there in the chopped-in-half living room with naked cherubs peering down from the ceiling. But the light and his mental focus were better at Hotel Palco. He sent a few emails from the business office, then settled into one of the lobby's deep armchairs and proceeded to make notes on everything he could remember about the guys he had taken fishing the day before: what they drank, their wives' names, whether they had kids, and, most importantly, anyone they had indicated who might be helpful, plus anyone they had mentioned who might oppose the idea of buying medical supplies and pharmaceuticals from the States. The ones on that last list he would try to meet soon, to charm and disarm them before they threw up obstacles.

It was still a little early to go back to his mother's place for dinner so he did what he often did: drove the winding streets of Cubanacán to admire the mansions with their beautifully tended lawns. They were government properties now, rented to ambassadors and such to earn hard currency. That would change as soon as Castro died. Without the old hero at the helm, the Communist Party would rip itself to shreds with political infighting, while capitalists from within and without quietly took over the Cuban economy. That same day, if not well before, Joe Lago would be in line to buy one of these houses from whichever government agency got bit by the privatizing bug first.

Joe arrived home as dusk was descending. As he parked the convertible and climbed the cracked marble steps, he envisioned the living room lamp making a circle of light over his brother's newspaper, with smells of food that recalled his youth wafting from the kitchen. He pushed open the door and it was exactly as he had pictured it, except that Luis was already at the table, waiting like a child for the meal to be served. Alma, hearing Joe enter, called out, "There you are, mi hijo. Sit down. It's ready."

"Smells great, Mamá," He slid into his place feeling altogether mellow. Luis, he decided, looked less tightly wound than usual too. Nothing like getting laid to take the kinks out. He probably should do the same for himself before heading back across the pond. God knows there were enough good-looking women around.

It did occur to him to wonder who Luis had bedded. Even at age nineteen, when Luis was doing his two-year stint in the military, he had been too much the puritanical commie to approve of whoring—or so he implied in warning his younger brother against it. The warning was entirely unnecessary. From age fifteen onward Joe had been able to bed, if not always the girl of his choice, at least one of the ones he knew and liked. Later he noticed that Luis also went after women he knew rather than strangers. The difference was that Joe moved one hell of a lot faster.

At this point in their life, Celia was the only woman both of them wanted. Joe was pretty sure that Luis realized he had been permanently ditched, which was probably what precipitated his little adventure last night. That made Celia fair game but Joe wouldn't put a move on her yet. Timing was important and now was the time to do absolutely nothing that might cause her to retreat.

Alma sat down at the table, crossed herself, and began passing food. Joe and Luis dug into the sautéed malanga and congrí with good appetite. Alma was the first to speak. "I called Celia's place but there was no answer. I wonder when they are coming home."

Luis looked up quickly at Joe, then down again at his plate. There was something accusatory in the look that clued Joe to the fact that Luis knew he knew her schedule.

"They're getting in on the Tren Francés at six in the morning," Joe said casually. "Shall we drive to the station to meet them?"

Luis seemed nonplussed. "As long as it arrives on time," he said stiffly. "I wouldn't want to be late for work."

"I was told that if it's more than an hour late, the fare gets refunded," Joe said.

"Goodness!" Alma exclaimed. "There's a first! I don't remember when Cuban trains ever ran on time!"

"So?" Joe queried again "Do we form a welcoming party? Luis, you want to be in charge of balloons and banners?"

"Sure." Luis gave him a crooked smile, and Joe could see that whatever was gnawing on him had let go.

EIGHTY

CELIA was pleased to see Liliana return from the ballet in a good mood. She was still cheery on Sunday when Franci drove them to the station to catch the Tren Francés back to Habana.

"Pourquoi le Tren Francés?" Josephine wanted to know. "Il va à Haití?"

"No," Franci laughed. "It doesn't go to Haití. They call it the Tren Francés because it used to travel from Paris to Brussels. There are people in both those places who speak French, just as they do in Haití."

"Nous irons." Josephine announced. "Dans ce train."

"Yes, we'll go on this train someday," Franci promised. "We'll ride it to Habana to visit Liliana and Tía Celia. And you'll meet us at the station, won't you, Liliana?"

"Here, Josephine. Let me lift you up so you can get a better look at the train." Liliana pulled the smaller girl away from the adults and lifted her into the air.

Celia and Franci looked at each other, both aware that Liliana had not answered the question. The two women hugged one more time, then each reached for the hand of a child and went their separate ways.

Liliana became euphoric when she saw that their tickets were for Clase Primera Especial. She settled into the red vinyl seat with obvious satisfaction, and said, with a touch of defensiveness, "I *like* travelling like this."

"So do I," Celia admitted. "Now that the economy is improving, I expect the government will start upgrading all the island's trains and buses. Needs of tourists just had to be met first in order to get the foreign exchange to make other improvements."

"At the rate they're going that'll take the rest of my life," Liliana grumbled.

Celia could have pointed out that Cuba might have recovered from the economic collapse much sooner if so many talented, energetic Cubans had not opted to go abroad in order to get back into an economic comfort zone sooner rather than later. But given that José was one of the Cubans who had taken his healthy, well-educated self and run, with no sense of obligation to the nation that had provided those benefits, and she and Liliana were travelling on his foreign-earned dollars, Celia said nothing.

For the first hour of the trip, the train's smooth ride and semi-posh surroundings kept Liliana's spirits buoyed. However, when a conductor came by to ask whether they would care for drinks or dinner and Celia declined, Liliana became withdrawn. She spent the next hour staring out the window. When it was too dark to see anything of the passing scenery, Celia opened the bagged supper Franci had packed for them. Liliana ate, but with an indifference that made it plain that a bagged supper, no matter how lovingly prepared, was not nearly as satisfactory as dinner served by a white-jacketed waiter.

Liliana then toured their car and several others. She was gone a couple of hours. When Celia, on the pretense of going to the toilet, went looking for her, she discovered Liliana socializing with some young foreign travellers. She was relieved that Liliana had found a diversion and slightly uneasy that the diversion she sought was with foreigners.

There were also Cubans on the train about Liliana's age. Liliana could as well have struck up an acquaintance with them, but she had chosen foreigners. Had it not been for recent worries Celia would have been pleased to see Liliana practising her language skills on young people from other countries, as she was not all that fluent in French and barely spoke English at all. As it was, well—Celia shrugged and went back to her seat. What could Liliana do now that *wouldn't* cause her to worry?

When Liliana finally returned to her seat, she announced, "I met some girls from England. They're going to Trinidad."

"I went to Trinidad when I was looking for you," Celia said. "We should go there together sometimes. I have friends we could stay with." Celia glanced at Liliana for her reaction. She saw a spark of interest, followed by a weary expression. Then Liliana turned her face toward the black window and soon was nodding.

Celia slipped an arm around her and pulled her close. Unresisting, Liliana pillowed her head against Celia's chest. But the movement had wakened her. Constantly shifting positions told Celia that she was unable to get back to sleep.

"Would you like to hear a story about your parents?" Celia asked.

Liliana's face tilted up to look into hers. "What kind of story?"

"One you have never heard. One you were not old enough to hear before."

"Is it a happy story?"

"No. It is sad. Possibly the saddest story you will ever hear."

"Is that why you never told it before?"

"Yes, and because there are things in it a child would not understand but a nearly grown girl would."

"Then I want to hear it," Liliana said. Putting her back to the window, she turned sideways in the seat, pulled her knees up against her chest, and waited for Celia to begin.

"Just before you were born Carolina took maternity leave from the military. She remained on leave for a year. Your papá was away, stationed in Angola. Cubans went there to help the Angolans fight for their freedom, to help the government they'd elected stay in office, rather than be displaced by a warlord backed by the United States and South Africa."

"I know all that; we studied it in school," Liliana cut in. "But Papí and Mamí went to Angola together, didn't they?"

"That was later," Celia said. "First your father was there. He came home when the war ended."

"Wait a minute!" Liliana held up a hand as if to stop Celia from making a mistake. "You mean they weren't in the war? Wasn't that how they were killed?"

"Your father definitely was in the war. But your mother, no. She stayed in Habana with you. Then your father came home. It was like a honeymoon. They were both just ga-ga over you."

"You've told me that a hundred times," Liliana said impatiently. "But—"

Celia took a deep breath. "But there were problems."

"Like what?" Liliana narrowed her eyes, conveying a readiness to challenge anything that hinted at sugar-coating.

"Your father had had an affair while he was in Angola. Carolina was not a particularly jealous woman, but when she found out she took it pretty hard. Like our mother, she had lots of men friends and could have had lovers while he was away if she had felt like it. But for her, your coming changed everything. From then on nothing was ever about her, only about what was best for you. She thought risking her marriage was not in your best interest, and she felt betrayed that he hadn't felt the same way."

"*She* felt betrayed?" Liliana interrupted harshly. "She *left* me!"

"Yes," Celia said. "She did. But you might not feel so bad about it if you understood why she made that decision. It was only supposed to be a six-month assignment. And not a battlefield assignment because, like I said, the war was over. Her job was helping the Angola government organize records related to people who had been killed or wounded in the war, so they or their families could be compensated. Carolina was good at clerical stuff, not just running an office but setting up systems so information was easy to retrieve. The data was to be computerized. Back then, in the early 1990s, not many Angolans, or Cubans, for that matter, were computer-literate. Carolina was, so she was a natural for the assignment, and the army wanted to send her. But that was not why she went."

"Then why did she?" Liliana's face, open as that of a small child, kept changing, reflecting interest, then anger, then skepticism, and now uncertainty.

"Because your papá was going back. She talked to me a lot, about whether she should go or not. I can tell you, Liliana, it was not an easy decision for her. In the end, of course, she went. But not for career reasons. It was because she felt that to be separated from her husband again, for half a year, might cost their marriage. She did not want you growing up in a divided family. She was only eight when our papá died. She wanted to be sure yours was around. We both thought she was making the right decision. I promised that your grandmother and I would take good care of you. It was only for six months. The war was over. Carolina thought they would be coming back."

Celia stopped speaking, allowing Liliana time to digest this new version of her parental history and hoping she would not ask for the rest of the story. Of course she did.

"You said the war was over. But you and Tía Alma and everyone always said she was a soldier in Angola and—"

"A soldier in Angola, yes. But not in a war."

"Then how?" Celia could see Liliana's lips trembling. "How did my mamí die?"

"It was a Sunday. They borrowed a jeep to go to the beach. Even though the war was over, people did not venture out of town very often. But this was a well-used route so they thought it would be okay."

"You mean there was still fighting? Like guerrillas?"

"Well, yes, there was that because the United States was still funding the warlord and he was continuing to attack. But that was in another part of the country. There was no fighting around the capital. What made it unsafe to go into the countryside were land mines—tens of thousands planted during the war. The route your parents took was considered safe. But something . . ."

Celia was forced to quit speaking in order to hold on to her composure. So many times she had relived the last minutes of her sister's life, had smelled the dust rising up from the dirt road on that hot day, had seen African women and their children walking to town because it was early morning on a market day, had heard . . .

"A boy screamed. His goat had run out in front of the jeep. Your father swerved off the road to miss the goat and the boy. Not even two metres, just to the outside of a path that people used all the time. The tire went over a land mine. Six people walking along the path were injured. And your parents were killed."

For a moment Liliana sat perfectly still, swaying gently with the movement of the train. Then fell forward into Celia's chest and sobbed, "I thought they were war heroes."

"They were more than that." Celia spoke into her hair. "They went back for humanitarian reasons. Not to fight, but to help people who had suffered most in the war."

Liliana continued to sob, and although Celia trusted Franci implicitly she wondered if she had done the right thing. How could it be right to say anything that would cause a child such anguish?

Eventually the sobbing passed. Without raising her head Liliana asked, "Did they die right that minute?"

"No," Celia said. "They were—" She paused, unable to say, Their lower limbs were blown off; they bled to death in minutes. "Their injuries were terrible and they died very quickly because you see, there was no way to stop the blood. Your father was not conscious but your mother was, for the few minutes longer she lived."

"Was she screaming?" Liliana asked, which seemed to Celia an odd question. But she knew that however awful, Liliana needed to form a picture in her mind, just as she herself had needed to do when she first heard the news.

"No, she was not screaming. She would not have felt much, because the body goes into shock at a time like that. There is no pain. They said she kept repeating, 'Por favor, mi bebé. Mi bambino.' Begging people, in Spanish and in Portuguese, to take care of her baby. At first they thought there had been a baby with her in the jeep. Only later did they realize that she had meant her baby back home in Habana."

She held Liliana's head close to her chest, feeling the trembling aftermath of the girl's sobs. Celia kept wiping away her tears to keep them from falling into Liliana's hair, not wanting her to feel the wetness, or to look up and see her own enduring sadness.

But Liliana did look up. "It's all true, isn't it?"

"Yes," Celia murmured. "Would you rather I hadn't told you?"

Liliana shook her head. "Knowing is awful. But when you don't know you make up things that are worse."

EIGHTY-ONE

CELIA watched Liliana anxiously over the next two weeks, evaluating skin colour, energy level, moods, posture, and anything else that might provide clues to her mental and physical condition. Some days Liliana was pert and flippant, almost like her old self. Other days she became uncommunicative and retreated to her room. Celia called Franci every day but became exasperated when she realized that Franci was paying more attention to Celia's emotional needs than to Liliana's problems. Finally, in frustration, she screamed at Franci to give her one, just *one*, suggestion for how she might get Liliana to return to school.

There was a long silence on the line. Then Franci said, "Give a party."

"A party?" Celia echoed in disbelief. "What good is *that* going to do?"

"I expect she is still ashamed about what happened, and she is hiding from her peers. If you dunk her in a social situation, she'll discover that the water is not as cold as she imagines. It will have to be a surprise, of course."

Celia was too busy at work to arrange a party herself, so she appealed to Emily and Magdalena. They understood the purpose and planned with gusto. Magdalena got permission from her parents to host the party and recruited a hip-hop band made up of friends from Alamar. Magdalena also recruited José—something she informed Celia of only after the fact. José's role would be to bring the band members from Alamar to Magdalena's house in Cojímar, then go get the unsuspecting Liliana. When Celia got home from work, he would pick her up and bring her to the party.

Despite Celia's uneasiness over continued dependency on José, she had to smile at Magdalena's audacity in recruiting Mr. Me-First to play taxi for a swarm of teenagers.

By the time Celia got to the party things were well underway. To forestall complaints from neighbours, the entire neighbourhood had been invited. The street was cordoned off and filled with kids gyrating to music that Celia found totally alien. The only thing she had come to see, and did see, was Liliana dancing. From all appearances she was having a wonderful time. Celia stayed as long as she could bear the overamplified music, then asked José to take her home.

She was grateful when he did not make a pass at her, and more so when he said he would go back and keep an eye on the party to make sure things didn't get out of hand. There was little possibility of that, since all of Magdalena's family—siblings, parents, and grandparents—were in attendance. Nevertheless Celia was surprised and charmed by a level of thoughtfulness she still found it hard to believe was in José's nature.

At two in the morning Magdalena phoned (waking Celia up, of course), to inform her excitedly, "It worked! Lili promised *everybody* she'd be back in school on Monday!" Celia hung up and fell asleep, the first sound, trouble-free sleep she had had in weeks.

The next day, Celia at the computer and Liliana humming in her room as she put together the things needed for school the following morning, José called. He said he would be heading back to Miami in a few days and wanted her to know that Luis had agreed to get the documents Liliana needed for the trip to México. Liliana deduced from Celia's end of the conversation that José was leaving and shouted from her room, "Ask him to leave the convertible with us again!"

Celia ignored her, but José must have heard because he asked, "Shall I leave the car with you? It's only in the way at Mother's place."

"No," Celia said. "Absolutely not."

At which point Liliana said loudly, "Our life is *boring*, Tía. Boring! I'd rather be *dead* than live such a boring life!"

"Let me speak to her," José said sharply, and Celia knew he had overheard that too. She motioned Liliana to the telephone.

José did all the talking. All Liliana said, twice, was, "Really?" She hung up with a beatific smile and told Celia, "He's going to bring me a present from Miami. A surprise."

That evening Celia called Franci to let her know that the party had been a success. Philip answered the telephone. "Tell her yourself," he said with a smile in his voice. "She's on her way to Habana right now."

"Oh!" Celia was dismayed. "I can't take off work tomorrow! I won't be able to meet her at the station!"

"She didn't expect you to. She has other things to do in the city. If you're not at home when she arrives, a neighbour can let her in."

Franci was in the apartment when Celia got home from work. Clad in shorts and tank top, she was sprawled in front of the television, eating chunks of pineapple from a bowl. She grinned and held the bowl out to Celia. "Hola, hermana. Want some supper?"

Celia kicked off her shoes and slid down beside her. She accepted the pineapple bits and polished them off. "Um. Have I ever told you what a good cook you are?"

"No, but I remembered what a bad one you are, so I brought my own snacks. I hear the party was a smashing success."

"Totally! Liliana left for school this morning without a whimper. You are a miracle worker, Franci!"

"What was the point of all those years of shrink training if I can't pull a miracle out of the hat once in a while?" Franci replied lightly.

"I never would have thought of a party. But you were so sure—"

"Not at all. That's why I came. In case it didn't work out and you needed help."

"Ay, Franci! What a friend! Who told you it went well?"

"José, whom I called and asked to meet me at the station."

"You did?" Celia was surprised. Franci had never been particularly fond of José.

"Why not? He's got a car and no job—at least, not while he's in Cuba. I knew you'd be at work, so it was a good time to visit friends in the old neighbourhood."

Celia gave her a narrow look. "And you wanted to check out the new Yanqui version of José Lago to see if he has what it takes to snare me again."

Franci looked sheepish, but rallied with a challenging, "So? Somebody's got to evaluate your prospects."

"My *prospects*?"

"Ex-fiancé pining away for you, ex-ex fiancé trying to lure you to Miami, and now you tell me—or did you forget you told me?—you met a new guy in Manzanillo. Who, I couldn't help but notice, sent you home limp as a noodle." Franci reached up with her toes and turned down the volume on the television. "Sounds like 'prospects' to me."

Celia was silent, sorting through the implications of what Franci had said. She had been so preoccupied with Liliana and work that Miguel had scarcely crossed her mind. At last she said, "I didn't meet him in Manzanillo. I met him at the Comandancia."

"Aren't you the cool one!" Franci exclaimed. "So is this something serious?"

"I wanted to fall in love," Celia confessed. "I thought I did. But it was not real."

Franci clicked her tongue disapprovingly. "You're talking nonsense, girl. You don't fall or not fall in love with somebody that quickly. Not past the age of twenty anyway."

"No, but you can tell when something you need is not there."

"Such as?"

"Look, Franci, you've seen me through all my romantic entanglements. You know I was passionate about José—back then, anyway. And I truly care about Luis. He is a good, socially responsible person. But what I *need* is somebody whose mind I can get into and vice versa. There was a brief moment when I thought this new person might be the one. But it was a . . . hallucination. I imagined it because it was what I wanted."

"Are you sure about that?" Franci asked gently.

Celia rubbed her temples with her fingertips. "Franci, I am working fourteen and fifteen hours a day, trying to get something done that, if the work is good enough, might push the government into developing policies that will prevent the suffering of millions of children. I have a child of my own who is far from well. I don't even *want* a man in my life now. I couldn't handle it."

Franci put a hand on Celia's neck and began to massage the iron-tight muscles. "So it's not that this new guy was wrong; it's that you dropped him without finding out?"

Celia allowed her head to flop forward in response to the soothing pressure of Franci's fingers. Recalling her last moments with Miguel on the train, she said, "To be honest, I think he dropped me. But just as well. I need to get things clear in my own head before I start looking for somebody with a mind to match."

Franci toes went to the TV volume control again, this time to turn it up. Luis was being interviewed about Cuba's alternative energy potential.

"Intelligent guy," Franci murmured when the interview ended.

Celia took her point. "Yes, but it's not just about being intelligent. It's about underlying premises. The ability to make connections. And . . ." She hesitated. "It's about me thinking for myself, not letting somebody I admire do all the work."

"'Miami Joe' is willing to do all the work. Or not, as you please. He told me so."

Celia grimaced and with her own toes turned the volume on the television down again. "One thing you can say for José, he is not sneaky. What you see is what you get."

Franci gave her an arch look. "I wouldn't be so sure about that. Everybody's got something under wraps." She jabbed Celia in the ribs. "Even you, girl. Sleeping with a stranger under my very nose!" She paused and considered. "Or was he a stranger?"

"Oh, yes." Celia assured her. "He was a stranger. Strange as a wild animal. And very likely to stay that way."

EIGHTY-TWO

LUIS and Emily spoke on the telephone almost daily during the three weeks of each month that school was in session. During the last week of the month, when students went home, Emily returned to her parents' home too. Because her family lived in Las Cañas, a suburb on the south side of the city, their outings were usually in that area. They spent a day at ExpoCuba, one at the Jardín Botánica, and despite their views on Hemingway, visited Finca Vigía, the writer's former estate. Most of their time, though, was spent in Parque Lenin. They strolled through the woods, went rowing on the lake, and visited the small aquarium and art gallery. Once, they rented horses, and although neither was an experienced rider they managed to walk sedately along the park's shady paths and return to the equestrian centre without mishap. They even went to the Sánchez museum, but its exhibits were so sparce that Luis couldn't imagine why Celia had bothered to go there more than once.

Since Luis could not very well make love to Emily in her parents' home or his, the motel in Parque Lenin where he used to take Celia once a year was where he now took Emily. He felt odd about it, but Motel La Herradura was convenient and Emily was unlikely to find out that he had ever brought another woman there.

Afterwards, if it was a rainy night, he and Emily might cross the motel parking lot to Restaurante Ciclista, named for a famous Cuban racehorse. On nice evenings Luis chose a less expensive outdoor café nearby. There they sat for hours in balmy night air. Emily sometimes chattered nervously and sometimes was shyly quiet, but she always hung on his every word.

She regularly reported on how Liliana was doing at school. "Not quite herself," Emily had confided the first week. "Less confident than she used to be. That may be because she is behind in her studies. I expect she will feel better once she catches up."

The following weekend, as they sat on the shore of the park's little lake watching children fly kites, Emily told him, "She is still withdrawn. Dark circles under her eyes, you know, as if she's not sleeping well."

And later, "She was quite keen on this boy Danilo before her . . . her time away. He is still interested in her, crazy about her, really. But when they meet, often right under my window at the far end of the building, he now does most of the talking. She is so much quieter than before. It does seem like she has other things on her mind."

"What about her dorm mates?" Luis asked. "Does she have many friends?"

"Oh yes. Especially Magdalena. Surprising, really. Of all the girls in the school, I would say that Magdalena is the one she has least in common with."

As Emily described Magdalena's in-your-face behaviour and penchant for gaudy fingernails and bizarre hairstyles, Luis recognized her as the same awful girl who had insulted him at the campismo, the one who had called him "Dumpee Number Two." Recalling the incident so infuriated him that Emily laid a hand on his cheek and asked timidly if she had said something to upset him. He assured her that she had not, but remarked darkly that if that was who Liliana had chosen for a confidante, her aunt could expect more problems in the not-so-distant-future.

Because Emily seemed both sympathetic and genuinely interested, Luis revealed more about himself than he had to any other woman: how he had been forced to assume many family responsibilities at an early age because of his father's injuries, and how that sense of responsibility had increased with the death of his father, and still more when his brother turned gusano, leaving him alone to look after their mother.

He also talked politics with her, explaining why he believed that socialism, with its emphasis on providing a safety net for the weak, was the only moral political system. "But the state can only meet material needs," he said gravely. "It is the responsibility of family and community to meet the emotional needs of their members, don't you agree?"

More than simply agreeing, Emily understood how it applied to him personally. She conveyed as much by saying, "It would be terrible for your mother if you moved out, when you are the only person she can depend on."

Gradually they reached an understanding of each other's needs that surpassed any understanding he had ever had of Celia's needs or, he believed, her of his. As weeks went by Luis told Emily many things—but not that he been engaged to Celia Cantú, and not that he had applied for permission for Liliana to travel abroad.

It took Luis less time than he expected to get the visa required for Liliana to accompany Celia to México. It was José who broached the idea, soon after Celia's return from Santiago. "Franci told Celia it would be good therapy," José had said. "Personally, I disagree. México City is not the safest place for Liliana to be unchaperoned, which she'll obviously be during the day while Celia is at the conference."

However, Luis respected the opinions of professionals. Because Franci had advised it—and because José said he didn't like the idea—Luis decided to do what he could to arrange it. He went to Quevedo and explained the situation. He described Liliana's apparent suicide attempt and said that if the captain wanted medical verification, he could call Dr. Franci Cumba, head of the psychiatric department at the Santiago medical school. With a disdainful smile, Luis added, "My gusano brother is willing to pay Liliana's travel expenses. Celia dislikes him as much as she dislikes travelling. But for Liliana's sake . . ."

Quevedo nodded understandingly, and in a stunningly short amount of time had arranged with the necessary departments to issue the visa and other travel documents.

The Friday Luis picked up the last of Liliana's travel documents, he waited until five in the afternoon, by which time Liliana would have arrived home from school, and drove to the apartment. Passing through the lobby he saw that Celia's bike was not there and guessed that she was still at work. Just as well. He wanted to get this over with as quickly as possible, go home, shower, and drive to La Caña to pick up Emily.

336

He knocked twice on the apartment door, feeling the mixture of annoyance and humiliation he always felt when it was not immediately opened to welcome him. He turned the knob and finding it not locked, pushed it open and called testily, "Liliana!"

There was silence, followed by a small noise in the kitchen. Liliana appeared in the doorway between kitchen and living room. She looked nothing like the rebellious teenager who had defied him prior to her disappearance, or the battered one he had seen only twice since. Still wearing her school uniform, but barefoot, she seemed small. Her skirt revealed not the well-muscled legs of an active teenager, but the thin white legs of a child. He was shocked by the amount of weight she had lost.

"Tía Celia's not here," she said in a frightened voice.

Although Luis had nothing to be ashamed of, Liliana's fear filled him with shame. "I have something for you," he said gruffly.

"Are you alone?" She edged out of the kitchen, eying the door as if she might make a dash for it if she could be sure that there weren't monsters lurking in the hallway.

"For God's sake, Liliana! Do you want these travel documents or not?" he snapped, settling himself on the sofa and opening his briefcase on the coffee table.

"Really? Oh, Tío Luis!"

The use of tío recalled a younger Liliana, one whom he had really cared about. It hinted at renewed trust—trust that he, with the best of intentions, had almost destroyed.

Liliana went down on her knees on the opposite side of the coffee table and with shaking hands received the visa and other pertinent papers he handed across to her. She handled and read them with more reverence than Alma showed for her religious icons.

Perhaps Luis should not have taken advantage of what seemed to be a moment of receptiveness, but he had, after all, gone far out of his way to get the documents. She owed it to him to at least listen. "Cuba is not a rich country, Liliana. After spending hundreds of thousands of dollars on each child, ensuring that they have the very best health care and education, I hope you realize how hard it is on everybody when young people leave the country without giving anything back."

Liliana looked up at him sharply. "What do you mean?"

What Luis had meant, although he was not about to explain, was that he did not expect her to bolt in México but it would not surprise him if she defected later, after she had got a university education—especially if she kept hanging around with trash like that Magdalena girl. He shrugged. "Nothing. I was just making a point."

Liliana's eyes narrowed, and in a split second he was facing not a frightened child but a challenging teenager. "So what's your point? That I'm a traitor just because I want to travel? Then Fidel's one too! He's been all over the world! And everybody knows José Martí lived in New York. And what about Che? If he hadn't started travelling he never would've become a revolutionary. He'd have been a boring old Argentine doctor nobody ever heard of!"

"That may be true," Luis began in a reasonable tone, "but not everybody—"

"Not *everybody* likes being penned up on this island like, like Raúl's prize cows!" she interrupted rudely. "Oh, it's great for you and Tía Celia. You get to go abroad almost every year. Even if it does take Tía Celia about a month to do all the paperwork."

Luis was tempted to remind the ungrateful brat that *he* had spent weeks getting *her* travel documents, and there probably weren't ten people in government who had the connections to do it so quickly. He swallowed the retort. He had not, after all, done it for her. He had done it for Celia. Or perhaps because it was the right thing to do. Celia could deny it if she wished, but the fact remained that Cuba's children belonged to Cuba, and as such, they were a collective responsibility. If a vacation in México was what it took to remove the threat of suicide, then like any other form of therapy, it should be provided.

"Naturally we have to get official approval. The state pays our expenses," he said in defence of government policies. But he knew that there was truth in her complaint that citizens were required to run a gauntlet of red tape in order to travel abroad.

"The state is not paying *mine*," Liliana reminded him.

Reminding Luis, also, that although there was no way she could have jumped the queue and got the documents without his help, José, who paid the fees and bought the ticket would get all the credit. Luis snapped shut his briefcase and headed for the door.

Liliana called after him with a half-hearted, "Gracias, Tío."

He did not bother to reply.

EIGHTY-THREE

CELIA called the next day to thank Luis. She was thankful not only for the trouble he had taken, but for simply giving the papers to Liliana and not using them as an excuse to see her. For she understood now, as she had not in the past, that that had been the pattern: Luis unobtrusively piling favour on top of favour until she was unable to refuse him the intimacies he desired. This, she hoped, would be the last great favour she would need or accept from him.

A week before their scheduled trip to México, Celia arrived home from shopping on a Saturday afternoon and found Liliana in her room stuffing things into large bags. She let out a mental shriek when she saw that it was the sexy jinetera clothing that had precipitated their crisis. For months the stuff had lain on the closet floor where Celia dumped it after Liliana's disappearance. Celia had not suggested that she put it away or that she throw it out. She had waited to see what Liliana would do. Whatever it was, she was now doing it.

Liliana looked up and smiled. "Come on in," she invited. "I don't want this junk anymore. I'm giving it to Magdalena."

"That's nice." Celia sat down on Liliana's bed, trying not to imagine the use to which Magdalena might put the outfits.

"She'll be *so* surprised," Liliana chuckled. "But I'm *never* going to want to wear this garbage again." She held up a micro-miniskirt and looked at it critically. "Tacky," she pronounced.

Celia noticed several English-language fashion magazines lying on the bedside table. "Is this what José brought you from Florida?" she asked, flipping through one of them. Most of the girls in the ads had a wholesome look, and none of the fashions were as outrageous as the clothes Liliana was now treating like the trash they were.

"Yeah." Liliana plopped down next to Celia. "Here's an outfit I really like. And this one too." She paged through the magazine pointing out her favourites, all of which Celia thought showed reasonably good taste, and none of which could be purchased in Cuba without dollars—or even with, for that matter.

"Tía Alma called to invite us to dinner on Sunday. Can we go?"

"I don't know about dinner," Celia equivocated, knowing as she said it that a visit was necessary. She hadn't visited in weeks, and Alma would be hurt if she put it off much longer. "We could drop by for a couple hours tomorrow afternoon, though."

Celia tossed the magazine back on the nightstand, and as she did so, knocked some of Liliana's travel documents to the floor. She reached to pick them up. "We should get a folder to keep these in. Losing one could cause all kinds of problems."

Before Celia could lay hands on the scattered documents, Liliana scooped them out of her reach. "I'll take care of them," she said brightly as she patted them together and placed them in the top drawer of her dresser.

They arrived at the Lago apartment as planned on Sunday afternoon. Celia had not been there since her break-up with Luis, which gave the visit a deja vu quality. Years earlier, when her relationship with José terminated, she had stopped visiting the Lago home for a time. As the need for family grew, she had gradually started dropping by again. Then as now, there was a debt owed that she had no way of repaying.

Several bulbs were burned out in the high overhead chandelier, so that the cherubs on the arched ceiling flitted about in dim light that contrasted sharply with the living room's bright lower level. Luis sat in his usual rocking chair, reading *Granma*. He barely nodded, leaving Alma to welcome them.

"That's what I like to see!" Alma exclaimed, hugging Liliana then holding her out at arm's length. "Roses blooming in my girl's cheeks!"

José came out of the bedroom and greeted them casually. Liliana turned her cheek to him for a kiss, then deliberately walked over to Luis and presented a cheek to him, as she had been taught to do as a child. He kissed the air next to it and without speaking, went back to his newspaper. He was, Celia saw, irritated about something. José must have seen it too because he motioned them toward the sofa and said, with rather too much cheerfulness. "Sit down, sit down. Where's the coffee, Mamá?"

"What do you mean, where's the coffee? Since when do I need reminding to serve coffee to my own guests? You want it on the table quicker, go tell your fancy coffee maker to perk faster!" Alma scolded, but smiled as she headed for the kitchen.

"Wait!" Liliana grabbed Alma by the hand. "Sit down, Tía Alma. I have something to tell you. All of you. Something really exciting."

"Ha! You think I can't hear everything that goes on in this house from my kitchen?" Alma protested. But she allowed Liliana to lead her to a chair at the old wooden dining table.

"Ven, Tío Luis and Tío Joe. Tía Celia?" Liliana looked beseechingly at her aunt.

Celia moved toward the table uneasily, having glimpsed something in Liliana's eyes that contradicted her gaiety.

Only when the other four were seated did Luis, with the air of a busy adult being asked to participate in a child's tea party, lay aside his newspaper and join them.

"As you know," Liliana said, "this time next week, Tía Celia and I will be on our way to México. That's because Tío Luis"—here she paused and blew a kiss across the table to Luis—"got me a visa."

Celia barely had time to wonder why she hadn't simultaneously thanked José when Liliana continued, "And Tío José has bought me a ticket to *Miami*."

All faces swivelled toward José. "You *what*?" Celia gasped.

"Like she said, I gave her a ticket to Miami. In addition to the one to México."

"Behind my back!" Celia shrieked.

"*Not* behind your back," Liliana and José responded in unison.

"He made me promise to tell you," Liliana said. "So I'm telling you, Tía. Telling all of you."

"That was the deal," Jose explained. "I'd get her a ticket—and it's a round-trip ticket, by the way—but she had to work the rest out with you. Which as far as I can tell is what she's trying to do."

Luis, who had taken the chair that had been his father's, gripped the wooden arms as if to keep from slugging his brother. "You treacherous bastard!" he hissed.

"No call to insult our mother," Joe snapped.

"You're the fucking insult! Is this what you came home for? Didn't do enough damage when you ran out on us? You have to destroy the family we have left?"

"I'll come back!" Liliana cried, clearly having not anticipated the turn things had taken. She grasped Celia's hand. "Tell them, Tía. I just want to . . . oh, don't any of you *understand*?"

Tears filled Liliana's eyes. Celia recognized them as not of manipulation but desperation. She did not think that she herself had ever wanted anything as badly as Liliana wanted this trip, unless it was for the notice of her own sister's death to not be true. But that was different, that was unattainable. What Liliana wanted, with a passion that none of them, with the possible exception of José, could understand, was a chance to travel abroad. The very thought of Liliana making such a trip terrified Celia. But even more terrifying was the gulf that she was certain would open between them if she should be the one to prevent it. In a voice so steady Celia could not believe it was her own, she said, "If Liliana says she will come back, she will."

Luis looked at Celia as if she was the biggest fool who ever lived. "From México maybe. But from Miami?" His mouth twisted into a sneer. "Or will *you* end up there?"

Celia knew the possibility, had looked long and hard at it before this moment. She squeezed Liliana's hand tightly, an unconscious promise, or plea, that they would not be separated. She looked beseechingly at Alma. "*Madrina!* Give her your blessing. Give us both your blessing. We will come home!"

"Let me give my blessing at your wedding," Alma begged. "To one of my sons!"

Celia sighed. "I will get the coffee." With that she got up from the table, leaving her niece to fend for herself. From the kitchen she could hear Liliana attempting to do just that. Surprisingly, she was doing a credible job of it under the circumstances.

"*Excuse* me!" Liliana wrapped her knuckles on the table as if bringing an unruly meeting to order. "*I'm* the one going. *Yo. Moi. Me.* So how come this is all of a sudden about Tía Celia?"

Another snarling expletive from Luis was followed by another rap on the table by Liliana. "Tío Luis, this is about *me*. So will you please stop bickering with Tío Joe?" She turned to Alma. "They are *so* dense! You'd think by now they'd have twigged to the fact that my *tía* is never going to marry either one of them."

"Why?" Alma wailed. "They are such good boys! The best!"

Celia served the demitasses of coffee, then laid a consoling hand on Alma's shoulder. "They are, Alma, and I love them both."

"Yet you won't choose! Why, mi hija? Why?"

Celia sat down without attempting to answer. Then she saw that Liliana, Alma, Luis, and José were all looking at her, waiting for a reply to exactly that question. Staring into her steaming coffee, Celia said softly, "They do not know who I am."

"Corazón de Jesús!" Alma stood up, anger stanching her sobs. "How can they? Did Saint Joseph know he was betrothed to the mother of Jesus? There is not a man alive who knows a thing about women!"

Alma stomped into the kitchen and returned with spoons, which she practically flung onto the table. She sat down and stirred an excessive amount of sugar into her coffee, clinking metal against the china cup until it was in danger of breaking.

"I'm ashamed of you kids!" she shouted. "Middle-aged you are and still believing in fairy tales!" She glared at Luis. "Communism!" And at José. "Capitalism!" And at Celia. "Romantic love! May La Virgen help you all!"

José rolled his eyes at Luis. "You hear that, hermano? She calls on the Virgin every second breath, and *we're* the ones hooked on fairy tales!"

For once, José's trick of defusing Alma's anger with humour did not work. Pointing a spoon at him, Alma hissed, "Just wait till you are on your death bed and see how much comfort your money and political 'truths' bring you. And you!" She aimed the spoon at Celia, "When you're an old lady, alone with your romantic nonsense!"

Liliana laid her head on Alma's shoulder. "Let's go to church tonight, Tía."

"Preciosa! You have more sense in one curl than the lot of them!" Alma stroked the girl's hair with a trembling hand, apparently having forgotten that it was Liliana's startling announcement that started the whole thing.

"No need to act like she's going to the moon," José said to the table at large. "It's just a trip, for God's sake. I travel all the time. Celia, Luis, so do you. The only thing unusual about this one is that it's Liliana's first. So how about we celebrate? Would you like a going-away party, Liliana? Not like that bash at Magdalena's, but you know, just family? Dinner at one of the new hotels, maybe?"

Celia did not catch Liliana's answer because at that moment Luis leaned across the table and snarled at her, "Do you really expect me to go along with this?"

Celia knew that whether Liliana would be allowed to leave Cuba would depend on what Luis decided to do—and that in turn would depend on her answer. It was a long moment before she answered.

"Trust," she said softly, "is all we have left. If we stop trusting each other, what else is there?"

There was a stillness, as if everyone was holding breath, waiting for a vibration that would reveal what Luis would do. Looking into his eyes, Celia saw that he himself did not know.

It was José who spoke. "Face it, Luis. Our charming niece has a mind of her own. And from all appearances, not a socially responsible bone in her body."

Luis laughed ruefully. From that laugh, Celia guessed that whether Luis knew it yet or not, he would not prevent Liliana from leaving.

Liliana, apparently confused by what she took to be a compliment followed by insult, moved her chair closer to Alma. Alma patted her hand and whispered something, probably words meant to reassure them both, and which seemed to do just that.

Celia picked up her coffee and walked to the window, unable to see the view for her tears. She did not know if the trip would be the right thing or the wrong thing for Liliana. She only knew what it could mean for her if Liliana should fail to return.

EIGHTY-FOUR

LUIS stood at the top of the cracked marble steps and watched as his brother backed the convertible out of the narrow space into the street. Luis could not have expressed his feelings as the gusano knight, not on a white horse but in a canary-yellow convertible, carried his former fiancée and her niece off into the sunset. Part of it was emptiness because, in truth, Luis could not remember a time when he did not want Celia Cantú. Yet there was relief too, as if he had been freed from the responsibility of doing something that was simply beyond his ability.

Of course it helped that there was Emily. He was still annoyed that Alma had insisted he be at home this afternoon when Celia and Liliana came to visit, as that had required him to drive Emily back to the school early, where she probably was as lonely in her room as he felt standing here on the steps of his family's home.

To erase the memory of Celia's firm buttocks under the worn denim of her bottom-tight jeans that lingered after she walked past him down the steps, he deliberately conjured an image of Emily's fragility. But it was not their physical difference that, for Luis, made all the difference. It was Emily's transparency. She explained herself in a shy yet straightforward way, but Luis didn't need the words to read her doubts, her delights, and, above all, how she felt about him.

He had never been certain of Celia's thoughts on any subject. He did not even understand her mental process. A lifetime of being around her, two years of which they had been on the most intimate terms, and he was still without a clue as to what she felt. Perhaps that was the attraction of Celia Cantú, why men as different as himself and José had gone after her in the first place. That air of mystery was so powerful that even now he was not released from the desire to know what was going on inside her.

As these half-formed thoughts and convoluted feelings swirled in Luis's head, he wandered out onto the street. It was really the only place to go, since he was not about to go back into the house where Alma would be kneeling before her altar to the Virgin, praying for the only thing she ever prayed for: the safety and unity of the family. Luis would never comprehend the triple deception that sustained her: the notion that she, little Alma, could call forth the grace of a non-existent god to protect a family that was a mere pseudo-family to start with, and which, after today, would have no more connection to theirs than palm fronds ripped from the trunk and blown out to sea by a hurricane.

A child batted a tattered softball in his direction. Luis caught it automatically and whipped it to the pitcher. The boy grinned and gave him a thumbs-up. He returned the gesture and walked on. At the end of the block, two neighbours were struggling to unload a sofa from a truck. Luis saw the need for another man and rushed forward. He helped them lower the sofa and lent muscle to the task of lugging it up an unlit stairwell to the apartment for which it was intended.

Minutes later, back on the street, one of the men called down to him from the balcony. "Amigo, you forgot something."

Luis looked up. The apartment owner was holding a can of beer, unopened. Although it was a clear invitation for him to join them on the balcony, Luis held up his hands. The guy read his signal and tossed the beer down to him.

Luis held the can away from himself to avoid the foam when he popped the top. He took a swallow, saluted his neighbour, and walked on. By the time he had walked a block the beer had been drunk and the can deposited onto a raked pile of garbage that a truck would pick up someday, whenever the gasoline supply permitted. He stopped at a kiosk and ordered a shooter of rum. Luis was not ordinarily a drinker. But this was not an ordinary day.

"Hola, Luis," greeted a neighbour standing at the outdoor bar. "Did you watch the game last night?"

"Didn't everybody?" Luis replied, although he actually had not because he had been with Emily. "What did you think of it, Alfonso?"

"It must gall the Yanquis that with twenty-five times Cuba's population they can't field a team to match ours," Alfonso crowed.

"Sometimes they do," chimed in a man Luis didn't know.

"Yeah, but we cleaned their clock at the Olympics," Alfonso gloated as if he personally had scored the winning run. "And we'll do it again at the Pan Am Games."

"Not if we keep losing players," Luis muttered. He swirled his rum and took another sip, noticing, not for the first time, that he didn't like the taste. "I wonder how many gusanos end up coming home."

"A lot," Alfonso said thoughtfully. "But ordinary people. Probably not that many who get their hands on big money."

"Money, shit!" Luis slammed his empty shot glass on the bar. "How can a man put a price on his country? It's like putting a price on yourself. 'Pay me and I'll be somebody else.'" He signalled to the bartender for a refill for the three of them. "They sell their fucking soul."

The bartender poured each another shot. Luis lifted his in a toast. "Viva Cuba!"

"Viva Cuba!" echoed the others.

EIGHTY-FIVE

JOE finished stowing Liliana's bundles in the trunk and put the top down on the convertible, knowing it would please the girls. When he slid behind the wheel, they squeezed into the front seat next to him.

"This is such a cool máquina," Magdalena cooed.

"Joe is a cool tío." Liliana cut her eyes at him and he grinned back, acknowledging both the compliment and her claim to a special relationship.

They had not gone more than two kilometres along the waterfront road when they passed four teens coming down the hill from the Estadio Panamericao. "Look!" screamed Magdalena. "It's Danilo and Osmani and—"

"Ymildeida and Yipsi!" Liliana finished. "Stop, Tío!"

Joe applied the brakes and backed up so the girls could chat with their friends. Or so Liliana could show off him and the car, which appeared to be the purpose of the stop. All four teens—two slender Latino boys with well-muscled calves and two tall black girls—were coming from workouts at the stadium.

"Jump in," Liliana invited. "We'll give you a lift. Right, Tío?"

One boy came to the driver's side and put out his hand. "You must be Liliana's tío from Florida. She told us about you. I'm Danilo Silva. Welcome home, compañero."

"Nice to meet you." Joe shook the boy's hand, pleased to be called compañero for the first time since his return to Cuba.

The other three followed Danilo's lead, each shaking hands before piling into the back seat amid the girls' giggling pleasure, masked by fake complaints, at being squished together in such close physical proximity.

"Where are you headed?" Joe asked over his shoulder.

"To the bus stop," one of the girls answered. "But we're going to hang out in Cojímar for a while first. You can let us out anywhere."

Joe glanced into the rear-view mirror. He could tell from the way they were relishing the rush of wind through their hair that they were having more fun right this minute than anything they might have planned to do in Cojímar. How many decades had it been since North American kids got a thrill out of a simple car ride with an adult at the wheel? On impulse he called back to them, "Where's a good place for ice cream?"

Several suggestions were thrown out, but he drove to where he had intended to go when he asked the question, a small shop a block from Hotel Panamericano that he had noticed the day he picked up snack foods for Celia and Liliana to take on the bus.

The boys pushed together two tables at the sidewalk café and Joe went inside to order the ice cream. As he waited what seemed an interminable length of time for the simple order to be filled, he looked through the plate glass window to the table where six high-energy teens were trying to sit but seemed physically incapable of doing so. The girls laughed and dodged as the teasing became physical. Osmani picked up Magdalena, carried her to the railing, and made as if to drop her onto the street a few feet below. Others rushed to her aid, and the girl called Yipsi, who was taller than Osmani by a head, picked him up and made as if to drop *him* over the railing.

Joe was so caught up in the scene, their exuberance reminding him so much of his own teen years with Celia, Carolina, Franci, Joaquín, and others in their neighbourhood, that the clerk had to nudge him to let him know the dishes of ice cream were on the counter, melting quickly in the afternoon heat.

"Thanks," Joe said, but stood there a moment longer, watching the kids, thinking, There's one thing wrong with that picture. There ought to be two pretty blond teenagers named Keri and Amy right in the middle of it.

He motioned for help in carrying the ice cream, then sat down at the table with the kids. It occurred to him that in the ten years since leaving Cuba, he probably hadn't spent thirty minutes in the company of teenagers. What surprised him about their babble was that none of it was about recent purchases or things they wanted to buy. This puzzled him. Even his four-year-old, in a five-minute phone conversation, would have mentioned something she wanted or had just acquired. His girls' most animated moments revolved around receiving gifts. Surely there were things these Cuban teens wanted to own; they were, after all, human.

Not withstanding the fact that Liliana had just given away everything she'd bought for herself in the past six months, there was, he knew, a strong current of acquisitiveness in her nature. And from what he had seen of Magdalena's home, her family was extremely possession-oriented. Yet none of them brought up the subject of having or buying. The theme—if there was a theme to their chatter—was people. The athletes exchanged views on how well others at their workouts had performed, or would perform in upcoming competitions. Magdalena went on at some length about the intrigue involved in keeping Liliana's surprise party secret and a guy in the hip-hop band she had dated since. Liliana went off on a thread about the school secretary, of all people, saying how Emily knew who met whom at night and stayed out past curfew, but you could trust her not to pass on things that might get you into trouble.

After half an hour Joe's interest in Liliana's friends flagged, so he took them to the bus stop, drove Magdalena to her house, and dropped Liliana back at Celia's. Then he headed home to dress for what he privately called Liliana's "maiden voyage" dinner.

But all the way back to Vedado he kept thinking about kids. Or more particularly, his kids and what it would be like for them to spend time on this side of the Florida Straits. It was not the first time he'd had such thoughts. However, in the past he had envisioned them at their present age, even though getting them over here anytime soon was a near impossibility. Now he found himself thinking of what Cuba would seem like to them, and they to other Cubans, if they were Liliana's age. Try as he might, he could not quite wrap his head around that.

Amy and Keri weren't athletic; not that they were old enough to exhibit talent in a particular sport, but Vera would certainly have them both in tennis lessons within the next year or so. Plus piano, plus dance. Then what? What did kids *do*, anyway? Whatever his kids learned to do in the course of their carefully controlled, thoughtfully guided, expensively purchased activities over there, would those activities translate to the relaxed, hang-out-on-the-beach and dance-till-dawn, make-your-own-fun activities he had enjoyed as a teen and that still seemed to be the norm for Liliana and her crowd?

Joe shook his head and decided to give it a rest. By the time his girls were Liliana's age, Washington's political razor wire would have come down and within five years of that Cuba would be culturally interchangeable with south Florida. The issue wasn't whether it was a good thing or a bad thing. It was simply—or not so simply—the world *his* girls would grow up in.

EIGHTY-SIX

JOE found Luis sitting on the bed half-dressed, holding a shoe in one hand. Considering the poor quality of the shoe, Joe could understand why a man might look glum, but he suspected that in Luis's case that wasn't the reason. He said hello and headed for the shower. When he came out ten minutes later, Luis was still sitting there, the only difference being that now the shoe was on his foot.

"Been sucking on a lime to get yourself in a party mood?" Joe needled as he pulled a dress shirt out of the cramped wardrobe.

"What, am I supposed to be happy with this crap you and Liliana cooked up?"

There was no answer to that that Joe could think of, so he put on his shirt and started buttoning it. Luis watched his fingers as if he was trying to figure out how his brother managed so complex a task. Luis seemed like a man betrayed, and when he spoke again, that was how he sounded. "You think that with Liliana in Miami, you can get Celia there to marry you."

"Yeah?" Joe countered. "Maybe you helped with the visa because you figure that with Liliana gone, Celia will get lonely enough to marry *you*."

Luis looked so ashamed that Joe took pity on him. He sat down on the bed opposite. "Ah, quit guilt-tripping, Luis. You know that's not why you did it. Not why I did what I did either."

"Then *why?*" Luis asked in a tone that Joe found just short of pathetic.

Joe sighed. "We already went through this out on the boat. We did it because we don't know what's in the kid's head. If she did off herself, we'd spend the rest of our life thinking we might've done something to prevent it."

"But it was set up for México! Why didn't you leave it at that?"

Joe considered carefully how to answer that question. He never lost sight of the fact that Luis could bring the whole thing to a screaming halt. What's more, he could do it in such a way as to make it impossible for him to do business in Cuba, ever. Finally, giving it his best shot, Joe said, "I did it because I think Liliana's past saving and Celia's going to ruin her life, or at least her career, trying. Or haven't you noticed how much time she has missed from work in the past few months?"

Joe paused, just long enough for Luis to calculate the weeks, then continued. "You cleaned up after Liliana this go-round, but what about the next time? Celia's career's not the only one on the line here, you know."

"José," Luis said, giving Joe a look that stopped his spiel in midstream. "Don't try to con me. You do not give a damn about Celia's career, let alone mine. So I ask you again, why did you do it?"

"You want the truth?" Joe asked, as if that wasn't what his brother had been asking for all along. "I did it because I plan to be going back and forth a lot from now on. I don't want to step off the plane into family shit every time. It wrecks my concentration. Liliana's antics could become as much an embarrassment to me as to you. Celia doesn't need it, you don't need it, I don't need it."

"De veras!" Luis exclaimed, and Joe knew that he had finally got through.

"So let her get a bellyful of Miami. I live there, man. It's a toxic culture. If she can handle it, fine. Then that's where she belongs. Me, I can handle it, and no, I do not wish I had stayed in Cuba. Maybe she will feel the same way. Or maybe she won't. But you know as well as I do that Celia is not going to follow her. Honest to God," Joe said again, only this time, he was lying, "I did not arrange for Liliana to go there in order to bait a trap for Celia."

Luis was quiet for a minute or two. Then he started lacing his shoes. "How *did* you arrange it? I thought the only way Cubans could get into the States was as so-called political refugees and all that caca."

"I paid six hundred bucks for a Mexican passport, which is what she'll be travelling on. As far as Uncle Sam is concerned, she will be another upper-class Mexican girl whose graduation present from her Florida relatives was a trip to Disney World."

"A sixteen-year-old?" Luis looked skeptical.

Joe clicked his tongue. "Use your head, Luis. If she's travelling under an assumed name and an assumed nationality, naturally she'll be travelling under an assumed age. I wasn't about to go through the red tape necessary to transport a minor across international borders."

"You think she'll come back? Stay a week and go home like an ordinary tourist?"

They stood face to face there in the small room they had shared for all but ten years of their life. Face to face and eye to eye, because physically, they were the same size. And, Joe conceded for the first time, perhaps equally intelligent. With that in mind, he did tell the truth, as he knew it to be.

"I have no idea, Luis. All I know is that Liliana thinks this is what she wants. She might be wrong about that, but she's right about one thing. It is her life."

"Ours too," Luis said quietly.

"Yeah." Joe pulled on his jacket. "But this is not a replay of the Elián story."

"What do you mean?"

"We're not a divided family."

Luis picked up his own jacket from the back of a chair and stood there with it dangling from his fingers. Finally he said, "Elián and his dad did come home."

Joe took the jacket from his brother and held it so Luis could slip it on.

"So did I," he said.

EIGHTY-SEVEN

CELIA expected the Lagos to arrive together to pick up her and Liliana, but José came alone. Celia wondered if Luis was so angry that he was not even willing to ride in the same car. However, when they reached Hotel Mundo Nuevo, Luis and Alma were waiting at the bottom of the broad steps. Alma, wearing a perky red scarf and a navy dress she saved for special occasions, saw them first and waved gaily.

"Oh, look!" Liliana cried. "Tía Alma's all dressed up. They both are!" She rushed forward and gave Alma and Luis each a huge hug. It was only then that Celia grasped how much it meant to Liliana that they were all here to celebrate her first trip abroad; that for her this might well be the equivalent of the coming-of-age quinceañero party she had not had. That was probably why Liliana had been so insistent that Celia dress up, even to high heels, which she rarely wore.

Celia embraced Alma and they climbed the steps to the main entrance. Liliana linked arms with Luis and José as if both were her escorts, and followed. They were halfway up the steps when Celia heard José ask, "Where did she get that?"

And Liliana's reply, "I don't know. I never saw it before."

Celia turned in time to see José cast a questioning look over Liliana's head at Luis, and heard Luis's sullen response: "She told *me* she didn't like jewellery."

Liliana called out, "Where did you get the anklet, Tía Celia?"

"Do you like it?" Celia asked, smiling down at Liliana.

Liliana hesitated. "It's a little old-fashioned. But it looks nice on you."

"My namesake, Celia Sánchez, wore one like this," Celia said and turned away from them to enter the hotel.

The Mundo Nuevo was one of Habana's newer hotels and not one Celia would have chosen, although she saw immediately that it would please Liliana. A broad curving stairway led to the dining room on the second floor—a mezzanine, really—that overlooked an enormous lobby. Massive chandeliers glittered and there were pillars at intervals across the dining room that Celia supposed could have supported the roof of the Parthenon.

They were shown to a table on the far side of the room. Alma, unpretentious woman that she was, sat down as calmly as if at her own table. Liliana pretended to the same calm, but her high colour showed that for her this was no ordinary outing. Celia kept her eyes lowered to prevent them from revealing to the others that the place represented everything she detested.

What kind of people built palaces such as this while children lay dying of hunger all over the world? How in Cuba of all places could such a hotel be built, while at the hospital they scrounged for basic necessities? Oh, she knew the answer: that without world-class facilities the tourists would not come, without tourists the dollars would not come, and Cuba would not be able to have the medical system it had, which for all its limitations was the best in the whole of the developing world. All that Celia knew, and still she hated this place.

As the others gazed around, commenting on this feature and that, she kept quiet and was grateful when a drinks menu was placed before her so she could keep her eyes lowered without seeming sullen. They ordered mojitos all around, even for Liliana. Celia did not protest because she saw José's surreptitious signal to the waiter beneath the level of the table, where Liliana could not see his hand, that her drink was to be weak.

The mulatto waiter, who looked to be in his sixties, suppressed a smile and murmured, "Perfecto, Patrón."

He replaced the drinks menus with food menus and moved away. Liliana entertained herself by reading the food menu aloud. "Can you believe these prices?" she exclaimed. "And in US dollars too!"

"Not for much longer," Luis smirked. "By November the convertible peso will be our currency, and pegged to the Euro, which will give Cuba an advantage in—"

"—trading with the States?" José chortled. "Come on, Luis. You know Fidel would give his beard to see the blockade come down and free trade—"

"You guys!" Liliana complained. "Can't you shut up about politics for five seconds?" She signalled the waiter, who was at her side in seconds.

"Yes, compañera?" the old man inquired solicitously.

"We would like to order now," Liliana said imperiously. "My tíos are much nicer to each other when their mouths are full of food."

Alma chuckled from behind her menu. "You wondered why I always nag you to eat, hijos? Now you know. Liliana has revealed my secret."

It took a long time to order, as Liliana had not yet completed her tour of the menu. The waiter described the entrees and Alma volunteered her opinions as to which dishes Liliana would like. By the time everyone had made their choice Celia was bored out of her mind and felt truly sorry for the old waiter, whose patience seemed limitless. She knew that employees in such establishments grew wealthy by Cuban standards on the tips they earned. It was said that restroom attendants at big hotels earned more from hard-currency tips than the minister of tourism earned from his peso salary. Still, watching the old mulatto in his stiff white jacket standing for long minutes while an overexcited teenager grew dizzy from so many choices made Celia feel bad for him and impatient with Liliana for her insensitivity. She ordered chicken cordon bleu, sipped her mojito, and gazed about the room. It had been almost empty when they arrived but now was beginning to fill with other diners.

"By the way," Luis addressed Celia. "Joaquín is in town. He phoned just as we were leaving. I invited him to join us but he and Sylvia had other plans."

"Too bad!" Celia exclaimed. "I would like to have seen them. Did you tell him Liliana and I are leaving for México in the morning?"

"He said he'd call you before you left," Luis said shortly.

"I'm *glad* he didn't come," Liliana said, looking at José. "All he ever wants to talk about is the crash of Flight 455. I have to listen to *that* at school every single year—unless I'm at home. At least Tía Celia never puts on the TV on October 6."

José shook his head in disgust. "After two decades the government's *still* harping on that?"

Alma sighed. "If they didn't, people would forget. But imagine, hijo"—she glanced at Luis—"how the co-pilot's daughter must feel. All these years, since she was a little girl, having to listen to that recording of her father's last cries when he heard the explosion and saw they were crashing into the sea."

Celia said nothing. She had met the daughter of the co-pilot, who was near her own age, and knew that the annual broadcast of his final words did indeed cause her anguish. And that Fidel's rant about the inhumanity of the men responsible and the US refusal to bring them to justice did not help. She turned to Liliana.

"Darling, tell us what you found in the México guide book that you want to do while we are there."

Liliana immediately began listing the things she had marked in the guide book José had given her. "The Zona Rosa, of course, which is where the beautiful people hang out. Tía Celia says we won't have time to do the Floating Gardens of Xochimilco, but we can go to Garabaldi Square, where mariachi musicians will serenade me—"

"That's only if you have a novio who pays them," José teased.

"Aye, plagua de Dios!" Alma grasped Liliana's hand. "Don't you dare come home with a Mexican novio!" She gave José the evil eye. "Or a Yanqui boyfriend!"

"You're kidding!" Liliana yelped. "Guys actually pay somebody else to sing love songs to their novias?"

"That's capitalism," Luis smirked. "You want anything there, even a love song, you pay for it. Not like here, where if someone has musical talent the state supports him so he does not have to go begging in the parks."

"Oh yeah?" José shot back. "If the Revolution is so supportive of artists, how come it took Ry Cooder to get Buena Vista Social Club made?"

"Because our focus is not about making one group or individual rich and famous," Luis retorted. "Music, and art in general, should serve the greater good."

"No, hombre!" José slapped the table. "It should provide what the public wants."

"Like that crap the entertainment industry serves up in the United States?"

"It's what people pay for! How would you like it if our waiter took it upon himself to bring you beans because it's healthier than that hunk of beef you ordered?"

"Silencio!" Liliana cried. "Or else talk about something interesting."

"I am going to the bathroom," Alma announced.

"I'll go with you." Liliana glared at the men. "When I get back you'd better be done with your silly arguments or I'm going to go tell the police that you're both CIA operatives."

Luis glanced around to see if other diners might have overheard. "Don't joke about things like that! Not when one person at this table is a Miami Cuban."

"A little paranoid, are we, Comrade?" José needled.

"Tío Joe," Liliana pointed a finger at him. "I'm warning you—"

"Come, Preciosa!" Alma took Liliana by the elbow and guided her across the dining room toward a sign on the far side indicating restrooms.

Celia watched Liliana walking away, wanting to scream after her, *Where are you going? Is there no turning back? What will happen to us?* They were the same questions that had consumed her night and day since Liliana announced her plans to continue from México on to Miami.

Celia had reviewed patient charts, sat through meetings with her doctors, come home to dinners that, now that the school term was over, Liliana cheerfully prepared. She had lain across Liliana's bed or Liliana across hers, discussing which clothes in her meagre wardrobe she would take, what things they might do in México (this a topic always introduced by Celia), and what Liliana wanted to do when she got to Miami (this a topic brought up only by Liliana). At bedtime Liliana had fallen asleep, often with a half-smile on her lips.

Celia, unable to sleep, had gone out on the balcony. There she sat staring at the ocean while hallucination after hallucination played with her mind. In them she was the courageous and competent woman she wanted to be. But when the hallucination faded she was no longer the Celia of her imagination. She was the one inside her skin, who felt utterly helpless in the face of forces beyond her control.

José laid a hand on her arm. "Do you want another mojito, Celia? Or wait for the wine? Our food should be here any minute."

Luis twisted around in his chair to look in the direction Alma and Liliana had gone. "I wonder what is taking them so long?"

"I'll go get them." Celia rose and wended her way between tables of well-dressed diners. At this early hour most were still drinking rather than eating, lifting glasses that caught and refracted shards of light spilling down from glittering chandeliers.

She was three-quarters of the way across the room when the strap slipped on one of her high heels. The shoe flopped on her foot, almost causing her to trip. She paused next to one of the Parthenon-like pillars, put a hand against it for balance, and lifted her foot to readjust the strap.

Blinding light struck her like a blow, followed by a noise that seemed to shatter the world. Blackness closed in around her and she fell . . .

. . . *was falling, while simultaneously watching from afar, the falling silver plane, bodies flung out into space, too far away to see the faces. Was her father among them? Bodies young and beautiful, glints of gold hanging from their necks, the blue Barbados sea rising up to swallow them. For all the sacrifices made, the other side had won. Cuba's children were dying. They and she were drowning in smoke, drowning in the sea, drowning in a noise like no other.*

EIGHTY-EIGHT

CELIA emerged into a hell she could not have imagined. Screams sliced into eardrums already ringing from the explosion, mingled with crashing chandeliers, breaking dishes, falling plaster. What had been cool clean air was a fine whiteness that she could barely breathe and burned her eyes like salt. People were running in every direction.

Celia stumbled toward where the ladies' room sign had hung, only to encounter the remnants of a blown-out wall. Shoes lost, feet slashed and bleeding, she clawed her way to the top of the rubble. Beyond, where the restroom should have been, lay a gaping hole. The room below was strewn with shattered toilets and other debris, drenched by water gushing from broken pipes.

"Liliana!" she screamed.

Arms closed around her waist and pulled her back.

"Let me go!" she shrieked. "Liliana is there!"

"No! She's below. She's okay!" shouted José.

Impossible! She could not be down there and okay! "Let me go!" she screamed.

He did not release her but half-carried her through the rubble to the stairs, which were packed with people flowing downward, some walking, some supporting those who could not. Luis passed them carrying an unconscious woman in his arms.

"Get out!" he shouted. "The ceiling's caving in. Celia, Come! You're needed!"

José gripped Celia's chin with one hand, forcing her to look at the people stampeding down the broad, curving stairway. "Look! There!"

Celia saw Liliana then, just two steps below, fighting against the downward wave of people, trying to get up to the dining mezzanine. Luis shouted at her to turn around and go down, but she was almost at the top and kept coming until she was in Celia's arms.

"Tablecloths!" Liliana screamed. "We need the tablecloths!"

"What the hell—!" José exclaimed. "Are you crazy?"

Liliana dove into the choking dust and Celia, wrenching herself away from José, followed. Liliana grabbed every napkin and tablecloth that came to hand and Celia, comprehending, did likewise. Arms full, Celia started for the stairs but Liliana pulled her to the railing and pointed. "There! See Tía Alma? Throw them down to her!"

Celia could not see Alma but Liliana let go her armload of white cloths and she did the same. José pushed both of them toward the stairs. Then turned aside to move an overturned table that lay on top of a waiter, pinning the man down in a pool of blood.

The stairway had become less crowded, allowing them to move swiftly down. At the bottom Liliana drew Celia away from the mob now trying to jam itself all at once out the front door. She pointed to a lounge area where some of the injured were being placed on sofas and carpet. There might have ten or a hundred, impossible to tell as friends and relatives milled about and those wanting to help tried to get to the most seriously injured.

"Over here, Celia," Alma called. "Liliana, bandages! Hurry!"

Celia knelt next to a person whose neck artery Alma was holding shut as best she could. Liliana stood over them and with a steak knife she must have picked up in the dining room began slashing a tablecloth into strips.

Alma continued triage, directing help to the most seriously injured. "Liliana, bandages!" she called again and again. And, "Celia, here! This one next!"

"Fidel." The word rippled across the room, like an echo coming from every direction. "Fidel. Fidel. Fidel."

Celia heard Liliana say, "Look, Tía! It's Fidel!"

But Celia did not look. She was staring down into the face of the old mulatto waiter. His crinkly black hair that she had noticed before has a few grey threads was now white with plaster dust, and his white jacket was scarlet with blood. She knew even as she opened the jacket that there was too much blood; too much. His eyes said he knew it too. Legs stopped next to her, tan trousers she saw from the corner of her eye without really seeing, because she was trying to find buttons beneath the ruffles of the sodden shirt.

"Comandante," wheezed the waiter, blood bubbling out of his mouth as he spoke. Celia could not imagine how he found the strength to lift his arm, but he did.

The legs next to her bent. A long-fingered hand, pale and age-spotted, enclosed the dark one in its grip. Celia looked up and found herself staring into brown eyes flecked with gold, eyes that she had supposed, from having seen them only on television screens, were much darker, but which in her hallucinations had always been exactly this colour. They seemed to be asking, *How could this happen? Where is their humanity?*

Hers answered, *Don't ask. Just carry on. We have no choice.*

His eyes widened, but whether in comprehension or because at that instant they both felt the old man's body give up life Celia would never know. Castro folded the hand gently onto the blood-soaked chest, stood erect, and moved away. Celia turned to see which patient she should attend next.

"Look!" Liliana shouted. "They got them!"

Across the lobby a knot of police prodded two handcuffed men toward the exit, one a young Latino tough, the other a short grey-haired man. When the captives glimpsed Fidel, the younger man tried to lift his hand in an obscene gesture, only to have it knocked down by the barrel of a policeman's pistol. The older prisoner spat at the officer and shouted at the top of his lungs, "Fuck you, Castro, and the horse you rode in on!" then, "Chinga tu madre, Pendejo!"

The crowd roared and surged toward them, forcing the police to form a cordon around the captives for their own protection. On the opposite side of the lobby, Fidel's security people pressed him toward the exit.

Celia turned back to the injured. She was about to bandage a child's leg when

Liliana appeared beside her. "I can do that," she said. "You take care of her." She pointed to a woman whose eyeglasses had imploded into her face.

"Oh God," Celia said under her breath, "I need—"

A pile of items rained down beside her—bandages, antiseptic cream, scissors, and more. She sorted through them and found tweezers, which was exactly what she needed. Behind her she heard Liliana ask, "Where did that stuff come from?"

José replied, "The boutique. Nobody was around so I helped myself."

"Santa María, Madre de Dios, Gracias!" Celia heard Alma exclaim. Seconds later she understood the reason for such fervent thanks. Teams of paramedics descended on them like a flock of white birds. Celia and other medical people who had been first on the scene fell back, letting the newly arrived professionals take over. The injured were eased onto stretchers and carried out, friends and relatives trailing behind.

Celia went down on her knees again next to the old mulatto waiter, who, being so obviously dead, had not been moved. It was pointless to close his eyes but she did it anyway. There was nothing else to be done

She felt a stabbing pain in one foot and gave an involuntary shriek.

"Be still," Liliana said in a soothing voice. "I have to clean your feet. They're bleeding all over the place. There's a piece of glass in this one."

There might have been more useful things for Celia to do just then, but she did not look to see what they might be. She lay forward on the carpeted floor, next to the old mulatto, and allowed Liliana to practise all the medical skills she had learned in the past thirty minutes.

When Liliana finished bandaging Celia's feet and informed her that she could get up, Celia sat down on a nearby sofa and looked around. Most of the people remaining in the lobby were in uniform, police or hotel employees. Luis was talking to the police. A hotel employee was coming their way.

Alma said, "Those *were* the terrorists. I know. I saw their shoes."

"Their shoes?" Celia said blankly.

"Young man!" Alma called out to the hotel employee. "Can you help me find a restroom? If there's still one standing?"

"Right this way, compañera," he said, taking Alma by the arm. "You were magnificent, by the way. Are you a doctor?"

"Ambulance driver," Celia heard her reply. "Retired."

EIGHTY-NINE

JOE had always seen Celia as attractive, but not in an eye-catching way. Earlier, though, she floating up the steps ahead of him as they entered the hotel with a breeze swirling the skirt of her pale blue dress high enough to expose tan skin from taut thighs to trim ankles, he had had second thoughts about her beauty.

If that had surprised him, what entered his mind as he crossed the lobby surprised him even more. As he walked through the wreckage toward a woman who looked pretty damned wrecked herself, that mysterious gold chain glittering on one ankle, something in the back of his mind crumbled like a piece of plaster disintegrating hours after the main explosion. It was the notion that Celia was going to haul him out of the wreckage of his marriage. That anklet. Not from him. Not from Luis. Not something she would have bought for herself. There was only one possibility: another man. Celia Cantú was not the woman he thought she was.

The woman she was now was a mess, hair white with plaster dust and the front of her dress as covered in blood as if she had been stabbed. She and Liliana sat, fingers entwined, staring at the old mulatto. He was one of three people, all dead, who had not been moved.

As Joe approached, Liliana looked up with reddened eyes. "He was our waiter."

Joe laid a hand on her chalk-dusty hair. "He was bringing our food when the explosion happened. It must have caught him broadside. How did you manage to get downstairs so fast? Celia thought she saw you go into the restroom."

"We did. But those men were in there."

"What men?"

"The terrorists. Tía Alma was about to go in a stall when I saw feet in the next one over. I pointed, and when she saw two pairs of men's shoes in the same stall we got out of there fast."

"But you couldn't have known—" Joe began incredulously.

"No. We just thought they were gay guys. So we went downstairs to find another restroom. That's when I saw Fidel."

"You saw Fidel? *Before* the explosion?"

"Yeah. He was in a conference room with a bunch foreigners."

"Where the hell was his security?" Joe wanted to know.

"They were there but they didn't take any notice of us until I tried to peek in for a better look. A guy in an army uniform with about a zillion medals pulled me back. Tía Alma asked him where we could find a toilet. He said upstairs and pointed over our head, where we'd just been. Tía Alma gave him one of her looks, and said, 'We prefer one that isn't being used by *perverts.*'" Liliana paused and shook her head. "You know, her attitude toward homosexuals isn't very modern." She glanced at Joe. "But maybe they were perverts. Normal gays would use the men's room, wouldn't they?"

"I don't know. Not my area of expertise," Joe said gruffly.

"Anyway," Liliana continued, "when she told him about the men in the ladies' room they all went crazy. Two ran in the room where Fidel was. One grabbed Alma and told her to show him which ladies' room and another one took me by the arm and dragged me the other way and—"

She stopped speaking as Luis walked up. "Where's Mamá?" he asked.

"Here," Alma said as she joined them. "Shall we go?"

Luis took her elbow and headed for the exit. As the others followed, Liliana slipped her arm through Joe's and asked in a shaky voice, "Is this going to change things, Tío Joe? Like make it harder to fly back and forth between Miami and Cuba?"

"Probably," Luis answered for him.

"There'll be a lot of grandstanding," Joe admitted. "Likely a lockdown on both sides for a while."

They passed through the lobby door and were standing at the top of the steps when Liliana stopped. Turning to face Joe, she said, "Then I guess, I think—I don't want to go to Miami."

"Wait a minute!" Joe grabbed her by the arm. "You're saying—"

Liliana began to cry. "I changed my mind, that's all!"

"That's *all*?" Close to two thousand bucks he'd spent to get her out and she'd changed her fucking mind? Joe lifted a hand. He wanted to slap the flaky little snit from here to breakfast but settled for a finger in her face. "Listen, if you're afraid—"

"So what if I'm afraid?" Liliana blubbered. "Who wants to live where kids carry guns to school to shoot classmates they hate and grownups go around blowing up—"

"Goddammit, Liliana! You don't judge a whole country by its lunatic fringe!"

"I know! I'm crazy! But they're crazier! They tried to kill us!"

"No!" José yelled. "We were just there. In the way!"

"Enough!" Alma admonished José. "Can't you see she's upset?"

As if Alma's diagnosis gave Liliana permission to abandon the calm she had maintained through the crisis, she suddenly and completely fell apart.

"Don't you get it?" she shrieked. "Tía Alma went off to show that security guy what toilet those perverts were in and there was the explosion and stuff falling all around us and I thought my whole family was blown up!"

Celia's arms closed around her. "It's okay, Preciosa. We are all here."

Luis said, "I don't see a doorman, José. Shall we go get the cars?"

Walking toward the parking lot, Luis placed an arm across Joe's shoulder. Joe could never remember him making such a gesture before, but somehow it felt right. For the first time in his life, he was glad to have a brother.

NINETY

CELIA, wet-haired from the shower, was cold. Rather than go to her own bed, she got in with Liliana, who had showered first and was already asleep. Liliana slept soundly in the way of exhausted children and did not stir when Celia lay down beside her.

Celia was exhausted too, but the adrenalin in her system had not abated. After a while she got up and headed for the kitchen to make herself a cup of cocoa. As she passed the telephone on the table at the end of the sofa, it rang. She picked it up. "Hola?"

Joaquín's hysterical voice came over the line. "Celia! Oh my God, is it really you? I can't believe—tell me it's you!"

"Calmate," Celia soothed. "It is me and I am okay. We all are."

"Luis said you were going to the Mundo Nuevo for dinner! The dining room— I'm looking at it now, on TV! So many injured!"

"I know. But we were on the far side. We were not—"

Joaquín was sobbing. "Let him go to trial. Burn in hell! But if you had been hurt I would have killed him with my bare hands! Oh, but they got him. This is a miracle!"

To Celia, it sounded more like a total mental breakdown. "Joaquín," she said sharply. "What are you talking about? Got who?"

"Luis Posada Carriles! Don't you have the TV on? Turn it on, for God's sake!"

Celia started toward the set, holding the telephone to her ear. But the cord was not long enough to reach, so she stood where she was, listening to Joaquín.

"Look, they're showing his picture now! It's him for sure!"

"You mean the man they captured, the older one?" Celia, although staring at a blank television screen, dredged up an image of Luis Posada Carriles from a photograph that had appeared in *Granma* at the time he claimed credit for the bombing of other Habana hotels back in 1997.

"See? For sure it's him!"

She could not speak.

"Celia? Celia! Are you there?"

"I'm here," she whispered. "Are they actually saying the older one is Posada?"

"Not yet." Joaquín admitted. "But you can tell! Look at the eyes! That's something that never changes!"

"What about the other man, the younger one?"

"A Salvadoran, like those who helped him before. He'll be convicted same as they were. But Posada, the old devil, he always got away. Not this time, though!"

Celia's hands were shaking, causing her to wonder at the unpredictability of her own body. She had remained steady through all that had happened, but now this—a fragment of unsubstantiated news—made her tremble. She felt as if she had fallen through the roof of her own nightmare into a place she never expected to be: a world where the spectre of her fathers' killers, still on the loose, no longer haunted her.

"Thank you, Joaquín," she finally managed to say. "When I get back from México we will get together. We will celebrate. Now let's just . . . watch the news."

However, when she hung up Celia did not turn on the television. She went into the kitchen and with unsteady hands, made the cocoa. How ironic it would have been if the man responsible for killing her father had, over a quarter-century later and by purest chance, succeeded in murdering his only surviving daughter and granddaughter.

If Liliana had not seen the shoes, if she had been standing at the mirror as she normally was in any ladies' room, smiling at her own reflection, and then . . . no more. Would there have been any way to go on? Celia could imagine Liliana's absence; she had lived the anguish of that absence not very long ago. More recently she had tried to come to terms with the possibility of losing Liliana in the sense of being physically cut off from her should she decide to stay in Florida. That had seemed intolerable, something she was not at all sure she could bear. But to imagine Liliana out of existence, that she could not do. Easier by far to imagine that she herself had been killed. For what was there, after all, to imagine? Just—the end. The nothing thereafter.

She thought of how her father and her sister had died in explosions half a world apart, and how her mother and Celia Sánchez, both of whom had been in the middle of a war for two years or longer with grenades, gunfire, mortars, and bombs exploding all around them, had not been scratched. They were survivors. She was a survivor.

With that thought came another one: *I am the woman they were.*

The cocoa was suddenly boiling. She poured it into a mug, returned to the living room, and sat down in a rocker. The room was dark except for moonlight spilling in through the balcony door. The cocoa was too hot to drink but it comforted her to wrap cold fingers around the warm cup and breathe in the sweet steam rising from it.

Directly in front of her was the television screen, empty except for a faint reflection of the white terrycloth robe that had opened to reveal her crossed legs. What she saw in that reflection, though, was a different pair of legs, much thinner than her own, but which, like hers, had a glint of gold about the ankle.

She was a ten-year-old child, sitting on the floor, waiting impatiently for the cocoa that had been placed on the coffee table in front of her to cool. She was not really listening to the conversation between Celia and her mother, would not remember it afterwards. Yet she must have heard what they said; how else could she be hearing it now?

"Dying is overrated," Celia Sánchez was saying. "A momentary thing, like giving birth or getting married. It's the afterwards that counts, if there is one. In the case of death, I strongly suspect there isn't. Not one we would recognize anyway."

"Ah, Celia, you are so brave." Her mother began to cry. "You always were."

"Katrina," Celia Sánchez spoke sharply. "You asked how I am. I am telling you. But don't burden me with your feelings—not at this point." She turned to the child on the floor and said, "How is the cocoa? Too hot, yes?"

"Sí, Compañera Celia," the girl replied. She was pleased to have been noticed by the lady with the very thin legs, so elegantly crossed at the knees. Then, shyly, "I like your anklet. Is it a present from Fidel?"

Celia Sánchez smiled and instead of answering the question, asked, "What is it you plan to do with your life, my little namesake?"

"Uh, be a doctor," the child replied quickly, knowing this answer would please the adults.

"That is a very noble thing to aspire to. But it is not easy. You must study hard."

"She's a very good student," her mother bragged, causing the child to duck her head with embarrassed pleasure.

"My father was a doctor," said Celia Sánchez. "He worked with the poor in the sierra and often took me with him. I watched him ease the suffering of many, and I myself held the hands of some who died. So I know"—here she turned away from the child to speak to her mother—"about death, Katrina. That is why I am not afraid."

"And you are not in pain?" Katrina asked anxiously.

"Some," Celia Sánchez admitted. "At times . . . so hard to breathe. But pain I can tolerate. It's the loss of energy that I find frustrating."

The women sat quietly for a few moments, having forgotten the child who thought she was not listening anymore, engrossed as she was in testing the hot chocolate with the tip of her pinkie and feeling a prick of pain because the cocoa was still scalding hot.

Celia Sánchez spoke again. "In the beginning we ask, as your daughter should be asking, 'What do I want to do with my life?' But at a certain age, Katrina, the question needs to change, and we must ask ourselves, 'What do I want to have done?' The Revolution—of course it has not been fully realized. But we always knew it to be an ongoing process, something that, if it was to be a success, had to be worked at generation after generation. It was only ours to begin, and that we have done, yes?"

Celia Sánchez coughed. The child could tell that talking was difficult for her. She wondered why her mother, who talked so much at home, was saying so little, why, in the presence of this older woman she was like a girl herself, shy and respectful.

"I have done all the things I wanted to have done, but for one, and it is almost finished. I have saved all the papers, every note, every instruction Fidel ever put his hand to. Now they are being organized into a national archive, and this I must finish. When we are gone this written record is all there will be, the only thing that tells what we did, how we did it, and why. Fidel said history would absolve him, but only if the history of La Revolución is preserved."

"Surely you're not still working on those archives!" Katrina exclaimed. "I heard that there are more than a million documents! There must be other people—!"

"Of course," Celia Sánchez said. "Not one task in my life have I set out to do that there weren't others—like you—who joined the struggle."

She looked again at the child. "That is what it takes if we are to make this island a better place for all of us. Right, little one?"

The child, sucking the finger scorched by the hot cocoa, looked up quickly and nodded, but Celia Sánchez was again speaking to her mother. "Do you understand what I'm telling you, Katrina? In the end, what makes death easy is being able to say that you have done what you wanted to do. That is why you must ask, and know the answer. Not at the last minute either. If you wait till the last minute to ask, and the answer is that you have not done what you wanted, then your dying will be a terrible thing. So I'm telling you." Again the spasm of coughing.

When it had passed, Celia Sánchez said in a voice that had become hoarse, "Ask yourself now, Katrina. Not the question of a child, 'What do I want to do with my life?' but the question of an adult, 'What is it I want to have done?' Then get on with it."

The child, finding the cocoa at last cool enough to sip, understood the words but not their meaning. All she grasped was that Celia Sánchez was behaving like a mother to her own motherless mother, and that she was going to die and was trying to teach her mother about dying, which seemed a silly thing to do, since her mother wasn't even slightly sick.

They never spoke of that conversation again, not on the walk home, not a dozen years later when Katrina lay dying of the same disease. It was not until now, in this darkened room with chocolate-scented stream rising from the cup in her hands, that Celia wondered, Did you, Mamá? You saved lives in the war, raised Carolina and me, loved our father while he was alive and other men who took your fancy later. Was that enough, or was there more you wanted to have done? You died so young—only a decade older than I am now. And I—what if I had died tonight? What is it I want to do that I would not have got done?

She wouldn't have wanted her research projects left undone. The studies were not long-term; they would be finished in two years and would contain data that she felt sure would force the government to stop ignoring the health risks second-hand smoke posed for children. She would also show Liliana all the beaches and rivers and mountains and mogotes of this beautiful island. That, for sure, was something she wanted to have done.

Celia listened to the whisper of surf, so ever-present that she normally did not hear it. She watched the patterns cast by moonlight change as the moon moved across the sky, watched the reflection of her legs on the grey television screen fade and disappear. She lifted the cup and sipped the cocoa.

After a while she conceded that there was one other thing she wanted to have done. But it would take a little longer.

NINETY-ONE

CELIA was wakened by a telephone call from Dr. Leyva. He said that in televised reports on the bombing he had glimpsed her and Liliana treating the injured and wanted her to know that after such an ordeal he did not expect her to go to México City today; that if she wished, Dr. Cohen could be sent in her place. Celia quickly agreed and hung up with a huge sense of relief.

The next caller was Alma. When Celia reassured her that they were fine, Alma called, "Luis! Come tell Celia what you found out."

Luis came on the line and in a tired voice informed her that if she had received a call from Joaquín claiming that the terrorist was Luis Posada Carilles, she shouldn't believe it; that he had just spoken to Captain Quevedo, who said neither of the terrorists were Posada Carilles. He said MININT had good intelligence that Posada was still in Central America and was expected to surface in the United States soon. There he would probably get the same protection accorded to Orlando Bosch, his accomplice in the Barbados airline bombing, who continued to live openly in Miami.

Celia was grateful to get the news from Luis rather than Joaquín, as it allowed her to deal with her frustration and bitterness in private and not have to cope with Joaquín's at the same time. Luis did not acknowledge her thanks and handed the telephone back to Alma without saying goodbye.

Liliana wandered into the kitchen, dark curls frizzy from the late night washing and no interim combing. She was in surprisingly good spirits and ate breakfast with the television on in order to watch constantly replayed scenes of the chaos following the bombing, some of which showed her assisting the injured with calm efficiency.

After a while Liliana said she was going to unpack. Celia limped after her and sat down on the bed. Simply making herself available had always been the best way to get Liliana to open up. That was especially important this morning, Celia felt, in the aftermath of the hotel bombing.

Liliana exhibited a certain seriousness as she set about unpacking, but did not seem upset or particularly interested in talking about the night before. Celia was about to leave when Liliana lifted the ballerina music box out of her suitcase, carefully unwrapped it, and put it back in its usual place on her dresser.

Celia's heart gave a painful thud. She knew that this final gift from Carolina was Liliana's most precious possession. She would have packed it only if she planned to stay in Miami. Celia reached out and touched the music box. In as neutral a voice as she could muster, she said, "You weren't intending to come back, were you?"

Liliana deftly moved the music box out of her reach. "No. But you'd have come there, wouldn't you? After a while?"

"No," Celia said with quiet finality.

Liliana stared at her, disbelieving. "You wouldn't? Not ever?"

"Never."

"Why not?" Liliana almost howled the question.

"Because what I want is here."

"*Here?*" Liliana pointed at the floor, indicating their small apartment or possibly the whole shabby building below them.

"I mean here in Cuba," Celia said, surprised by how surprised Liliana seemed. Surely the girl had known! Then retracted "surely" as she recalled that even she had not been positive that she would never go to Miami. Only now was she certain that, although she would have grieved for Liliana as she had grieved for Carolina, she would not have given up her work, her nationality, and her island.

"I like my life here," Celia said mildly. "What about you? What was it over there that you wanted so much?" She picked up an issue of *Granma* lying on the bedside table and pretended to scan headlines so Liliana wouldn't feel she was being grilled.

"Well, the stuff I can't have here. Like a car. Or even a good bike."

Inadvertently, both of them glanced toward the music box that, as far as Celia knew, still contained enough cash to buy a nice bike. She thought she saw a flush come to Liliana's cheeks. Liliana flopped down on the bed next to her and said petulantly, "You don't make enough money to buy anything and when I'm a doctor I won't either. It's not *fair.*"

"What is not fair?"

"Having to give up some things to get others. Like, if I moved to the States I couldn't afford to go to medical school. Tío Joe did say he could get me a job, but it wouldn't be an important job like *that.*" She thumped the newspaper in Celia's lap.

Celia looked down. The article was about Operación Milagro, a new program in which hundreds of Cuban doctors were being sent abroad to work in poor countries.

Liliana continued. "Fidel personally shakes their hand when they leave, and everybody tells them what a great thing they're doing for humanity. They feel *proud.* At least, I would." She stared glumly at the ceiling. "But they don't earn diddly. Tío Joe said even in the States, do-gooder work—that's what he called it, do-gooder work—is done mostly by volunteers. He said if I wanted to own a car I'd have to take a *real* job."

"It sounds like you've been thinking about moving to the States for a long time," Celia ventured.

"For a while," Liliana said noncommittally.

"What caused you to change your mind?"

Liliana gave her a surely-you-know look. "The hotel getting bombed!"

"Well, yes. But what difference did that make? What did it change?"

Liliana pulled a brown curl into her mouth and held it between pursed lips. It was a moment before she replied, in a dreamy voice, "It's like all of a sudden I could see myself actually being what I want to be."

"Which is?"

Liliana let go of the strand of hair and brushed it away from her face with a laugh. "You know. A doctor. Like you."

Neither of the Lago brothers contacted Celia in the month following the bombing. Her first inkling that Luis had also been jolted into making a life-defining decision came when Emily Solana telephoned to say she and Luis were engaged and gushingly invited Celia and Liliana to the wedding.

At first Celia worried that Luis's decision to get married was some kind of rebound behaviour. However, at the wedding reception Emily recounted how they had met during Liliana's convalescence, and Celia realized with considerable surprise that they had been seeing each other for many months.

Alma, whose looks and personality had changed little in Celia's memory, flitted among wedding guests looking more like a woman in her forties than one in her sixties. Unselfconsciously, she repeatedly thanked God for protecting her family and bestowing this blessing: the marriage of a son and promises from her new daughter-in-law that she would soon be surrounded by grandchildren.

Liliana, who regularly visited the Lagos, had passed on to Celia the news that the couple had moved in with Alma. As a wedding present José had given them a king-sized bed to replace the two broken-down single beds that had furnished the brothers' room for as long as anyone could remember. He had rented an apartment for himself near Hotel Palco and had not called Celia or stopped by since the hotel bombing. She wondered, watching him work his way through the wedding guests toward her, whether it had a noticeable effect on him too.

Apparently something had changed because when they were finally face to face, he barely acknowledged her, and instead, addressed Liliana. "I wonder if you'd mind helping me out with the car?" he said abruptly.

"The car?" Liliana looked as puzzled as Celia felt.

"There's no parking at my new place and I hate leaving it at Mother's when I'm out of the country. If you'd learn to drive you could use it when I'm not here."

Celia supposed this was his way of apologizing to Liliana for having got so angry with her the night of the bombing. But she also sensed that it was another attempt on his part to keep her in his orbit and instantly protested.

"No, I don't think—"

José interrupted. "Celia, for God's sake. It's the twenty-first century. Driving is a skill she needs, and Alma's perfectly capable of teaching her."

Liliana laid a hand on José's sleeve. "Really, Tío? When can we start?"

"All right." Celia grudgingly offered the consent that neither of them had bothered to seek. "But leave me out of it. Whatever you decide is between you two."

Driving lessons began almost immediately, and by fall Alma pronounced Liliana a competent driver. José presented Liliana with a credit card issued in her name by a Mexican bank, along with a stern warning that its use for anything other than gas would cause her driving privileges to be revoked. After that Celia could hardly deny Liliana the right to practise when the car was available. However, she drew a line at Liliana running around in a convertible loaded with other teens. Her solution was to work straight through during the three weeks each month that Liliana was at school, and then take off work the week Liliana was on break. If José was in Miami and they happened to have the car, she would let Liliana pick a place on the island to visit and they would drive there, Liliana at the wheel.

All José asked was that Liliana drop him at the airport when he left and pick him up on his return—unless she was in school, in which case Alma performed the service. José told Celia he liked the convenience. Liliana told Celia that what Tío Joe really liked was not having to take a taxi like an ordinary traveller, but being picked up by "a classy chica in a classy máquina."

Celia smiled at Liliana's description of herself as a "classy chica," and mused that José might have been less pleased with the arrangement if he knew that Liliana relished details of his personal life and loved sharing them with Celia, Emily, and Alma.

"I found a woman's shoe in the car," Liliana would exclaim. "And it's not the same size as the pair left in the car last month. Are these women so sprung on him that they forget they got in the car wearing shoes? Or leave them on purpose so he'll see how worn out they are and buy them a new pair?"

Celia listened with a smile and never asked for details. Thus there was a several-month delay in hearing a tidbit of gossip that did interest her. One day at the hospital Esther Cohen popped in, and in her abrupt way asked, "Which of those Lago brothers are you seeing, Celia?"

Celia looked up from her desk, surprised by the question. "Neither one. Why?"

"Oh yes, you know—the one who calls here all the time. Or used to."

"Oh. Used to." Celia wondered what had prompted the question, as it had been months since Luis had telephoned her at the hospital. "That was Luis, the older one."

"The one who recently got married?"

"Yes. I grew up down the street from the Lagos. I didn't know you knew them."

"Slightly," Esther said airily. "I met the younger one at services."

"Services? You mean church?" Celia must have looked dumbstruck.

"Synagogue." Esther gave Celia her competitive, one-up smile and was gone.

The exchange so intrigued Celia that she could not resist asking Liliana, "Do you know if José is seeing a doctor from my hospital?"

"Oh yeah!" Liliana brightened at the opportunity to demonstrate more in-the-knowness about her playboy tío. "Doctora Cohen. Emily told me. One day Tío Luis couldn't pick her up after church so he asked Tío Joe to do it. Emily said she was crossing the street to where he was parked when Doctora Cohen came out of her synagogue and Tío Joe whistled at her. Emily said Doctora Cohen stopped and looked him and the máquina over in this really bold way. He called out did she want to go to lunch with him, and what do you suppose she said?"

"I cannot imagine," Celia admitted because she really could not.

"Doctora Cohen said, 'That depends on how good a conversationalist you are, and whether you have anything interesting in mind for later.'"

Celia chuckled at the very thought of comedy/dramas likely to be played out between those two as they clicked and clashed. "Is he still seeing her?"

"Her and about twenty other women. I guess he's pretty good to all of them, though, because he does get a lot of repeats."

"I am sure he is," Celia said and kept to herself the rest of that thought, which was: As long as he gets a lot of high-energy, low-hassle sex geared to his bio-rhythms rather than those of his partner and no questions as to whom he bedded the night before.

According to Liliana, much of José's time in Miami was spent fighting with his ex-wife, trying to get permission from the court to take his daughters on vacation out of the country. Knowing how Alma ached to know her grandchildren, Celia hoped he would find a way to bring them to Cuba—preferably not one of the illegal ways that Liliana said he often threatened when he returned from Miami in a really foul mood.

"Sad," Celia mused. "Given half a chance I think José would be a good father."

Liliana, who was sprawled on the sofa with a textbook propped on her chest, said casually, "He told me that if you moved to Miami and married him, he might be able to get custody of his kids. At least part of the time."

"Oh really?" Celia sat down in the rocker and looked at her niece speculatively. "And you would have two little sisters. Was that what you wanted?"

"I wouldn't mind. But it doesn't matter so much now."

"It mattered before?"

"Well, yeah. Before he started letting me drive the convertible."

In a voice that carried a hint of disgust, Celia asked, "Is that what he promised you if we moved to Miami? A car?"

Liliana reddened and did not answer. All Celia could think was, A car! She was willing to abandon Cuba and me for a car!

After a moment Liliana sat up and, textbook clutched to her chest, said with a mixture of apology and defiance, "The car wasn't the main thing. I just wanted to see what it was like over there. You know, like people used to."

For a second Celia failed to comprehend "like people used to" since not in her lifetime had it been possible to hop over to Florida for a mere look around. Then she grasped that Liliana didn't mean the recent past but the whole of Cuban history—or almost all of it. Five hundred years during which residents on both sides of the Strait travelled both ways for business, vacations, family visits, or just to get a sense of what it was like "over there."

"You never wanted to travel so you don't understand how I feel," Liliana stated with the assurance of an adolescent that no adult can possibly comprehend their passion.

Celia almost smiled. If only you knew, she thought. I travel to places so far in the past that the only way to get there is in my head. And similarly transported, there's hardly a night in the last year that I haven't travelled into the mountains to be with a man who finds all his meaning there . . . and only come back because what I have to do is here.

"There is Operacíon Milagro," Celia ventured.

"Do you think it'll still be going on when I get out of medical school?"

"Almost certainly. Maybe even expanding by then."

"I saw a list of the countries where doctors are being sent," Liliana said thoughtfully. "I wouldn't care which one as long as it was, well, *some* where."

Celia had a sudden image of Dr. Leyva's daughter, whose desire to go "somewhere" had led to her death and a lifetime of sadness for her family. It was followed by an enormous sense of relief that a travel option had opened up for Liliana—or would be open if she pursued her education.

Celia crossed a leg over her knee to expose the sole of her foot. "So, Doctora Liliana. What do you think? Are my feet healed enough to go to the beach?"

Liliana studied the scared sole. "Not barefoot," she pronounced. "And not alone. I have to go with you." She pushed the book aside. "I'm burnt out on studying anyway."

"What are you reading?"

"*La Historia de la Revolución.* It is *so* boring." As she headed into her room to change, she added, "Except for the part when they were in the sierra."

Celia dressed for the beach and waited for Liliana. She came out pulling up her swimsuit. "When I'm living in Santiago, could we visit the Comandancia de La Plata sometime?"

"Funny. I was just wondering if that was something you might like to do." Actually, Celia had thought of it more than once when they were doing their "every weekend a different place." She had never suggested it, though, being not quite ready to share it—or Miguel—with anyone.

"I wish the book had more about Celia Sánchez."

"She was a very private person. Only Fidel really knew her."

"Magdalena says even though he has Dalia now and all those sons, he still goes to Celia's place late at night and sits there for hours because he misses her so much." Liliana turned her back so Celia could tie the strap at the neck. "You think it's true?"

"Possibly. Lift your hair out of the way."

"I wonder if I'll ever meet a guy who loves me that much," Liliana mused, her bright dark eyes going dreamy. "Lots of women risked their *lives* for him. And that was when he was still a grungy revolutionary. But Celia was his true love, wasn't she?"

"So they say," Celia murmured.

"Imagine living with one man—how long?"

"Well, it was in 1957 that she went to stay with him in the mountains, and January 1980 when she died. Twenty-two years, I guess."

"Awesome! There must be a million women in the world who would like to sleep with him. Even now, when he's a dottery old man."

"Not so dottery," Celia protested.

"Would *you?*" Liliana challenged, smirking over her shoulder.

Celia laughed and headed for the door. "Maybe—in another life."

EPILOGUE

CELIA could feel that the cabin was empty. She knocked on the door, which was slightly ajar. There was no answer so she pushed it open and stepped inside. Although she had only been here once and that was almost two years ago, she did not feel like an intruder. However, the juita sitting under the table may have felt otherwise. Fat as an overfed cat, he watched Celia watching him until she backed out, having ascertained that but for the big tree rat, the cabin was empty.

The hour-long climb up the trail from the parking lot had left her hot and thirsty. She drained the last of the water from a bottle she had brought with her and took in her surroundings. She had not paid much attention to them on her previous visit, yet the place seemed familiar. This, she knew, was because of details included in the more than one hundred letters she had received from Miguel in the past fifteen months.

Besides answering her questions and remarking on things she had written him, each of his letters contained detailed descriptions of aspects of his environment that he found intriguing. Thus when she walked to the end of the porch she knew that if she looked hard in a certain place she would not immediately be able to pick out what would seem to be a brown leaf dangling near the end of a thin branch. Yet if she waited she would see the movement of a bee hummingbird sitting on her nest.

Actually that was not what she saw because that description had been in a letter from Miguel the previous week. What Celia saw was the iridescent colobri zip up to the brown thing that was not a leaf but a nest the size of a bottle cork, and perch on its rim to feed her newly hatched hummingbird babies.

Celia stepped off the porch and circled the cabin. Trees grew close on all sides, as if the builder had not cut any but found a spot between them to squeeze the cabin in. The structures at the Comandancia had been built like that too: trees left standing to prevent buildings from being seen from the air and to provide protection from the blazing sun.

Behind the cabin she saw a rain barrel on stilts. That, Miguel had explained in one of his letters, was how he managed to have running water in the sink. She found the outhouse where she expected it to be and knew to duck as she entered to avoid disturbing an elaborate spiderweb that Miguel liked to observe when he was using the facilities.

Completing her inspection of the immediate vicinity, Celia went back to the porch and collapsed into one of the rockers. She knew that Miguel went out at first light but did not know when he came back. That might be one of the few things about him she did not know. He knew as much or more about her. After all, why bother to keep secrets from someone to whom you had revealed your darkest secret before even learning his name?

She knew he called himself apolitical, although he had also told her that nature was both his politics and his religion; that he would lay down his life, take up arms, or even pray if he thought it would protect the natural environment for all time. He felt that the state capitalism of Cuba had been as destructive to the environment as corporate capitalism, and despised them equally for it. The one difference, he said, was that the former was younger and as such, perhaps more amenable to learning, self-awareness, and change. At least he hoped so and did the research he did and wrote the books he wrote in an effort to facilitate that process.

She had learned that Miguel rarely ate meat, read all sorts of books, played just a bit of guitar, and, like the poet José Martí, "el arroyo de la sierra me complace más que'l mar"—"the mountain stream pleases me more than the sea."

He had made it clear that he would never live in a city or even a town; that when his research in the Sierra Maestra was completed he would move on to another wild mountainous place where, as he had so pointedly reminded her, there were no hospitals. She knew that in about three months' time he would be leaving here to begin a project in Parque Humboldt on Cuba's northeast coast. Did she know more than that about him? Did she need to know more than that, plus what her own senses had confirmed? Had he told her less about himself than she had told him about herself?

She had told him what it was like growing up in a Habana suburb, and of course, about Carolina and Liliana. She also told him about the Lago brothers whom, oddly or predictably, she rarely saw anymore. He knew that Liliana was now in Santiago, living in the Morceau household and attending medical school.

According to Franci, Liliana's biggest adjustment had been the return to foot power. However, being her usual resourceful self, Liliana wrote to her ever-indulgent Tío José. Soon thereafter Philip was called down to the train station to pick up what turned out to be a bicycle for each of the girls. That silenced Liliana's complaints while ensuring that she got regular exercise. Her grades, of some concern during the first two months, were now being maintained at an acceptable level.

Naturally Celia had written Miguel a good deal about her work, how each of the clinical trials had taken on a life of its own and every page of paperwork seemed to generate more. And how, when she asked to be relieved of administrative duties so she could resume working with patients, Dr. Leyva had refused. He explained that while there were innumerable younger pediatricians well trained in patient care, the "internal brain drain" caused by doctors leaving medicine to take up careers in tourism had left him with no senior doctors to replace her in administration. He reminded Celia, in words reminiscent of what she had told José about why she didn't want to leave Cuba, that, "Our mission is to serve the Revolution's goal of making Cuba a better nation. We do that by contributing our services where they are most needed."

Celia had very nearly asked the question José had tossed out in that same conversation by the pool there in Viñales, as to why, exactly, it had to be *her*. But the more she thought about it the more the question evolved in her mind until it became, Why is it somebody else, and not me, who decides what my contribution should be?

371

All this and much more Celia shared with Miguel in the letters they exchanged once a week for a time, and more often now that Celia lived alone. She had felt very close to him writing those letters, knowing that he was alone too. Only now, sitting on the porch of his cabin, did she realize how different living alone was for each of them. She lived in a cement block tower many metres above the ground, with a vista of rocky coastline and vast light-reflecting ocean. He lived in a thatched-roof hut barely one step above the ground, so close that she could smell the earth. It was surrounded by tall trees that blocked the view and filtered the sunlight.

Directly in front of her, the largest tree of all was not one tree but two; a marañon wrapped tight by a strangler fig. It was one of the things Miguel had described in a letter, explaining how the fig grew up as a light vine, twining itself around the larger tree, then, upon reaching its full height, began to thicken and squeeze. Eventually the tree that had supported the fig when it had no sturdy trunk of its own would cease to be, having given up its life to sustain the seemingly weak but actually stronger fig.

Was this a metaphor for relationships? she wondered. Did one always hold the other in such an inescapable embrace that the weaker one ceased to be its own life form? Looking up at the strong but dying marañon, she understood that this was what she had feared all along, first from José and then from Luis. She had no such fear of Miguel, but was that sensible? It was true that he had never held her too tight, but Luis had seemed gentle too, had he not? And yet she had had a harder time extracting herself from Luis than from José. Perhaps she should be afraid of Miguel, but she was not. There were two sides to that coin, she reasoned, or rather, two people in any embrace. Both had a choice.

As she stared up into the intermingled leaves of the marañon and its strangler mate, she knew there was something else that made a man and a woman's relationship different from this great tree and the smaller one that was swallowing it. The marañon had no defences, no thorns or toxic bark to fend off its subtle attacker. But she, Celia, was not so helpless. A warrior mother she'd had, a warrior sister, and yes, a warrior soul—the soul of her namesake who became a commander not to command men but so none could command her. No one would ever again take from her what she did not want to give.

She caught a movement from the corner of her eye, turned her head, but saw nothing. She ceased rocking and as she had learned to do from Miguel's letters, sat very still, watching until she saw the movement again. It was Miguel, who had stopped when he saw her sitting there, now striding forward. She went to the edge of the porch and he, standing on the ground below so that they were the same height, greeted her in a full-body hug.

"Have you been waiting long?"

"About an hour."

"You didn't tell me you were coming."

"It was kind of last minute. I have been working weekends, hoping to get a few days off in a row. As soon as I had permission, I caught the next train to Santiago to see

Liliana. Then came here because—well, this will be my last chance before you leave."

"Yes." The single word told her he was in waiting mode, waiting to find out whether she had come to say goodbye, or if not, why exactly she had come.

"I want to visit the Comandancia again," she said in a low voice.

He looked at her for a long moment, looked into her, she felt, and understood exactly what she was asking.

"I know now," she said hesitantly, "that I went there to find my*self*, not . . . the other Celia. I couldn't accept the choices I was being offered and, well, I guess I hoped the past was something I could . . . disappear into."

He listened to her self-analyze, neither nodding nor contradicting. He was silent a moment, then looked up the mountain toward the Comandancia, and said, "If we wait until sunset when the guides have gone down we could stay the night up there."

"Even if I do not know . . . ?"

She did not finish the sentence, did not know how to finish it. She still had occasional feelings of deja vu but had not had a full-blown hallucination in more than a year. That did not mean that there was no Sánchez left in her psyche. It might reappear at any time and if it was going to, where more likely than at the Comandancia?

It was not that she needed to know whether it could happen again because to her, the Sánchez persona, whether large or small, real or imaginary, was an integral part of her being. What she needed to know was in a question she did not ask, but which Miguel answered with a very soft kiss. "Don't worry. I'm not afraid of her ghost. Or yours."

She would have fallen off the porch into his arms, but he stepped up and past her. "I've been out since before sunrise and I'm starving. How about breakfast?"

She laughed. "At three in the afternoon? How about *lunch?*"

"If you insist," he grinned, washing his hands and reaching for a skillet.

Celia looked around the room. It was smaller than she remembered. Miguel must have guessed at its impression because he said, "If I had known there would be two living here, I might have built a bigger cabin." He paused and added, "A juita takes up more space than you'd think."

"You built the cabin yourself?" Celia was impressed.

"I did," he said over his shoulder as he broke eggs into a bowl.

"And the bed." The reason the room seemed cramped was because in addition to the narrow cot where she had napped before, there was, leaning against the wall, the headboard of a double bed, new and intricately carved. "So this is the 'little woodworking project' you wrote about!"

She knelt to study the birds, leaves, and vines carved with such painstaking care, a design that echoed elements of the Sánchez memorial. "You do fine things to wood."

"Wood does fine things to me. I love working with it." He set two plates on the table, each heaped with yellow eggs, a brown splat of beans, and slices of red tomato.

"Here you go. I may not be the best cook in Cuba but I am the fastest."

For a few minutes they ate in silence, ravenously. When he had almost cleaned his plate, he flipped the last bit of egg over her head. She turned around in time to see the big tree rat gobble the tidbit. "What will you do with the juita when you leave?" she asked.

"Do with him?" Miguel looked surprised. "Nothing. He doesn't need me. I'm not even sure he likes me. He just doesn't want to waste energy looking for food. Most animals don't."

"Interesting," Celia said, but in truth, she was not much interested in the tree rat. "What about your things? That headboard looks heavy. How will you get it down the mountain?"

"On the mule, I hope."

"What mule?"

"There's one that hangs around up there." He waved a hand vaguely toward the Comandancia. "I see him in the forest now and again, and if I've got any food on me, we share it. Some of the guides tried to catch him but so far I'm the only one who has got near him. I might be able to put a rope on him and persuade him to pack some of the heavier items down. But I'd let him go again. That animal should not be domesticated."

"Why not?"

"You know how long a mule's legs are, right?" Miguel held his hand to a little above her knee. "A metre or less. But this mule, I swear I have seen him put a hoofprint into something two metres behind his rump."

"I *know* that mule!" Celia exclaimed.

"You do?" Miguel looked at her quizzically. "From where?"

"It's a story," Celia said. "I will tell you sometime."

So she had not, after all, told him everything there was to know about her, nor had he told her everything about himself. How long would that take?

"I applied for a transfer to the hospital in Baracoa," she said abruptly.

"Really?" He reached across to touch her hand. "Did you get it?"

"No."

He swallowed hard and looked away. "Too bad. Baracoa's a nice town."

"Your hometown," she said.

"Yes. There is Moa farther west, but it's out of the question. With the nickel smelter and all, a filthy place."

"I know."

He walked to the door and gazed out into the forest where, although she saw only a wall of trees, he must be seeing a universe. "I'm looking forward to Parque Humboldt. There is a little bay with manatees." He smiled at her but it was not the happiest smile she had ever seen. "Humboldt is a habitat of the ivory-billed woodpecker. They say there are none left in Cuba. I'm going to be the one to prove them wrong. However long it takes."

She followed him to the door and put her arms around his waist. "What about

Playa Maguana? It's only twenty-four kilometres from Parque Humboldt."

He stepped back as if to get a better look at her. "Have you ever *been* there? Or even to that part of the island?"

What was he looking for? To see if she was crazy? Well, no, she could have told him. I am crazy often enough that I know perfectly well when I'm not. "I went there with Liliana, when we were doing our around-Cuba, every-trip-a-different-place thing."

"You didn't tell me!"

"Um, no." She had not told him because she was not sure she would get the job and did not know how he would feel about it if she did. Or because she did not *want* to know how he felt about it—not until she was sure of what *she* wanted, and exactly why. Three days there, staying at a nearby campismo, had revealed that Playa Maguana was a community where she could get back to the hands-on care of children she missed so much. At Playa Maguana she would have an opportunity to compare the difference between children's health in rural Cuba with that of the urban children she had always treated. She could use skills she had learned and learn things she did not know.

Of course it mattered that the move would give her distance from Luis and Jóse. More importantly, it would put her closer to Liliana and Franci; she'd be only six hours from Santiago instead of sixteen. And of course, close to Miguel. She doubted that he would want to live with her in Playa Maguana, or that she would live with him in Parque Humboldt. But with only twenty-four kilometres separating them, she did think he would come, often, or she would go to him. They would be close enough to find out just how close they wanted to be.

He was staring at her, dubious if not incredulous. "Then you know Playa Maguana isn't a town. Just a scattering of houses. There is absolutely no place to live."

"Actually, there are quite a few families. And a clinic that has only a nurse, no doctor. At least, not until I get there in January."

"Until *what*?"

"They said I could live in a room at the back of the clinic. Or build a cabin of my own. The government provides some building materials free of charge. And local people help each other with the construction. I saw some of their bohíos. In the forest, like this one. But I need one on a hill where I can see the ocean."

Suddenly Miguel was laughing. "You know, I have never been too sure about this other Celia you think you are, but I can just hear her explaining to Fidel why the Comandancia was the perfect place for them to build."

"She did!" Celia exclaimed. "That is a historical fact! She found the place and designed the buildings and supervised the construction—Che's hospital, the cookhouse, the cabin she and Fidel shared—everything!"

Despite Miguel's amusement, for just an instant Celia felt a ripple of uncertainty. She was not all that practised at taking the lead and leaving others to follow or not as they pleased. Had she pushed things beyond where he wanted to go? Might he feel threatened? He had not, after all, said any of the traditional things.

Before the fear could be fully realized, he leaned against the door frame and pulled her to him. "Compañera Celia, have I told you that you are an amazing woman?"

"Not lately. In fact, not ever."

"An amazing, hot, sweaty woman," he said, licking beads of sweat from her neck. "Not to mention salty."

"I would have washed up but—where do you bathe anyway?"

"In the stream." He jerked his head toward a trail that disappeared into the forest. "It's the one that flows down from the Comandancia, you know, that one below Celia and Fidel's cabin. Come, I'll show you."

She did not need to be shown . . . *mossy green boulders with that stream spilling down from a height of three metres, into a pool where dappled light passes through clear water to create ephemeral patterns on a sandy bottom.* She saw it already in her mind, and laughing, began to run.

"Wait!" he shouted. "It's not an easy trail. You'll get lost."

No. There are many ways. I will find one.

ROSA JORDAN grew up in the Florida Everglades and earned degrees from universities in California and Mexico. She immigrated to Canada in 1980 and currently resides in Rossland, BC, with her partner Derek Choukalos. They have co-authored two travel guides to Cuba, *Cycling Cuba* and *Cuba's Best Beaches*. One section of Rosa's autobiographical travel narrative, *Dangerous Places: Travels on the Edge*, is also about Cuba.